THE CUTAWAY

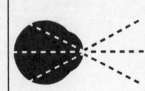

THE CUTAWAY

CHRISTINA KOVAC

THORNDIKE PRESS
A part of Gale, Cengage Learning

GALE
CENGAGE Learning·

Farmington Hills, Mich • San Francisco • New York • Waterville, Maine
Meriden, Conn • Mason, Ohio • Chicago

GALE
CENGAGE Learning®

Thorndike Press® Large Print Basic.
The text of this Large Print edition is unabridged.
Other aspects of the book may vary from the original edition.
Set in 16 pt. Plantin.

LIBRARY OF CONGRESS CATALOGING-IN-PUBLICATION DATA

Names: Kovac, Christina, author.
Title: The cutaway / by Christina Kovac.
Description: Large print edition. | Waterville, Maine : Thorndike Press, a part of Gale, Cengage Learning, 2017. | Series: Thorndike Press large print basic
Identifiers: LCCN 2017007390| ISBN 9781432839260 (hardcover) | ISBN 1432839268 (hardcover)
Subjects: LCSH: Women television producers and directors—Fiction. | Women lawyers—Fiction. | Missing persons—Fiction. | Criminal investigation—Fiction. | Georgetown (Washington, D.C.)—Fiction. | Washington (D.C.)—Fiction. | Large type books. | GSAFD: Mystery fiction.
Classification: LCC PS3611.O74942 C48 2017b | DDC 813/.6—dc23
LC record available at https://lccn.loc.gov/2017007390

Published in 2017 by arrangement with 37Ink /Atria Books, an imprint of Simon & Schuster, Inc.

Printed in Mexico
1 2 3 4 5 6 7 21 20 19 18 17

For Joe Loebach

CHAPTER ONE

It began with someone else's story. In the beginning, a woman went out to meet a man, and on her long walk, she disappeared. I didn't know the woman. I'd never met her. But I could see her clearly in my mind, walking the streets of Georgetown, her heels striking the sidewalk to the percussive music booming out of city bars. That same path I'd traveled many times myself.

Her married name was Evelyn Carney. She'd been born a Sutton, small-town country club people hailing from the cold north. I didn't discover much about her people, except they seemed to have no time for her or to care very much about what she did, and when she disappeared, gave a collective shrug. Had she fled them, or was she like so many other young women, women like me, who'd come to DC with dreams of making herself anew? She had none of the typical means to success in the District, no powerful sponsor or academic prowess or massive wealth. She had no family connections, either. But she had ambition and a powerful appeal to men, and she wasn't afraid to use either.

I never figured out how that captured my sympathy, but somehow I got hooked by that first glimpse of her. My mind is devilishly quick to fasten itself to an image, and I should've been more careful. I'd certainly been warned. When I was a young and reverent girl making those gestures that good girls must make, my parish priest had told me: "Be careful what your eyes take in. What you see becomes a part of you."

It might have been advice worth heeding, but I didn't, not when I was a child or a cub reporter, or much later, a too-young executive producer playing with the power of pictures. By then, I was hip deep in my quest for Evelyn Carney, and it was too late.

On an early Wednesday morning, her story arrived in a stack of press releases left on my desk. I'd been flipping through the papers when the big, bold letters — MISSING — caught my attention, and then the text:

The Metropolitan Police Department is

seeking the public's assistance in locating a missing person identified as Evelyn Marie Carney. She was last seen at approximately 9:48 p.m., on Sunday, March 8, in the twelve hundred block of Wisconsin Avenue, NW.

The MPD lingo description — thirty-year-old white female, five four, 115 pounds — could have fit any woman. It almost fit me.

Maybe thirty seconds of airtime, no more, but then I thought: Georgetown? No one went missing from Georgetown. Not with police officers standing sentinel every couple of blocks, protecting the expensive houses and trendy restaurants and upscale shops.

Beneath the text was the missing woman's photograph, blurred by a bad copy job. Her face was grainy and gray with two white spots for eyes — like a mask, creepy as hell — and I thought she was probably dead. It happened with sickening frequency: a woman killed by someone said to have loved her, or less often, by a stranger preying on her. Throughout the decade I'd been in the District, I'd worked different variations of this same story with sickening frequency.

There was a tap on my office door as Isaiah came in. He was the managing editor, my right-hand man, and he knew everything — changing technology in broadcasting, history of the city, local politics and crime stats, who's who, and what's what. Nearly forty years ago, he was one of the first black journalists to break into television. He was a great newsman.

"You're late for your own meeting," he said, looking at me over the top of his black horn-rims. "What happened to your Virginia Knightly early-for-everything rule?"

It was a rule he'd taught me, along with everything I knew about reporting. I glanced at my watch and was surprised to see he was right. "Let's go," I said.

As we cut through the newsroom, I got that rush of joy that comes at the oddest times — in the quiet moments before an editorial meeting, in the midst of my shows if there was a beautiful shot of video. Sometimes it came at the end of the day after everyone had gone home and only I was left to turn out the lights.

In the conference room, Nelson Yang, our best young photographer, stood with his shoulders pressed against the glass wall and his Dodgers cap pulled low, covering his mop of dark hair. He had a careless disposition and a penchant for gossip. Now he was telling a lewd tale of a competing news director caught with a female employee on the floor of the Graphics Department. "Talk about graphic," he muttered.

"No news director would risk his job in such a way," Isaiah said, taking his seat next to me.

I lifted my hand, ever the traffic cop. "True or not, it's unprofessional to talk about our colleagues' personal lives."

"But, Virginia," Nelson whined, "it's what we do."

Moira swept into the meeting. *Swept* is the only way to describe how Moira moved. She was built like a runway model, and her loose bohemian clothes trailed behind her as if she were caught in a constant headwind. She was the perfect female anchor, defying demographics of gender and age and race. She had the androgynous beauty of a Greek statue and the warm toast-colored skin of newly baked bread.

"They're laying off people at Channel 5," she said in her perfectly articulated voice.

"Coming soon to a theater near you," Isaiah said.

Here we go again. Every week there was some new anecdote about the demise of broadcast television. Now it's true that awhile back when the sponsors were losing money and pulling their ads, I panicked a little. Our fate was tied with theirs. But you didn't cry disaster in the face of disaster. You put on your game face and dug in harder.

"They're offering early retirement," I said. "Not layoffs."

"Same thing." Moira shrugged one of her shoulders, as if she didn't care enough to exert both. "The experienced people lose their jobs."

"Not nearly the same," I argued. "Early retirement comes with a big, fat paycheck that no one would take if they didn't want to."

"I'd love to get money for nothing," Nelson said, and then he leaned across the table toward me. "What are you huddled over?"

"It's called a press release. Maybe you've heard of them."

"A press release of what? A Rorschach test?"

I studied the eerie eyes of Evelyn Carney again. "It's supposed to be a picture of a woman missing from Georgetown."

"It's the picture that's missing," Nelson said with disdain. "That ink stain could be anybody. You, Moira, anybody."

I rubbed the back of my neck. "Yeah," I said, and then to Isaiah, "Get the police to email a color photo, will you?"

When he opened the glass door to go, I asked Isaiah to find Ben. "Ask him to call his cop buddies. See what they think of the case."

He gestured to the digital clock above the bank of televisions, meaning Ben was late, as usual. "I'll try to find him, but you know how it is with the beautiful people," Isaiah said. "No offense, Moira."

She did her one-shoulder shrug.

Later, when the evening news was under way, I left the control room and climbed the stairs to my office, where I turned off the overhead lights. The soft yellow desk lamp threw shadows over shelves holding my mother's antique tea set and my books, waiting like old friends. There were shadows, too, on the awards hung on the walls — some from stories with Ben, some all my own — and on the framed articles I wrote during my early days at the *Washington Post.*

I kicked off my shoes, and lifting the remotes from my desk, turned on the monitors showing newscasts from each competing station, leaving them on mute. At the end of the hour, the color photograph of the missing woman flashed across the row of monitors simultaneously.

Evelyn Carney was young and pretty, with shoulder-length brown hair, thick and wavy, wilder than my own. Her skin was rosier, too, and her face rounder, and her green eyes tilted up in the corners like a Disney princess.

I'd seen her before, but not in person. She'd been in a video, although I couldn't place the clip. It'd been brief, maybe two seconds long, three at most. Probably a cutaway shot, one of those quick flashes of video used to show a reaction, but I couldn't be certain.

I went to my desk and clicked on the database for archived video on my computer and ran a search for Evelyn Carney. Her name brought up no hits. I was expanding the search when Ben knocked on my door.

He must've come directly from the anchor desk. His face was still covered in makeup, and his dark hair had that perfect gelatinous sheen he'd mess up as soon as he hit the street. He was giving me that look of his, his smile slow and dark eyes direct, as if I were the only woman in the world. I was pretty sure he looked at all women that way.

"I'm in the mood for some Russian lit," he said, and I waved him in. He bent his big body to the bookshelf, pulling out the hardbound copies of *Anna Karenina* and *War*

14

and Peace and grabbing the bottle of vodka they hid. He poured a hefty shot into the teacup from my mother's set. His hand eclipsed the cup as he swirled it. "I always wondered what you kept behind your *Ulysses.*"

"Stay away from my Irish," I said. "The alcohol isn't a good idea anyway."

He lifted his cup. "To all the bad ideas that make life worth living," he said and tossed back the shot, a momentary grimace on his handsome face.

I rotated the monitor with its picture of Evelyn to face him. "Where have we seen her before?"

One eyebrow shot up. "We have?"

"On video," I said. "Somewhere."

He dragged a chair stuttering across the carpet, flipped it backward, and sat with his elbows on my desk. He angled the monitor for better viewing.

My nails drummed across the top of the desk.

"Shhh," he said without looking away from the monitor, pressing the tips of his fingers against mine, stilling them. He had thick-veined, red-knuckled hands marred by a half-moon scar; strong, capable hands. When I pulled mine away, a corner of his mouth lifted. He continued to study the photo.

Finally, he said, "I've never seen this woman in my life."

"And you'd remember because she's beautiful." I'd meant to tease him, but it came out like a complaint.

He looked up. "But you remember?"

"I've seen her in a short clip. I can't place it."

"What goes on in there?" he said, tapping his forehead. "How does that work?"

As I concentrated, my eyes grew heavy, and the memory isolated, sharpened: "It's two seconds of video. A crowd-reaction shot to a main story that I can't see. She's clear, though, dead center in an audience of some sort, seated. The rest of the room, or any identifying feature, is beyond the frame."

My forehead scrunched up. "But the woman, this Evelyn Carney — she's got the photographer's attention. It's the way she leans forward, some intense emotion . . ." My voice drifted off.

"You can't read the emotion?" he asked softly. "Or you can't see it clearly?"

"I don't understand it. Whatever it is, she's alone in it. No one around her acts as she does." I blew out a breath of frustration. "All I got."

He eased back in the chair. "You think she's going to be a big story?"

"Not sure. I need more information."

"That's why you had Isaiah hunt me down, nagging me to make calls."

"Isaiah asked you to do your job. You used to love reporting." I paused. "That was before the anchor desk ruined you."

He laughed. "Poke at me all you please. I know about your soft underbelly. Besides, men like mean women. Mean or crazy, not both at the same time. Not even I could handle that."

"Not true."

"You're right. I probably could handle that."

"About what men like, I mean."

"Truest thing I can tell you, Virginia."

I lifted my hands impatiently. "Did you get information on Evelyn Carney or not?" If I let him, he'd draw the whole damn thing out all night. He had to be the slowest newsman I'd ever met.

He had discovered that Evelyn was a recent law school graduate. She worked at a prestigious firm. On the night she disappeared, she had dinner at a restaurant in Georgetown. His source didn't know the name of her dinner date, but she left alone. Police recovered her car, abandoned not fifty yards from the restaurant. I asked if we could get a shot of the car.

"It's in the garage at Mobile Crime," he said.

"So investigators think something bad happened. What does your guy think?"

"My guy always thinks something bad happened. He says the chief took the case out of the district today. She assigned it to detectives up at CID."

Criminal Investigations wouldn't normally handle a missing persons case so soon, not unless there were special circumstances. I wondered what those might be.

"How about we grab some dinner?" Ben said.

I gazed up, still lost in my what-ifs about Evelyn Carney.

"Someplace quiet," he went on. "You could expense it, we both get a free meal, and we could talk. We need to talk."

"About the case?"

He stretched his shoulders, pushing outward, as if fighting some terrible constriction, before he hefted himself from the chair and made his way to the door.

I waved helplessly at the spread of papers over my desk. "It's only that, you know, there's so much —"

"Work, yeah, I know."

After Ben left, I searched again for that video of Evelyn. It was maddening. I began to question what I'd remembered. Maybe the video hadn't even been on our news. Maybe it was video from a competing station. That was especially worrisome.

By the time I looked up from the computer, bleary-eyed, it was late. So I sorted my work into piles of what I'd done and what I'd yet to do and made a note about assigning someone to resume the video search tomorrow, knowing in the end, that someone would probably be me.

It was a five-minute drive to my neighborhood in Cleveland Park. I parked a half block from my house, the closest spot I could find. The night was cool and clear and the street was cast in blue. A full moon was over the National Cathedral tower.

From beneath the seat of my car, I pulled out my three-cell flashlight, heavy with a patterned grip that felt good in my hand. It was the kind beat cops carried not for illumination but as yet another weapon, the same reason I carried it up the brick walkway and onto my porch. I went inside and locked the door. The click of the security bolt echoed through my empty house.

CHAPTER TWO

My memory isn't exactly photographic. For instance, my mind doesn't collect reams of newsprint or prose, and numbers are a completely foreign language. Only pictures burn a permanent place in my memory, a terrific gift at deadline. I can remember the angle of every frame I've used, where it was shot, what time of year, if there were leaves on the trees or snow on the ground, tourists mingling in the foreground, that sort of thing. But here's the flip side of that shiny coin: you can't get *rid* of a picture, either. Not even when it hurts you.

That's how I got into trouble about five years back. During what would become my final stint as an on-air reporter, I'd been working the story of a mother and daughter gone missing from a DC suburb. Turns out, the husband had refused to pay back a debt to some really bad guys. I don't remember all those details. Only what happened to the mother and her girl. The police requested help from the FBI, and one of the agents assigned was a guy I often used as a source, so I pretty much owned the story. But soon the story owned me, too: long days and sleepless nights, the meals I went without — nothing mattered except finding that mother and her daughter.

One morning, my source tipped me to a search in a remote park north of the city. It was large and densely wooded and leaves covered tangled paths that merged into one another. In my hurry, I got lost. When I found the crime scene tape, I was no longer certain which side I was on, so I followed the tape until I heard the growl of an engine.

About a dozen searchers circled a crane, which was lowering a steel drum to the sand. The drum was wet with pond water. One of the searchers struggled with a crowbar to break the seal. Finally, there was a loud crunch as the drum opened and a thud as the heavy lid fell on the sand. The crane operator cut the engine, and everything went silent as the searchers clustered.

I moved closer. The top of a woman's head was visible, the white line of her scalp glowed against shiny black hair. Her body was curled inside, chin tucked to one shoulder and arms held outward, protectively it seemed. And then I saw what — or rather *whom* — she'd been trying to protect.

A child cradled in her arms.

It came to me at once: the last moments inside that drum, the mother trying to soothe her little girl, both trapped inside that black, cramped, airless space with the water sloshing outside. And then I heard another thing, too. It was soft as the breeze through the tops of the trees, an echo of a woman's whisper: *It's okay. Mama loves you. Someone will come for us.*

And no one had come.

Well, I couldn't do that live shot. I couldn't even lift myself from the path. My limbs felt heavy, waterlogged, and my heart thumped in my ears, competing with the *huh-huh-huh* of my choppy breath. When someone tried to help me up, I had to sit back down again. That's really all I remember.

Isaiah covered for me. He sent the new guy at the station, a reporter named Ben Pearce, to take over my story. When the live shot was over, Ben drove me back to the station, where Isaiah lectured me on my *susceptibility to certain stories,* on letting myself *get all run down. You don't take care of yourself,* he'd said. *You can't do field work if you don't take care of yourself, simple as that.*

That story marked my fall from the highest of highs, and yet I learned to love producing. For me, it has always been about telling stories, no matter where you do it — in front of the camera or behind it — and it's the best gig going. You hold on to it for as long as you can, knowing that one morning you can wake up at the pinnacle, and by nightfall, you're clinging to your career by your fingertips. In a snap, just like that.

The next morning, I cut across the cathedral grounds on my walk to work. At Wisconsin Avenue, someone had taped Evelyn's missing persons poster onto a bus-stop enclosure. The edges of the poster were already curled in the cool, moist air. Another poster hung in the window of my favorite coffee shop. I opened its door, assaulted by the strong coffee smell. You could get a buzz just standing there.

The barista, Alonzo, was a tall guy with dreadlocks. I'd been coming to his coffee shop for years. When he greeted me from behind the espresso machine, I ordered my usual — a black coffee, the biggest cup they had.

"That poster in the window," I said. "Do

you know her? Evelyn Carney?"

"Yeah, actually, I do. She's a customer." He talked as he worked the espresso machine. The line behind me began to swell. "Her friend handed out posters yesterday and asked us to hang one up. I said, sure, I'm happy to help."

"So Evelyn lives in the neighborhood?"

"Probably works in an office around here," he said. "She and her friend come in for a coffee from time to time, always with a stack of files they're going through. They're all about the work. Her friend *Paige*" — intoning her name so you could tell what he was thinking — "she can wear a suit, believe me."

I laughed. "You got a number for your Paige?"

"She gave me her business card. Give me a minute to clear the line. I'll get it for you."

I moved over to the bar and sat, my heel resting on the rung of the stool, and warmed my hands on the cup. The coffee was deliciously hot and bitter as always. A well-thumbed *City Paper* was spread across the bar. I flipped through it while waiting for Alonzo's break. Finally it came. He strutted out of the back room, waving a little card.

"You don't think something bad happened to her?" he asked.

"I don't know. I'd like to find out."

He hesitated, saying, "Paige didn't say I could give her number out. But you'd be helping, right? Put her picture on the news, do a story or something, then she comes home?"

"That's the idea."

I copied the phone number onto my notepad, double-checking the spelling of the law firm, then handed the card back.

"You get the story and find the girl, be sure to make me the hero," he said, smiling. "Paige gives me her digits, and I get my just desserts."

Our newsroom and studios were housed on the top floors of a square building erected during the ugly era of American architecture. It sat atop the highest point in Washington, a hill shared by other news stations to the south of us.

A delivery cart blocked the building entrance. Some boxes had fallen from the cart and into the automatic door, jamming it. The delivery guy was struggling and people behind him complaining, but no one stepped forward to help the guy. I didn't, either, distracted as I was by my expanding list of priorities for the morning: the video search for Evelyn, follow-up calls to police for the latest in the investigation, and now this contact number for Evelyn's friend Paige Linden. I'd assign my best reporter, Alexa Lopez, to call her. Alexa had a softness that disguised her tenacity and a wonderful way of making people talk.

Once the deliveryman cleared out, the guard waved me through, saying, "Good morning, Ms. Knightly." His attention went to someone behind me.

A woman stood in the entrance. She wore boots the way a cat arches its back, her face was something you'd see touched up in a magazine — big eyes, small nose, cheeks curved like a Ming vase — and her blond hair swung in the light. She had TV written all over her.

The elevator doors opened, and inside, Isaiah stood slack-jawed. I got in and pushed the button. "You might want to close your mouth before the drool runs out," I joked.

He looked at me over his horn-rims. "Do they get younger every year? It's a terrible thing to grow old in a young person's business."

"You are *not* old. You are experienced, respected, and skilled. You are necessary."

He gave me a gentle smile. "Your affection blinds you."

26

The elevator arrived at our floor. We stepped into the cold air made for machines, not men. Across the newsroom, Alexa Lopez was rapid-fire cursing in a way that sounded like beautiful Spanish poetry, if you didn't know what she was saying. I didn't *habla*, but in a Washington newsroom, you picked up gutter words in many different languages. I moved quickly for damage control.

Alexa was waving a camera media card beneath Nelson's chin. "He shot me fat," she said.

Nelson leaned into her, his mop of black hair falling over unshaven cheeks. His checkered scarf wafted against her. It looked like the beginning of an embrace except for those two sharp chins pointing at each other and the card she used to slash at the scarf.

"I shot her," he said, "She's —"

"Don't you say it." Her face was flushed, her dark eyes wild.

"I was going to say —"

"Don't even think it," she said, and then to me: "This is how he gets back at me."

"I'm an artist," he sneered. "Not a plastic surgeon."

"Chinga tu madre." We all understood that one. The newsroom went silent, except for the chirping police scanners and ringing phones, which no one answered.

27

"No arguing in the newsroom," I said, trying to push Alexa along. She wouldn't budge. I said, "Show me your stand-up in my office. I'm sure you look great. If you need a retake, we'll get someone to do that, but it has to be fast. I have a more important story for you."

"It's killing him," she said. "He still hasn't gotten over me."

Great red splotches colored Nelson's cheeks. "Gotten over you? You dumped me *last night.*"

They were shouting now. My efforts to come between them had failed miserably. Several writers lifted their heads from their desks, and there was a grin or two but no help. At the far side of the newsroom, Ben came out of the elevator, pushing his mountain bike. I walked as quickly as I could without appearing to run to him.

"Alexa and Nelson are fighting," I said. "Get your buddy out of here before I haul them both up to personnel."

"No kidding." He pulled off his helmet and ran his fingers through his hair. "Look at this newsroom. They look like prairie dogs poking their heads out of the ground." He pushed his bike leisurely past the cubicles. "On Sundays my grandma used to get all gussied up in her church hat and grab her favorite rifle and go prairie dog hunting. Hell of a shot, my grandma. Too bad we had to take away her gun."

We crossed the newsroom. Ben leaned his bike against his hip as he pulled off his gloves. "You guys fighting?" he asked Alexa.

"He's trying to kill my career."

"No one can kill your career," he told her. "You're a great reporter."

She gave Ben a disbelieving look. "Don't let him shoot you. He'd turn you into a hunchback. The great Emmy Award–winning Nelson Yang who shoots women —"

"Lower your voice," I warned her.

"— and turns them into pigs."

Nelson gasped. "She thinks she can wear white," he told Ben. "How can she not know it makes her wide as a billboard?"

Ben whispered into Alexa's ear. She blinked up at him from beneath thick lashes and sucked in her cheeks, biting the folds. It was a wicked, knowing look that had Nelson kneading his scarf. She walked away with a pronounced swivel in her hips.

"Nelson," I said in warning.

He ignored me.

"Nelson," I repeated. "Let her go."

He chased after her.

"It'll blow over now," Ben said. He

29

pointed across the room where Nelson had caught up with Alexa. Soon they were huddled in a corner.

As we strolled down the corridor toward my office, I told Ben about the phone number in my notepad, how I'd planned to assign the story to Alexa and Nelson.

"You could ask me to report," he said. "I'm still pretty good in the field."

"Try not to be absurd. You're the anchor now." A superanchor, if truth be told, as damn near celebrity as you could get in Washington, and it embarrassed the hell out of him.

"I'd take a field assignment if you ask nicely," he teased. "You could produce for me, like back in the day. Write all the boring stuff I'm no good at writing."

"You mean, like your script? Do your work?"

"Why not?" He grinned. "But I'd need you in the field with me, not stuck here. I may not be the deepest-thinking man on the planet, but even I understand you shouldn't hole yourself up here day and night."

"I can't go out in the field," I said in a cool voice. And I couldn't. There was too much to do here at the station.

"Lost your nerve, didja?"

"My — *nerve*?"

"Settle down now. It happens." He gave me his Anchor Ben look, his smile wry and dark eyes crinkled in the corners. "You used to be great in the field, but that was years ago, and now you're not so sure of yourself. You're afraid you're rusty."

"I am not —" And then I stopped. Hell, I probably would be rusty, now that I thought about it.

"We can shake off the rust together. All I'm saying."

"I have responsibilities to the shows," I said, hesitating. "And there's the video of Evelyn I have to find."

"Isaiah can cover the shows. He's more than capable. Assign the video search to a couple of editors. Let them do what they do best." His voice went low and slightly mocking, but of whom I wasn't sure. "Come out and play. We can bust the story wide open. You know you want to."

The idea was tantalizing.

I thought about the press release of Evelyn with those strange white spots for eyes, Evelyn who might need someone to help her, and this feeling crept up on me, catching me by surprise. It made no sense, and yet I couldn't shake it. It was the loneliest damn feeling.

31

In my office, I pulled out my reporter notebook and Googled Paige Linden's name with that of her firm, and bingo, her portrait was staring back at me. Bright smile. Direct gaze. Ash blond hair and darker blond eyebrows that slanted upward, giving her a shrewd look.

Her bio was impressive. Extensive bar and court admissions, good-sized list of memberships and boards, half page of representative experience. She'd graduated magna cum laude from law school and clerked for a federal appellate judge. Midthirties, I guessed, and already a partner at a firm that billed itself as one of the most experienced and respected practices in Washington, providing counsel to political candidates and elected officials, nonprofit and ideological groups, as well as major corporations.

Paige Linden was listed as Lawyer of the Year by *Best Lawyers* magazine. She was an *up-and-comer, the one to watch.*

I expanded the search with Paige's name and found several blogs mentioning her. A snarky posting referred to Ms. Linden by her courtroom nickname, "Ana," as in anaconda. *Lovely and charming she may be,* the blogger wrote, *but stealthy. You don't realize she's crushing you until the air leaves your lungs.* Jocular comments followed, many in the vein of: *Sour grapes?* and *Paige trounce your sorry ass in court again, did she?*

A *City Paper* blog described Paige as a whisper candidate to replace the retiring delegate to Congress. Other blogs went further, shaking the Magic 8 Ball: Would she run or wouldn't she? And more seriously, who might back her? Whether she wanted to be the DC delegate was immaterial if she didn't have the money to run.

From a news search of the *Post*'s archives: *DC lawyer saves drowning boy,* with a dateline from several years ago. A young boy from the Midwest had wandered off from his tour group near the Jefferson Memorial. He had been playing along the granite ledge when he slipped and fell into the Potomac. Bystanders wrung their hands. Paige Linden had been jogging on a nearby path and heard the commotion. She jumped in after the boy.

Our coverage of the rescue included a taped interview with Paige, her hair slicked back with river water and a gray blanket tossed like a cape over her shoulders. When asked if she'd been afraid to jump into the Potomac, a treacherous river known to claim lives every year, she shrugged. "I didn't want the boy to be swept away," she said, her modest words at odds with her defiant stare.

I dialed the number written in my reporter pad. Paige's secretary put me on hold. After a short wait, Paige picked up. I told her I was producing a story about her friend's disappearance. She didn't say anything. I explained how the story could assist searchers by broadening the reach for potential witnesses. She didn't want to talk.

"The police said I shouldn't." Her voice was like a tuning fork, resonant and pure pitched, and what she said perplexed me. She had to know how important it was to find a good witness. She was a lawyer after all. And then she explained, "The investigators said the media would turn it into a circus."

My news ping went off. A circus to police equaled Big Story to us.

"But you understand the police are talking, right?" I paused for effect. "What they're saying makes little sense. How does a woman go out to dinner in the heart of Georgetown on a Sunday night —" I flipped as noisily as I could through the blank pages of my notebook. "I'm sorry, who was she dining with?"

Her lovely voice became defensive. "Her husband, of course."

"The police said she left the restaurant alone. Why would she leave without her husband?"

"You're not going to report he did something wrong?" she said in a hard voice.

"Why don't you tell me so I get it right?"

There was a long pause I didn't fill. Most people were uncomfortable with silence, but not Paige. Finally, I prodded gently: "If Evelyn were my friend, I wouldn't be concerned with helping some detective avoid a circus. I'd do whatever it took to bring my friend home."

"Let me think about it."

I told her about confidentiality and off-the-record sourcing. She could tell me anything, even what she didn't want me to report, all to get a clear picture. "The clearer the picture, the more we can help Evelyn and her husband. What's his name?"

"Peter. Peter Carney."

"How can I get in touch with him?"

"I could give him your number. Maybe he'll call. He might be too upset."

"Lots of upset people talk," I told her. "It's the best way to find their loved ones."

She wanted to check with detectives. I knew where that would leave me, but I let her go. I hadn't been so long from the field that I forgot you couldn't push. You had to let the game come to you. Before she hung up, she took my phone numbers and agreed to let me check in with her.

But I was puzzled. For one thing, investigators seemed to be acting against their best interests. Paige Linden seemed the perfect spokesperson for her friend Evelyn, so why hold her back? How could this become a circus?

Alexa hurried into my office without knocking. She had the media card in her hand again. "Need to chat," she singsonged, coming around my desk and handing it over to me. "Listen, I adore Nelson, I do."

"Less I know about that, the better," I said dryly.

"His talent is amazing," she went on as if I hadn't spoken. "Same time, he's too emotional, and all those emotions get in the way of my work. Now, I don't want to upset him more than he already is."

"Meaning, you want me to separate the

two of you."

"Yes."

"Reassign him without looking like you're behind it."

She huffed out a breath. "Take a look at what he's put together. You'll see."

It was an audition reel of Alexa's stand-ups. These kinds of reels were usually sent with an accompanying résumé to prospective employers, people other than me, maybe my competitors. She was prowling for another job. I tried not to feel betrayed.

As she sped through the images, one clip caught my eye.

"Stop," I told her.

The frame froze on Alexa talking into a microphone in front of a historic stone building now used as a community center. Police cruisers were parked in the background. "What's the story here?" I asked.

It was from her report of last summer's Big Story, a serial rapist stalking the jogging paths of Rock Creek Park. One of the victims had died from her injuries, and the police set up a task force with undercover female police officers jogging the paths. No one had been arrested. The attacks had stopped with the cold weather.

"Where's the rest of the video?"

"I don't know," she said, dismissive. "This

is the stand-up reel Nelson put together for me. But it's the perfect example of how great he makes me look when he's not trying to sabotage me. Wait until you see the next one."

My phone rang. I was being cordially summoned to a meeting with my boss, the news director. I tried to buck it — pressing issue with a reporter, I said — but his secretary said he wasn't having excuses. Mellay was in a mood, she warned.

Nick Mellay's office had swallowed the sun-filled side of the newsroom. He'd had a wall removed, cutting into our conference room, and filled his cavernous space with extravagant furniture, a ridiculous expense for a station struggling to stay on budget and for a news director who probably wouldn't last.

He was a small man behind a big desk, his chair raised to its highest notch. He always seemed to be bursting with something. With Mellay, you never really knew what that something was. He was often brilliant, sometimes lacking judgment, but most of the time he wasn't around, which was fine by me. In my eight years at the station, I'd survived five news directors. One had been very good. Naturally, he'd gotten fired. The rest had neither helped nor hurt anything. They'd gotten fired, too. Two months ago, we got Mellay.

He was blathering on about his glory days in network news, and I tuned out, having heard it all before. Instead, I was thinking of Evelyn Carney. I had to get her address. Maybe I could get an interview with her husband. If he wasn't home, I'd check out the neighborhood, ask around about her.

Mellay had stopped talking and was staring at me.

"I'm sorry?"

"What do you think?" he said. "You help me get the ratings up, and when I go back to network, you get all this." He spread his arms wide. "I can make it yours."

I kept my expression blank.

"You don't like my offer?"

"Of course I want the ratings up," I said carefully. "I'll work as hard as I can, whatever it takes."

His head tilted to the side, and the overhead lights glinted off his glasses. "You want something else?"

I wanted what I had. Editorial control. Not only what stories to cover but how to cover them. A news director had the business of news, the endless chess match of ratings and demographics, lead-ins and audience share, courtship with advertisers.

That wasn't for me. I loved stories for their human foibles, their pulse and their heat, and in the best stories, their mystery. It was the unknowable that hooked me.

But I wouldn't tell him what I loved. That's when it was always taken away.

"I wouldn't presume to know your job," I said carefully.

"Then I really can't understand your announcement in yesterday's meeting."

"What announcement?" I didn't remember making one.

"You promised no layoffs." He shook his head, mugging disbelief. "In this difficult economy? Particularly with the ratings your shows have been posting?"

"Oh, well, I did tell my staff —"

"Not *your* staff."

"There's word all over town about newspapers folding and television stations laying off employees, but I told them — your staff — that our shows are still number one. The budget's in good shape, all things considered, but they worry about competition from nontraditional content providers."

"By whose authority were you speaking?"

The authority I'd always spoken with. I was executive producer, second in command who oversaw day-to-day operations, the afternoon and evening newscasts, the

40

person who made the shows happen. But I held my tongue.

"There's going to be some reshuffling," he said. "Some contracts won't be renewed. Others might lose their jobs."

My mind automatically went to the names and faces of the most vulnerable among my staff. And they were *my* staff. He didn't love them. Not like I did.

But I said nothing. Showing emotion would get me nowhere.

"Now that that's out of the way," he said, "what have you got for tonight? What's the lead?"

For a moment I considered showing him Evelyn's missing persons poster, and then I stopped. I had this vague feeling I should protect Evelyn or my idea of what Evelyn's story might be. Instead, I rattled off a handful of news stories probably every other newscast would have, and in the midst of it, mentioned the woman who hadn't been seen since Sunday night. "Police aren't saying much, certainly nothing to indicate foul play. If they don't find her today, we can run her picture again."

None of that was a lie, I reasoned.

"That's the problem." He stood up and leaned over his desk, his palms on the blotter. "None of those stories have any chance

41

of increasing the number of viewers, which our survival depends on. Now I like you. I admire your work ethic. But I just don't see the vision."

And then he gave me a cool smile and his dimple appeared. That dimple gave me a bad feeling.

"Meantime, there's inefficiency in upper management I've got to rectify," he went on. "We don't need two people overseeing content and production of the shows, right?"

"We don't have two people," I said warily. "We have me."

"Starting today, the shows have me." He came around the desk to me. "I need to get in there and see what's going on. You'd only be in the way."

He was demoting me, firing me — I wasn't sure which — but certainly he was stealing my shows. I concentrated on my breath, my smile, how the act of smiling was supposed to change your inner chemistry. It didn't change a damn thing. Still, I held on to that stupid smile.

He sighed. "I'm not firing you, okay?" He lifted his jacket sleeve and checked his watch, not even bothering to hide it. "Once I get us on the right track, maybe you get your shows back. Meantime, you won't lose face. Keep your parking spot and your memberships we pay for. And at the correspondents dinner next week, I'll seat you at the big boy table with me."

"But if my shows are gone, what do I do?" It was my beggar's voice, and I could've kicked myself, except he'd already done it for me.

He wasn't listening. He was gazing over my shoulder. The blond beauty queen from the downstairs lobby was now posing in his doorway, her shiny black boots crossed at the ankle and one knee bent out provocatively. A yellow umbrella was swinging from her wrist. It was quite the look, all for him.

"Later," he said, as he brushed past me to get to the girl.

I held on to my anger for as long as I could. It was my easiest emotion, all wrapped up as it was in virtue or maybe self-righteousness. Sometimes it's hard to tell the difference. I sat hunched over my desk, forehead resting on clenched fists, telling myself I'd find my way back to my shows. There was always a way. For now, what I could do was the work.

I called the Metropolitan Police Public Information Office, better known as the Lack of Information Office. The officer who picked up the phone asked if I'd gotten the press release about Evelyn.

"Did you send one today?"

"No. Yesterday."

"I got yesterday's," I said. "What's new today?"

"That's all we got."

"But investigators must be doing something. I want to report it."

He didn't say anything. I wasn't sure he was still on the line, and then I heard a yawn.

"Let's start with the basics," I said. "Who's Evelyn Carney? What was she doing when she disappeared? Where was she going?"

"I don't have that kind of information."

"All right, put me on the phone with someone who does."

"This office is handling all inquiries."

Now I remembered the other reason I'd come in from the field. "You don't know the answers," I said. "Or you're not doing anything to get answers? Maybe you have no one investigating the case?"

He hung up on me. I called back.

"Did we get disconnected?" he said.

"Very cute. May I speak with your boss? Captain Andrews?"

"He's not in."

"Then I'll leave a message," I said. "Please

tell him I need concrete answers to specific questions directed to his office in time for my newscast." I listed them, all simple and easy, the basic who-what-where type, and told him if I didn't get a response by my deadline, I'd be asking the next logical question: why wasn't the investigation moving forward? Or, as he seemed to suggest, was there no investigation? And I'd be asking those questions on air.

He cursed. "Give me a break, will you? We get at least ten thousand reports a year for missing people, almost all of them runaways. Tell me how this woman rates."

"If she doesn't *rate,*" I said, keeping my temper on a leash, "why'd *your* office put out the press release? You guys asked us to help you, remember?"

"Upstairs wanted it out, so it gets out. I don't ask why. I just do what I'm told."

Upstairs — now that piqued my curiosity. *Upstairs* meant the top floor of police headquarters, which housed the offices of the command staff, the chief, and all of her deputies. If it had been atypical for Criminal Investigations detectives to lead the investigation of a missing persons case, it was much more so for the command staff to get involved.

After I hung up, my fingertips clacked

across my computer keyboard as I ran more searches, this time for anything linking Evelyn Carney to the Metropolitan Police before her disappearance, particularly to its chief, command staff, or to any of the District's community or neighborhood crime watch groups whose meetings police officials frequent. Nothing. If she had a footprint on social media, I couldn't find that, either.

My fingertips tapped the desk as I thought it through: how did a young lawyer at a prestigious law firm that dealt in business and politics make an impression on a city police official? I'd covered political stories and crime stories, even the occasional political that became a crime story (usually over sex or money), but generally speaking, the two were worlds apart. So how had Evelyn Carney encountered a police official? Had she reported or witnessed a crime? A search on the databases for the DC courts came up blank. I left a message with a friend in the Clerk's Office at DC Superior Court.

Through one of the pricey databases linked to public records, I typed Evelyn's name with her age and came up with an address on the southeast side of Capitol Hill. A man named Peter Carney also lived there. I printed the information and tossed it into my satchel, along with a notepad and my phone.

And then I thought *Mellay*? Should I tell him? Or . . . ask him? I'd always found it more palatable to seek a man's forgiveness than his permission. Then again, Mellay was a pretty unforgiving guy.

I went back and forth, worrying my lip with my teeth, until I decided: the answer was always the story. I'd help Evelyn and Evelyn's story would help me, and by extension, my station. That was the calculation, anyway.

The hell with Mellay.

CHAPTER FOUR

The sun had come out and the air was crisp. To the east, the cathedral bells tolled noon.

From the underground garage, Nelson's blue Chevy Tahoe rolled up. The thumping bass of alt rock strained the windows. I jogged over and banged on his passenger window, which inched down, blasting me with music before Nelson turned the radio off.

"Can you go with me to the Hill?" I said.

He put on his sunglasses and settled back in his seat, stretching his legs. "You asking or telling?"

"I don't know if I have the authority to tell you." I paused. "I think I was just demoted."

His mouth dropped open. "You were *what*?"

"Mellay just —"

"Demoted *you*?" He pushed open the car door and I slid in. "Tell me everything," he

48

said with excitement. "Does anyone else know yet?"

"You're the first."

He hit the accelerator. As we crossed town, weaving in and out of traffic, running red lights and veering within inches of other cars and bicycle couriers, he peppered me with questions. If I was going to prevail against Mellay, I had to get my people together. I could count on Isaiah and Ben, and where Ben went, so went Moira. The beautiful people always stuck together. I'd hired Nelson, so maybe he'd side with me, too. I'd have to wait and see where the others lined up.

"So if you're not still executive producer," Nelson said, "what are you?"

I frowned. "Not sure."

"You need to talk or anything, let me know. In my car, we observe Four Corners Rule. Nothing gets repeated outside these corners."

We were driving through the residential side streets of Capitol Hill. Our pace slowed with the narrowing streets. Nelson's hand beat the steering wheel to some rhythm in his head. "So what's Ben say?"

"Hmm?" I said, absently, looking for parking. The cars were bumper to bumper, no spots.

"He must be steaming. No way he's happy his woman gets the ax."

I turned to Nelson, confused. "His . . . what?"

"No need to pretend. I admire how you guys keep it under deep cover, even though everybody knows."

"Stop the truck."

As the Tahoe jerked to a halt, I grabbed my bag and the two-way radio on the console between us, and then I was out of the truck and in the gutter. "Look at me and listen." I pointed the radio antenna at him. "I am not one of Ben Pearce's women. I belong to no one except myself. Spread that around, okay?"

I slammed the car door shut and stomped off toward Sixth Street. He called out: "You want me to shoot anything?"

I raised my two-way radio over my head and waved it.

Evelyn Carney lived on a street of two-story row houses with trimmed yards and gravel-lined driveways disappearing into alleys behind the houses. Thick black bars caged basement windows. The cherry trees were nice, though, with their tiny green florets shivering in the breeze. At the west end of the street, the Capitol dome peeked above the tree line, and to the east, the distant wail of police sirens. Here, the neighborhood seemed to hold its breath.

A man was working in the yard in front of Evelyn's house. He was crouched down, pulling ivy from the base of a tree in a bust of angry jerks. The bill of his blue USMC cap shaded his angular face. I asked if he was Peter Carney.

"Who are you?" he said suspiciously.

When I told him, his eyes changed, as if they were windows slamming shut.

"I'm doing a story about your wife. I wonder if you'd talk about her."

"My *wife,*" he spit out. He rose from his crouch and pulled off his cap, wiping a forearm across his brow. His blond hair was buzzed short and bristly looking.

"Police say she hasn't been seen in several days. Do you know where she might have gone?"

"How the hell should I know?" He glared toward the Capitol dome as if it had done him wrong.

"But you're her husband," I said. "Why wouldn't you know?"

He crouched over the ivy again. His hands were long and narrow and got lost among the leaves. He kept his back to me. I stepped out of my shoes and set them away from

51

the ivy. My skirt hiked high when I kneeled next to him. We pulled ivy together.

"I'm not going to talk," he said. "You're wasting your time."

"Maybe you could give me just one thing and send me on my way."

"I'm the last person to know where she is," he said. "And that's a fact."

"You had dinner together the night she disappeared. You were the last person seen with her."

The tips of his ears flushed. "Miss — what did you say your name was?" When I told him, he said: "Miss Knightly, if I tell you one thing, will you get the hell out of my yard?"

"I will."

"There's no news here. She left home, that's it." He paused. His mouth was moving strangely, almost like a child's moves when he's trying not to cry.

I sat back on my haunches, my knees sinking in the cold, moist earth, and waited.

"She traded up, got herself a better man," he said.

"Who?"

"She wouldn't tell me. But you need to find Evie? Look for him."

Nelson's Tahoe idled on the far side of

Seventh Street where I'd left him. Someone was bending over the passenger door and that someone straightened. It was Ben. He skirted the hood and ambled across the street to me. He wore his field clothes, a charcoal-gray suit jacket — Italian, no doubt — perfectly tailored to show off his wide-shoulders-to-narrow-hips ratio, the top button fastened over a white shirt as bright as his grin. His torso was camera ready, but his beat-up boots and faded jeans told you everything you needed to know about him: *I'll give you what can be seen. The rest belongs to me.*

"What are you doing here?" I asked.

"You roamed pretty far afield to make that call." His dark eyes narrowed on my legs. "How'd you get all muddy?"

I told him about Evelyn's husband, how he didn't deny being at the restaurant with his wife minutes before she disappeared and that he believed there was another man. To my mind, this suggested opportunity and motive, and I should've been suspicious of Peter. In truth, all I felt was sympathy. He seemed broken.

"Sounds like we've got a lot of ground to cover," Ben said. "Better get started."

"What do you mean, we?"

"Meaning you and me. I'm your talent."

53

This wasn't a good idea for a variety of reasons, but I stuck to the most obvious: "The evening newscast needs its anchor."

"I'm sick of being an anchor." He folded his arms across his chest and raised himself to all his height. "It's so damn boring being stuck inside and reading a teleprompter all night. I don't know why I ever wanted it."

"If I remember correctly, you wanted anchor money."

He grinned. "Well, I'm not giving *that* up."

"You can't leave the anchor desk now. I can't afford the ratings to fall."

"Let them," he said softly. "It'd be Mellay's fault for taking you off the shows."

So that's why he was here. I didn't know why I was surprised. Nelson had probably been sitting in his Tahoe all this time hitting rapid dial. Ben would've been his first call.

"I don't want your sympathy," I said.

"Good. I'm only offering my help. You might as well agree to partner up. I already persuaded Mellay to put me on the story." He lifted an eyebrow. "It's a done deal unless you refuse. I don't partner up with the unwilling."

He looked amused, as if this was a game to play, one he'd surely win. I could feel the inevitability of him working the story, and it didn't make me happy.

54

"Make the deal," he said, holding out his hand, and when I didn't take it, he wiggled his fingers impatiently. "Come now, *tempus fugit.* Deadline's approaching."

When we shook, he said: "My source told me some pain-in-the-ass TV chick was saber rattling. His quote, not mine. Threatened to do a story on police incompetence if she didn't get the information she wanted. Threw a real tizzy, again his quote, so police are holding a press conference at three."

"Jesus, Ben." I checked my watch. "That's in less than a half hour."

I looked around for Nelson's Tahoe, but he'd driven away. I jogged across the street to Ben's truck.

"Plenty of time," he said, following me. "Nelson's en route to headquarters now. He'll save us a seat."

He opened the truck door and helped me in. It was no easy thing to climb into that truck in a skirt and heeled shoes. Before he closed the door, he said, "Did I mention? They've got a new commander up at Criminal Investigations."

I didn't like that particular gleam in his eye.

"Your old boyfriend. Commander Michael Ledger. That's quite a few promotions since you two parted ways. I understand he's running the news conference."

Michael. I forced my lips into a firm line.

He leaned in closer. "Why'd you blanch? Not chicken, are you?"

"Try not to be ridiculous," I said, to him or to me, I wasn't sure. "If you're done having fun at my expense, maybe we could go gather news?"

He laughed as he pointed to the seat belt. "Don't forget to buckle up. Might be a bumpy ride."

CHAPTER FIVE

The lobby of DC Police headquarters was crowded with people waiting to pass through the magnetometers, which were a huge pain in the ass. I was cooling my heels at the back of the line, trying not to worry about seeing Michael again, but the memories came without warning — Michael as I'd first seen him in the bright floodlights behind the crime scene tape, walking like a priest, touching nothing and nothing touching him. Michael tossing his tie over his shoulder as he bent over a dead man, searching for that one elusive clue.

There were other, more dangerous memories. Michael in the morning light, his body against mine as he said, *"See how we're made from the same swath of cloth?"* My skin scorched by his stubble, the lethargic tangle of limbs, how peaceful it felt. How it drugged me.

All of it was from a regrettable past I was

beyond caring about. I would've told Ben, too, except he'd know I was lying.

I glanced up at him. "Could you please stop smirking at me?"

"Not smirking." He was doing that tall-guy posturing, tucking his chin to his chest, looking down at me from beneath lowered eyebrows. His mouth formed what was clearly a smirk. "Just wondering how long it'd take to get your head back in the game. Aaaaand she's back," he drawled. "Good. What's the plan?"

We decided Ben would question the chief, since like most women, Chief Hayden found Ben charming. Me, I'd work the room. The best information came off-podium, and those were the answers I wanted. I jotted questions for Ben to ask and ripped the paper from its spiral.

He shook me off. "Got it all right here," he said, tapping his temple.

Soon an officer searched my satchel and waved us through the mags. We took the elevator to the fifth floor, where we were ushered into a storage room converted for news conferences. Our competitors were already here.

"We're the last arrivals," I complained. It was so typical of Ben. He was the slowest person I'd ever met, he really was, and now

58

he was slowing me down, too. Forget the fact that he told me about the news conference. I didn't have time to play fair.

"Why bust ass? My guy promised they'd wait for us to start and they have." He clapped his hand on my shoulder and leaned down, whispering: "Looks like you've rattled the hornet's nest, huh? If your missing girl wasn't a story before, she sure as hell is now."

His laughter boomed over the buzz of too many cops and reporters. He sauntered to the front of the room and shook hands with the captain in charge of the Information Office. They put their heads together, as if sharing gossip, which they probably were. Nelson had already set up in the line of cameras behind folding chairs. I kept my back to the wall nearest the door.

An officer shut the door beside me. Another door across the room opened, and Chief Joyce Hayden stepped through. She wore her dress blues, a navy jacket over a white shirt and black tie, four stars glittering on each shoulder, her hair bound as neatly as her body. She took her place behind the podium as a couple of plainclothes detectives filed in behind her.

There was no family joining them. In missing persons cases there was always family — parents or siblings, spouses or lovers — someone to ask for help, someone who cared.

Evelyn Carney had no one.

The last official came through the door. It was Michael. He assumed a detective stance, hands clasped behind back, weight on heels. His suit was straight from a Zegna ad, tightly fit to his runner's body. He looked the same as the day he left me. A weird pounding in my ears made the chief's words drop out like bad audio. I put my head down and, with a shaky hand, took notes on her opening statement.

The chief said that investigators were canvasing the area where Evelyn was last seen, with cadets expanding the search to the Chesapeake and Ohio Canal and adjacent woods, so far yielding no leads. Police had spoken with a witness who saw Mrs. Carney leave the restaurant and walk alone to the corner where she turned south on Wisconsin Avenue. She'd worn a long black coat and tall boots and carried a small black purse on a cross-body strap. The weather that night had been cold and messy, with patches of slush still on the ground from last week's snowfall. Not a lot of foot traffic, but police hoped more witnesses would come forward.

During the question and answer, the chief

said there'd been no recent cases of women assaulted or robbed in or around Georgetown. While there were other open cases of women missing from the District, none bore similarities to Mrs. Carney's.

No calls had been made from her cell phone. Neither her credit card nor her bank card had been used.

More hands went up.

Come on, Ben. Ask our question.

A television reporter asked the chief to describe Sunday's dinner at the restaurant. Chief Hayden stepped aside and introduced Michael, even though everyone in the room knew him. Since his early days as a young homicide detective with a gift for solving intractable cases, his superiors had assigned him to high-profile murders. He had forensic training at Quantico and a PhD in criminology. An actor in a crime drama once rode along with Michael for a month to get into character, and after that, so his fellow detectives nicknamed him "Hollywood."

Now they called him sir.

I looked away, listening to his speech, the tough, clipped sound of New England, low pitched, well remembered. "Evelyn Carney had dinner with her husband, Peter Carney," he was saying. "She left the restaurant

61

alone, and he remained behind. We've talked extensively with Mr. Carney and found him helpful and forthcoming."

Someone else asked if Peter Carney was a suspect. There was no indication a crime had been committed, Michael said, and therefore they could have no suspects. He stepped back from the podium.

Ask the damn questions, Ben.

As if he heard my thoughts, Ben turned in his chair and made a sweeping gesture in my direction, indicating my turn to speak. It was infuriating. Michael and the chief were heading to the door when I called out: "Wait, Commander. I have a question."

Michael stopped, squinting past the camera lights, and then smiled. "Miss Knightly."

"Who notified police of Evelyn Carney's disappearance? When was the notification made?"

"I believe the call came in Monday, maybe late morning, early afternoon."

"Who made the call?"

"I'd have to check the case file and get back to you."

"If Evelyn Carney's is a missing persons case, why is it being investigated by CID, rather than the district detectives who usually handle such cases?"

"We're working with district detectives,"

he said. "As you know, collaboration between the districts and headquarters is nothing new."

"Not in criminal cases it isn't, but you say there's no indication of —"

"Excuse me," he said, and whispered something to the chief. When she nodded, he ended the news conference by escorting her to the door.

Instead of following the chief, he turned back into the throng of reporters that circled him, talking to him all at once. He pushed past them, heading my way. My stomach went cold. It was just nerves; the kind anybody would have seeing him again, especially here, where everyone knew Michael and me and our history, where everyone was watching, and if I showed that I still cared, they'd tell everyone, it'd be everywhere.

The room had become loud with the clacking and banging of equipment as the photographers broke down their gear, and now Michael was close enough that I could see the stubble along his jaw. My fingers itched to rub it or slap it, I couldn't decide. My heart punched once, twice, and I bolted.

The ride back to the station was brutal. There was nothing worse than Ben's giving me the silent treatment. I'd almost prefer his bucolic tales of family and farming out west or his ear-bleeding theories of human mating based on the biological imperative, or whatever he called it. Hell, I'd even let him yammer on about the pioneering use of sheep to rid cattle-grazing lands of noxious weeds, if only he'd say something.

"Why aren't you talking?" I asked.

"Didn't want to interrupt all that noise in your head. It's pretty loud. Even from over here."

After another long moment, I told him, "Just say it."

He shrugged. "Got nothing."

Ah, the dumb cowboy routine. I hated that routine. He reserved it for folks he disdained, and that had never before included me.

We were stuck in traffic on Massachusetts Avenue by the old convention center before he drawled out: "If you really want to know? It was bad, you making calf eyes —"

"Calf eyes?"

"Getting all moony over that cop who played you for ten kinds of fool."

"That's enough, Ben."

"I'd have thought so, too. But there you were, running out."

"I got what I needed and left."

"You *ran*. Like some lovesick schoolgirl." His face remained calm, but his voice gave him away. It'd gone low with the throaty *R*'s and the flat *O*'s of the high western prairie, an almost Canadian sound that returned when his temper was riding him. "In front of every damn reporter in town. Hope to hell nobody shot video."

I hunkered down in the seat.

"If you hadn't run," he said, "you'd know I got the name of the hostess at the restaurant, the last known person to see Evelyn that night. A source told me off the record that Evelyn wasn't having some disagreement with her husband. She left him for another guy, just like the husband told you. Police know who the guy is and want to talk to him."

That got me sitting up straight. "Who?"

"They won't give up his name, and isn't that interesting? Who knows what else we could've gotten if you hadn't run?"

"You're right."

He was downshifting, and his mood went with it. "You've had a tough day. I get that. But you can't go batshit crazy on me. I need help with this script. I'm slow. I can't make deadline without you."

"We'll make it."

"People depend on you. If you fall apart, I

don't know what happens to the rest of us. I'm locked into a contract. I've finally got you broken in the way I like —"

"You *what?*"

"For the most part," he said, laughing. "And I don't want to work for anyone else."

And there it was, how I could never remain annoyed at Ben — his oaths of loyalty hidden in humor.

It was slow going through Dupont Circle. I pulled out my notebook and cleared my mind to conjure the story, and there it was: Evelyn on the dark street, her black wool coat flapping in the wind, her hair as wild and tangled as her feelings. I jotted a lead and read it under my breath. Not bad. The rewrite rolled off the tongue better. The next graph was inevitable, so I wrote that, too. Insert chief's sound bite here. Cover with video there. The rhythm of the story carried me along, drowning out everything else.

Done, I thought happily, dropping my pen in my lap and stretching my fingers. The spine of the live shot was written. I blinked Ben's profile into focus — his hawk nose, his eyebrows drawn together, a shade against the late-afternoon sun. When I blinked again, we were pulling in front of our building.

I read him the script. "Pretty good, right?"

"Damn good." His voice contained some emotion beyond respect, maybe even admiration, and I was glad. He'd forgiven me. It was the first rule, after all. If you got the story right and by deadline, how you got there was largely forgotten. The daily redemption.

CHAPTER SIX

The best part of the day is show time. I
always watched the show from the control
room with its wall of monitors and flashes
of video feeding in and the *boop-boop-boop*
of the countdown to each story. In the
control room, the work came together, alive
with sound and color and movement, and it
gave a wondrous feeling I tried to hold on
to, because also lurking was the ever-present
fear that somehow we'd missed a story or
that some news might break and bust the
show's rundown all to hell or that something
would go wrong — because something
always went wrong — and I would have to
fix it fast. That was my job.

But today I skipped all that and went
home. Not that I'd been told to stay away
or anything. I just didn't want to see Mellay
doing my job. Problem was, sitting around
the house made me fidgety, the silence
sharpened by the bare white walls and hard

surfaces of my few furnishings, when what I really wanted was the thrill of the control room or even the shouting and chaos of the newsroom — so much that it felt like withdrawal.

At six o'clock I ate supper in front of the television. Ben was the lead of the show. I'd written the script, but he brought it to life, talking to the camera like he was telling a friend a story about a lost woman. How Evelyn had been late meeting her husband at the restaurant, and when she arrived, told him she no longer wanted to be married. How she'd left her husband stunned with a table full of food. The hostess watched a distressed Evelyn stumble from the restaurant. Where did she go from there, investigators wanted to know. Had anyone seen her after she'd turned that corner?

My cell phone rang. It was Paige Linden, Evelyn's friend who hadn't wanted to talk. Now she was telling me about a vigil she was planning for Evelyn. She had printed out fliers and asked some coworkers to hand them out in Georgetown tonight. "Could your station do the story?" she asked.

Of course, I'd send a photographer to shoot pictures. "What I'd really like is to interview you on camera."

She hesitated. "There's so much to do,"

she said. "I haven't even contacted other news outlets yet."

"Maybe I can help." I flipped open my laptop. From an old press release in my email, I copied the email addresses of reporters at other stations and pasted the list into the body of an email, along with the draft of a typical press release for a missing person vigil. It was the work of a moment. It might seem a little out of the box, giving Paige a template to invite my competition, but she'd have gotten them anyway. In the time she saved, maybe she'd talk. Besides, it was important to establish reciprocity. A relationship with a potential source is like any other relationship. You couldn't just take. You had to give a little, too.

"Use this if you like," I said, typing her address into the line and clicking send. "Press releases follow this format. If you email them to a reporter's phone, it's more efficient than trying to chase them down by calling their newsrooms. Especially during happy hour," I joked. "You receive the doc yet?"

She hummed. "This is exactly what I need. Thank you."

Before we hung up, she agreed to meet after the vigil, no cameras. And yes, she said

70

in her lovely melodious voice — *yes, yes, yes* — she'd speak only with me.

I took a cab to Georgetown, getting out at the corner where the hostess had last seen Evelyn, and followed the route Evelyn must have taken. The brick walkway sloped toward the waterfront, past pretty shops and restaurants in historic buildings. This part of the city was usually busy, and tonight there was a mix of middle-aged professionals and couples on dates and some hard-faced teens in hoodies. A group of college guys who'd been drinking pretty heavily brushed past me. Among the crowd, a man's voice cried out: " *'Where, O death, is your victory? Where, O death, is your sting?'* "

Goose bumps rose along my nape. Ahead of me, the college guys staggered around a homeless woman rocking herself on the sidewalk. She had a face the color and texture of a peach pit, and her eyes were so pale they appeared milky.

From a distance, the street preacher called out again: " *'Why do you endanger yourself every hour? I face death, even as I pray for you —'* "

Someone started playing the plastic bucket drums. My feet picked up the rhythm. At the corner of Wisconsin and M streets, the

Corinthian columns of the bank framed the vigil.

I found a spot in the shadow of the bank column, where I could study the group. There was a young guy darting out at the cars stopped at the busy intersection to hand out posters. The others were dressed in business attire and chatting as you might if you'd just left those same people in the office moments earlier. They held lit candles, and there were flashes from the print photographers and lights on top of television cameras, and the lights were all moving. At the center of it all was Paige Linden.

She was taller than I'd expected, standing chin to chin with the men. Her strong face was framed by ash blond hair tucked behind her ears, and she wore silver hoops that swung as she shook her head vigorously, arguing with a blond man whose back was to me.

Someone bumped me from my blind side, knocking the satchel from my shoulder. "Sorry," I said, reflexively, to the pale, doughy-faced girl who'd come up from behind.

"Better watch yourself," she warned before rounding the column, soon out of sight.

When I turned back to the vigil, the man Paige had been arguing with was gone. Now

Paige was chatting with a female police captain and a tall, middle-aged man with the sloped shoulders and husky frame of a laborer. He wore a brown tweed blazer and a pink tie. The cameras circled them.

I showed my press passes to a man in an overcoat who was stuffing leftover candles into a box. "That's Paige Linden in the middle of everything, right?"

He glanced over. "Sure is."

"And the man she'd been with a few moments ago? Blond hair cut short, medium height, thin?"

"You're probably talking about Ian, I guess? Ian Chase?"

Of course I recognized the name. He was an assistant US attorney downtown. A few years back, he'd gotten a lot of press for the successful prosecution of corruption within the city government. The mayor had been implicated, but only his cronies had been charged. It had been a very big story. Since then, Ian Chase had been promoted to the Homicide Section as its chief.

"I don't see Ian anymore," I said, standing on my toes.

The stout man glanced around. "Huh, no. Must've left."

I asked around about Evelyn, but few knew her. They were mostly acquaintances

73

or friends of Paige Linden, who was working the crowd. She touched one woman lightly on the sleeve. To another, she gave a soft, sad smile. When her eyes locked with mine, she cut through her admirers with an easy confidence.

"Virginia Knightly, right?" she said, holding out her hand. Her grip was strong. She looked down at me, unblinking, and her eyes briefly unfocused. It gave me a weird feeling, almost like a premonition. Then her face lit with a wide smile, and the feeling was gone. She was really very lovely when she smiled.

"Thanks so much for helping with the press release," she said. "We got a good turnout, didn't we?"

"You did, yes."

She agreed to let me buy her a warm drink. When we got to the coffee shop across the street, I reached for my wallet, but it was gone. I dug deeper in the satchel where everything lost always turned up, but no wallet.

I never carried credit cards in the field, so it wasn't a complete catastrophe. My press passes and identification cards hung safely in plastic sleeves on a lanyard around my neck. But I'd lost cash and the business card I'd wanted to give Paige.

Could I have left my wallet at home? No, I had it when I paid the cabbie.

"Is something wrong?" Paige said.

And then I remembered the girl who bumped me. It must have happened then. "My plan was to treat you," I said with an apology. "But I'm pretty sure someone lifted my wallet."

CHAPTER SEVEN

The coffee shop was nearly empty. I chose a table at the back, far from the windows and the prying eyes of my competitors, and watched Paige Linden place our order at the counter. She wasn't beautiful, but was something better. She had sharp cheeks and a strong nose, a chin that could crack ice, and there was a glow about her, as if she revved at higher throttle than the rest of us mere mortals.

She walked toward me, her confident stride laced with swagger, and when she held out my coffee, she winced. I jumped up. "You okay?" I said, helping her with the drinks.

"Sparring injury." She rubbed her shoulder in an annoyed manner. She was a runner, she said, but on off days practiced martial arts for self-defense. During practice last night, she'd let down her guard and taken a hard right to the shoulder. "It was stupid to work out when my thoughts were so scattered. I kept worrying about where Evie could be."

Gingerly, she slipped off her jacket and settled it on the back of her chair before seating herself. She wore a silver necklace with a circle pendant. It glittered over a black sweater that was tightly fitted to show off her muscular arms and neck. She appeared capable of great athletic feats, and I could tell she took pride in her body. It was the way she held herself, tall and straight, pointy chin lifted.

"I can tell from your reports that you're getting good intel from the authorities, aren't you?" she said. "Are they saying anything you're not reporting?"

It was as if she was the producer, and she was interviewing me.

"You were talking to a police official tonight, too," I said. "What do you hear?"

"Do they think Evie was abducted?" she asked, ignoring my question.

I hunched over my coffee, warming my palms on the cup, and thought about it. "There's no evidence pointing that way, not that I'm aware of. Investigators seem more interested in Evelyn's marital troubles. They say she left her husband for another man. What do you know about that?"

"It doesn't explain why she hasn't been to work," she argued. "If Evie separated from her husband, how does that keep her from her job? She's been a no-show. No calls. Nothing. If she's not sick or hurt, she'll be fired."

"Would that be a big deal? Does she like her job?"

"Evie was thrilled when I hired her." She explained how a colleague had called in a favor last year, asking Paige to give Evelyn a chance, and as these things happen every day in the District, Evelyn was hired. Evelyn was smart and hardworking. She'd been a good hire, Paige said defiantly, even if Evelyn wasn't like the other associates and didn't have Paige's Ivy League education or résumé full of clerkships or family connections to help her along.

"It's so boring how top firms pick candidates from the same schools and backgrounds and who all look and act and talk like all the other partners." She paused, waiting for me to agree, as if I was someone with Paige's background, as if her firm would pick someone like me — which it wouldn't.

That I kept to myself.

"Personally, I like to think out of the box," she went on. "And Evie does make a different impression. The first day I introduced her, you should have seen my coworkers, all respectable middle-aged men, well informed about workplace rules, reduced to fawning idiots. At first glance of her, their brains checked out, one by one."

She described Evelyn's dress as conservative enough, her suits the right color and length. "But when you're built like Evie, you have to be concerned with fit. I showed her how to camouflage. We softened her makeup, tidied her hair. We even nixed her shoes, which were a little too *Sex and the City* for a law firm in Washington."

That I understood: there was the District, which was young and hip, and there was Washington with the white buildings, which was anything but. The two never mixed comfortably. The big law firms belonged resolutely to Washington.

"But she's great with clients," Paige said. "Especially the men. The more powerful they are, the better she is. I think she sees them as a challenge, like a puzzle to solve, and they love her for it."

"Anybody love her a little too much?"

"Stop right there," she said quietly. "Maybe Evie has a certain appeal, but she has never behaved inappropriately with a client."

"How would you know?"

She lifted her cup and leveled an icy gaze at me over the rim. The steam pinked her cheeks. I caught hints of cinnamon and cardamom, a bite of pepper.

"I've already told you," she said. "I'm her mentor. I'm also her boss, and those clients whose behavior you're questioning are my clients."

"Any way I could get their names?"

Her cup clanked down on the table and she leaned toward me aggressively, saying, "This is about Evie. Not my clients."

I wasn't so sure. According to Ben's source, Evelyn left her husband for a man whose name the investigators weren't ready to give up. This suggested the police were giving him special consideration. Perhaps one of the clients Evelyn won over?

"Did Evelyn mention being afraid of anyone in the workplace?" I said. When she ignored the question, I went on: "How about the husband, Peter?"

She rocked back, seemingly content that I'd backed off about her clients for now. Her long fingers tapped on the arms of the chair.

"I really don't know," she said. "We work long hours, without break, often through shared meals. A few times, I took her out to celebrate after a win in court. You'd think all that time together would create intimacy, but she never spoke of her personal life, certainly not of Peter, except to mention when he was away. Apparently he goes overseas for months at a time, some kind of military deployment. That's when she'd ask for extra work, more hours to bill out."

"You called Evelyn your friend," I said, disappointed. "You gave the impression that you were close."

Her stern expression was replaced by a smile. It was a really lovely smile. "As friendly as work allows. Have you ever worked in a law firm?"

When I admitted I hadn't, she explained her firm's rigid social structure. It was much like a caste system with the three founding partners at the pinnacle, presiding over everyone else. Beneath them were the partners and then the associates ranked according to their years in service to the firm. Evelyn was a first-year associate, barely above the support staff — paralegals and secretaries, and the like.

"So we really can't hang out," she said. "It's frowned upon to socialize with anyone except your peers, and no one moves up and down, except by the whims and follies of our founding partners. A stupid system,

81

if you ask me, where three people have such power, even determining who I can be friends with. Still, I let it be known in no uncertain terms that Evie, as my hire, was under my protection."

"So you were concerned about Evelyn? Someone was a threat?"

"That's not what I mean." She glanced over her shoulder, even though we were the only patrons left in the shop, and the barista had ducked into the back room. "As I said, I brought Evie in, but last fall she was reassigned to work for my nemesis. A real piece of work, believe me. Makes every woman at the firm feel she has no future. I didn't want her to chase Evie away, too."

"Wait. *Her?*"

She leaned forward on her elbow and said in a confidential tone: "Bernadette Ryan."

I shook my head. The name didn't ring a bell.

"Founding partner," she went on. "A very big name in the political world with extraordinarily big money clients. When she tells the other partners to jump, they jump."

"You worried for Evelyn?"

"Yes."

"Because this Bernadette has gender preferences?"

"For men."

"Yet here you are, a partner."

"Here I am," she said, and laughed. It was a triumphant sound, full of the same music in her voice. "Bernadette tried to cheat me out of the fast track to partnership that I'd been promised, the sole reason I chose my firm. She went behind my back, actively campaigned against me, pressured the other partners into voting for anyone except me."

"And she lost?"

Her intense eyes seemed to glitter. "Oh yes. I won."

"Why would she try to cheat you?"

"I don't question why some women are competitive with others," she said, shrugging. "It's too stupid to contemplate. I only wanted to protect Evie from enduring what I'd had to. Evie's an intelligent woman and a good lawyer, but there's something gentle about her. That makes her more vulnerable to office politics than I ever was."

The barista came out of the back room and began wiping down the espresso machine. I glanced at the clock on my phone. There was only an hour until deadline, and I had little to show for it — some non-reportable background, a better feel for Evelyn in her workplace, and video of the vigil I had yet to carry uptown for editing.

"What about Ian Chase?" I said. "What

83

does he think?"

That surprised her. "You know Ian?"

"Sure, he's an AUSA downtown. I saw you talking with him tonight. You seemed at odds."

"I asked him about the search," she said, "but he denied knowing anything. Investigators aren't talking to him."

Now I was surprised. Police and prosecutors were on the same team. They gossiped and shared information, formed alliances and friendships. Even if Ian's office hadn't formally discussed the Carney case with police yet, Ian should've been able to find out anything he wanted with one phone call to headquarters. It would be considered a professional courtesy. It was also the way the city worked.

"He's probably lying about what he knows," she said. "Look, Ian and I go way back. We dated eons ago, and we're still friends — because you want to be friends with a guy like Ian — but truth is, that's typical Ian, hitting me up for information, needing to be in the know."

"Because Ian's office has an interest in the search?" I said. That would mark a significant change in the case if the Homicide Section had become involved.

"No, he didn't say that." Her fingers

twisted the silver necklace as she thought about it. The longer she thought, the more agitated she appeared. "The questioning was pretty casual."

"What's his interest?" I said. "If it's not professional, it's personal?"

Now the pendant was swinging back and forth on the necklace, like the flick of a cat's tail. "No, I don't know," she said slowly. "If his office isn't involved in Evie's search, I haven't the foggiest idea why he was here."

With my wallet gone and no cash for a cab, I called our news desk and begged a ride from our courier, who dropped me off in our station's horseshoe driveway. I hurried inside, heading straight for the edit suites, where I found my editor, Doug Fordham, waiting in the doorway with his hand out.

"Not much time here," he said.

I slapped the video into his palm. "Enough."

We picked out a good shot of Paige Linden talking to the police captain at the vigil, and then we were searching for the video of Ian Chase. If the head of the Homicide Section was at a missing woman's vigil, I wanted to show him, even if I had no idea why he was there.

Doug paused at a shot. "That him?"

85

"No."

He scrolled through more video. "If you could describe him better."

"Blond? Hell, I didn't get a good look," I said. "Pull up file footage on the server, so we can see his face."

"We're up against deadline," he muttered as he swung his chair from the edit machine to the computer. He typed with a fury, complaining about how any minute someone would call down to yell at him about missing his slot. "I'll blame it on you," he warned as he stopped on a still photo. "That him?" When I said, "No, I don't think — no," he began typing and talking under his breath: "I'll sell you out in a heartbeat. Don't think I won't."

I laughed. "I'll take the fall."

A headshot filled the monitor. I got up dizzily and moved closer to the screen: there, Ian Chase's official portrait from the Department of Justice. And then another of Ian standing in front of DC Superior Court, and Ian at a black-tie fund-raiser.

Ah, of course.

He was in the story with the cutaway shot I was looking for. I remembered the podium shot of Ian addressing a gathering. Behind him were several feds in suits and a white shirt from US Park Police. Cut to an audience shot of Evelyn Carney, gazing outward, rapturously — maybe at Ian? I didn't know. I couldn't see beyond the frame.

"Virginia? You okay?"

"Can you finish without me?" I said, already out the door.

I ran back to my office and logged into my computer and there, the story slug:

Rock Creek Serial Rapist

Dateline: August 5

Location: Community Center, Rock Creek Park, NW DC

Summary: Police task force meets community leaders, re: sex assaults of female joggers in park. Latest victim, twenty-year-old Susan Wilkes of NW DC, died Tuesday from injuries.

The news package opened with footage from a lonely park path, a shot of a gurgling creek surrounded by summer foliage and yellow crime scene tape fluttering in the breeze. Next, a wide shot of police officials glad-handing like the politicians they could be. A jump cut to Ian Chase speaking at a podium — *yes!* — a handsome man with narrow patrician features and short blond hair, perfectly coiffed. I turned up the volume for his talk about the attacks, but couldn't concentrate on his voice or the words, because I knew what was coming next . . .

And there she was — *hallelujah!* — in that cutaway that'd been nagging at me: Evelyn Carney, a young woman caught in an unguarded moment, her face flushed with excitement, all big eyes and wild, dark hair. She might wear a plain charcoal suit and high-buttoned blouse all she liked, but she drew the eye and kept it. Those near her were a background's afterthought: the gray-haired man mopping sweat from his forehead, and on her other side, an elegant older blonde in a gold brocade jacket, the rest of the crowd blank faced and bored looking, wilted by the summer's heat.

The generic crowd shot, I thought, except for her. Evelyn Carney was different. Her delicate shoulders were thrown forward, her attention riveted.

Who was the object of it?

It might be Ian Chase. It might not be. During the editing process, video was routinely taken out of sequence, so that in this shot, Evelyn could be looking at anyone.

It was impossible to know from an edited story.

The raw video would tell, but it wasn't in the system. Had it been accidentally deleted or trashed to make space? Maybe someone had forgotten to load it. These things happened all the time.

I went back to the edited story and copied it onto a flash drive and clipped that drive to a lanyard around my neck. Before shutting down the computer, I took one last look at Evelyn. The video only brought the same questions: *Who are you looking at? What is it that you so obviously want? Did you get it?*

And then, probably the most difficult to answer: *Why the hell do I care?*

CHAPTER EIGHT

I didn't want to talk to Commander Michael Ledger. In fact, my plan had been to avoid him for the rest of my life and go nowhere near the circle in which he moved, and if I saw him on the street, turn and go the other way. That was the intention, anyway. The story made him unavoidable.

Next morning, I called police headquarters and put in a request for a meeting with Michael. Within the hour, Michael's secretary was escorting me into his office. It was a dreary place with dark paneled walls and old furniture more suited for a curb. The secretary's bracelets jingled as she pointed me toward a sofa, where I sat between two punctures in the vinyl, careful not to snag my stockings. As soon as she left, I got up and went straight for Michael's desk.

Photos stood at attention on its top, each in matching silver frames: Michael at the helm of his boat; Michael with a marathon race number pinned to his chest, crossing a finish line; Michael with the movie star who rode along with him for months, studying how to play a detective from the expert. My stomach twisted at the pictures of his two small children, a boy sporting a cowlick and glasses, a toddler with Michael's pale gray eyes. There were no photographs of the woman he'd recently divorced.

Evelyn's case jacket would be somewhere among the files on his desk. Not that I'd go digging through them. It was unthinkable to rifle through a police official's desk. I wound my arms around my waist and bent over the desk, and there it was. The mud-brown jacket with Evelyn's name and case number typed in the corner. It was on the top of one of the stacks, in plain sight. I opened it.

Clipped inside, the picture of Evelyn on the missing persons poster, as well as a wedding photograph of Evelyn and Peter Carney on a dance floor. Peter seemed so young, bulky with a corn-fed wholesomeness, and he was smiling broadly, at ease with himself and his place in the world. Evelyn was in profile, her arms clinging to his neck as if trying to lift herself from the drowning layers of her dress.

It was an odd picture for a case jacket. It

showed more of the husband than the woman that police were searching for. I wondered why it'd been chosen.

The door banged open, and Michael strode in. He stopped midway, hands in his pockets, rattling coins. For a long moment, all I could hear was Michael with his money.

"You haven't changed at all," he said.

But he had. Vertical lines were dug deep between his eyebrows. The arrogant line of his jaw had fallen. He appeared tired and unhappy, maybe even worried, and then I reminded myself, Michael Ledger's moods were not my concern.

"I see you found the file," he said.

"I'd like to read it. With your permission, of course."

He laughed.

"Will you talk to me about Evelyn Carney?" I said. "I need help."

He went to the sofa and plopped down, sprawling his legs. He patted a spot on the vinyl next to him. "Come. Sit."

I crossed the room and chose the farthest spot on the sofa, teetering on its edge. The smell of his musky cologne was strong. When he'd been with me, he'd never worn it. Even after he'd come home from the Medical Examiner's Office and had to scrub himself down with lemon soap and steam clean his pores and shampoo his hair twice, he'd gone without cologne, knowing I didn't like it. I preferred men to smell like men, for better or worse.

"You look prosperous," he said, smiling. "I hear you've done well. Aren't you some big-shot producer now?"

My heel tapped impatiently. I caught him staring at my legs and stopped tapping.

"I wanted to call you after the chief's press conference," he went on. "But I was afraid you'd slam the phone in my ear. Maybe you held a grudge?"

"You mean, for the way you dumped me."

It gave me great satisfaction to see him so uncomfortable in his beautiful suit, yanking at his silk tie. "Well, I wouldn't say —"

"If this has to be done before we can get to business, let's be accurate. You dumped me and married another woman within six months. You had a wedding that took at least a year to plan."

"And a marriage that took several more years to fall apart," he muttered under his breath, and then: "Look, I know how it seemed."

"That you were duplicitous or that I was an idiot to trust you? Both seemed that way because that's how it was, but the past bores me. I'm here about Evelyn Carney. What's your working theory of her disappearance?"

He nodded once, as if to say, okay, if that's how you want to do this.

"Could be a robbery gone bad," he said, scrubbing at the stubble on his jaw. "More likely a street snatching with intent to defile. Probably by a predator." He paused. "No evidence of that. Just my gut."

"You see any connection to the open cases of sex assaults on joggers in Rock Creek Park?"

The lines between his eyebrows deepened, as he considered it. "Different MO," he said as his eyes unfocused and he slipped into his Zen mode and talked softly, as if to himself: "Rock Creek suspect lurks in the remote parts of the park, away from cars. He uses a knife. Not impulsive, he waits patiently, choosing his ambush at a blind turn in a path, places accessible only by foot, far from help. This eastern section of the park he knows well, feels comfortable in. Probably lives or works east of the park, close to where he hunts his victims."

I imagined his thoughts traveling across the separate crime scenes, flying from the lonely park paths to the busy street in Georgetown from which Evelyn had disappeared, searching for coincidence, intersection, clues investigators might have missed.

"Now, a snatching on a busy street," he went on softly, "that's an entirely different thing. Daring. Decisions made quickly. No time to lurk. Not when there could be witnesses, security cameras. A victim fights back, cries for help, and someone would hear her. Most of all, a Georgetown abduction would require a vehicle. We don't know if this guy has one."

"But you're not ruling him out?"

He got up from the sofa and started pacing. "If this is the same guy, there's been a change in his needs, more risk taking — an escalation."

The security cameras interested me. There were thousands of cameras across the city, some owned by the feds, others by the District, but most were owned by private companies — paid for by the merchants. For years, police had argued for their full access to private cameras, to no avail. The merchants had dug their heels deep. I asked Michael if there was security video showing Evelyn that night.

"Not that anyone's shared," he said sourly. "There seems to be a distinct lack of trust in authority these days. Cooperation tends to go hand in hand with trust."

My palm slid across my press passes. The thumb drive with video of Evelyn was still on the lanyard around my neck. "Is it a coincidence that Evelyn Carney attended a meeting in Rock Creek about the attacks?"

"What meeting?"

"Some task force question and answer with the community. The mayor was there. Ian Chase, too."

"Intriguing, this rumor —"

"Not rumor. Fact."

"That Evelyn was at that meeting? Who's the source?"

"Don't need a source," I said. "Not when I have video."

It was subtle, the faint pink spreading across his cheekbones. "I'd like to see this video."

"Not a chance," I said, and then: "So tell me about the US Attorney's Office. They involved in Evelyn's case yet?"

He was watching me silently, steadily, with a cunning look. I could almost hear his thoughts. Finally, I burst out laughing. "You're trying to figure out how to compel my video."

"Wrong," he said with a sly smile. "I already know how to get it. Is it worth my time? Describe it."

"Not until I hear an offer."

He asked what I wanted, and I told him everything, what I could report and what I could not, details both important and those seemingly irrelevant. I wanted to know the players, who Evelyn knew and loved and hated, and especially those who loved and hated her. I wanted to know about Peter Carney and the marriage and about the investigation.

"That's a lot of wanting," he complained.

"Not really. Start with her workplace. Anything suspicious about the firm?"

His eyebrows went up. "Simmons, Mc-Fadden & Ryan? The gold standard, extremely well regarded from what I'm told, and yes, we've checked."

"Any creeps or stalkers or weirdo clients?"

"We've done interviews, routine stuff. So far, everybody checks out."

"All right," I said. "How about Ian Chase?"

He gave me a surprised look I'm not sure I bought. "I thought we were talking about Evelyn."

"Exactly."

"Well, I'm not the right guy to ask. Ian and me, we don't exactly move in the same circles." But he shrugged as if to say, if *you wanna waste your time, fine by me.* "Word is, he comes from loot and clout with judges and politicians on both sides of the Chase family tree, and you know how that plays around here. Golden boy was born with the keys to the kingdom, and all the ass kissing that accompanies it. It's only gotten worse since he's up for US Attorney."

"But not you? You don't kiss his ass?"

He frowned. "His coattail is not my ride."

"You don't like him?" I prodded.

"Didn't say that."

"Then why withhold information about Evelyn's case from him?"

Again, a look of surprise, and this seemed genuine. "You got a bad source on that one."

Or Michael's investigators were keeping him out of the loop. I'd have to look into that later. "Ian Chase attended Evelyn's vigil last night, because he knows her, right?"

"He does?"

I always admired how he answered a question with a question, as if he were truly puzzled. He made it so believable.

"I have video of them at that meeting, remember?" Not that I had video of them *together,* of course, but when fishing, sometimes it was hard to get off the boat.

"Christ, I need caffeine to keep up with you," he complained, crossing the room to some shelves where an old coffeepot sat. He carried the empty pot to the door. "I have to step out for water. That file does not leave this office, understand? You disappear with it, I'll arrest you."

I opened the file. Among the first pages, a curriculum vitae in neat block type:

Peter Lawrence Carney, age thirty-one, native of Oneida, New York, currently residing at 600 A Street SE, Washington, DC. College grad, Syracuse University. Upon graduation, officer candidate school, four years active-duty USMC, enlisted USMC reserves (see career below).

No arrests, no convictions, no records of calls to present or preceding home addresses.

Status: Married to Evelyn Marie Sutton Carney. (Marital separation requested by Evelyn Carney on March 8, night of disappearance, see statement attached).

Career: Currently working in Office of Civilian-Military Cooperation, USAID, at Reagan Building. Active-duty reservist, Captain USMC, attached to civilian affairs unit at Headquarters Marine Corps. History: multiple tours of duty in Afghanistan; six months deployment, expeditionary crisis response force. Civilian and work patterns fluctuate: tends to follow six- to nine-month deployment overseas followed by year of civilian work in States.

Comments: Since return from Afghanistan January 17, Carney reports insomnia and frequent headache, some weight loss. No prescription or illegal drug use or abuse, uses alcohol for insomnia but "not excessively." No history of domestic abuse, says he has never struck Evelyn Carney or any woman. Does not believe he suffers from PTSD, but says he's not been tested. No physical ailments or injuries. To this detective, Peter Carney appears in good overall mental and physical health. His demeanor is direct, forthright, and exhibits worry for Evelyn Carney's well-being and willingness to assist investigators —

The next page highlighted part of the interview of Peter Carney by Detective Miller dated Tuesday, March 10, at 2:45 p.m.

I waited for her at the restaurant. She showed up sometime around 9:30. She looked nervous. I held out my hand and asked what was wrong. She said she had to leave me. This time, for real. I told her she didn't. There's always an adjustment when I get home, but we always worked things out. She put her head down and cried. Here we were in the middle of this restaurant with all these people pretending not to watch the spectacle of my wife with her face in her hands. I lost my temper. I told her to stop crying. It was bad form. Get ahold of yourself, I said. She got up and left.

From beneath the door, I could hear Michael talking to his secretary. I put my head down as the audio guys do when they need to focus. Other sounds registered — a door opening and closing, light steps across the tiles, water pouring into a carafe and glass striking a metal plate, and finally, there was Michael moving quietly across the room to me. He took the file from my hands and closed it. From the top drawer of his desk, he pulled out a brown leather notebook.

"Needless to say, everything's off the record," he said.

I tilted my head. "What does 'off the record' mean to you?"

"Ha, nice try." He balanced himself on the edge of the desk, tapping the little notebook, and listed his demands: I could report nothing unless he okayed it beforehand, and if I did have something to report, he was to be described as a source with knowledge of the investigation, nothing more specific. If I used his information to get someone else to talk, he wanted a heads up. "You don't agree to everything, you might as well leave now," he said. "No video in the world is worth my ass."

I agreed, for now. We could renegotiate at a later time.

"Tell me about Evelyn," I said.

"First the video."

"Uh-uh, nope. Don't want to prejudice you. I'll email you the clip and you tell me what you see. Now Evelyn."

"Seriously good-looking woman," he said.

I rolled my eyes. "Yeah, yeah, yeah. What does she do? What is she like?"

"Like the kind of sexy that smacks a man in the face." He pursed his lips, more serious now. "One thing everyone agrees on, she's smart and ambitious. Worked her way through law school, landed a great job. She and the hubby have known each other all their lives, high school sweethearts who married out of college. If you can believe people still do shit like that."

"Sounds all right to me," I said, and then frowned. "Unless he killed her. You think he killed her?"

102

"Hope not. The guy's damn near a freaking war hero." He slapped his thigh anxiously, the brown notebook making a *thud thud thud*. "Besides, a restaurant full of witnesses place him at the table for a good half hour after Evelyn left, zoned out."

"What about the man she left him for? There was another man, right?"

"So Carney says," he said dryly. "We don't know where she was going that night. We certainly don't know where she ended up. Our witness saw her walking to the corner of Wisconsin Avenue and heading south. After that, she's gone, poof, into thin air."

Sighing, he got up and moved to the window, where he opened the blinds to his view of Indiana Avenue from five floors up, quite impressive for a former detective. The brown book was thudding against his thigh again. When he turned back to me, he wore a humble expression that didn't suit him. "I'm not a guy who wallows in the past, but the other day when I saw you — well, let's just say, I don't feel right how it all went down with you. Maybe I have . . . regrets." *Regrets,* as if he was just discovering the word. "I'd like to make it up to you. If you let us, we could be friends."

That was impossible. In many ways, the District is a small town. Everyone knows

103

everyone else, and they'd all known Michael was in love, but not with me, long before I did. The rumors had swirled. When Michael's engagement announcement was made public, my colleagues had treated me with kid gloves. Some had even pitied me.

"You can be my source," I told him. "See how that plays out."

He nodded once. "All right, how does this source keep you from airing that video of Evelyn?"

"You don't."

"What if I asked you to wait?"

"I'd need a compelling reason, an issue of public safety, or if the video compromises Evelyn's life or the investigation in some way. Whatever it is, you have to articulate it."

"You couldn't just trust me?"

Suddenly I understood. "This case has you worried."

"What if I offered you a deal?" he said, gazing down at the brown book. He held it out to me. "Take a look. Tell me if you want it."

CHAPTER NINE

The book had been recovered from the glove box in Evelyn's Volvo, still impounded at the police lot off of South Capitol Street. It was small and covered in soft textured leather, and fit my hand as if made for me. Best I could tell it was some sort of journal.

The red satin ribbon opened to a page filled with wild loops pressed hard into paper. Evelyn's handwriting, presumably. There were descriptions of marble buildings against a gunmetal-gray river and boats that raced on long white wakes. The best views were from across the river, this writer believed — the spires of Georgetown University reaching heavenward, the star-shaped lanterns illuminating the Key Bridge, and farther still, the Kennedy Center like a tidy shirt box nestled along the river.

Favorite haunts were mentioned: an upstairs room at a speakeasy, a piano bar in a club with no name, dinner parties she couldn't imagine attending — and yet, here she was, in the famous wine cellar, no less — a private room at a steakhouse on Pennsylvania Avenue, where she charmed clients —

"This is Evelyn's writing? You're certain?"

"Certain as we can be," he said dryly. "You want to deal or what?"

I wanted the journal. What I got was its copy. In return, I promised to email him the video of Evelyn at the meeting with Ian, and give him a few days before we put the video on air. Why he'd dealt so fiercely for that reprieve, I didn't much care. I got my glimpse into Evelyn.

After leaving headquarters, I walked the block to my car, which was parked across the street from the US Attorney's Office. I tossed my satchel and the journal copy onto the driver's seat and called up to Ian's office. No answer on his line. No room to leave a message on the voice mail, either. His spokesperson said that Mr. Chase was out of the office, and no, she couldn't say when he'd be back. The office had no statement regarding the Evelyn Carney case. All inquiries were being handled by the DC Police.

"Ian Chase was at a vigil for the missing

woman last night," I told her. "So the US Attorney's Office is investigating, I take it? And he's the head of Homicide Section, right? That means —"

"There are no statements at this time," she said, and hung up.

I got into the car and sat staring at the phone in my hand, thinking about the conversation. Its tenor surprised me — the spokesperson's evasion, her defensiveness that seemed almost protective, the abrupt hang up. It was rare for the US Attorney's Office to be anything but coolly professional. Of all the press offices in the city, they ran theirs best.

The clock on the phone showed it was midmorning, long past time to get back to the station. I called into the news desk to give my ETA. Isaiah picked up on the first ring. "Where the hell are you?" he said. "I've had to cover for you all morning."

I told him about the detour to police headquarters and the interview that ran longer than expected and was about to tell him about the journal when he interrupted me. "Well, heads up, Mellay's on the warpath," he said angrily. "He's been looking for you and can't figure out how I don't know where you are. Makes me look like I'm not doing my job. And oh, by the way, he announced layoffs this morning. Stacey is already gone —"

"What do you mean, *gone*?" I said, shocked.

"She was escorted out of the door like some kind of criminal."

It was outrageous. Stacey was our receptionist, the most thankless, ill-paying job in all of television, and yet she was competent and patient, dealing with the crazy callers and the on-air egos. She worked hard, and she was loyal. There was no reason for her to be gone. I imagined her dead-man's walk as she was escorted out, carrying her personal belongings, the school pictures of her small children —

The images made me so angry that my hands shook and the phone slipped from my hand. "You still there? Isaiah? I dropped you."

"You certainly have," he said, and hung up.

The traffic was heavy on Massachusetts Avenue, so I ran a couple of red lights on Thirty-Fourth Street to make up time. I pulled into the garage and then my parking space. The elevator to the newsroom was crowded.

At the receptionist desk, a new intern out of J-school handled the phones, ringing

108

more frequently than she could answer. She vibrated with nervousness or excitability — I was uncertain — and then I noticed four empty cans of diet soda on her desk.

She handed me a pile of yellow while-you-were-out messages. The last note gave me pause. "What's this about my mother calling?"

"She called a couple times," she said, snapping her gum. "I tried to put her through to your cell, but you didn't pick up."

"My mother's dead —"

"Oh my god." Her gum dangled on her lip. "And you didn't get a chance to talk to her?"

I handed the note back to her. "No, this is a crazy caller. You have to recognize them. They sound sane and their stories real, but they're not. Be polite. Don't engage. Get rid of them."

"Uh-huh. I had to hang up on some drunk girl this morning. Said she wanted to sell her story about a missing woman."

"*What?* Where's her number?"

She gawked at me, her face reddening, and then: "Maybe I wrote it someplace." She sorted through scraps of paper strewn across the desk. When she peeked up again, she was teary eyed. "She had a weird name, and she wanted money. That's not right, is it?"

"No, we don't buy stories, but this is my story. Those calls go to me." I pulled a tissue from the box and handed it to her. "First lesson is there's no crying in news." And then I thought, no, that's the second. The first is to get someone with experience to answer my damn phones. "You're a female journalist. Under no circumstances can you show emotion. Do you understand?"

She nodded tearfully.

"Okay, good." I glanced at my watch. "I have to find Isaiah, and we'll get you help with these phones. Meantime, find me that number."

The newsroom was deserted. The studio sign requesting Quiet Please blinked on. It appeared we were getting ready for a live shot. I stood over Isaiah's empty desk, watching how the studio lights overtook the darkness and bathed everything in a soft golden light, and then Moira swept into the room, and she, too, was in the light. It was all so beautiful it hurt.

The teleprompter spun the words on its wheel like a slot machine before steadying. Moira squinted at the teleprompter and then to the script that lay on the anchor desk before crushing the script in her fist.

I stepped under the lights, which warmed my hair.

"You're here, oh thank god, fix this," she said, shoving the balled-up script in my hand. "Hurry, I'm on in ten minutes."

I couldn't imagine the script was bad as all that, and then I read it. The diction was meant to sound hip, slangy, except I'd never heard Moira talk like that. Worse, there was an absence of facts. I picked up a Sharpie and scribbled changes.

Behind me, a throat cleared. "What's the problem, Moira?" Mellay asked.

"This needs a few adjustments," I said, marking copy.

"I approved the script. You'll read it."

She lifted her chin. "I won't."

The seconds on the clock ticked. "Can we just get through this live shot?" I said.

He cut me a narrow-eyed look, and then said to Moira: "If you don't read the script I've approved, we'll have dead air, and I promise you, we won't have it a second time. I'll call one of the dozens of experienced reporters who can't find a job. Someone who'd be thrilled to read whatever I give them and *who won't threaten me with dead air.*"

She read flawlessly. When the studio lights winked out, she crumpled the script and tossed it in a high arc onto the black carpeting and walked off the set. She glided past Ben, who was leaning against the farthest wall, his arms across his chest, watchful.

"Come out everyone," Mellay shouted. He stepped onto Moira's chair and climbed onto the anchor desk. "Isaiah, call everyone in. Let's get this said, once and for all."

The editorial staff shuffled in — what used to be my staff — along with photographers and editors, studio techs and engineers. Ben remained with his back against the wall.

"I look around this room," Mellay said, "and I see the best in the city. We're number one because of you. It's important to recognize your talent." He nodded, smiling, even as he held up a hand. "*However,* being the best does not exempt you from what's happening all over the industry, competition from nontraditional news content providers, from culture and entertainment websites and bloggers. The audience for traditional news is dwindling, and with it, money. News requires people and equipment, and people and equipment require money. That money comes from advertisers who pay according to our audience. We have to bring in the audience to pay for our jobs, right?"

He was nodding again. A few nods were returned, and then it went through the room like a wave and everyone was in the wave with him. Except for me. I was waiting for the other shoe to drop.

"I know how to bring in audience," he said. "That's what I do."

Someone raised her hand. He ignored her.

"The audience wants change," he said, surveying the room that had gone silent except for the distant chirp of police scanners. "Change I cannot make with the resistance I've been encountering. Each of you must make your own decision. Do you want to keep your job, or not? Think about it."

He hopped down from the anchor desk and everyone filed out. He crossed the room to me. "This morning I requested an update on the missing woman story, but you were MIA."

"Actually, I was out working that story," I said.

"Join us in my meeting," he said. "Get everyone up to speed."

"I have to meet with Isaiah."

"He'll be there."

CHAPTER TEN

The conference room was crowded. Ben was at the far end of the table, his head down with his ball cap flipped backward, scribbling dark lines across a reporter pad. Nelson slouched next to him, chin on palm, half asleep. In my chair was the blond beauty queen from the lobby the day before.

"We haven't met," I said.

She took my hand. "Heather Buchanan."

"You're new, so you probably don't realize you're in my chair."

"There are others," she said, looking through me.

She had TV starlet written all over her, and I was pretty sure, Mellay wrapped around her finger. Maybe I couldn't help my meeting being stolen by Mellay, but I'd damn well keep my seat at the table.

"Yes, there are," I said. "Choose one."

Heather glanced beyond my shoulder to where Mellay was fidgeting noisily at the

114

head of the table. She got up and took a seat next to Isaiah.

"Let's start with Virginia," Mellay said, smirking. "She's working the woman missing from Georgetown. What have you got today?"

Around the table there were curious glances. Ben kept his head down to his reporter pad, so I spoke to the tuft of dark hair spilling from the hole in the back of his cap. "As you know, MPD received a missing person report for Evelyn Carney on Monday afternoon. This afternoon marks the fourth day of their investigation. Nelson has fresh video of police cadets searching the C&O. Detectives canvased the neighborhood around Prospect Street where Carney was last seen. We'll pursue the latest in the investigation —"

"Not what you're pursuing," Mellay interrupted. "What we're reporting. What's the lead, Virginia?"

"There are several angles we're *pursuing*," Ben said without looking up from his doodling. "But the longer we sit here *talking*, the less time we have out there *confirming*."

Mellay jerked his chin toward where Heather and Isaiah sat. "We've been working the story at this end. Heather has uncovered some interesting details."

115

Ben looked up from his reporter pad. "Who the hell is Heather?"

"My trainee," Mellay said. "Isaiah's been showing her the ropes."

Isaiah ran his palm over his scalp, nervously. The staff was taking it all in, rapt.

To diffuse it, I smiled. "You're in good hands," I told Heather, before my gaze settled on Isaiah. He wouldn't meet my eyes. "Can you tell us what you have?"

"I have a source," she said in a low breathy voice, holding both hands out, as if the camera were already rolling. "Apparently Evelyn Carney was having a secret love affair with a coworker who killed her and dumped the body."

This contradicted what Michael had just told me. "Who's your source?"

"I'd rather not say."

"We need to confirm it," Mellay said. "I want to lead the six o'clock with it."

"Everything is protected within these walls," I explained to her, "but if you can't give a name, you can categorize. You know, is your source a police investigator or family member? That sort of thing."

She shook her head.

"You understand it's our story?" Ben said. "If you don't tell us who or what's the relationship, how can we determine reli-

116

ability? For all I know, you're talking to some nutcase or someone with an ax to grind. Could be some yahoo trying to get on TV."

"Don't attack her," Mellay said. "It's not her fault she's dug up more than you two award-winning journalists."

Ben flipped his ball cap around and tugged the brim low over his eyes. "It's my face going on the air," he said.

"Not necessarily."

Ben rose slowly until he towered over us, pressing his knuckles into the table. Here we go, I thought: Hurricane Ben ready to unleash his fury. I didn't know what he meant to do, but it was as exciting as a summer storm — and likely as damaging for him. Mellay had settled back in his chair, waiting for Ben to do something stupid.

I dialed my phone quickly. "Gentlemen, please," I said, holding up a hand for silence.

When he answered my call with a curt "Michael Ledger," I pressed the phone closer to my ear and told him: "I'm in a crowded meeting and can be overheard, but I need a quick yes or no. Is it true investigators believe Evelyn Carney was having an affair with a coworker who killed her and dumped her body?"

He snorted. "Where'd you get that?"

"Yes or no?"

"We've uncovered no evidence of any sexual relationships with any coworker."

"And you've looked?"

"Of course, although we're still in the process of interviewing."

"Okay. And the body-dumping theory?"

"Can only be speculation," he said shortly. "Now, where's my video?"

After I hung up, Mellay demanded to know who was on the phone.

"An official with knowledge of the investigation," I said. "He warns that Heather's source is engaging in speculation not shared by investigators assigned to the case."

A flush ran across Heather's cheeks, and I winced. I'd shown her up in front of everyone, which was not my intent. My only thought had been Ben.

"You did a good job asking the right questions," I said in apology. "Before we go on air we always confirm information with an official or someone within the inner circle of the investigation. Sometimes Ben confirms my information, sometimes I'll check yours, that's how it goes."

She flushed again, but thanked me.

Ben rapped his knuckles twice on the table. "Well, allrighty then. I'm going to head on out and find us a lead." He sauntered to the door and stopped, turning to me. "You coming?"

"Will you excuse me a moment?" I asked Mellay, and then to Isaiah: "I'll be right back."

When we got into the hall, I grabbed Ben's elbow and walked him out of the line of sight.

"Nice temper," I hissed. "Where's your trademark cool?"

He ignored my scold, laughing. "Calling your *official with knowledge of the investigation.* What a cocky little show-off you are."

"You should not taunt Mellay," I said, pointing up at him. "He's got more power than any boss we've had, and he uses it. He's not intimidated by your celebrity status or your big contract. That makes him dangerous, Ben. I don't want what happened to me to happen to you."

"We're getting your old job back," he said, slapping my shoulder, flip as hell, and then he laughed again. "The way you shushed us — *excuse me, gentlemen* — in that queen-to-commoner voice you get. You see Mellay's face? Looked like you kicked him in the —"

"It's called *deflection,*" I said dryly. "From your reckless behavior, I might add. Keep it tight, anchorman. I can't always be around

119

to save your ass."

After the meeting, I met up with Isaiah at his desk. He didn't want to talk, not about the layoffs or the entire day thus far, which was for shit, he said. So after trying and failing to engage him, I begged for help. There was a connection between this missing woman and a prosecutor downtown, but no one would tell me what the connection was. We had to get to the prosecutor. Could he find me a home address and private number for Ian Chase without telling anyone?

"Who wants the interview — Ben?"

I hesitated. "Actually, it's for me." And when Isaiah yanked off his black horn-rims and waved them about furiously, I argued: "I just want to see how this Ian Chase guy reacts — get a read, you know? It's my hunch to run down, and it won't take long, I promise."

"Where are your priorities?" he said. "You're needed here. You need to watch our backs. Can't you see what's going on?"

I saw plenty. Wasn't I the first demotion? But instead of arguing, I counted to ten before telling him I'd get Mellay what he demanded — the show's lead. "So please, if you get me the address for this prosecutor,

120

I'll break news. Everything will be better once we get good stories on the air. Trust me."

CHAPTER ELEVEN

I put my feet on the desk, making myself
comfortable for a long read. The journal
was fascinating, frustrating, full of flowery
and effusive descriptions of people and
places, and not one damn name or date to
fact check any of it. Evelyn Carney was
either naturally discreet, or she was being
secretive. In either case, it seemed she worried she'd have a reader. Who? What did she
have to hide?

In one entry, she wrote fondly of a man
and how he told her boyhood stories of
summers spent at his family estate by a
river, bow hunting and fishing in the shadows of the pawpaw trees, reciting the work
of the Lost Poets to his grandpa, whose vision was deteriorating.

And later, she described the opera, which
she hated but attended anyway, accompanying a powerhouse of a woman she wanted
to please. Paige, I wondered? At intermis-

sion this woman chatted with a Supreme Court justice, as if they were old friends. How did she get to this place, within striking distance of rubbing elbows with the elite, she wondered yet again, and more important, how to hold on?

I flipped back to the beginning and started again, reading more slowly this time. The earliest entry mentioned a teacher's great kindness to her, how he'd helped her land a job and given her good advice. He thought she was smart. No one had ever said she was smart. She liked being admired for her mind.

This teacher appeared on CNN, wearing a pinstripe shirt that she described as jumping on the screen, and she warned him it was too distracting, a bad wardrobe choice. This seemed to me an intimate observation, the kind a wife or a girlfriend might make. Assuming this teacher was one of Evelyn's law school professors, I had two data points — finally, something to work with.

On CNN's website, I searched the transcript section for *George Washington University Law Professor.* The query brought up too many hits, so I restricted the field to the last two years, since Evelyn's journal appeared to have been written fairly recently. Of the legal analysts listed, two were men. I eliminated the senior legal analyst who appeared frequently, thinking he'd know how to dress properly for air. The other was Bradley Hartnett, constitutional law professor.

His profile was on the law school's website. At the top, screen right, was a portrait of Professor Hartnett. I'd seen him in the crowd at Evelyn's vigil. No one answered the office number listed on the website, but his voice recording referred me to a cell phone number, which I dialed.

"Hartnett here." He had a big voice, deep and booming. I barely got out who I was and what I was working on when he agreed to meet. "If it's about Evelyn, I can talk now. Not sure if I'm up for a taped interview. Mind if we do off-camera?"

I sighed. Only in the District would you find a professor well versed enough in TV lingo to jam me up. Fresh video was desperately needed, but I told him we could begin any way he liked, as long as he talked.

Bradley Hartnett lived in the Kennedy-Warren, a condominium wedged between Connecticut Avenue and Rock Creek Park and to its south, the National Zoo. It was a beautiful prewar building made of limestone and had eagles carved on its colonnade. The setting sun flashed across the windows, gilding the glass.

Hartnett was waiting by a fountain in the courtyard. He was a large, barrel-chested man, and his thick neck sported a green tie, carelessly knotted. As we shook hands, mine disappeared into his.

"Not sure how you do these kinds of interviews," he said nervously. Whether his nervousness had to do with Evelyn or the interview remained to be seen. "If we need privacy, we can go up to my apartment. Otherwise, there's a lounge in the building, members only; no one will see us."

That gave me pause. "Why would we need privacy? You're not asking for anonymity, right?" I still needed someone to go on the record, for god's sake.

"Let's hit the lounge."

We went through the glass door and into the lobby, where I found myself gawking like a tourist. The lobby was wonderfully glamorous with its brass zigzag railings and deco lamps brightening the rich green walls. Ornate columns soared to high ceilings cut into geometric grids.

Hartnett led me to a bar that belonged in a black-and-white movie. Club chairs surrounded little tables scattered around the room. There was a shiny black piano that no one was playing, and a mahogany bar where a man in a suit polished glassware. We were the only patrons. Hartnett ordered sparkling water for me, a scotch for himself, and we carried our drinks to a corner. He was clinging to his drink like it was a life raft.

I tried to soothe him with chitchat. "What a lovely place to live, and so close to the zoo. Do you ever hear the animals?"

"In the morning sometimes," he said. "My wife and I used to get up at dawn and listen for lions."

"Is she here now? Your wife?"

He looked at me strangely. "They didn't tell you?"

"Who?"

"The police. They told you about me, right?" He had an ankle over his knee. His wing tip oxford was kicking in agitation. "I'm widowed almost five years now. They should have told you that, too. They made me look like a dirty old cheat, didn't they?"

"A . . . cheat?" I thought about the intimate way Evelyn had written of him in the journal. Had I stumbled on the guy I'd been looking for? "You had a relationship with Evelyn Carney?"

His chin lowered. He gazed moodily into the glass. "No, we weren't in a relationship," he said, and then, choosing his words carefully: "We were . . . friends. She confided in me, shared her worries. Why won't they believe that?"

"Who?"

"Police detectives."

There are many reasons people talk to a journalist. To help a person find their reason, I've played good cop and bad, confessor, psychologist, fellow mourner, and friend. But Bradley Hartnett needed only a willing ear. For him, talk was catharsis, and his words rushed out.

He repeated what he'd told police: he'd never been involved with any student, not even a former student, he swore it. Not that he was any great arbiter of morality, but he took pride in his work. He had always maintained an open-door policy, and while popular with students, he kept firm lines. Besides, those bright young women with their ironed hair and diet-starved bodies held no allure for him. They had no mystery. No depth. They gave voice to every idea, certain theirs were inarguably right. All that youthful sincerity made him feel ancient.

Then one day, Evelyn Carney walked into his lecture hall. She was older than the others, more mature. She always sat in his front row, center seat, all alone, and — it seemed to him — lonely; her serious eyes lingering on him as he lectured. Her loveliness was to him a thing incandescent.

As he wove his story, I wondered if Professor Hartnett was a romantic, and his view of Evelyn was idealized, except for this: I'd *seen* Evelyn in that cutaway video, and she *was* incandescent.

During the fall that Evelyn was his student, Brad Hartnett became infatuated beyond reason. His life condensed to Thursday afternoon lectures, those ninety minutes he could gaze on her in his front row. Sometimes she'd cross her legs, and he'd get lost in midsentence, but his discipline held firm. If she approached him, he would treat her no differently. He would speak to her as any other student. Every Thursday before the lecture, he made these promises to himself, but she never approached. He never even heard her voice. He only knew her work, and then the class was over.

Months later, she appeared in his office doorway. "She wanted to know if I remembered her," he said with a humorless laugh. "There she stood, her small hand gripping her opposing wrist, which I'd later learn she did when she was nervous. She was far from home and knew no one in the city. She needed help with her career, and, I like to think, she also needed a friend. I told her she could drop by my office anytime, and she did, frequently. Those visits became the best part of my day. The more we talked, the more dazzled I was."

When he went silent, I gazed at him with sympathy. "You grew to care for each other?"

His face flushed. "Not the way I had hoped, but yes."

"You loved her?"

He winced. "I do."

The present tense, I noted. "But you never had a sexual relationship?"

"She's married," he said quickly. He took a gulp of his drink and balanced the glass on his knee. "Besides, I don't believe she has ever thought of me in that way."

"Understood," I said, and then I asked him to help me understand the timeline. "She began visiting you, when?"

"Last winter. She was in her final year and needed help on the job search. She wanted to prove to her folks back home she could make it on her own merits."

"They expected a lot?"

"They expected nothing at all, except for her to be pretty and harmless. They thought even less of her ability to have a successful career in the law. Marry the boy next door. Keep a nice home. Join the local country club. I think their disregard hurt her."

I understood that, too. "She's a lawyer, that's who she is. She wanted recognition for being good, right?"

"Yes," he said, and then in a defensive tone: "I only arranged the interview. She landed the job herself."

It was Paige Linden he turned to. Paige had been a schoolmate of his wife, Maggie, who'd been quite a bit younger than Hartnett. He'd always admired Paige's talents as a litigator and her support for other women in the workplace. Paige also knew firsthand the difficulties working in a male-dominated field, so he'd hoped she might look out for Evelyn.

After Evelyn began working at the firm, he'd planned a celebration that never happened. Evelyn was too busy. Her new bosses were demanding, so he gave her the space she'd asked for, even though he missed her.

Then, several weeks ago, she rushed into his office as though there'd been no time apart. By then, the fog of his infatuation had lifted, and he saw her as he'd never been able to: nearly twenty years his junior, so young it broke his heart. Beneath her makeup, her cheeks were blotchy from crying. He begged her to tell him what was wrong.

"What did she say?"

He glanced up as if he'd forgotten I was there. He gave me a troubled look before he said, "What happened Sunday night? Do you know?"

"Investigators say she argued with her husband and left the restaurant alone. She hasn't been seen since."

"Yes, yes, that's what the police say. What really happened?"

I sat back in my chair and watched him. "You don't believe the police?"

"Take the chief's press conference on the news yesterday," he told me, lifting both eyebrows suggestively. "She described Evie as if she were some silly girl who'd wandered aimlessly into the dark. What a ridiculous caricature."

"How so?"

"Evie's small and delicately built, and she understands she's in a city dangerous to women. She's far too intelligent to have left the restaurant like that, alone."

This line of reasoning always mystified me. How did people think we lived? Were we supposed to lock ourselves away the moment night fell? Refuse to leave a restaurant without a man to escort us? Besides, a decade of reporting news in the District had taught me a woman's intelligence — or lack thereof — had nothing to do with becoming a victim, with influencing who was picked out as the lion locked on one antelope while the rest of the herd moved on.

His eyes shifted away from mine. "What about Evie's phone?" he said. "Have you heard anything?" A range of expressions played across his face — anxiety? Worry? Guilt? "If she had her phone that night? Do you know?"

There it was again, that look — was it guilt? Suddenly everything he told me took on a darker tone. He had said his infatuation for Evelyn Carney was beyond reason. She cared for him, but not the way he wanted. He was in love with her. He couldn't have her. He gave her space and was not happy about it.

Investigators had questioned him. *Why don't they believe me?*

"Where were you the night Evelyn disappeared?" I said.

"Are you asking if — if — *I* did something to Evie?" he sputtered.

He had thick wrists and hands that were fisted in anger. They were the kind of hands that could crush a small woman. Hell, they could probably crush me.

I kept an eye on his fists. "Could you answer the question, please?"

"On the night Evelyn disappeared, I was at a dinner party," he said. "The party was at a friend's weekend house in Annapolis. I drank too much and stayed overnight. But aside from that, use a little logic, would you? I could never hurt Evelyn. It's Peter Carney I wanted gone."

CHAPTER TWELVE

Outside of Hartnett's condominium, the late-afternoon sunlight cast the courtyard fountain in gold. I propped my hip against it and thumbed through the texts that had piled up on my phone. Most were from Ben, starting with a couple of *trying to reach you's* and *return my call ASAPs* and escalating to *I need something new or my live shot's gonna die* and *where the hell are you, anyway? Chasing you can wear a body out.*

Ben was my friend and also my responsibility, but it wouldn't hurt if he got his own leads every now and again. It really wouldn't. Instead of complaining, I replied: *Got nothing to report yet. Call cops for latest & lead with whatever they say.*

There, that ought to buy me some time. The last text was from Isaiah with Ian Chase's phone number and home address across the river in Arlington, Virginia, as well as the tags for his Mercedes, according to DMV records.

I ask you for the world, I replied to Isaiah, *and you give me the moon, too.*

Rush hour was slow going through George-town, and traffic on the Key Bridge was at a standstill. The bridge walkers with their pink cheeks, blowing hair, and flapping coats were making better time than I was. Finally, I was across the river, and a few blocks later, turning into Ian's neighbor-hood. It was a quirky mix of 1920s Sears kit houses and contemporary townhouses surrounding a park that overlooked the river. Across the street from the park was Ian's condo building, an all-glass high-rise, very modern and luxurious, and consider-ing its looks and location, expensive as hell.

I parked where I could keep an eye on the entrance door and the garage, and dialed Ian's number. When there was no answer, I crossed the street to the condo and buzzed the concierge, watching him through the glass as he picked up the phone. Mr. Chase wasn't in, he said, and no, I couldn't wait in the lobby.

I went back to my car and settled in for the stakeout. My notepad was angled against the steering wheel, so I could tran-scribe the interview with the professor while keeping a lookout for any movement.

Later, my cell phone rang. It was the intern at the receptionist's desk. She told me the woman claiming to be my mother had called for me again. This time she'd asked for driving directions to the station. She threatened to talk to me one way or another. "Sure you don't know her?" she said. "Called herself Doris Knightly."

Christ, I thought. These wacko callers couldn't even get my mother's name right. My mother had been Diana, as in Roman goddess, lunar virgin, guardian of wild creatures and protector of young girls, and it was this image I carried of her always. Diana.

"Put me through." My voice was gruffer than I'd intended. "Go through the switchboard, so it's the station's number, not mine, that shows up on the caller ID."

"Want me to stay on the line?" the intern asked as a woman joined us, and then the intern said, "I have Virginia Knightly on the line returning a call."

"Is this Ginny?" the woman said.

The back of my neck tingled. No one called me that, not in more years than I could count. I told the intern to hang up. "My name is Virginia," I said.

"Oh, honey, thank the Lord." Her voice

had that downstate Delaware sound, the country drawl with a mid-Atlantic nasal twist. "These people answering your phone, they're so rude. They won't let me talk to you. I'm about a minute from driving down myself, but I don't care for big cities."

"No, wait, don't drive anywhere," I said. "Tell me what you want."

"Oh." She paused. "You sound so . . . maybe a little hard, honey. Not that I'm criticizing. Your daddy says you're on TV in the nation's capital" — *nation's capital,* she said, as if it were some den of iniquity — "one of them mainstream media always being talked about. But I always say, folks got a reason for being what they are."

I interrupted. "Who are you?"

"Didn't your people tell you?"

"You claimed to be my mother. That's a rotten trick."

"Maybe I shouldn't of said it, but that nasty girl had it coming. Acting like I got no right to talk to you. I got plenty of right. I think myself mama to all your daddy's babies."

All his babies.

Lovely.

I pinched the bridge of my nose, saying, "So wait, you're married to my father?"

"He wants to see you, honey."

137

The memory struck fast. The beach on a hot summer's day, the sand scorching my feet, and then, being lifted in powerful arms, the world tilting and righting itself as he set me on his wide shoulders, high, oh so high. I clutched at his mane of hair warmed by the sun, and we frolicked in the waves, the spray of ocean mist cooling my sunburned skin —

The old ache settled in my chest. "Not a good idea," I said. "It's been twenty years since I've seen the man." And I stopped. There was really nothing more to say.

"He's sick." She gave the name of the hospital he was in, but I didn't need the address. It was where my mother had died.

"If you came, it'd bring him — it'd be kind, that's all." She had a voice that was hard to hang up on, matronly and sweet, full of sad pauses. She did good phone, I'd give her that. "It would mean the world to him, and it's such a teensy bit of effort, just to come on by and say hello."

A red hatchback pulled in front of the glass building. It had one of those green-and-red roof domes advertising an Italian restaurant. From its hatch, the driver lifted a tall stack of pizzas. Doris was saying *"think about it honey, but not too long,"* and I was nodding "yeah, uh-huh" sort of absently, watching the driver as he struggled with the pizzas.

I said goodbye as politely as I could under the circumstances before I hung up and ran across the street. At the first set of entry doors, the delivery guy was lifting the boxes he'd set on the floor to make his call. The door buzzed loudly, and a latch clicked.

"Here, let me help you," I said, grabbing the door. I drafted behind him.

Past the now-empty concierge desk, there was an alcove with puffy chairs grouped around heavy wood tables in a decor reminiscent of a high-end hotel. An enormous potted tree with broad leaves shielded the chair farthest from the concierge desk. I chose that chair and pulled out my notebook, pretending to write while watching through the leaves for Ian Chase.

The pizza deliverer nodded on his way out. After that, time passed slowly. The concierge who returned to his perch was a different man from the one I'd spoken with earlier. He glanced my way several times, as if trying to decide whether he knew me or if he should know me, and if not, should he approach? Just as it seemed he might, Ian Chase came through the atrium doors. He walked heavily with slumped shoulders, clutching his arms at the elbows. He ap-

139

peared to be warding off a chill.

I followed him around the corner to a bank of elevators where he waited. An arrow lit up before the doors opened and he got in. I was conflicted. Should I follow him up or let him go and try to raise him by phone now that I knew he was home? He put his hand on the door, holding it for me, and I got in.

The elevator was made of glass. As it rose, the street lamps flickered through bare trees, and then we were above the rooftops and the trees, and I could see the lights of the city across the river. It was an incredible view, probably a multimillion-dollar view, but Ian Chase had his head down and saw none of it.

"Mr. Chase?" I said, breaking the silence. His head shot up. I told him who I was and what I did. He slapped a button on the control panel. The elevator lurched to a stop.

"You're a reporter?" he drawled.

"A news producer, yes."

He stepped closer to me. It was intimidating, as it was meant to be. "You can't follow someone onto private property without permission," he said through his teeth. "I can have you arrested."

"I'd prefer if you didn't," I said. "Look, I've been trying to reach you all day and hadn't meant to follow you up. Could we can go down and talk in the lobby — or on the street, wherever you like. I just need to ask you about Evelyn Carney."

He was studying me from beneath long lashes, the same way I was studying him. "Who gave you my name?" he demanded.

"I saw you at the vigil in Georgetown. You were talking to Paige Linden about the investigation."

"There must have been fifty people at that vigil, and you're here, questioning me? Why?"

I was taken aback by how angry he was, and how quickly that anger had come. It seemed out of proportion to the question asked.

"Wait, can we start again? I need a do-over." I blew out a frustrated breath and held out my hand. He frowned down at it. I said, "My name is Virginia Knightly, and I'm working on the story of the missing person Evelyn Carney, who has been seen with you in a video —"

"I don't believe that," he snapped.

"A news video of remarks you made to a community group in Rock Creek Park last summer," I said patiently. "And then I saw you again at her vigil. The press office said your office isn't investigating the case, so I figured if your interest wasn't professional, you must be friends with Evelyn or that you in some way care about her and the fact that she's missing. I'm looking for people who will talk about her. I'm trying to find out about her. No one will tell me who she is."

And then I glanced over his shoulder and lost all train of thought. We were suspended a dozen or so flights up, and through the elevator's glass walls I could see the spires of Georgetown University and the star-shaped lanterns that illuminated the Key Bridge and beyond those lights, nestled along the river was the Kennedy Center. It was just as Evelyn had described it.

"It does look like a tidy shirt box," I murmured, and then, still lost in the wonder of it: "Evelyn kept notes. She described the Kennedy Center as seen over the lights of Key Bridge. It was from this angle." I turned my attention to him. "She was here, wasn't she?"

It was quick, his flare of panic, before he wiped his expression clean.

"She came here to visit you?" I said, and when he seemed at a loss for words, I went on: "If I banged on your neighbors' doors and showed a picture of Evelyn, they'd say they'd seen her here, wouldn't they?"

He hit the control panel again and we descended. At the lobby level the door opened, and he held the door for me. I dug into my satchel and pulled out a business card. "When you're ready to talk," I said, handing it to him.

I got out of the elevator and made it a few steps when he called out. He was slumped against the open door, holding my card. He looked nothing like the cool and sophisticated golden boy in the glossy pictures of the local magazines. This guy looked like he'd been kicked in the gut.

"When you're given something so private, never intended for your eyes, you might consider why you were given that kind of access," he said. "Ask yourself, what did your source want? How did she or he hope I'd appear? As we know, appearances are not truth. Take your Kennedy Center, for example. From this side of the river, sure, it might *look* like a shirt box, but it is, and always will be, the fucking Kennedy Center."

CHAPTER THIRTEEN

The dashboard clock in my car read 11:48, which meant, if I had any hope of catching up with Ben, my next stop would be one of the northwest bars featured in his nightlife. Ben's philosophy boiled down to this: people were pack animals and it was unnatural for such animals to be alone. Above all, one must live according to one's nature. Or some such bizarre reasoning. The result was Ben on a barstool after the show every night, talking and drinking and (if rumors were accurate) womanizing, each night a specific bar. Tonight was Friday. Friday meant Chadwicks.

Chads, as we called it, was a basement bar filled with shift workers, mostly journalists, some cops and firefighters. From the platform above the hostess stand, I scanned its long crowded bar and faces in the mirror behind the bar. A couple rose from their barstools, and the crowd shifted like starlings on a wire, creating a path. At the end of the path was Ben.

Nelson was there, too, sitting with his back to Ben, talking with a group of college-age women, probably from American U. But Ben seemed very much alone, his big shoulders hunched over his drink. In the mirror, he wore a sullen expression and his thick hair was a disheveled mess. When his dark eyes met mine, he scowled in a way that made the back of my teeth tingle, and don't ask why a bad-tempered Ben wooed me. It was something I tried very hard to ignore, but never could.

At the bottom of the stairs, Nelson greeted me with a sloppy hug. "You see our story tonight?" he yelled, as he always did when he drank a lot. The louder he yelled, the farther I wanted to be from him. He had a terrible habit of knocking into people when he got drunk.

"Our generous producer, or whatever you are, should buy us a drink," he said, ushering me to the bar.

Ben put his palm over the longneck. "I'm good. Thanks."

"Sorry for missing your calls," I told him. "I was —"

"Yep. Okay. Forget it."

"He's been cranky all night," Nelson said,

smiling crookedly. "Should've known it was you. Come on, Virginia. Dish it. What'd you do?"

I lifted my hands, helplessly. "Can you tell me what we reported?"

"You missed the *live shot*?" Ben said.

Nelson let out a long, high-pitched whistle.

"That's why I'm asking."

"I should've figured you'd blow me off," Ben said. "But never the story. When's the last time you missed a live shot?"

I sighed. It'd been a long day and all signs pointed to a longer night, and clearly self-medication was in order. I signaled the bartender and ordered a round, whether Ben would accept it or not. After that first wonderful bite of vodka, I asked again about the script.

Ben leaned back against the bar, elbows on the glossy top and long legs sprawled like he owned the place. "You know, I don't think I will tell you," he said. "Not till you explain why you were ducking calls."

"I was working the story and lost track of time."

His eyebrow shot up as his mouth turned down. "Yeah, right. The woman who lives her life to the seconds."

The bar was noisy with people feeling no

pain, but you never knew what sound traveled. I leaned in close with my hand on Ben's shoulder and my lips close to his ear. "Tonight I talked to Ian Chase."

"The AUSA? In charge of the Homicide Section?"

"The very same. And it was weird, let me tell you. First I'd seen him at Evelyn's vigil, when allegedly his office isn't working on her case. So I'm trying to figure out, if he's got no business being there, why is he? And that video of Evelyn I've been tearing the station apart for? Well, I found it. Guess who's in the head-on shot leading up to the audience reaction shot featuring Evelyn Carney? Yep, you guessed it, Ian Chase. Coincidence or something else, I wonder? So let me go talk to him. See what he says. Even the attempt to talk pissed him off to no end. Once he was over the surprise of me being there, don't you think he'd answer simple questions? Nope. Not even why he was at the vigil."

Ben was gaping as if he'd been poleaxed.

"What are you two whispering about?" Nelson shouted.

"Over the phone you talked to him," Ben said, "or what? How'd you talk?"

"Isaiah found his address, so I staked out his apartment. Or condo, I guess. He probably owns it. He's richer than God, I'm told."

"Who's rich?" Nelson said.

Ben blinked, as if just noticing Nelson. "I have to talk shop with Virginia. How about you treat those friends you abandoned to some drinks?"

"You guys are always cutting me out," Nelson whined. "Disrespecting me, like I'm not on the team. I'm as much —"

"Put it on my tab," Ben said.

"Really? Well, all right then."

Nelson scampered off happily and I settled onto the stool he'd vacated. Ben turned to the bar, and we sat shoulder to shoulder, drinking quietly, sizing up each other's moods in the mirror. He was in a strange one tonight.

"All right," he said. "Spill it."

I got him up to speed on the day's events. When I got to the part about my talk with Professor Hartnett, Ben frowned, and then when I got to the stakeout at Ian's, he frowned deeper. I pulled out my phone and showed him the video clip of Evelyn at the meeting in Rock Creek Park.

"I could've used this video in my story tonight," he complained.

It would have been a scoop. He was right. "I don't want to use video that I don't understand yet."

"Come again?"

"There's a connection between Ian Chase and Evelyn Carney," I said. "What the nature of it is, I'd prefer not to speculate. The video begs for that kind of speculation. When we put it on air, I want to say definitively what they are to each other. If I had the raw tape to show the progression of events at that meeting, or to see how they talked to each other, if they talked directly at any point . . ." My voice drifted off on a wistful note. "The conversation with Ian tonight? It was volatile. We couldn't have been in the elevator for more than five minutes, and in that time he went from angry and paranoid to lonely and hurt. The whole gamut, which says to me he cares."

"Or that Ian Chase is playing you."

"I'm so easy to play?" I said, smiling ruefully.

"You're not, but you've got your blind spots. One is for girls in danger. Know why you do that?"

"Nope," I said, and it was true.

"Just as well. Reckon you wouldn't do it if you knew. Same vein, your blind spot for kicked dogs. Ian Chase takes one look at you and figures he can't push you around without you pushing back, and harder. So

149

he pretends to be hurt and alone."

I sipped at my drink, considering it. Over the top of my glass, I said, "Interesting theory. Why go to the trouble?"

He put his head down, bent over the pocket knife he'd pulled from his jeans, and was now spinning like a compass on the bar top. The ivory handle was worn smooth, although I knew he kept a keen edge on the small blade that did little more in an office than open letters. Certainly it wasn't much of a weapon. But the knife had been a gift from his father and he carried it with him always.

"Tonight I reported that investigators believe there's a romantic link between Evelyn Carney and the man who reported her missing," he said, seemingly transfixed by the spin of his knife. "That call came in the day after she disappeared. Police aren't calling this person a suspect because they haven't determined if her disappearance is a crime, but he isn't cooperating. He's already gotten himself a big-money lawyer, and that lawyer won't let him talk."

"Well, if that man is Ian, I can believe he's romantically linked. There were some pretty strong emotions coming off of him."

"Textbook kicked dog," Ben said cynically. Under his hand, the knife stilled. He scooped it up, and leaning back, slid the knife into his pocket. He put his elbows on the bar and regarded his beer thoughtfully. "He wants you feel sorry for him. Know why?" And before I could answer, he said: "He's trying to prolong the moment before you take the next obvious step. When his name is reported. When the relationship becomes defined. And when it all goes down, don't be surprised if it turns out he killed Evelyn Carney." His lips thinned, and his dark eyes took on a hard look. "If true, that means the guy you ambushed all alone in an elevator is a *murderer.*"

"Well, of course I considered that," I said with impatience. "I'm not an idiot."

"Nope, just reckless. Which leads me to what I've been sitting here all night itching to tell you."

Pinpricks of anxiety tickled my spine.

"You made me unhappy today," he said.

Those words. *You made me unhappy.*

"You agreed to partner up," he went on. "You shook my hand and gave me your promise, and what'd you do first opportunity? You ditched me."

He picked up his beer, swinging the empty bottle as he talked, but I'd already tuned out. I was too busy chastising myself for teaming up in the first place. Temperamentally, we were a bad fit. What he called reckless, I considered resourceful fact finding. I had to follow the lead where it would take me, and frankly I was glad to have gone alone. There was no way I could have sneaked up on Ian with an anchor and crew.

Besides, if I had evidence that Ian had hurt Evelyn, I'd *have* to question Ian before we reported it. Ben knew that. He was being emotional. It was better not to talk about it now, of course, since it could only make Ben unhappier. I got up from my barstool, ready to bolt.

"Don't even consider it," he said calmly, sliding his bottle onto the bar. "My legs are longer and faster and it'd only embarrass the both of us."

I sat down again.

"Now tell me why you're upset," he said, "when anybody can see I'm the injured party here."

"I don't want to argue. Not with you. That's why I don't do this."

"This?"

"Partner up. I'm no good at it."

"Know what I think? All that time you spent buttoned up in management is to blame here. But we're only talking a few minor adjustments, and the first is the easiest. Ready?"

He was no longer unhappy but frowning in a way that barely held back his grin.

"Repeat after me," he said. "*I will keep Ben in the loop.* Come on now."

"Try not to be so melodramatic, Ben."

"You can do it," he teased. "You run an entire newsroom and all its people and you even handle, or mostly handle, pain-in-the ass divas like me. Surely you can learn a simple mantra."

"To be honest, it's that — well, I'm just better at being alone, that's all."

I'd meant *working* alone, not *being* alone. Jeez, that vodka had gone straight to my head. I signaled the bartender for another.

"You think being alone's the problem?" he said.

"Mostly."

He shook his head slowly and he smiled. "Problem is this. You're used to *thinking* you're alone. I've been here the whole time."

When the bartender approached, Nelson sidled up to the bar and added some German beer I'd never heard of to our order. "Girls went to some party," he explained to Ben. "Figured I'd hang with you."

"You can't stand next to me and drink a Hefeweizen," Ben told him, and then to the bartender: "Don't let him have it. You know what he'll do."

"The lemon adds zest," Nelson whined.

Ben cut him a sideways look. "How many times have I told you? Any beer you put fruit in is not a beer. It's an affectation."

The bartender banged our order on the bar: my vodka, Ben's longneck Bud, and Nelson's Hefeweizen, cloudy gold in a tall delicate pilsner glass. Then he set out a saucer with two slices of the offending lemon. The bartender winked. "That enough fruit for you?"

Nelson gave an impish look. He held the lemon aloft, pinching it between thumb and forefinger above the rim of the pilsner as he began a long, rambling story about shooting pictures for Ben at his family farm out west, a big snowstorm, ATVs in the backcountry, and some animal caught in a trap. I had a hard time following, worried as I was by his hand hovering close to the pilsner glass. He was going to knock it over. I just knew it.

"So we follow these tracks," Nelson was saying, "and there's this god-awful hollering in the distance. Beyond the tree line we find caught in a trap this — this —"

He snapped his fingers to jog his memory, his hand barely clearing the beer glass.

I pushed it away.

"What's that animal again?" he asked.

Ben shifted uncomfortably. "How about enjoying your fruity drink in quiet?"

Nelson snapped his finger again. "A bobcat, that's it. So Ben swings his rifle off his shoulder and goes over to the trap. He starts banging on the trap with the rifle butt. Well, that cat goes wild, making these hair-raising yowling noises, and Ben's all bent over, dodging claws while beating on the trap —" He gasped with laughter. "And the cat," he wheezed, "the little cat —"

"Little cat my ass," Ben said. "That was full-grown mature wildcat. If you thought it was such a nice kitty, where the hell were you?"

"Hiding behind your skirts, of course." He laughed. "So Ben, he frees her, praise Jesus, but does she run off like a good cat? No, she makes one last lunge, and Ben, he's screaming — like a —"

"It dug its *claws* into my *scalp.*"

"That little cat knocked big old Ben *flat — on — his ass*!" With that, he flung his arms outward, fist slamming into the pilsner glass that went rolling, fancy German beer pouring across the bar and dripping onto the coat of a woman behind him.

The woman jumped up with a shriek and fled to the hostess stand.

Ben and I were tossing white towels onto

155

the bar to help the bartender clean up, while Nelson scrubbed his jaw, looking down at the mess as if he had no idea how such a disaster could have occurred. It was so typical. I told him to give the woman some dry-cleaning money. Naturally, he had no money. So I gave him my wallet, and Ben called him a cab.

"Why do we love him?" I was serious. Sometimes I wondered.

"Because he's ours," Ben said grimly.

A yellow cab filled the picture window overlooking Wisconsin Avenue. Nelson gave Ben a bro-hug. Before he turned to go, he slapped me on my back, knocking me a step forward. In my ear he whispered, "Later, bobcat."

When the cab drove away, Ben tried to make Nelson's excuses. Apparently, Nelson was brokenhearted over Alexa's imminent departure. She was determined to find work in South Florida, which was home for her, and had gotten serious inquiries from several stations, including our Miami affiliate. Nelson thought it was only a matter of Alexa's deciding which station offered the best deal, and if Nelson could persuade her to take him.

"Everyone who's got a place to go is going," Ben said. "Hell, I've thought of going home."

"You'd go back to *Montana*?" It was like another country, a place beyond comprehension, and he was thinking about it. With Ben, thinking meant he was already halfway there. "Good god, Ben. What market is that?"

"If I went, it wouldn't be for television. I've got years of hay baling to catch up on." He took a long sip of beer, savoring it, and in his eyes there was a faraway look, all softness and yearning, where he wandered a bit before slowly coming back. "But I can't leave just yet."

My back sagged with relief. "Good, I still have some use for you," I said, smiling, and made a silly attempt at mimicking his deep voice: "I've got you broken in the way I like you —"

"Yeah?"

I laughed. "No."

We picked up our drinks at the same time and drank simultaneously, and for some reason, Ben found this funny. I started laughing again, too. Maybe the intense feeling of happiness came from that last burst of energy at the end of a draining day or maybe from that perfect balance of vodka in my blood, but I had to figure it came mostly from Ben. He made you believe the illusion you weren't alone any longer.

His warm eyes crinkled at me. "You know what happens to a man on a fast approach to forty?" he said. "He gets this idea he wants to *talk* to a woman. What's worse? He decides he wants a woman who can talk to him, too."

"I should warn you. That's called a conversation."

"Now don't think he wants talking more than he wants other things, being what he is, but enough that when he comes up for air, it's not to put on his hiking boots. Young and dumb doesn't cut it anymore. He wants to know a woman, and he needs a woman smart enough to know him, too."

He gave me a tender look that had my heart racing, even as huge warning sounds started going off. "Ben, wait —"

"I've waited long enough," he said. "The woman I want to know is you. Maybe you've been thinking about it, too?"

There was a punch of heat to my chest, unbelievably pleasurable or painful. I couldn't tell which. I couldn't tell much of anything. I think I was in shock.

"You want to know a woman — to know me." I was feeling all kinds of thick-tongued drunkenness now. "You're talking sex, right?

That's what you mean?"

He exhaled equal parts laughter and relief. "Christ, you take all the romance out of it."

The overhead lights flickered. It was past last call and the bartender was polishing the wood of the mostly empty bar. There was a crash of ice, a busboy scooping out a bin.

I breathed Ben's name like an apology.

His eyes narrowed. "I'm asking for a simple answer here. Yes or no."

"I — no."

He nodded once. "Okay," he said, and lifted his hand for the check.

"Wait. Don't go." And then I stopped, having no idea what else to say.

The bartender dropped the bill onto the bar. Ben rolled onto one hip and pulled out his wallet.

"Do me a favor, though," he said, looking down at the wad of cash he dropped onto the bar. "From now on, be more careful. You ambush any more suspects in Evelyn Carney's disappearance, don't go alone. Take Nelson or Isaiah or whoever."

But not him, I noticed.

"Ben, please —"

"It's okay," he repeated, still not looking at me. "See you Monday."

He grabbed his jacket from a hook beneath the bar and tossed it over his shoulder before climbing the stairs. I watched help-lessly as he went out the door and passed the big picture window in a long-legged stride, and then he was beyond the frame, disappeared on the dark street, gone.

During the darkest part of the night I woke with a start in a pitch-black bedroom. The darkness itself had a heartbeat, and then I realized no, the sound came from my own heart loud in my ears. I sat dizzily, gulping air, my fists curled around the edge of the tangled sheet until my eyes focused and the shapes took form and I put names to them — *bed, lamp, table* — and by naming them, got a sliver of control.

I'd been thinking of my father. Not a dream, but the kind of remembering that comes like a dream in your half sleep. It had been as if I was really there again, hid-ing in the wings of my mother's faded chair, my first grown-up novel, *Gone with the Wind,* heavy on my lap, and upstairs, my father was yelling and Mama crying. Then there was a new sound — *thump, thump* — of duf-fel bags dropping at the top of the stairs. The steps creaked under the weight of my father as he descended, then the screen door thwacked and moments later, a muscular engine roared to life. I heard the old Firebird as it bottomed out at the end of the driveway one last time.

On that day, I learned the sounds of betrayal, and I learned, too, that you always had a choice. I ran after my father as fast as my skinny legs allowed, until there was a cramp in my gut and I couldn't run anymore and couldn't call out for lack of breath. Not that it would have mattered. The old Firebird had already pulled up to the intersection, its turn signal winking at me. Across its rear window, there was a flash of sunlight, and in that flash everything became suddenly clear and hard and blindingly bright.

My father had turned.

I uncurled my hands from the sheets, lowered my feet flat to the floor, and put my head between my knees, letting the blood rush back. When my breathing calmed, I got out of bed and belted my long, soft robe and went downstairs, flipping on the hallway light as well as the kitchen light and every other switch I encountered. My whole house lit up.

The kitchen was strewn with white papers from Evelyn's file glowing beneath the spotlight. I gulped a glass of water, cooling my throat, and poured myself another. I car-

161

ried it to the table and logged onto my laptop.

The Amtrak website listed a ten o'clock Acela Express from Union Station to Wilmington, Delaware, only an hour-twenty ride. This was no time to travel. I was in the middle of an important story. Not to mention the serious mop-up operation I had to do with Ben. Except that I had no idea how to mop that up. I'd never known how to deal with Ben, not in that way.

My hands hovered over the keyboard. My heart punched once, twice, before I booked it. I printed out the train ticket and laid it on my satchel and climbed the stairs wearily to bed. The rest of the night, sleep came in fits and starts. The old nightmares had come back.

CHAPTER FOURTEEN

Ten o'clock Saturday morning. It was a short trip and the Acela is a comfortable ride; that's really all there is to say. The view from train journeys along the northeast corridor are all the same anyway, the same industrial parks and suffering waterways and graffiti-scarred bridges; the same trash along the tracks. But I wasn't looking at the landscape. I was looking back, trying to remember my mother's face. I could get parts of it: the splash of freckles across her nose, the high arch of her eyebrows, her skin that was pale, except in the summer when it burned a coppery tan.

Her voice was equally difficult to remember, except that it was soft and it drawled and she'd called me Ginny and sweetie, except when I disappointed her. Then I was Virginia.

From my satchel I pulled out my reporter pad and flipped pages until I found some blank space. With a felt-tip pen, I wrote a list of childhood resentments: our furniture hauled out, the yard gone to bush, the pantry bare except for the line of Campbell soup cans — I liked tomato, she liked chicken noodle — the boxes of herbal tea that'd settle her stomach, the days-old stale bread. The nighttime when she thought I was asleep, her fingernails tapping calculator keys and the machine humming out white tape with red ink that curled across the table and dropped to the floor, and the sound that bothered me most of all, her strange whispers in her empty bedroom.

Those words, the way she'd whisper his name, calling out for him when she was dying, I didn't know if I could bring all of that up. But the rest I'd throw in his face I could always see so clearly — his ruddy-cheeked good health, his thick-legged, strongly built body, powerful enough to carry any load. And clearest of all memories: his green eyes looking through me as he'd made his way to the door.

The train slowed and the stop for Wilmington was announced. I stepped onto the platform and walked down the steps and into the station, which had a surprisingly clean and lovely interior, having been renovated since I'd been through last. I went out and stood under the same gray sky with that low ceiling I associated with my childhood. After a deep inhale, I tasted the sweet polluted air and coughed. I was home.

Several taxis were queued. As I lifted my hand, the first taxi pulled forward and I jumped in. On the way to the hospital, I tried very hard not to anticipate. Above all, not to prepare any speeches. *Just walk in, take a look, hand him your list, and walk out, you leaving him this time.*

At the entrance to the hospital I lost my nerve. The automatic doors whooshed open every so often for the sick people and their visitors and some deliverymen. I'd take a step forward and the doors would open again. I'd step back and watch them close.

I left the hospital and wandered down the road, actually a split-lane highway dotted with the kind of megastores seen everywhere. There was a huge bookstore with a café, where I ordered a chai tea and carried it to a puffy green chair next to a table of sale books. The tea grew cold as I paged through books, unable to concentrate on the words. After a while of chastising myself for my great stupidity and even greater cowardice, I walked back to the hospital.

The young woman at the information desk gave me his room number on the eighth floor. I was surprised and a little worried he was on the eighth floor, not that I cared about him being in any particular place, of course, but only because it was a bad floor. That was the floor my mother had been on. I clipped the visitor tag to the lapel of my jacket and reminded myself *no speeches,* and crossed the spine of the hospital to its bank of elevators. The numbers ascended on the panel and then the eight lit up and the doors opened.

The old game I played when my mother lay dying here came back to me. In it, I'd walk through the hallway holding my breath, and when my breath ran out, I'd gulp quickly, pinching my nose, and then I'd hold my breath again for as long as I could. It was pretty childish even as a kid and ridiculous now, but I couldn't quite help it. It wasn't the cancer that was contagious, it was the fear. You could smell it over the stink of chemical cleaners and hothouse flowers, and in this ward, it smelled infinitely worse.

The cul-de-sac had a nurse's station in the center, which I circled to the farthest room where his number was displayed. I went in. It was small and cramped with beeping equipment. In the bed, an old man had an oxygen mask over his face. That was not my father. A middle-aged woman sat beside him, caressing his wrist, and when she looked at me, she put a hand to her mouth. I walked past them to a dividing curtain.

On the other side, a young black man reclined in a bed beside the window. His hand cupped the back of his head and his other held a television remote. He glanced from the TV to me. "Hel-*lo* pretty lady," he said. "You here to visit me?"

I backed out of his portion of the room, murmuring my apologies, thinking the damn hospital can't even get a room number right, when the beep of the heart monitor sped up in the room behind me. I turned slowly. The old man was pulling off his mask.

"Ginny," he said.

But this guy was not my father. First, he was the wrong color. My father had been a big red-faced man with strong cheeks and full lips and thick black hair and eyebrows that grew in a straight line. This guy had gray skin and thin hair combed over his head, shiny beneath the fluorescent light. This guy is someone else, I thought, and then I noticed his hand picking restlessly at the sheet. He wore a gold ring with a black onyx, the same my father had always worn, only now it was on his thumb.

The woman rushed at me. Her chubby arms crushed me to her ample chest in an awkward embrace. "Oh bless you, sweet girl," she kept saying. "I knew you'd come."

"Leave the girl be, Doris," he said, whistling the s in her name.

The afternoon light was coming through the blinds, projecting a shadow like a huge ladder on the wall, each line a rung. There were fourteen rungs. Beyond the shadow was the door, which I eyed greedily.

"You look like your mama," he said.

Yes, like Mama.

I thought of the list of his transgressions. I should pull it from the top of my satchel and throw it in his sick gray face on my way out the door. I was good at leaving, too. Me, the queen of all departures, the one thing I learned from my father. My mouth formed the words but my mind tumbled and my hands refused to grab the list. And anyway, those transgressions filling two pages of reporter pad, none of them seemed applicable to this frail old man staring up from his bed.

"Thinner than your mama," he said. "I'm not one to talk." He smiled at his joke. At least I think it was a smile. It was hard to tell. He had no teeth. "You ever eat?"

"Yes. Of course."

"Oh you're so sweet," Doris gushed, clutching at my jacket. "Couldn't I take this for you, you look overly warm, your pretty face all red, you sweet girl —"

"Doris," he said. "Stop it."

A nurse came in. She was a big woman wearing a baggy, flowery shirt, and her dyed auburn hair was cut short and gelled up all over, burned looking at the ends. "How are ya, handsome?" she said as she bustled about the room, moving in an off-balanced way, and then I noticed she had only one breast.

"He's doing very well," Doris said. "He has a visitor. You see his visitor?"

The nurse glanced up at me over her black-rimmed glasses, taking me in and dismissing me in that one glance. She leaned back over her patient. "She the prodigal daughter?"

"This isn't my home," I said a little stupidly. "I live in DC."

"Aren't these kids too much?" she said to no one in particular, stretching to the wheeled tray and grabbing a tissue she handed to Doris. She did all that without taking her eyes from him. "All right, tough guy. Let's get to business. I've got good meds."

"No meds now."

"On a scale of one to ten?" she said.

"It's manageable."

"I need a number for the chart, handsome. You know the drill."

"What's manageable?"

The nurse rolled her eyes. "How about an eight? It wouldn't surprise me if you felt an eight."

"Seven's good." He whistled his seven.

"You're such a toughie." Her thick, clumsy hands touched him gently, and for all of her gruffness, she seemed like a gentle woman. "There's no reason to suffer more than you have to."

"I have to talk." He looked right at me.

"All right, toughie," she said, "but you get tired of talking, push this button here." She gave me a quick glance that held a warning before she left.

"Come closer," he said. "My eyesight is shot."

Doris went to his side, whispering in his ear, all the while smoothing his ugly blue gown. When she straightened, she tugged at the gown snaps covering his shoulder, and then she leaned over and kissed those snaps.

When we were alone, I said: "This is not what I anticipated. I shouldn't have come."

"Closer," he said. "Please."

I stepped away from the curtain to the foot of the bed. Beneath the blanket, he was so much smaller than I'd remembered. I felt big and awkward. In all my imagined confrontations over all the years, I'd never considered this. I wouldn't have wished this on my greatest enemy, which I suppose had always been him.

"Will you tell me about yourself?"

"No."

"Are you married?"

"Is this an interview, by chance?"

"I wondered if I had any grandchildren."

"Maybe from someone else," I said. "Not by me."

"But you have family."

"No."

"Someone you love?"

I shifted from foot to foot. There was only one chair in the room, but it was next to his bed. I was thinking about the futility of this, glancing again at the door, when he closed his eyes. I thought he'd fallen asleep, but he opened his eyes again. They were wet looking but focused. "Will you tell me your story?"

"I don't have one," I said, and realized it was true. I chased other people's stories and ignored my own. I had work and all the stuff that work had gotten me — a house, a car,

171

a wardrobe, and shoes — but stuff never constituted a story. I thought about bragging about all that stuff, but it seemed such an effort, as all lies were.

"You hate me."

"No." *Hate is such a clean, precise word. I no longer had the clarity of hate.*

"I'm sorry. Can I say that?"

"You can say whatever you want," I said slowly, trying to find my way through this idea. "And then I'd accept it, because that's what people do. But what can it matter? It was long ago. We're totally different people now."

"It matters to me."

It matters to me.

"You needed me," he said. "I let you down."

You let me down. "No, wait, that's inaccurate," I told him. "I never needed you and I got out just fine."

"You were so young. Thirteen."

Twelve years and two months, a couple of days.

"Will you tell me about after I left?"

After you left —

"I don't talk about that," I said. *Not ever.*

He seemed to struggle with his breath, and then: "You went to your mama's people."

"No."

"She said that's where you'd go."

"We were estranged from her family." *There's a precise word. Yes, estranged.* "I was here and then I went to college."

"Your mama must've been proud."

"Would've been, I imagine."

The room got very quiet except for the beep of his heart monitor and the whoosh of the compressor that fed his oxygen mask and the murmur of the television behind the curtain.

"I don't understand," he said. "Your grandpa didn't come for you?"

"I told you. I don't talk about those years." *The lost years. When you lose a thing, you let it go.*

"But a child can't live alone."

"A family took me in." *As you'd take in a dirty, scruffy stray.* "A foster family. We don't need to talk about it. Everything was fine. They were a good Christian family." *Into their good deeds. I was their good deed — until I wasn't.*

"You were happy?"

"Sure."

"You still talk to them?"

"No."

He was plucking at his sheet again. "You're not going to be able to forgive me."

The ladder-shadow on the wall had thickened so that it barely resembled a ladder anymore but had taken on the shape of a door closing swiftly.

"You're getting yourself all worked up," I said. "Should I get a nurse for you?"

"Stay."

"This isn't any good for you. I didn't come here for this."

"Why then?" he said, and when I couldn't answer: "Curious?"

"My motivation wasn't heroic." My hand sifted nervously through my hair. "I treated someone I care about badly, my friend, a man. I don't know how to deal with him or with what he says he wants, and part of me thinks that's your fault. You know, all that Freudian crap about absent fathers? So I came all this way to kick your ass."

"It's already kicked."

"I'm not going to feel sorry for you." But I could feel myself being lulled by the rhythmic beep of his heart monitor, the whoosh of the oxygen compressor, up and down, making my harsh breaths match his ragged breaths, my heart beat to his.

"Okay."

"You can't make me."

"You said that when you were six."

"You expect me to believe you remember

that long ago?"

"Blink of an eye," he said. "I remember your mama like that, too."

I brushed angry tears from my eyes. "I have to go." When I got to the door, he said something about negotiating. I spun around. "What did you say?"

"Can we negotiate?" he repeated.

"No, *I* do that."

"What?"

"*I* negotiate."

"It's a good tactic."

"No. Not for you, it isn't. It's a good tactic for me. It's mine." I exhaled a bitter laugh. "When I feel small and someone's got leverage over me. When there's something I have to get but I can't get it. It's *my* tactic. It cannot be your tactic."

"Apples don't fall far —"

"*I fell!*" I shouted. "*Far.* After you *dropped* me."

A nurse peeked into the room, asked if everything was all right. I nodded without speaking, and she went away. I took a deep breath and relaxed my fists and ran my hand over the bed railing, which was shockingly cool. I pulled my hand away.

"I shouldn't holler at you when you're unwell." My voice was calmer now. "It's only that I'm not you. Nothing personal. I just wanted to be something else entirely; maybe all children do, and that's all I meant, not to upset you."

"You have the leverage here."

"Hardly." I snorted, and then: "I'm not in shape for this and you're definitely not."

"This is as good as I get."

"And if I stay much longer I'm going to say something that'll rattle around my brain for years and I don't need that. I want to be better. I'm really going to try."

His hand moved across the blanket, restlessly. "I was afraid —"

"I don't — want — to hear it," I said through clenched teeth.

From the other side of the curtain, the television's volume was turned up suddenly, and sports talk blared. The man in the other bed was trying to give us privacy, and he was sick, too. It was wrong of me to bring my anger here. I picked up my satchel from the floor and slipped it over my shoulder.

"Wait," he said, and after a deep breath, "How about I give you something you need?"

"Christ, you sound like I do." I put my head down and rubbed my temples. "I'm sorry, but you don't have anything I need. Not to be cruel, but I never needed anyone."

"I could tell you about your mother."

I lifted my head and stared. His face was thin, his lips dry, but his eyes were full of purpose. He did not blink.

"You probably don't remember her when she was well."

It was true, even the old photographs were gone, the last stolen a decade ago when my bag got lifted from a club downtown, and all that remained, was a wavering memory of a blank-slate face. I thought of that other blank face — the first picture of Evelyn Carney, the one with the white spots for eyes — and then the pictures were moving around in my mind, one sliding across the other, suggesting disturbing similarities I couldn't name and that made no logical sense.

"I have this stupid photographic memory," I said in a slow, thick voice, "except for her. I can't see my mother's face. I don't know why that is."

"Ah," he said. "Her beautiful face. Let me tell you."

My hand gripped the rail of the bed again. The band of my watch skimmed noisily across the cool metal as I made my way toward him. In the chair next to the bed, I sat elbows on knees, my head lowered.

The stories took the rest of the afternoon. He spoke slowly, whistling his words, and he had to stop often to catch his breath. Sometimes he'd ask me to put the mask over his face and he'd rest, his watery eyes blinking slowly and I figured painfully, until his hand would pluck at the rubber band cutting indents in gaunt cheeks. I took the mask off, careful not to snap the band against his waxed paper skin. Sometimes he'd ask for a cup of water, which I'd lift, pointing the straw between his parched lips, careful not to push too far, and I'd wait. I would've waited hours, days. I felt I'd waited my whole life for this. He was a gifted storyteller, and he made my mother come alive. Not the beautiful woman who'd held a little girl in awe, nor the dying woman whose strange prayers for deliverance terrified me, but the living, breathing, hot-blooded, soft-talking, happy, clumsy — if you could believe it, he laughed, *clumsy* — proud woman I'd have liked to have known.

They were good stories, his gift to me.

After visiting hours were over, I made my way to the hotel a block from the hospital and asked if they had a room, thinking if they had one, I'd stay the night, I was so tired, but if not, fine, I'd hop the train home. They had a room. It was small and dark with blackout curtains covering the view of the highway and beyond the highway, the interstate back to DC. On one of the double beds, I sat with my back to the headboard and wrote everything I could remember of what he'd told me. When room service came, I was still writing. For the first time in a long time, I took off my watch and laid it facedown and wrote well into the night and maybe morning, I don't know.

I wrote about the day my father had left. Fairness dictated a report not through the eyes of a girl who was being deserted but through those of an impartial judge, the eyes of a god who flings his wealth and suffering widely but without bias, I could now see. I wrote about *Gone with the Wind* on the lap of the girl hiding in her mother's chair and about the sound of arguing in the parents' bedroom upstairs, of duffel bags dropping and the engine roar as he drove away. I rewound the memory to the bags.

Thump, thump. Two bags — tell the truth — one for him and one for her, the girl had wished that day. Because the girl was afraid of sickness, too. Because it wasn't until the girl was betrayed that she learned not to betray, she would have left had she been given the choice. Thank the father she hadn't been given that choice.

I stared down through tears at the black marks trembling on the white page, breathing hard, scarcely able to believe I'd finally admitted it. There it was. The girl would've abandoned her mother. She would've left her for dead. And there, that girl was me.

The next morning I returned to the hospital. The nurse warned me my father was having a bad day. When I went into his room, he was asleep. The dividing curtain had been drawn back and the bed next to him was empty. The morning light poured through the window and made his skin appear more taut and gray than it had the day before. One of the snaps on the shoulder of his gown had come undone and his collarbone protruded. He wore his mask, his breathing labored even in sleep.

I touched his hand, avoiding the needle and the tape over the needle and the bruising all around the tape. He opened his eyes and lifted two fingers, which meant he wanted his mask off. I tugged the band carefully, resting the mask beneath his jaw. I told him I was leaving now. I had to get back to the District. I had a job there, and they wouldn't tolerate my ditching work. He was whispering, so I huddled closer. He said he'd made a mistake when he was afraid and he'd never known how to fix it. It kept growing until it wasn't fixable.

"It's okay," I said. "I get afraid, too. Right now, in fact."

"I was young. I wanted to live. I tried to run but it got me anyway."

"It?"

He picked at his blanket, restlessly, the onyx ring turning on his thumb.

"I should never have run," he said. "I'm so sorry."

I put the mask back over his face and he breathed easier. I did, too. I told him I forgave him and the lost years were finally gone now and I'd remember only the great gift he'd given me, which I'd carry back to DC and wherever else I roamed.

He pulled the mask down himself.

"You're a good girl, Ginny." He smiled a weary, toothless smile. "I'll tell your mama when I see her."

CHAPTER FIFTEEN

Cabs idled beside the main entrance to the hospital. On the far side of the driveway, a familiar gray pickup truck was parked. A tall man got out of the truck and came toward me, his jacket flapping open, the long, unhurried sauntering gait I knew so well. An apparition, too good to be true, but no, it really was Ben.

"Need a ride?" he said.

Christ, he looked good. He wore aviator sunglasses that changed him somehow, made him look older, the strong contours of his cheeks and nose and jaw more pronounced.

"How did you know where I was?" I said.

"Isaiah forwarded me your travel info. I wish — Well, it doesn't matter what I wish, as long as somebody tells me what's going on, I guess. Let's go."

His palm cupped my elbow and I leaned into him for a moment, the hardness of his arm against mine, and something in me relaxed. He led me to the truck and opened my door. When he settled into the driver's seat, he shoved his keys into the ignition without turning the engine over. "Your dad will be all right?" he said.

"No."

He swung his dark glasses on me. "Ah, Virginia, I'm sorry."

"It's not like I know him or anything."

"I know it," he said. "That's why I'm sorry."

We drove in silence for a bit. The interior of the truck was cramped, intimate. I turned the radio on low. News radio competed with engine hum. I pressed my face to the passenger window and burrowed deeper into the leather seat. Outside, the broken white road lines became solid with speed, and it seemed we were traveling through time and space, sailing south, making our way home. My eyes became heavy and I slept.

A loud, humming noise jarred me awake. I rubbed my eyes to the yellow light of the harbor tunnel outside of Baltimore. The earthiness of being awakened while submerged and the hum in the tunnel and the yellow lights casting Ben's skin darker — all of it made the truck interior electric. I watched him while pretending not to. His long-fingered, knuckle-scarred hands gripped the wheel, and I imagined those hands on my body. When he glanced over, we were out of the tunnel.

"We should probably talk about the other night," I said softly.

"Not today."

"To clear the air, so we can work —"

"Leave it alone." When he glanced up in the rearview mirror, I noticed the heat on his skin, his lips in a stubborn line. He appeared as hard and remote as the place from which he'd come and to where I'd figured he'd one day return, and I couldn't understand how I'd known him all these years without really seeing him. Maybe I'd been looking too long through the lens of the camera that made him pretty, almost boyish; the camera that lied.

"It's okay," I said. "I get it."

"You do?"

"Sure, I can be patient."

He cut me a sideways look of disbelief. "You — patient?"

"Uh-huh, right now we're both off-kilter. You, because you want to do what you'd typically do for a friend who needs you. But you're not sure what we are — friends, coworkers, something else — and you dislike that kind of confusion. And I imagine,

184

although I'm not entirely certain of this, you also feel bad because you idolize your father and can't imagine a world without him, and you're projecting that feeling onto me."

His mouth dropped open.

"So it's okay," I said. "We'll work it out later. See? Patient."

By early Monday morning I was back to work. I hated Mondays. My desk was always buried under a weekend's worth of paper-work, newspapers, press releases, and sticky-note messages of missed calls. This particular morning I felt about as tired as I'd ever been, my mood still low from the visit with my father, and the pile on my desk seemed insurmountable. I ignored everything except the *Post,* which I scanned for weekend developments on the Evelyn Carney investigation. The print guys had nothing.

Evelyn had been missing for over a week. During that time, I'd been making the same calls to her family, leaving messages for her parents in upstate New York, neither of whom had returned one damn call, and to her husband, Peter, from whom I expected no return call. Next, I called Paige Linden and left a message. Despite her busy schedule, she let me check in with her each day, even if she had nothing new to tell, nor I to tell her. But the relationship had been established, and I liked her.

As I hung up, my cell phone rang. "I'm hungry," Michael Ledger said without identifying himself. "Come out for breakfast."

"I don't recognize this number."

He laughed. "Meet me at our coffee shop?"

He was so arrogant I nearly laughed, too. "We don't have a coffee shop."

"Sure we do," he said. "You remember."

"Don't play games. If there's something new in the investigation that I can report, tell me now, so I can rush it on air."

"The way sources are treated these days. Can't even get a cup of coffee." There was a loud, dramatic exhalation on his end of the line. "I'm sure I can get better treatment from your colleagues at the *Post,*" he mused. "They've got coffee, though it hasn't gotten any better since you were there. Or maybe I'll go to Channel 5. They're always quick to feed a fellow."

I sighed. "Give me a few minutes to get there."

Michael was already at the register, pulling his money clip from his pocket, running his hand over the bills as one might caress a lover, before he slid the clip back into his pocket. He carried two mugs of coffee to the table and went back to retrieve a scone for me and two glazed donuts for himself.

"Have to keep up the stereotype," he said, shoving a donut into his mouth.

Michael Ledger was no stereotype. He wore a bulky fisherman's sweater that no fisherman could afford. It bulked up his slim frame nicely. He had color in his pale face, and his gray eyes flashed with humor. He looked good the way an actor looks good. I could appreciate it, but it no longer hurt me.

"I talked to Ian Chase the other night," I said. "He was awfully skittish. You think he was in a relationship with Evelyn Carney?"

"Of course he was. We're talking about me first."

"You *knew*. Goddamn it, Michael. I specifically asked you."

He went on as if I hadn't spoken. "I find myself all jammed up in this situation," he said, elongating each syllable: *sit-you-ay-tion.* "I figured you could help me work the angles. You're pretty clever. It involves this news exec I like."

My back tensed. "Let me hear it."

"Top-of-the-line newsperson, well known

187

for her *fair dealings* and all that. She comes to me for sensitive information — sensitive being the understatement here — and trustful fellow that I am, I give her the goods, thinking I like her, she likes me, we'll watch each other's backs. A good deal in a case that could go bad in a hurry. And did I mention? This news exec and I, we've got history, so all the better. You still with me here? You look bored. I'm not putting you to sleep with my situation?"

"Too much caffeine pumping through my system." I lifted my cup. "Get on with it."

"So I trust this *fair* and *honest* newsperson and give her access to info as well as a copy of my victim's journal — which, by the way, I see in that overgrown handbag of yours."

I dropped the satchel to the floor and kicked it under my chair.

"Flaunting what you learned from that journal is pretty ballsy," he told me, "given you have *not* watched out for me. I haven't received one call. Imagine my surprise when I turned on my TV and that prick Ben Pearce was reporting romantic intrigue involving my case."

"Ben was never a great fan of yours, either."

"Smug as hell, that one," he said, shoving

188

the last of the second donut into his mouth and talking through it. "Don't know what you ever saw in him."

"I never saw anything."

He lifted his eyebrows at me, chewing all the while, and his eyes gleamed.

"Ben's got plenty of sources willing to dish," I said. "One of them dished. Nothing I can do about that."

"Yeah, yeah, whatever. This is about me, remember?" He pulled his phone from its holder and turned it in his hand. "You gave me no warning. No explanation. All weekend, I kept checking my phone, perplexed. It's got power. There's no problem with the signal. I ask myself, why won't she call?"

"I'm not checking in with you," I told him. "You can't make me do it."

"Seriously —"

"That deal we made is absurd. I don't need your approval to report what doesn't come from you."

He clasped his hand to his chest. "You *lied* to me," he said, laughing. "You've become *ruthless.*"

"Yeah, and you've been holding back." I took a sip of my coffee and considered the agreement. "Besides, I would've said anything to get that journal and you knew it."

"No, I didn't. You *used* to be the most

annoyingly honest person I'd ever met."

"You can relax," I said. "I have no intention of annoying you with the truth anymore."

He laughed again. "As long as you remember I'm the source and you need me. I expect to be courted. You have to court me."

All this talk was curious. Sure, I needed him, but it was becoming increasingly obvious he needed something from me, too. What that was specifically, I'd have to figure out.

"Why'd you hold back on Ian?" I said. "You think he's responsible for Evelyn's disappearance?"

He finished the last of his coffee, blinking at me lazily, making me wait. "Couldn't say one way or the other," he said finally. "Got himself a lawyer who's not letting him talk. Until he explains himself, he stays on the short list."

"Of suspects?"

"Persons of interest. Remember, no evidence —"

"Of a crime, yeah, yeah," I finished. "So talk to me about this short list. Who else is on it? Peter Carney?"

His whole demeanor changed. He talked admiringly about Peter's heroics overseas, his multiple tours in Afghanistan and other exotic places Michael refused to name. He also noted Peter's apparent worry for his wife and helpfulness with investigators, how Peter gave permission for the police to search the Carney home and car. Most important, he said, Peter's alibi checked out.

"Now, there might have been some marital problems," he went on. "Fairly typical for a married couple that spends so much time apart, I hear, and when you factor in the stresses of war? Not just this physical stuff. There's psychological trauma, too."

He was talking as if Peter was his victim. What's more, he or his investigators seemed to be viewing Evelyn's disappearance through Peter's eyes, and it was Peter's take that was driving the narrative. Understandable as a starting point, given Peter's willingness to talk, but maybe not the whole story or even the real story.

"You sympathize with Peter?"

His face screwed up, as if he'd tasted something bitter. "Hard not to. Poor guy's off getting his ass shot at while his wife's running around DC having her little sexual adventure."

Ah, there it was. "Her sexual *adventure*?"

"With Ian, certainly," he said, thumbing the handle of his coffee cup. "What we don't know, are there other men? You know, there's a reason sometimes these women go missing."

My blood went hot. *These women.*

He shrugged. "Evelyn Carney got around. All I'm saying."

It was almost laughable — almost. I mean, this was Michael talking — *Michael Ledger,* who was shockingly promiscuous. Of course, he would say he was just doing what fellas did, while women *got around,* and if sometimes these women went missing?

Through my teeth, I said: "And how about him?"

"Who?"

"Peter. The husband. Did he indulge in extramarital relationships? Anything that might have caused Evelyn to get gone?"

"Not that I'm aware of."

"Meaning, your investigators haven't checked, have they?"

He waved his hand in dismissal, and my temper whipped dangerously again, even as I understood that anger was a waste of time. Michael's attitude about sex when a woman's body was the crime scene was so commonly held among investigators that I shouldn't bother fighting it, except for this: Evelyn Carney depended on Michael's good will. If he thought she "got around" and was unworthy of his precious time, he might stop looking for her, and her case would fall to the bottom of his tragically long list of cold cases.

I also knew there was no use pointing out the flaws in his worldview that was already baked in. Without a word, I got up and ordered a coffee to go. He followed me out of the café and up Wisconsin Avenue.

"You mad at me?" he said.

"Nope."

"You're acting like it."

I cut him a sideways look.

"Well, if you're not mad, take me to that big-shot dinner at the Hinkley Hilton tomorrow night," he said.

The White House Correspondents Dinner had been on my calendar, and every year I got two tickets, but this year I'd forgotten about it, which was pretty remarkable. It was *the* black-tie event for TV folk. At the Hilton, you could walk a red carpet, wear beautiful clothes, get drunk on the cheap, and rub elbows with celebrities, the real ones from Hollywood. I wasn't into celebrities, but they attracted the Big Fish, the holders of information, and that was the objective of the game. You invite a Big Fish, and they allow you access to their information, quid pro quo— although I'd long since grown weary of that game and in recent years went with Ben instead.

Now Michael, my own hooked Big Fish, was talking about being invited by some crime reporter who'd had the prudence to invite him. "But I'd ditch him in a heartbeat if I could go with a beautiful, *ruthless* woman."

"Yeah, all right, I'll take you."

"Try not to sound so excited about it," he said in a dry voice. He stopped at the corner that turned toward my station. "So tonight? Got any plans to go back across the river?"

That was Michael-speak for Arlington, where Ian Chase lived. "What time you talking?"

"If you get there before sundown, you'll be good. Techs will go in with the blue lights, search for blood, that sort of thing. Maybe you get yourself some pretty pictures."

Now that was worth the dinner ticket — and more. "How'd you get the warrant?"

"Ian's attorney gave permission."

"The attorney that wouldn't let Ian talk?" I said with suspicion. "He's letting your investigators search Ian's home? Why?"

"Because, my love, our fine AUSA is trying to finagle his way off my list." His smile was long and thin like the blade of a knife.

194

"Trust me, that list is nowhere you'd want to find yourself."

195

CHAPTER SIXTEEN

Here's the problem . . .

Nelson and Ben hovered over me, one on each side of my desk. I pointed to the computer monitor that showed an aerial view of Ian Chase's neighborhood. Google Earth was a wonder that allowed you to consider stakeout locations without ever leaving the office.

"The investigators will most likely go through the front," I said, and clicked on the street view of the glass condo. The entrance was as impressive as I remembered.

Nelson whistled. "Check out his crib," he said with awe. "Know what that building needs, though? Hip Asian guy. Lend it some of my cool."

"Sure, you're what it needs," Ben said. "But what it requires? Lots of money."

Nelson scratched his chin. "More than my artist salary, you think?"

"Can we drool over the real estate later?"
I said, tapping my stylus to the monitor.
"So here's the first camera's position, staked
out at the front door. We'll need a second
camera for the garage entrance. The big
question: how to get video of Ian's apartment on the fourteenth floor. If I'm calcu-
lating correctly, this is his unit — the
penthouse on the northeast corner."

"Dude's got river views," Nelson said,
whistling again. He pushed back the brim
of his ball cap and scratched his scalp as he
thought about it. "You need me to get
interior video of the police searching an
apartment fourteen floors above the street?"

"Even if you can only get the reflection of
the blue lights off the windows," I told him.
We'd gotten this kind of video plenty of
times by shooting through the window —
child's play for Nelson, really — but never
in a location so high up. This required more
ingenuity. "It's a shot we may never use.
Hopefully, Evelyn Carney will turn up safe
and sound. But if Ian Chase did something
to her, I need the picture to write to. How
do we make it happen?"

"Get me in a helicopter, and I'll get your
shot," Nelson said.

Ben said, "A boy can dream."

"Yeah, restricted air space this close to the

District," I said, and then to Nelson, the biggest gossip I knew: "Did I mention? No one can know we're shooting video. An F-16 escorting a news chopper out of airspace might attract some attention."

We were quiet for a moment, staring at the monitor, when Ben pointed to the part of the map that showed parkland across the street from the condo. "What if we put a microwave truck in this lot for the park?" he said to Nelson. "We could use the camera on top of the mast?"

It wasn't my favorite option. The truck was big and obvious, with our station ID painted on its side. When the mast went up, it created a lot of noise. The video from the mast camera was always shaky and blurry, borderline unusable.

Nelson did a quick calculation using his fingers. "Yeah, no. If the dude's penthouse is on the fourteenth floor, it's at least a hundred twenty feet up. Mast is maybe a little over sixty feet, max. It won't get the shot." He gazed at me, his lips pursed. "If you got in the building before, why not again? I could get you up to speed on a camera, something hidden —"

"Not an option," Ben said, folding his arms across his chest. "She no longer has the element of surprise, it's not legal, and

Mellay won't have her back. Last thing I feel like doing is the two-step with a bunch of corporate lawyers. Or bailing her ass out of the Arlington County Jail."

Some girls got all mushy from flowers and jewelry and professions of eternal love. I got warm and fuzzy when Ben talked about bailing me out. It meant we were ourselves again, a team.

"What's the farthest point from which you can get usable video?" I asked Nelson, noticing no one had mentioned my idea yet.

"Baby has a seventeen-to-one ratio," Nelson said proudly. "She's got the most amazing lens."

"Baby?"

Ben rolled his eyes. "He named his new camera. Don't ask."

"All right, dumb it down for me," I said. "On this map, where does Baby have to set up for a shot that's worthy of her?"

"If she's on tripod or otherwise steady, she can shoot from three hundred feet away and the video would look like she's fifteen away. At that distance, you won't see wrinkles on a face, but you see the face." He bent over the monitor. On the map, his finger circled a radius around the condominium. "That means she can handle anything within this area, if this map's scale is right. The closer to the condo the better, obviously."

"What about this building here?" I pointed with the stylus. "The one with the parking garage?"

"Hell yeah," Nelson said. "Get me on that roof, Baby gets your shot. What is it?"

I grinned. "A hotel."

There'd been no small rooms on the top floor of the Marriott, only a corner suite at a budget-busting rate that would've flagged Mellay had I charged it to my corporate account. But it was the perfect location for the stakeout. I booked the suite with my personal charge card.

My satchel was packed and I was ready to go when Mellay stopped by my office.

"Got a minute?"

I cursed inwardly. "Sure."

"Isaiah just told me about your father's illness," he said, crossing the room to me. "I wanted to make sure you got the time you needed. You need anything, you have only to ask."

My brow creased. He was being nice to me. I scarcely knew how to take it. "Thank you," I said.

"You look flustered. Maybe you came back too soon."

"Just feeling a little pressed for time."

He squinted at me through his glasses. "Oh yeah? Working on something for the show?"

"I . . . no. Well, no, not for tonight's show." I felt my face getting red. "Just a tip that maybe needs checking out. Not sure yet."

He went silent, strolling around my office. At the bookshelf, his fingertips strummed the spine of my books, stopping at *Ulysses,* and tapped the book twice. "Girl with this many books is looking for something," he said, turning back to me. "Can't say I understand you, but I know this: it's not smart to hide things from your boss."

"If anything pans out, I'll call you."

And I planned to. I really did.

Inside the hotel suite, Nelson set up his camera at the window. Over the tree line, we could see into Ian Chase's apartment. Its windows were floor to ceiling and had no curtains or blinds to obstruct our view. The interior space was lit up.

Nelson was gawking through the camera's viewfinder. "This Ian Chase guy is living my dream," he said, stepping aside. "Take a look."

I could see the main room, a stunningly elegant and open space. Abstract paintings hung above wainscot, and minimalist furniture scattered around what appeared to be an Adams mantel. A gourmet kitchen with high-end appliances ran the length of the far wall.

"No way the techs keep those curtains open," Nelson said. "We can't be this lucky."

"Your camera stays on that window until investigators leave, okay? If there's even the hint of blue light, I want it."

He gave me a crooked smile. "Never in my life have I missed the money shot."

When the sun went behind the trees, it grew cold by the open window. A westerly breeze swept in. I went into the sitting room and made a pot of coffee and slid on my jacket before pacing with restless excitement. Finally, my cell phone rang. Ben told me the techs had just gone in through the lobby.

"Your photographer got video?"

"Parking and unloading equipment. Two detectives accompanied them. I checked the video. It's good stuff."

I hurried back to the bedroom where Nelson was bent over the camera again. His slender frame was taut with an alertness that said something was going on in the apartment. I stepped away from his blind side,

202

softly, so as not to startle him. "Police inside?"

He grunted.

There was nothing to do except stand there, watching Nelson shoot whatever the hell he was seeing. Finally, he straightened from the camera and stretched his back, grinning. "We're getting freaking everything," he said. "Take a look."

In the foreground, a technician worked over a small table in front of a window, holding a book by its binding and shaking it out. Another was working over a kitchen sink. I couldn't see what he was doing.

From behind me, Nelson was saying: "I got to hand it to you, Virginia. This is serious access. You got some kind of pull with that source of yours."

It made me nervous. Ian Chase was a well-regarded, politically connected federal prosecutor. "I thought Ian was one of them," I murmured.

Nelson snorted. "Guess not. They're hanging their boy out to dry, for real."

Later that evening, I parked my car in a spot at the end of the street, the last remaining space, and grabbed the Maglite from beneath my seat. Under a sky bright with stars, I walked toward the darkness that was my house. I'd forgotten to leave lights on again.

The trees behind the streetlamps threw weird shadows across the porch. The largest shadow in the corner moved. It appeared to be a man rising from the Adirondack chair I kept chained to the railing. I pointed the Maglite at him. It was Peter Carney.

He lumbered across creaky slats and down the steps to meet me on the walkway. His clumsy movements made me wonder if he'd been drinking. "I got your messages earlier," he said, talking as if it were perfectly normal to be waiting for a near stranger outside her house late at night. "Would you like to talk now?"

"You should have called before dropping by," I said warily.

"Yes, of course. You're right." His short hair stood on end, and he was looking everywhere except at me, surveying the dark corners of my yard and the line of cars along the curb to the end of the street, where music played faintly. "I just started walking. I wasn't thinking about where I was going. Next thing I knew, I was here."

"You walked all the way from the Hill?"

"It's easier to walk at night," he said. "There's not as much color. Over there — where I was in Afghanistan — everything is muted. All that rock and dirt and concrete, it changes the light, spreads it out, and then I come home, and all the bright color gives me headaches. Today it was bad."

He was shivering, despite the temperate air. I didn't like him being here, but it felt unkind to send him away.

"You want something warm to drink?" I said. "Or I could grab you a blanket?"

"Huh, look at that," he said, holding out his hand, watching it shake. On his ring finger was a wedding band. When he looked up again, he said: "Detective Miller let me pick up Evie's Volvo today. I wanted to tell you that. You know Detective Miller?"

"Not personally. He's the lead detective on the case."

"He said the guy who reported Evie missing was some prosecutor she was seeing when I was overseas. She never told me his name, just that she was in love. Now this detective tells me she's not with him, either. It's so confusing."

He told me a rambling story about going with Evelyn to high mass at St. Peter's. It was a frigid morning about a month ago. The place had been packed with swells of people, kids in the choir, everyone wearing bulky winter coats. He was afraid of what was beneath everyone's coats. He told Evelyn what to do if there was an explosion, and he warned her, too, that there's often a secondary device that goes off. He curled his fingers over the lip of the pew, pushing his weight on the wood, making sure it was solid. Yes, it was good cover, until she could get to an exit. Help as many children as you can, he'd told her.

She'd reached across the pew, holding his hand, letting him fiddle with her rings, and it calmed him. Later that night, when he couldn't sleep, she sat with him by the window and watched the snow falling beneath streetlights. "That was the night she promised she'd never leave," he said. "And then, a few weeks later she left. I don't know what to think. Where could she go? She doesn't even have her car, and now the blackjack is gone, too."

"Blackjack?"

"A weapon." He described it as a short, leather-covered club with a coil spring and a heavy ball of lead at the end. It was small and easy to conceal, and in the District, quite illegal. He always kept it in the glove box, but it wasn't in the car when he picked up the Volvo. "Detective Miller had me file a report."

"It was stolen from the lot?"

"Miller thought it the most likely explanation. But I can't stop thinking about how jittery Evie was at the restaurant. What if she took the blackjack from the car and carried it because she was frightened?" He frowned, considering the idea. "Although that's confusing, too. Who takes a weapon to meet a man she supposedly loves?"

CHAPTER SEVENTEEN

Early the next morning, my cell phone woke me. It was Michael. He told me a bass fisherman had found a woman's body in a shallow cove on the Maryland side of the Potomac, just south of National Harbor. The fisherman had gone out with the tide in the early golden light and found a body swaying in the current. Her long dark hair had gotten twisted in the reeds.

I rubbed sleep from my eyes. "You think she's Evelyn?"

"Evidence suggests."

"Hang on." I reached for my notepad and pen on my bedside table. "Tell me where to go. I'm ready."

The lot was marked only by a brown sign saying Overlook. Gravel crunched beneath my tires as I turned in and parked across from several Maryland state police and county cruisers, and a couple of Crown

Vics, the typical unmarked DC Police car. There was an ambulance that wasn't going anywhere. The medical examiner's wagon blocked the entrance to a path, presumably leading to the overlook. The river was beyond the curtain of trees, some still leafless and broken by winter.

No other media had shown. Not even my own people, Nelson and Ben and the satellite truck I'd requested. Beside one of the cruisers, a big-bellied detective was interviewing a thin man wearing a floppy-rimmed hat and a Bassaholic sweatshirt beneath his windbreaker. The detective kept his head down, flipping through his notepad. The rolls on the back of his neck were pink in the morning sun.

I slipped on a ball cap and pulled my ponytail through the loop before climbing out of the car. Michael lifted his hand and walked toward me in muddy hiking boots; Michael who never muddied his shoes. His field coat was dirty, and there was tightness about the corners of his mouth, a closed look I'd seen before. It was his death-scene look. "You got here fast," he said.

"Where's the body?"

He pointed behind him. "In a cove. You have to climb a pretty steep path about thirty yards. From the bank, it's about ten, maybe fifteen yards out."

"Okay, let's go."

He shook his head. "The area's been taped off. Even if it wasn't, you don't want to see. The river does terrible things to a body."

"Then why do you think it's Evelyn?"

He told me about the ATM card with her imprinted name tucked neatly in the nylon stocking worn beneath the boot on her left foot. Her purse and coat and much of her clothing had been swept away. The coat, he surmised, may have gotten snagged on debris washed down the mountains from earlier storms. Maybe that's why she'd been down so long. Or maybe she'd been caught on something else. People dumped all kinds of stuff in the river. "We'll wait for the ME to positively ID her," he said, "but yeah, it's her."

"Take me as far as the crime scene tape," I pleaded. "I need to see where she is, not necessarily her, but where. Maybe if I see —"

"No can do," he said. "We can come back later, after the scene is clear."

"I'll owe you."

We locked eyes for a long moment. His were cool and gray and narrowed with calculation.

"Any favor at all, it's yours," I repeated. "No expiration date."

He jerked his chin. "Come on," he said.

On the path beyond the medical examiner's wagon, the heels of my boots sank into the steep moist slope as we descended. It was slow going. The tall grass slapped at my jeans, and dried branches cracked beneath my boots. Somewhere in the distance — *kee-ahh* — the call of a raptor hunting, a hawk or an osprey, maybe an eagle.

We cleared the trees. The river was dark and moody and filled the air with smells of mucky matter breaking down so that new matter could be born. I picked up my pace, skidding as we went downhill. Michael put his arm out. "Far enough," he said.

We were on a small clearing like a shelf above the river. Out of the pocket of his field coat, he drew binoculars and aimed them at a cove where men waded among waterweed. Several boats bobbed in the tide. From this distance, the faces of the men were indistinct, and I couldn't pick out Evelyn at all. The land curved around the cove, protecting it, and above the land, a tree spread its wide branches. A heron roosted on a branch. It was a big bird, its neck stunningly white, and it seemed to preside over the hopeless work of the men below.

Behind us, a couple of workers from the Medical Examiner's Office were making their way down the slope. They struggled with their bag. Michael greeted them and then put his binoculars up to his eyes again.

"Evidence techs are blocking the view," he said, still looking through the glasses. "I hate all this damn mud, but I better go down. You go back up to the lot."

"Let me use your binoculars."

His brow furrowed, but he handed me the glasses. "Quick peek, that's all, then you're out of here."

There were plenty of reasons I should listen to him. He was a police commander, and this was his case. It was at his pleasure I was where I was, and if I caused him displeasure, he could give me the boot. But I gambled he wouldn't do it. I ran, half falling down the slope, sliding a couple of yards before he grabbed me again, cursing me with really foul language. But I already had his field glasses to my eyes, and I could see.

One detective took pictures, as another placed something dark like hanks of hair or weed into a plastic bag held by another technician. Someone else waded through hydrilla swirling around his thigh-high boots. I could see the backs of two guys from the ME's office and the black body bag, and the tech in the thigh boots stepped back and there she was — Evelyn — or what was left of her, a bloated naked back and one leg floating across the surface of the river, the other leg submerged. Someone pulled a reed from her tangled hair that was black with river water and adorned with clusters of branches and leaves. She was facedown, her hair all about her, her body swaying with the current and the yanking of the men trying to free her, and then they turned her over.

Her eyes were gone.

I dropped the binoculars and turned to tell Michael, but then I heaved. Nothing came out. There was a voice from very far away that seemed to be getting louder. It was Michael. "All right now," he was saying. "That's right, breathe." He was rubbing my back, talking to me in a gentle voice so unlike Michael's, saying it was okay to be a little crazy, a perfectly normal response at a death scene; he was equally so at his first. He told stories about his "fool self" and about other detectives nicknamed Bull and Murph who had also lost their nerve. His words were soothing, and I started to feel like myself again, and then he said: "We got company."

I wiped my mouth with the back of my

hand and straightened. In the tree above the cove, the heron still roosted, seemingly transfixed by the men from the Medical Examiner's Office trudging up the slope with the heavy black bag. When the bag was out of sight, the huge bird lifted its great wings and launched itself from the branch, lifting itself high, higher. It tipped its wing and disappeared beyond the curve of the river.

"No, there," Michael said, pointing.

At the top of the hill, Nelson had his camera on his shoulder and was shooting from behind the yellow tape. Ben was frowning down at me, as if he expected me to fall apart. I pulled the brim of my cap low, shielding my eyes, and started my way up the slope. Without looking at Ben, I walked past him.

At the top, I called over my shoulder: "Come on, guys. We've got news to break."

CHAPTER EIGHTEEN

After the live shots were complete, I drove back to the station and took a long, hot shower in the locker room before heading to my office. The blinds were closed and the overhead lights off, making the office shadowy and cool. I clicked on my bank of televisions, keeping each on mute, and tidied my desk. There was my stapler and my set of pens lined in a row and my press releases stacked beside messages I'd read when I was ready. My newspapers were open, waiting like old friends. All was as it should be, now that I was where I was supposed to be, and if I stayed out of the field and here in my office, I would be all right.

I crossed to my bookshelf and pulled *Ulysses* from its row, dropped it to the floor, and grabbed the hidden bottle. The first shot burned all the way down. My thoughts calmed a little. I tried to rest but when I closed my eyes, all I could see was Evelyn.

No way could I go to that dinner tonight. But when I tried to call Michael, he didn't answer. With a sigh, I kicked my shoes under my desk and walked barefoot over the rough carpet to the coat rack where the garment bag hung.

Inside the bag were several dresses I'd packed when I had no idea what to wear: a couple of sleek black gowns similar to what every other woman in the ballroom would be wearing, careful dresses for a careful woman. I needed a vacation from that woman. The third dress was long and red and had to be shimmied on. My never-dared Jimmy Choos, the gold ones with the ankle buckles and four-inch heels I'd bought on a lark, winked from the bottom of the bag. Those, too, I thought as I pulled them out and stepped into them.

The heels propelled me hips-first to the mirror where a strange woman was reflected. She wore a red dress that clung to her body, which was surprisingly long and lovely, and her face was made up heavily to hide worry lines. The woman was pretty, maybe even beautiful, and I did not know that woman.

There was a melodic rap at the door. When I opened it, Nelson was still in his street clothes, his skullcap, and the khaki vest with the oversized pockets. He was obviously just back from the river. He gawked at me, open-mouthed, before he recovered. "Hey, that's some dress," he managed to say.

I waited for him to tell me what he wanted. When he didn't, I said, "Do you need something?"

"Oh yeah, you got a minute to chat in private?"

"Shut the door behind you." I went back to my desk. "Come. Sit. Commune."

He slouched in the chair across from me. "Mellay grabbed me on the way into the newsroom. Said he wants an inventory of my equipment for an audit. I asked is the station being sold and he gives me the typical runaround, chuckling the whole time, like it's some big joke. What do you think? We're getting sold?"

"I have no idea. Mellay doesn't confide in me."

"Moira is certain they'll sell us," he said darkly. "Tear a good thing to pieces to make money for a few fat gray-hairs. Which makes my decision easier, right?"

"I'm not following."

"Alexa knows people with a production company in South Florida. They do big stuff, you know, for cable channels like

Discovery Channel and National Geographic, the kind of shooting I've always dreamed of. I sent them my audition tape. They made an offer."

"Oh," I said, and my throat constricted. I put my head down until the constriction went away.

"I want the job," he went on, "but I feel terrible. Like I'd be deserting my friends when things are really bad and I'm supposed to be doing my best work for you. Ben's my foxhole brother, but you — you gave me my start in big market TV. You believed in me first."

He had sad brown eyes that looked through the lens with the eye of a god, and I knew that when he left, there'd be no replacement for him, not ever.

"You were born to shoot video," I said. "That's who you are and what you have to do. Your allegiance has to be to your talent."

"I only want to shoot."

"Then that's what I want, too." I lifted the whiskey bottle and pointed the top at him. "How about a celebratory drink? There's another teacup on the shelf. Bring it here."

He glanced at the closed door. "What if Mellay finds out?"

"Who cares? You're migrating south." I poured our drinks and lifted my cup. "Water of life," I said, and downed it.

After that second drink, I kicked back in my chair, rocking it to the rise and fall of Nelson's voice without actually listening to his words. He had a pleasant voice. His chip-toothed smile was endearing as hell, too. Maybe it was the whiskey, but he seemed to me the youngest, most endearing photographer in the world, and it hurt. I worried about him in a business that could be so brutal, but maybe someone would look after him when he flew south.

"Nobody gets hurt by a little dish," Nelson was saying when I tuned back in, "but that kind of video gets you fired. That's what Moira's hoping. It's risky, so she gave it to me. Since I'm probably leaving and all."

The whiskey gave my brain a nice, slow hum. "What video?"

He folded his arms over the big pockets of his khaki vest. "Surveillance of the garage downstairs. You can see Mellay with a woman. Grainy stuff, but best guess? Looks like Heather."

"What are they doing in the video?"

"You know," he said, smirking.

My eyebrows were up to my hairline. "Seriously?" If somebody sent it to corporate, Mellay would be fired. If so, I'd get my gig back, and honestly, it couldn't happen to a nicer fellow. "I can't believe Mellay is that stupid," I said.

"My network buddies tell me women are Mellay's weakness. He preys on the young girls straight out of college. Tells them he's some big-shot news director taking special interest, reeling them in with talk about their star quality and shit. Except it's against policy to reel them in like that. What's that called? A conundrum?"

"A lawsuit."

"I know, right? Sources say that's how he got kicked out of network. I triple-checked that one."

"You guys spend all your time in the field gossiping?"

"It's called 'news you can use.' If I didn't hate him so much, I'd feel sorry for the guy."

"If what you say is true," I said with disdain, "he created his own burden."

"No, I mean, because of his sister and all. It must be tough. There's his gimpy leg, too."

I rubbed the bridge of my nose, frowning. "Why do I never know what you're talking about?"

"I'm talking about his accident. Word is, it was bad. He complains how his foot hurts and everybody says how it left his sister in a

wheelchair with only him to take care of her
—"

"Wait," I said. "Are you making this wheelchair up?"

"The sister I've seen with my own eyes. Didn't you see her last week?"

"I must've been out in the field."

"He was wheeling her everywhere, showing her around the newsroom. He was a whole different person with her." He described the sister — small, dark-haired girl, pixie face, pink blanket over her legs — and he made me see her. I wished he hadn't.

"You're not joking, are you?" I said glumly.

"Why would it be funny?"

"It's just bad news, that's all." The mirror still held that strange, red-dressed woman with the melancholy eyes. She thought it bad news, too. "You have to keep your dog out of that nasty fight."

"I disagree."

"Listen, we can let Mellay crash and burn on his own bad behavior, but you can't plot against a guy who's caring for a handicapped sister. Do you understand? If you do, you're responsible for hurting the sister. You do something like that, and you're as bad as Mellay. Ethics 101."

"But he made it so I can't work here anymore."

221

"He made it so you don't want to," I said. "That's a big difference. Now give up the video."

I held out my hand. He grumbled but reached into the pocket of his vest and pulled out a media card, slapping it onto my palm. I dropped it into the bottom drawer of my desk and locked it.

"But the network guys tell me it's true," he whined.

"Doesn't matter. And Moira shouldn't talk you into doing what she won't do herself. Think about it."

"But she's leading the newscast, which proves reward for favors given."

"You're blowing my buzz, Nelson, you really are. Moira's not leading the newscast. She's anchoring."

"Not Moira. *Heather.* That's what I'm trying to tell you."

"Heather is not on air."

"Turn on your monitor," he said, his arm sweeping toward the televisions. "She graduates straight from college to on-air at the number-one station in a top market. Even I had to start small. And I'm a real Michelangelo."

Just then, Isaiah came in, holding a script. "That dress is a five-alarm fire," he said with a gentle smile. "My girl's all grown up."

When I asked about the show, he pushed at his glasses nervously. He said he needed something new to freshen the Evelyn Carney story.

"Ben's story is in the can, ready to go," I said. "I oversaw the edits."

"Mellay wants the story live."

"Can't have it," I said. "Ben has worked since early morning. I won't make him work a minute longer. Tell Mellay to take Ben's edited spot and deal with it."

"Mellay assigned the story to Heather."

"What?"

Isaiah didn't say anything.

My palms went flat across the desktop. "Assigned her to *my story*? It's the goddamn lead. Has she been on-air? Ever? In any market?"

"Some on-air stuff at her university, I think." He wouldn't look me in the eye. "She's not bad, just inexperienced. Mellay wants to give her some experience, that's all."

Nelson cackled. "I bet he does."

"Look at this." Isaiah handed me her script. "Pretty good, actually."

I only had to glance at the script with her name in the byline. "Sure it's great," I said, my voice rising. "Because *I wrote it.*"

He hesitated. "I told her to go through

the rundown and study how the good writers write."

"Oh, she went through it all right. She stole the script I wrote for Ben. Every word is the same." I caught the last graph. "Except, no, wait, there are seven — no, eight words that are different. Hey, Nelson, you want to hear the words?"

Nelson was punching buttons on the remote, toggling to find the channel for Heather's live shot. "Hit me with 'em."

" *'Her and her husband met at the restaurant.'* That's the change she made." I turned to Isaiah. "Well, *me and my photographer* are appalled. I can't believe you let her steal my work."

"It's no different than you writing for Ben."

"Hell it isn't. Ben puts my name in the byline. You ought to explain plagiarism to your girl."

"Too late anyhow." Nelson had found the channel for Heather's live shot and turned up the volume. He rubbed his hands together with excitement. "She's getting ready to go on."

"This should be good," I said. "I've never seen a train wreck as it happens."

We crowded around the monitor. At first glance, Heather looked as if she belonged.

The studio lights warmed her already flaw-less skin. She sucked in her cheeks and lifted her chin. The camera matured her, made her more elegant and beautiful — I had to admit it — a terrible beauty. She opened her mouth wide, stretching it, like a snake about to swallow its prey, and then she must've heard the countdown in her earpiece. She got an arrested look before she adjusted her mouth, slightly pursed with the smallest hint of a smile, the serious journalist look.

"Man, would I like to shoot her," Nelson said.

And then she was on.

She read my script as if it were her own. It was a perfect delivery, as if she was born for reading news, as if she'd been reading for years and our anchor desk had been waiting only for her. After she tagged out, she murmured her thanks for what could've only been congratulations from the control room. She pulled out her earpiece and slipped off her microphone and got up from the set.

I stared in disbelief at the empty desk on the monitor.

Nelson let out a low whistle. "Well, Jay-sus. You ever see anything like that?"

"Not since Ben," Isaiah said. "All she

225

needs is someone to put together the story for her."

I ushered them out of my office, leaving the door ajar, and strolled past the bank of monitors. My fingertips swept across dusty buttons, turning each off. The hush of no television. Emptier than silence. Like floating in the river.

I sat on the windowsill with my hot forehead against cool glass and peered down at the empty driveway below. Michael was nearly an hour late. He'd always been late, except when he hadn't shown at all, and it'd be a waste of time to wait for him. I wasn't going to waste anything anymore. Not the night, not my beautiful dress, not the whiskey buzzing through me. The hell with Michael. I turned from the window.

Ben was in the doorway.

He had one arm raised, white-knuckling the doorframe above in an attitude of climbing or falling, I wasn't sure. He wore a tux tailored beautifully, tight in the waist and across the shoulders, making him long and sleek and dark. I had the hazy feeling of standing on the edge of a dream with a strange man in a beautiful tux.

"Come in."

He shut the door and leaned against the back of it, his hands clasped before him.

"You all right?" he said.

"I've had several predinner cocktails, but unfortunately, I'm not drunk."

"You're not?"

"No, I'm very clear tonight."

And I was. Clearly from across the room I could see the long muscles of his throat where I could press my mouth and feel his words pulse against my lips. His shoulder twitched in that way particular to him, and I reminded myself, this was Ben. There was a rule about Ben. What was the rule?

Oh yes. *One does not use one's friends.*

"Tell me what you're thinking," he said.

"You already know."

His expression remained calm, eyes steady, but the doorknob rattled as he fumbled with the lock. I squared my shoulders and pushed off the sill, my shoes carrying me in a slow, perilous saunter, the spiked heels feeling thinner and higher with each step.

"I'm going to wait until you get out of this mood," he said, nodding to himself or to me, I didn't know.

"You should."

"I can't figure you out."

"Me, either."

He wore no cologne, only the faint smell of soap overcome by his heat and his heft. My thumb pressed into the hollow at the

227

base of his neck. It throbbed like I knew it would.

"I can't wait," he said.

He lifted me onto the desk and laid me across its top. With that first shock of his weight, I felt a surge of excitement, the zing of fear. And then his hand was in my hair, as he whispered what he wanted, how long he had waited. The newspapers crinkled beneath us.

CHAPTER NINETEEN

"I'll get you off this floor," he murmured, his fingers playing along the knots of my spine. "Give me a minute to catch my breath."

I lay all tangled up in him, loose boned and hulled out, slowly gathering myself — smarting knee against the rough carpet, left shoe lost, dress askew and beyond all redemption. No sense of time, except his heart punching in sync with mine. No sense of sadness, either, the kind that was sure to come, that had always come, even in the blue hours with Michael. Instead, a feeling so unexpected I feared its pronouncement.

I lifted myself on elbows, pondering the enigma of his face at rest. It was all dips and planes never seen from this angle. His mouth was soft and relaxed. I asked if he knew about the frog that survives arctic winters.

He smiled. "Tell me."

"When winter sets in, the frog makes her heart stop and she doesn't breathe. Her eyes go white from cold. It must look terrible, I think, this frog encasing herself in ice. But the false death protects her. Then spring comes, as I guess it always does, and the ice melts. The frog's heart starts beating again. Those first heartbeats, though, they must be painful. They worry the frog. Now she's at her most vulnerable."

"I know all about that frog," he said.

"You do?"

"I've been learning that frog for years. I can promise you. That frog's got nothing to worry about, except this drafty floor."

He groaned and said, "up you go," and guided me hobbling one-shoed to the leather sofa where we both dropped, me onto his lap. "I have only a dim recollection of falling off your desk." He laughed. "Who the hell knows where we'll find your shoe?"

His tux jacket had come off. His black tie was undone and loose from his collar. I spread open his shirt, discovering his shoulder that bore the mark of my teeth. My finger circled the mark slowly, wonderingly, and trailed lower. His waist had a thickness that surprised me, hidden always by his tailoring. It showed love for food and drink by a man who enjoyed life.

The bar-shaped metal cuff link was trickier, but I got it off and rolled up his sleeve and caressed the inside of his wrist, so much thicker and darker than mine. My fingertip trailed the tough skin of his bulky forearm, the kind a man acquires not from a gym but from physical work in the elements, work that now seemed a great secret.

"Tell me about your farm." My voice was halting, not mine at all.

"I've told you, it's a ranch," he said. "And I'm having a hard time recalling anything right now."

"How'd you get this?" It was a long T-shaped scar on the underside of his forearm.

He lifted his head and glanced where I pointed and let his head fall back again. "Barbed wire, beer, and Bandit. My horse when I was a boy."

"Sounds like an animal with behavioral issues."

"He liked to steal feed, a habit I secretly admired, me being the middle of five growing boys." He was watching me now from beneath lowered lids. "This particular scar came from checking fences. I'd been sneaking beer with my brothers. I was maybe sixteen, can't remember. Bandit got spooked or I'd had too many, or both, but it felt like he bucked a little on my dismount. I put a hand out for balance and got snagged on a barb. Damn stupid thing to do. Hurt like hell from the inside out."

The phone on my desk rang. He wrapped his arms around me and tightened. The ringing stopped, but after a moment, started up again. It had the effect of an alarm clock going off. "I have to fix my medusa hair," I said.

"I like it like that. Besides, I'll just mess it up again." He lifted my chin as if to kiss me, but he didn't. He was merely perusing a face of pure wreckage, my makeup long gone. I jerked my chin from his hand.

"Don't get shy on me." He blinked lazily. "I remember how everybody said the camera softened you when you were on air, made you so pretty. But I prefer you like this. Your skin rubbed pink. All your sharp edges."

"You're making no sense."

"I know it." He laughed again. "You've blown my mind."

When I got up and pulled at the hem of my dress, he helped me, tugging and straightening and smoothing in a way that made me consider wrecking it again. I walked in a silly one-shoe-on stroll to the phone on my desk and checked the caller ID.

Oh no. Not now. Not him.

I looked up from the display. Ben had eased back onto the sofa. His eyes were closed and his head thrown back, the long curve of his neck exposed.

"That dinner tonight," I started. "I don't want to go."

"Let's skip it. I can't get back in that tux. It'd suffocate me."

"I can't go with you anyway."

He stretched his legs, settling noisily on the leather, and he smiled, his eyes still closed. "Sure you can. Nobody will be surprised."

"I already have an escort."

He lifted his head and locked eyes with me. From behind the closed door, distant newsroom noises hummed.

"It was prearranged," I said. "I take Michael to the dinner and he gives me information. That's the deal, which is no big deal at all. I can meet up with you at the after parties, if you like."

"You're taking *him*?"

"I need him for Evelyn," I said.

"I can still feel you on me and already you're talking about him."

"Don't be nasty. I'm talking about the

story and you know it."

"Tell that to someone who doesn't know the game." He slid to the edge of the sofa, his powerful shoulders bunched on the arc of his arms. "You don't see me snuggling up to sources and taking them out on dinner dates. You don't see my sources demanding personal favors in return for information."

"That's not fair."

"What kind of person does that? Who won't give any damn thing away without expecting tenfold in return? Who holds friendships for ransom and trifles with women? That's your beloved Michael."

But this was about Evelyn, not Michael. Forgetting about Evelyn felt like the ultimate betrayal, another kind of death, and I wouldn't do it. Not even for Ben.

"Tell me how to make you happy without endangering the story," I said.

"Michael Ledger wants to hobnob with celebrities at the dinner? Fine, give him both tickets and come home with me."

"It won't work."

He pushed up from the sofa, advancing toward me. "Because you don't want it to work. You never do anything you don't want to do."

"No, I mean, that won't be acceptable to

Michael. What he wants is for me to take him to this dinner, that's it. And it's so easy to give."

"I guarantee that guy wants more than a meal."

There was a knock at the door. We both went still. Another knock, louder this time. I wedged open the door. Isaiah said I had a visitor in the lobby.

"Please tell him I'll be down in a few minutes," I said.

Ben sauntered up behind me, his TV Ben mask on good and tight, the rest of him looking like the cover of *GQ* except for his half-buttoned shirt and tie undone. He reached over my shoulder and flung the door wide. "Who's in the lobby?" he said.

Isaiah looked from me to Ben and back to me again.

"I'll make your excuses?" Isaiah asked.

My teeth grit so hard they hurt. "Tell Commander Ledger I'm finishing business."

"Don't tell him anything." He shut the door on Isaiah and leaned against the back of it, blocking it. His cheeks were red, as if someone had struck him, and maybe I had without meaning to.

"I don't know how this got so crazy, but I'm sorry. You're important to me."

"Important," he scoffed.

"And tonight was — it is — and I don't want to upset you. If I made a mistake."

"Don't you dare —"

"If I've said something wrong . . . Give me a minute. I can't think."

I turned from him, striding hippy and off-kilter in my absurd shoes to the mirror where I made a big show of ignoring him. I smoothed my wrinkled dress. My shaking hands combed through moist curls clinging to my forehead.

From the corner of the mirror, he said: "You're rejecting me for that — that *cop*."

"This isn't about you."

"The hell it isn't." He snatched his jacket from the floor and threw it over his shoulder, stalking to the door in several long, angry strides. The knob was in his hand and then his grip loosened and he turned back to me, his face gray despite his perennial tan. "I'd love to hear how you spin it," he said.

"There's nothing to spin."

His eyebrow shot up. "That newspaper ink all over the back of your dress tells the whole tale. Maybe your detective won't detect it. But I wouldn't count on it."

He slammed the door behind him, rattling the awards on my wall.

CHAPTER TWENTY

At the entrance to the Hilton, a glamorous crowd in evening finery waited to walk the red carpet. Behind the rope line, photographers shot the dinner guests as they crossed. The mayor stopped to whisper a few words to Michael before slapping hands with a Sunday talk show host. Michael pointed out a movie director I'd never heard of. Some reality TV stars were chatting up a congressman. Everyone was mugging for the cameras, holding up the line, but I didn't care. I'd gotten Michael to the party. If we made it no farther than this entrance, I'd have kept my word.

The cameras all swiveled for a freakishly tall woman whose face I'd seen on countless magazine covers. Michael was watching her in a sort of glazed-over, lustful way. When I laughed, he startled, and turning back, said automatically: "Have I said how lovely you are tonight?"

This was inaccurate. I was a wreck, my hair and makeup a mess, and my high-necked black gown was a dowdy sack compared to the red dress now wadded at the bottom of my desk drawer, locked away with thoughts of Ben.

"Nice recovery," I said. "You're quicker than you used to be."

"I learned it in that short-lived misery known as my former marriage."

My sympathy surprised me. "Relationships must be hard when your work is so demanding. I was sorry to hear of your divorce, though. I hope your children are well?"

He smiled down at me appraisingly.

"What?" I said.

"We're talking like friends."

He was right. For a moment, I considered whether this was good or bad.

"It was only a matter of time," he said, grinning now. "Face it, Knightly. My charm should be listed as a dangerous weapon, am I right?"

Before I could answer, he grabbed my arm. "Waiting bores me. Come on." He steered me through the crowd, skirting the edge of the red carpet, and shouldered our way into the corridor, which pulsed with constant shout-outs and flashes of camera phones and the high, keening laughter of guests who'd already knocked a couple back.

Everyone was doing the Washington-party scan, eyes roving, never lighting on the person they were talking to, waiting for someone more important to come along. The other constant: media viciously bashing itself, the so-called mainstream media ribbing on the right-wing media and vice versa. Good times hating on each other. And the excited whispers: *Is POTUS here yet? When does he arrive?*

Because the big draw was saying you had dinner with the president of the United States. Of course, nobody really had dinner with him. He might be on the dais eating a meal at the same time you were seated across the ballroom eating yours, but that was as intimate as it got. Maybe that was why my colleagues called the correspondents dinner "the prom" and acted like they were too sophisticated to attend, when of course they always attended. I never mocked the dinner. It was always a heady experience, and as Michael and I entered the wide expanse of the ballroom, I found myself trying to take in everything at once: the Big Fish bunched in groups, the round tables set with gold-edged china that circled

239

centerpieces of yellow roses and gold carnations, the women glittering in sequined gowns beneath great chandeliers, the men strutting about in their power tuxes. How many years had I been coming to the dinner? Always I had this same intense feeling as the first time I stepped through these doors a decade or so ago, the wonder of being a part of it all. How did I get here? Was this all some strange dream?

As with everything in Washington news circles, the tables were assembled according to pecking order: the networks and big magazines at the tables in the front row closest to the dais, and in the back, the struggling local television stations and the small papers, radio news, and bloggers. My table was somewhere in the middle.

We stopped at a cash bar. Michael handed me a flute of champagne, and with his glass, he pointed to a city council member under criminal investigation — but don't tell anybody yet, he warned — and over there, an aging columnist sent to therapy last year for anger management or sex addiction, he couldn't remember. He wagged his finger at me. "You ever get jammed up, that's what you say. 'I had to have it, couldn't help myself.' Popular ailment right now."

I laughed. "How do you know all this?"

"Keep my ear to the ground. Never know what you might need."

"Really," I said, cutting him a sideways look. "And what do you need here?"

"Ah-ah-ah," he chided. "We agreed. No talking about work tonight."

It was true Michael knew more people than I did: legislators and business leaders, activists and television celebs, law-enforcement officials from distant jurisdictions. He was constantly scanning the room, lifting his hand to someone he knew, then pulling me along to introduce me. He was charming, telling his outrageous tales out of school, and everyone we met seemed to like him.

He wanted me to introduce him to a particular news director from a competing station. Leila Gupta was a couple of tables over, a small woman in a coral-colored gown, speaking to a circle of admirers. I knew her only by reputation, which was for no-bullshit news, and admired her work tremendously.

We crossed to Leila's table. She told Michael in a breathless way that she was pleased to meet him. Someday he'd grace her newscast, she hoped.

"But not too soon," he said. "When I'm on TV, someone's had a bad day. Much as I enjoy attention, I prefer safe streets more."

She invited him for a tour of her station and to wine and dine him after. It was so outrageous I laughed. "That's outright poaching of my guest."

"And what about you?" she said, winking at me. "My station is on our way up. We only have to bump yours off, which would be easier if you were on my team. Consider it: the rise is more fun than the fall. And it'd be a coup to steal you from Nick."

It was a no-brainer to dump Mellay, but my staff I could never leave. To be polite, I took her card.

Michael's hand was on his hip, and he turned at the waist, surveying the room. "Where's your guest?" he asked Leila. "I was hoping to catch up tonight. We're old friends."

"I was stood up," she said, flatly amused. "Can you believe it? I haven't been stood up since college. I wonder if some big case kept him?" She raised her eyebrow at Michael. "Something I should know about?"

The lights flickered and then dimmed, signaling the dinner was soon to start, and we headed back to our assigned table. Michael pulled out my chair for me. Before he took his seat, he leaned down and whispered, "I'm gonna ghost. It's been a long day."

"Really? You haven't had dinner yet."

"Motorcade's on the move by now. I better leave before Secret Service locks us in."

With that, he walked away. I stared at his back, confused by his abrupt departure, as he weaved past the tables and climbed the rise and went through a set of doors. My attention turned to Leila Gupta and the empty chair next to her.

Where's your guest? he'd said. *I was hoping to catch up.*

Damn.

I moved as fast as my four-inch heels allowed. A server with a tray of breadbaskets came through the door as I reached for the handle, and we nearly collided. "Pardon me," I said, holding out my arms to steady the tray before moving on.

The lobby was empty except for two federal agents. They were checking me out — not in a good way — and it occurred to me it might not be the greatest idea to appear to be fleeing a room in which the president was momentarily expected. I slowed down, tossing them a jaunty wave and a "good evening, guys," and went through the door. When I hit the dark street, I started running. At the end of the block,

Michael was sliding into his cruiser.

I shouted his name.

He climbed out and stood in the open door until I reached him, panting. I held up one finger. "I — hang on —"

He stared at me, bemused. "Need a ride or something?"

"I need . . . to know . . . it was Ian. Right?"

"What did I say?" he said. "No work talk. This is my well-deserved respite. A nice dinner with a charming companion."

"But you didn't come for the dinner. All night long you were scouting the room. For Ian Chase, right? He was Leila's guest who stood her up, wasn't he?"

His fingers drummed impatiently against his trouser leg.

"It was clever of you," I said. "How did you know Ian was supposed to be here?"

He exhaled with impatience. "I told you. Keep my ear to the ground. Never know —"

"What you might need," I finished for him. "Right. But what were you hoping to accomplish if he showed? It's a party. What's he going to do? Stand on his chair and shout he had an affair with Evelyn Carney?"

He stepped around the door. When he closed it, metal creaked loudly. The edge of the front quarter panel was bashed in where

244

it met the door. It was a huge dent on a new-model Crown Vic.

"Of course not," he said. "Ian Chase doesn't talk."

His profile turned toward the streetlight, which illuminated his lips pressed together and his jaw gone taut, a cunning look I remembered well. It was the look of the hunter and meant Ian had become the focus of Michael's investigation and that Michael would show him no mercy.

"So you wanted him to feel you stalking him," I reasoned aloud. "Why go to the trouble? He knows he's a suspect. On your short list, as you say."

He shifted his weight to his heels and rocked a little, feigning nonchalance. All the while he was studying me beneath lowered lids. I could feel the weight of his thoughts and also his reluctance to voice them. Softly, I prodded: "Or do you have new evidence you wanted to present to him?"

After a long moment, he said in a low voice: "She was pregnant."

I blinked. A disoriented feeling came over me again, something akin to what I felt by the river when the heron launched itself from the tree and disappeared beyond the river's end — although the revelation shouldn't have caught me off guard. From the beginning, I *had* wondered if she was pregnant. It's one of those things you always have to ask when a woman goes missing, especially when you learn she had a complicated relationship with a man. But hearing it now after the way I'd seen her in the river, the way Michael announced it, abruptly, in such a harsh way, the hopelessness of it all —

I gave him a vague sort of nod, like *go on.*

"Peter Carney thought the ME's prelim had to be wrong. When we assured him it was not, he explained he and his wife had not been intimate since his return to the States." He paused, shaking his head solemnly. "Anyway, you can understand the husband's confusion, since the ME says she was seven or eight weeks along."

"Conceived when Peter was out of the country?"

"Yep."

"Did you ask Ian about it?"

"Another question on the list that Mr. Chase's attorney has refused to let us ask. But I'll get to him. Don't worry." He looked off into the dark street and sighed, and in a voice suddenly weary, he said: "Since you're going to ask, yes, you can report it, but not tonight. I need one night's rest. It's been a shit day — the river, the visit to the ME, all that pretense at the dinner — and I can't deal with reporters calling all hours or the chief asking why I don't already have an arrest warrant. Bright and early tomorrow I have to figure out whether a guy I work with offed his lover while she carried a baby likely his and dumped her in the river like yesterday's garbage, and if he and his celebrity attorney thinks —"

He turned into the light again. His profile was grim and pale against the night sky. The line of his arrogant jaw had gone flabby, and the streetlights picked out the gray in his hair, but he was still one of the most handsome, tough, and determined men I'd ever met. I understood then why I'd once been so hung up on him, and also the distance of the feeling, which told me I wasn't anymore and probably hadn't been for quite some time.

"Okay, so the information is embargoed until the morning news," I said. "What can we report?"

"The medical examiner found water in her lungs," he explained. "That means death from drowning, but how did she get in the river? There's also evidence of perimortem trauma — a head wound with no time to heal — meaning she'd been struck near the time of her death. Was she knocked out and thrown into the water? That's supposition on my part, but you can report this as fact: however Evelyn Carney got into the river, whether she was tossed, fell, jumped, or chased into it, we'll find out. We'll close the case and charge the suspect, no matter who he is."

He'd practically written tomorrow's script for me.

My thoughts slowed and focused. "I want the exclusive for as long as it will hold."

"Fine by me, but our person of interest is a federal prosecutor, and a politically connected one at that. How long do you think it's going to hold?"

He was right. Naming Ian Chase took the story into an entirely new territory. "I'm going to need to name you as my source."

He laughed unpleasantly. "Not happening."

"Then I need another source, and that source needs to be high ranking. Who else is in the loop who will talk to me?"

"You still don't trust me?" he said.

"Not a matter of trust. With something like this, I need at least two sources with direct knowledge."

He opened the driver's-side door. The metal groaned again. "Get in," he said, before crossing in front of the hood of the car and coming around to the passenger's side door. He unbuttoned his jacket and pulled his phone from his waistband before climbing into the seat. After he hit speed dial, a voice came over the speakerphone: "Mike."

"Hey, Doc." Dr. Robert Weller, chief medical examiner for the District of Columbia, precisely the source I needed. In his decades of work in the city, through the worst years of the drug epidemic and crew wars, he'd probably seen more bodies than soldiers on battlefields, and in the hot summer months when tempers frayed and shootings occurred with sickening frequency, his office got overwhelmed. Yet he was always cheery and competent.

"You're on speaker," Michael said, telling him who I was and that I was in the car with him. "Ms. Knightly has come to me with rumors in the Carney case. I'd like to set her straight on the prelim, at least. For one thing, she's good people, and we can trust her. For another, I don't need misinformation making this investigation harder than it has to be. That jackass lawyer will certainly use it as another excuse to keep his client from talking."

The jackass lawyer I understood to be Ian's.

"As long as she understands not to use my name," Weller said. "It's the policy of our office that we don't make statements until the report has been finalized. But if she wants to overhear us talk about some aspects of the prelim, meh, I don't mind."

They chatted about closed head injuries and temporal bone fractures and intracranial bleeding and striking objects, forensic information that was its own language. After asking them to dumb it down, what I got was this: the medical examiner believed Evelyn had been struck on the side of her head with some sort of blunt object — like a stick or bat, that sort of thing, nothing that pierced her skull.

"A weapon like a blackjack?" I said, interrupting.

Michael turned quickly to face me, his expression keen, but said nothing.

"There are many objects that could create that kind of trauma," the medical examiner said. "Yes, a weapon shaped like that certainly would."

He went on to describe the blow was to a space between her temple and ear and involved enough force to cause bleeding within her skull. Yet the head trauma hadn't killed her. The Doc surmised it was possible to have survived the injury, if she'd received medical attention.

It had been the river that killed her, after she'd fallen unconscious into it, or had been thrown in. In any case, the manner of her death would be ruled a homicide.

"One more thing, Doc," Michael said. "Given the state of decomposition, is it possible to extract DNA from the fetus? To test paternity?"

"We believe so, yes," the chief medical examiner said.

Michael was looking at me with eyes that caught the streetlamp and gave an odd glow. "Thanks, Doc. See what you can do."

CHAPTER TWENTY-ONE

Last night I dreamed I was swimming in the river. In the distance, a woman was drifting facedown. I wanted to help her, but the tide was working against me, and with each stroke, she seemed farther from my reach. It was hopeless, there wasn't enough time, and suddenly I was there, as happens only in dreams. My hands were on her shoulders, turning her, the long and tangled hair covering her face. I brushed her hair away to find her eyes were alive and open, a summer-sky blue, and she gasped a deep gulp of air.

It was my mother.

I jolted awake. It had all been so clear. The briny river smell. The push of the tide. The blue of my mother's eyes. *It's just a dream, breathe through it, it's not real* — and then my alarm went off.

Four o'clock had come early this morning.

After showering, I slipped on jeans and a faded American University sweatshirt and pulled my mop of hair back into a tight ponytail that I covered with a red Nationals ball cap and went out the door. My dashboard clock read 4:30 when I parked in the garage at the station.

Ronnie Morton was our morning editor. She was also the grande dame of the early news desk. She knew everyone in the business, having been in it since the days of shooting on film. But over the years her nerves had become a little unreliable, and breaking news fairly unhinged her, which was why — despite her talent and oversized contact list — we kept her on the zero-dark-thirty shift. It was simply quieter. These days, quiet made Ronnie happy.

Which was also why I approached Ronnie with caution, even though she'd obviously caught sight of me and was becoming noticeably disturbed, tugging nervously at the ends of her hair.

"Why are you here?" she called out in a falsely chipper voice. "Let me start over. Hello, Virginia, I'm pleased to see you. Now, how are you going to ruin my morning?"

"We're going to break some news, Ronnie." When she started to fidget anxiously, I held up my hand. "But no worries, I've

253

already written the script and isolated the video, and it's being edited as we speak. Now I have to get back down to the edit suites to oversee it, so I need you to get ahold of Ben. Tell him there's a new development in the Evelyn Carney story, and the show needs him live on the set. He's the lead."

"Ben's not a morning person."

"So don't call him before five," I told her in a firm voice. "Make sure he knows the script's already approved; he doesn't have to write a word. I left his copy on the set for review. If he could call the police chief as a courtesy heads-up for the story we're going to break, that'd be great. If the chief will give him a statement, that's even better. Tell him I've already put in calls to a man named Ian Chase, but if he could get a response from Ian's attorney, that'd be super. If not, I can do that, too." I handed her a sheet of paper with the attorney's contact info, wondering what else. "Oh, and tell Ben there's a fresh pot of coffee waiting for him. That'll get him here faster. Your assistant can fetch cream from my office fridge. He drinks it light but hates the artificial crap in the break room. I think that about covers it, but if Ben gives you any trouble, transfer him to me in edit suite two. Not to my cell phone. I seem to have misplaced it."

She nodded, smiling warily.

I was halfway across the newsroom before I stopped and turned back. "And, Ronnie? Do yourself a favor. Call in extra help to answer phones."

Her smile disappeared. "All hell's going to break loose, isn't it?"

"It might feel that way for a short time. But don't worry. After the story's edited, I'll be beside you the whole time."

As I entered the suite, the editor, Doug, spun in his chair. "This video you've called for," he said, talking about the cutaway shot of Evelyn Carney in the meeting with Ian. "I can't find it on the server."

"The raw video is MIA. The on-air version is here." I pulled the thumb drive from the lanyard around my neck and handed it to him.

"You removed it from the server?" he said.

"Yeah."

He paused, thoughtful. "Highly irregular."

"Sure is."

He inserted the drive. When he brought up the video of Evelyn, he whistled. "But wow, great shot," he said. "And here's the dude who killed her?"

"Person of interest, right."

He glanced furtively my way. "I can see why someone might want to keep it to herself."

"Yeah," I said, and left it at that.

Soon we were in the zone. It was no longer about Ian Chase or Peter Carney or Michael Ledger. In a certain way, it wasn't even about Evelyn anymore. It was about the process of making the story come alive with movement and sound: Ian Chase talking behind a podium, the police searching his condo, the blue light blazing across his walls —

"Stop," I said, leaning over and tapping a fingernail on the monitor. "Over this video of Ian we lay his statement. I don't have that yet. I'll go upstairs and put in the calls and get something. Leave enough room."

And then he laid the rest of the video: the haunting river shots and the body bag carried away, and that final poignant shot of Evelyn, the cutaway shot, when she was still alive with want —

When it went to black, Doug leaned back in his chair and exhaled. "Hell of a story," he said.

"Yeah."

He scratched his chin absently. "You know, you might check Nelson's locker for that raw tape you're missing. He's been

256

storing his best material for the audition reel he's putting together for Alexa."

That reminded me of the stand-up Alexa had shown me. *He shot me fat,* she'd complained, but on that stand-up, she'd been radiant against her backdrop, the old stone meetinghouse in Rock Creek Park that was still used for community gatherings. That was the meeting Ian Chase and Evelyn had attended, I realized.

"Of course this is Nelson's work," Doug was saying, as if he took my silence for argument. He pointed at the monitor. "Here, the soft focus around the edges, so you can't help but look at the woman at the center. It's his signature. Nobody shoots women so beautifully. It's like he's in love with their form."

"Yes," I said, lost to the memory, trying to hone in on the details: Alexa speaking into the microphone, and behind Alexa, people dressed in summer clothes, fluttery dresses and light-colored suits, some in shorts and T-shirts leaving the community center, walking past a line of police cars. One unmarked police cruiser was a beige Crown Vic, a newer model with a shadow in the front quarter-panel —

No, not a shadow. It was a dent.

Ronnie burst into the editing suite. "I

found Ben," she said, flush faced and excited. "He can't do the story. He's out of town. The Blue Ridge."

That snapped me out of it. "The blue what?"

"Mountains," she told me. "Backcountry camping. Said he's been at sea level too long, and had to get out. So late last night he requested a few days off. *Isaiah*" — she hissed his name — "granted them."

"Slow down. Let me think."

How could he be out of town already? Just last night, not even twelve hours ago, he'd been in my office and we'd — what? Had sex? Made love? Oh, goddamn it all to hell. I rubbed the spot over my heart that hurt every time I let myself think of him.

"He can't make it back in time," she said, her voice rising. "It's five fifteen now. The lead of our show, the entire first block *is in jeopardy.*"

I got up and put my hands on her shoulders. "This is mine to fix," I told her. "I'll call Mellay, and when we form a plan, I'll let you know. Now go back upstairs and wait for my call."

When Ronnie left, I asked Doug to check Nelson's locker for the missing video. If he had to, give Nelson a wakeup call. "Whatever raw tape you guys can find related to that August meeting in Rock Creek Park. Can you ask him about that?"

That left me alone in the edit suite to place my call. Mellay picked up on the second ring. He sounded clearheaded and chirpy, delighted about the exclusive story and unconcerned about Ben's time off. "Glad you called to discuss," he said. "You done good, kid."

"The story needs someone to voice it. What do you think of Alexa? At least until Ben gets back in town?"

"Nah, let's not. Get Heather on the phone."

I put my forehead on the editing console and banged it. Her inexperience was a burden, one more person I'd have to worry about. I needed a partner, not another hindrance.

"Heather's most familiar," he was saying. "She reported the story last night."

"This is the big break in the case," I argued, as calmly as I could. "And it's mine — ours, exclusively. It's a complicated story with moving parts and places to make mistakes if we aren't careful. Look, Heather's got talent. There's no denying it. But how can anyone with so little experience be ready for a story like this?"

I waited for him to see it, but he didn't.

"Your job is to keep Heather from making an error," he said, and then recited her phone number, as if committed to his memory.

CHAPTER TWENTY-TWO

With little more than thirty minutes to air, I worked the phone for last-minute statements, putting in calls to the police and the attorney representing Ian Chase, who was unavailable. I dialed the home number for Ian Chase until he picked up the phone. I read him a summary of our report and asked if he would comment. He told me to go to hell and hung up.

My final call went to Paige Linden. "An affair?" she said, groggily. "Evie and — and *Ian*? That's . . . I don't believe . . . are you sure? Who's saying?"

"Police. Did Evelyn ever talk about Ian Chase?"

"No, that's just *bizarre.* Ian? I've never even seen him with Evie." She was moving around, banging into things, and then there was the sound of water running, a clink of a coffeepot onto its burner. "And you say Evie was . . . *pregnant*?"

"The medical examiner says so."

"The night she disappeared, she was going to see Ian about a baby?"

"That's the theory."

She didn't say anything.

"Paige?"

Still nothing.

"Are you there?"

"It's just . . . wow . . . you think you know someone," she whispered, and then: "I wish she'd told me, that's all. I could have helped her. At least warned her off."

I moved to the edge of my chair. "About what?"

She blew out a breath. "You didn't hear this from me, but . . . Ian? He can be . . . a little rough."

"What does that mean?" I said quickly, "and yes, this is so far off the record it's already forgotten."

"Okay. So. Ian and I dated years ago, and I was into him. Why wouldn't I be? He's smart, good-looking, politically connected. I thought we made a great couple. Come to find out, he's into stuff. Now what, I don't know exactly, but with me, he was a little rough. Just playing around, he called it, pushing boundaries. When it went beyond a certain point, I stopped seeing him. Now we're friendly, because you want to be

262

friendly with someone like him, and there's this fear. What if he tells someone what he did to me? My colleagues would never take me seriously." Her voice had trailed off. "Even so, I would have warned Evie."

"You're saying Ian Chase had a tendency toward violent sexual encounters with women?"

"Yes," she said.

"But consensual?"

"For me, yes, until he went beyond a certain point. That's when I broke up with him."

"What was that point?"

She exhaled softly. "He hit me. Just missed my eye. That was the last time."

After Heather finished the live shot and the studio lights went out, the newsroom staff mobbed her with congratulations. Objectively, I couldn't complain. She'd done a fine live shot. She could read news in the most natural of ways and she would go far as long as she had good people to support her. She had *it,* whatever that magical, mysterious *it* was. That had to be admitted, too.

Sighing, I got up from the desk, and the group that had swarmed Heather now turned in unison to me. One person clapped, and the rest followed. Someone let out a whistle. My mouth started working funny, and I felt near tears. From fatigue, I told myself. After all, one does not cry in a newsroom. So I gave a pageant wave, mocking myself, and began a retreat to my office. I never made it. The phones were lighting up. Phase two of the game had begun.

Affiliates begged Heather to file reports for their stations. Friends from radio and print news called, poking around for information — like, yeah, I was going to offer up free dish. I told them to watch our news. A network correspondent I revered called *me* to ask for *my* help.

In the midst of all this chaos, I still couldn't find my cell phone. So I was stuck at a desk in the newsroom, putting in calls to the US Attorney's Office for comment, as well as calls to Michael, none of them returned. I didn't worry that Michael was ducking me. Surely the investigation had sped up on him, and he was busy with it, but I needed to ask him about his car. If it was his cruiser parked in the background of Alexa's standup, then he'd been at the meeting Evelyn Carney had attended. Wouldn't he remember seeing her?

Isaiah approached my desk, waving my cell phone. "Yours, right?"

"Gimme." I cradled it to my chest. "Where was it?"

"Manager from Chads said someone turned it in at the hostess stand. He recognized our station logo on the lock code screen and dropped it off with our front guard."

"Really?" I hadn't been to the bar since Friday with Ben. My phone had been with me all weekend. How had it gotten to Chads?

He tilted his chin down, looking at me over the top of his horn-rims. "You should take better care of what you love, my dear."

My phone showed several missed calls from the same unknown number. The caller had left a message, and when I listened to the recording, it was Evelyn's professor, Bradley Hartnett. He needed me to return his call. He had information about Evelyn. But when I hit return call, I got the voice mail of another man whose voice I didn't recognize. I left a message anyway.

Later, Mellay ordered a celebratory lunch. He even gave his puffed-chest speech about what a great team we were, thanking Heather and me (in that order) for our exclusive reporting. We were stringing together reports that brought the viewers and slayed the competition. His speech was sprinkled with these kinds of warlike metaphors, how we can use this momentum to crush the enemy but watch our flanks and blah blah blah.

Heather stood up and said in her low, formal voice how grateful she was for everyone's hard work and how much she loved being on Team Virginia. I found this particularly clever. Everyone knew Ben and I were partners. Not only because Ben could pull his own weight but because we'd worked together for years. Now she created confusion. What did it all mean? Was Heather now aligned to me? Where did that leave Ben? Where was Ben anyway?

Curious looks drifted my way.

And oh, how I missed him, today of all days. He would have loved the carnival atmosphere, the joking and camaraderie, and especially the free food. He'd yuck it up with the network execs and do live shot after live shot for affiliates. At his most elemental, Ben Pearce was a screen hog.

My chest constricted again. So I tried to do what I'd always done, pack away the feeling in the box containing disappointment and error and grievance, a box I labeled Distractions, but this particular feeling overflowed the box.

■ ■ ■ ■

Just before the deadline for the afternoon show, the spokesperson for the US Attorney's Office returned my call. She wouldn't comment on our report, but confirmed that Ian Chase was not under investigation by their office. She repeated the policy not to discuss personnel issues regarding employees, current or former.

That piqued my curiosity. "So are you saying he's a *former* employee?" I said.

"Ian Chase is no longer employed by the Department of Justice."

CHAPTER TWENTY-THREE

We were halfway through the six o'clock newscast, and our exclusive held. The newsroom was in high spirits. I was nervous. No official had yet gone on record. There weren't even the typical Washington whispers from low-tier sources, people repeating gossip to appear in the know. Yes, Michael had promised not to tell anyone, and I'd never doubted his professionalism, but was he capable of keeping the lid on such an explosive story? I'd ask him if he returned one damn call.

Finally, one of the calls I'd been waiting for: J. Thomas Winthrop, the attorney representing Ian Chase. He invited me for cocktails at a private residence in a working-class neighborhood near Catholic University. I was to come alone and without a camera. It was a meeting he'd deny if asked and located in a curious part of town for a K Street attorney whose client list consisted of dirty politicians, bad-boy entertainers and athletes, businessmen with more money than sense, those sorts.

I couldn't recall a case Winthrop lost. These days he mostly "fixed" reputations, which in this city was a far greater challenge than getting a jury to acquit. His success relied mainly on discrediting anyone whose narrative contradicted his portrayal of his client as an innocent lamb slaughtered by an overzealous government, incompetent police force, biased press corps, and you fill in the blank.

Winthrop was also famous for holding his tongue, and if he did talk to the media, it was only under circumstances he could control. I was worrying about those circumstances as I sped past Rock Creek Cemetery and the Old Soldiers Home, and then I was beyond the basilica and turning into the neighborhood. There was parking in front of a tall, narrow building that appeared to be an old chapel, replete with stained glass and arched windows. An attractive gym-fit forty-something opened the door. He wore pressed jeans and a navy hoodie of a texture that screamed comfortable affluence.

"Hey there, come on in," he said, as if he knew me. "Jay's getting cleaned up, long day. You're early."

269

"Occupational hazard, sorry." I smiled and put out my hand, introducing myself.

"David," he said. "Jay's partner."

I followed him into an astonishing place. Ceilings soared over twenty feet. One grand room combined a kitchen and living area with sculpted furniture, two love seats facing each other, a chair. A spiral staircase led to a loft. One wall was made up of massive arched windows framed in dark wood, its opposing wall with paintings of varying sizes, bright reds and vivid oranges that seemed to quiver with movement, arresting and sensual, hotly alive.

"I'm often late," he was saying wryly as he flicked his wrist carelessly toward the wall of paintings. "Occupational hazard for us creative types — especially when the work's going good." He glanced upward and smiled, and his voice softened: "Ah, the man himself."

J. Thomas Winthrop was shorter, thinner than I'd imagined, an older man with a shock of red hair brushed over his forehead. Wire-rimmed John Lennon glasses drew attention to the wonderful laugh lines around his eyes. There was something birdlike about the way he descended the stairs, quickly, in energetic hops.

After David let himself out, Winthrop and

I got to business. He congratulated me on our most recent newscast. "The reporting is remarkably more detailed than what I've seen elsewhere. That can only mean you're talking to someone within the inner circle of the investigation."

"Mr. Winthrop —"

"Please call me Jay," he said, moving behind a sleek black countertop that separated the kitchen.

"I don't discuss sources. I'm here to negotiate the terms of an interview with your client."

He tsk-tsked me. "Now that is where your youth shows," he said affably. "Charging right out of the gate without looking both ways."

"My youth?" It annoyed me. As if my age meant malleability, some weakness to exploit.

"I do my own research," he said with modesty. "You are Virginia Diana Knightly, aged thirty-four, from a blue-collar town in a small state, and during your formative years, you were a ward of that state. Despite the foster home shuffle and different high schools attended, you managed to graduate top of your class with a full ride to J-school at American. Perhaps more impressive, your quick ascent in a cutthroat industry, if you don't mind my calling it so, in which you are widely regarded as both intrepid and honest." He took a breath, smiled charmingly. "It is this final attribute that gives me hope we can come to an understanding."

So he did his homework. Big deal. Although it was nice of him to reveal I'd worried him enough to look me up.

"You know the name of the first boy I kissed, too?" I said dryly.

He laughed. "Now that I do not know. But I'm aware of a certain police official you've been seen about town with. Tongues are wagging, perhaps unfairly. You know how this city is."

It made me furious. Those kinds of rumors devastated the female half of my profession. As if the only way we could get information was by having sex with a source.

So J. Thomas Winthrop was going to try to discredit me? Well, he could give it his best shot.

"Know what? I'd like to record this interview after all," I said. "I'm a reporter of record, Mr. Winthrop. I only work against my interests when no other options exist. But you came to me. You want to talk to me."

"No recording."

So that was that.

"We've gotten off to a bad start," he said, "and I can see I've disturbed you."

"As you intended."

"Actually, I had hoped you would deny it." He lifted a glass full of ice and shook it. "But where are my manners? I haven't even offered you a drink."

"Nothing. Thank you."

He poured club soda over the ice, squeezed a slice of lime, and carried his drink to the chair across from me.

"Do you care for David's work?" he said, gesturing with his glass to the canvasses surrounding us. "A bit wild, I admit. But then David has a passionate soul."

The paintings were wild and beautiful, and they made me feel. What I felt mostly was whiplash. I was angry this lawyer thought he knew something about me and could imply something about my sexuality, which belonged only to me — that pompous, self-righteous bastard — and now all the hot emotion of his partner's work was trickling into my temper.

After a long swallow of his drink, he grimaced, thoughtful. "I cannot begin to comprehend what drives David to such agonies of creation, hours spent struggling with his whirlwind visions. If one brushstroke displeases him somewhere along the oh-so-fallible route from brain to hand to canvas, something that doesn't live up to what he envisions, he destroys it all, shreds it. And though I am a person most comfortable with the constraints of reason, of rules, I find this turbulence attracts me. Of course I'm not alone. In this city, where the intellect is currency, I find most of my clients are like me, reasonable, perhaps even boring men —" Here, he gave an elegant lift of his hand again, smiling ruefully. "They are simple people who chase the passion they scarcely understand, and sometimes it gets them into trouble. And yet, it's important to remember: a man cannot escape his nature. If by his nature, he's not violent, no storm of passion could make him destroy what he loves."

"You're talking about Ian Chase."

He leaned forward, elbows on knees, and gave me an intense look over the rims of his Lennon glasses. "My client did not kill Evelyn Carney."

"Let him tell me. I'll put him on camera, and he can shout his innocence to the world. Can you arrange it?"

"You've got the wrong guy," he went on evenly. "What's more, you're being led onto a weak limb that will surely break beneath the weight of lies you're being fed."

Ah, so that's why he'd invited me here. He thought to frighten me off.

"All right," I said, "if not Ian, then who killed her?"

He lifted his hands again. He would very much like to speculate, those hands seemed to say, if it were possible. "My client has asked me to relay his overwhelming grief for his friend's death —"

"Isn't 'lover' more accurate?"

"This point should also be made clear: my client has attempted to make himself available to investigators. But as you're probably aware, negotiations with MPD have devolved due to their egregious line of questioning. These experienced detectives, led by the celebrated Michael Ledger, ask little about events on the night of March 8. They care even less it seems about Mrs. Carney and her violent death. Instead, they obsess over this one lurid question: Who was my client having sex with? That is the great mystery rocking the capital. Naturally, it makes one suspicious."

"Isn't it routine to question the relationship of a person calling in a police report for a missing person? Why not answer that question?"

He went to the black granite countertop in the kitchenette and lifted a sheet of paper and carried it to where I was seated. "We provided this written statement to the investigators," he said, handing over the paper.

Much of the document had been redacted with a black marker. At the top was the firm's letterhead and date of the document, March 13. The last statement described a brief phone call to Ian Chase from Evelyn Carney on the morning of March 8. She asked if she could visit him at his home that evening. She did not give a reason. She also never showed. He waited all night at his home, alone. Late that same evening, he placed a call to her cell phone near midnight. Her voice-mail recording picked up on first ring, suggesting she'd turned her phone off, so he left a message. The next day, he called her office, only to be informed she had not shown up for work. Peter Carney answered her home phone, stating that Evelyn no longer resided at that address. This struck Ian Chase as worrisome, possibly suspicious, and so he called an official at the First District police station, asking if as a courtesy, a uniformed officer could do a welfare check.

"And a patrol officer went by Evelyn's home?"

"Yes," he said. "That courtesy led to a

missing persons investigation almost immediately taken over by Criminal Investigations. Soon thereafter, my client's sex life became the focus of their probe. Makes one wonder."

He had a point, and yet: "The investigators know that your client had a sexual relationship with Evelyn Carney," I said. "So why not admit to the relationship? Is it because Ian Chase is in the lifestyle?"

His long nose lifted, as if scenting something. "What's that?"

"Ian enjoys hurting his sexual partners during . . . role play?" There, I said it like I knew what the hell I was talking about. "Sex games with a woman's consent. And so on March 8, the night she disappeared, Evelyn comes over to Ian's condo —"

"Didn't happen," he interrupted.

"And things get out of control. Maybe they're playing around and he hits her harder than he intended. The brain's so fragile, you never know. These head injuries. Maybe it was just an accident?"

"My client did *not* kill her," he repeated. He looked at me as if he could will me to believe him. But I'd already gotten the feeling that J. Thomas Winthrop could tell an elaborate lie while staring you in the face. "This is how the MPD gets around the bother of presumption of innocence and standards of proof. Leaking vicious lies to the press in order to convict my client in the court of public opinion. Don't you see? You're being used to destroy my client."

When I wondered aloud why investigators would do such a thing, he explained what everyone knew: Ian Chase had been at the top of a short list for a presidential appointment to replace the outgoing US Attorney for the District of Columbia. What I hadn't known: the District's mayor had sent the name of his own choice for top prosecutor to the White House, and Ian Chase was not that guy. There was bad blood between the mayor and Ian, stemming from a long-ago public corruption investigation led by Ian, an investigation that resulted in the resignation of several of the mayor's cronies. The mayor hadn't been charged with a crime, but fault lines were drawn.

Simmering beneath the bitter political maneuvering was the District's ongoing grievance: a federal government that ruled over the city, often with no regard for the votes of its citizens or the preferences of the city's elected officials. Winthrop was not unsympathetic to the mayor's position. As a principle of self-governance, the city should be allowed to choose (among many things) its highest-ranking law-enforcement official. But a whisper campaign against Ian Chase to knock him out of the running, whether originated at the MPD or the mayor's office, was untenable.

It was a compelling theory with one big problem: it relied on Michael Ledger doing the dirty work, and Michael risked his ass for no one, certainly not the mayor, who would sell him out in a heartbeat, as Michael knew.

"Those are some pretty serious allegations," I said. "What's your proof?"

He shrugged delicately, indicating nothing. "For now, let me say this is a very dangerous game being played. A game that can quickly turn, I might add. In this city, far too many officials are fucking someone they shouldn't, and your source isn't the only one who can spread word of who has been with whom."

I was trying to decipher his meaning, when it hit me: "You aren't threatening to slander *my* name, are you?"

His eyes went wide, the laugh lines like sunbursts. "Oh dear, no. Not you." In his tone, there was genuine mirth. "Ask your source who I mean. He'll know."

CHAPTER TWENTY-FOUR

On the drive back to the station, I put in another call to the number Bradley Hartnett had left. This time he picked up. He had borrowed a friend's phone, he explained, in case someone was monitoring his. "Like what happened to Evie," he said.

That had me easing my foot off the gas pedal and looking for a place to pull over. "What are you talking about, Professor?"

"Didn't detectives tell you? Evie thought her phone was hacked. This fellow, Detective Miller, wanted me to keep that tip to myself. It was to protect the integrity of the investigation, he said. After your report about that prosecutor, I can only think he was looking to protect something else. I think Evie got caught up in a conspiracy, and it looks like it involves the feds."

Hartnett was agitated, not at all like the man I'd spoken with at his club last week. Who drank expensive brandy and listened for lions in the morning, and though he'd spoken romantically about Evelyn, had been down to earth, no nonsense. Not that I was dismissing him, but . . .

"A conspiracy?" I pulled into a lot for a convenience store and parked under the light. I dug a pen and reporter pad from my satchel and said: "Start from the beginning, Professor. I'm ready when you are."

"Evie dropped by my office a week before she disappeared."

"I remember," I said. "You told me."

"She suspected someone hacked her phone. She worried she was being followed."

"Why would she think that?"

He hesitated. "She told me she'd made some kind of mistake. At the time, I'd assumed she meant at work and was too ashamed to say, after I'd put in a good word for her. Anyway, she wanted an expert to look at her phone, so I called my friend who heads up IT for the university. She was supposed to take her phone to his office for a scan, but she never showed, and then she disappeared." He was breathing heavily now, as if struggling with emotion, and then he said, "We have to find her phone."

I thought of Evelyn in the river, what the river had done to her, how it had washed

away her purse and coat and taken everything, except her ATM card and a boot.

"Professor, I'm very sorry, but everything
she carried that night was lost in the river."

"Did you specifically ask about her
phone?" he said angrily.

"No, but —"

"Then you don't know what they have."

"Who?"

"Did you ask about police surveillance?
You know, the Justice Department doesn't
need anything physically to put on your
phone."

He went on a rant about IMSI catchers, a
controversial device used by law enforcement that acted like a fake cell phone tower,
but was small enough to hold in your hand,
like a police radio. The device locked in on
a phone number or range of numbers,
capturing data and eavesdropping on conversations. According to his IT expert, some
IMSI catchers could override the phone's
commands, turning the phone on or off
from afar. This haunted the professor. What
if Evelyn had tried to call him? What if she'd
needed help?

"Back up a second, Professor. Why would
the United States government —"

"Not the entire government," he said.

"All right. Why would someone from

Justice, FBI, or whatever put a first-year lawyer at a top law firm under surveillance?"

There was a swift intake of breath before he blasted me: "For the goddamn soon-to-be US Attorney for DC. So they could track and grab her off the street. *So Ian Chase could kill her.*" He was crying in loud gulps. "Sorry, I'm just so furious about what that bastard did to Evie. That bold, beautiful girl."

"Okay, Professor, I hear you," I said, and then gently: "The story was upsetting, and made you consider some theories that we don't have evidence for? Or can you back up any of those claims?"

As he tried to get control of his voice, I got the basics: he had a couple of screen shots of Evelyn's phone and some documents that she asked him to keep safe for her. "But I can't make sense of them," he said, sniffing. "They appear to be some kind of spreadsheets, maybe financials, except they're in code. Maybe you could take a look at them?"

"Can I see them tonight? I'll take the screen shots, too."

He blew out a breath. "Yeah, that's good. I'd feel better if you held them anyway. Nothing feels very safe with me."

"You feel vulnerable because you're

alone." How well I understood that sentiment. "Give me some time to get across town. There's a diner by the Avalon Theater on Connecticut. You know it?"

"I'll borrow my buddy's Pathfinder. I'll be there, thirty minutes."

The diner was south of Chevy Chase Circle, in a neighborhood of expensive restaurants and trendy shops and grocery stores. In the District, that's how you knew you were tucked in a nice upper-class enclave — you got a grocery store. This neighborhood had two.

I parked on the street and walked to the diner. When I opened the door, I glanced around for the professor, who hadn't yet arrived, and then above the metal counter at the hands on the neon clock. It was 9:07. That's when I heard the gunshots.

A woman behind the cash register put her hand to her throat. "Fireworks?" she whispered.

"Call the police," I said.

I jotted the professor a quick note and left it with the hostess before I went outside to call Isaiah. "Send a camera crew to" — I spun around, looking for a street sign — "fifty-five-hundred block of Connecticut, cross street McKinley or Morrison, I can't tell. Shots fired."

"On Connecticut Avenue?" Isaiah said sharply.

"I'll check it out. If I don't call back in five minutes, send a live truck and Ben."

"He's out of town."

Still? *Christ.* "Send whoever," I said through my teeth. "Then call the police. Make sure they know."

"Police aren't there yet? *Virginia.*"

I hung up and ran across Connecticut Avenue, my phone in my hand. Some asshole BMW swerved around me in the crosswalk, putting a hitch in my stride, but I stayed the course in the direction of the grocery store. South of it was an Exxon station. The gunshots came from that direction. A holdup or a street robbery, I figured. Either made sense.

A waist-high brick wall enclosed the parking lot of the grocery store. At the far end of the lot were two very young men: both medium height and narrow in that way of men in their late teens or early twenties, one wearing his hair in long braids, the other in basketball shorts and flip-flops, in mid-March. For some reason, the flip-flops engrossed me rather than the behavior of the teen waving his hands in obvious distress. Maybe because my mind couldn't accept — it seemed utterly implausible — what I was seeing as I crossed the blacktop.

An older-model green Nissan Pathfinder had backed into a parking space. Across its windshield there was a dark cloud of what appeared to be blood spatter. My feet became heavy, my pace slowed. My breath tingled behind my teeth.

Through the gaping hole of the shattered glass of the side window, I could see a large man lurched forward in the driver's seat, his cheek pressed against the steering wheel. His hair was wet with blood.

It was Professor Bradley Hartnett. The back of his head had been blown off.

Chapter Twenty-Five

The catalogue of details came slowly: the pebbles of broken glass crunching beneath my feet, the passenger door ajar and the car's dome light on, illuminating the windshield —

No, look away from the windshield.

Behind me, one of the teens was saying, "Aww, man, I can't believe this. You believe this?" and the other teen saying, "No, cuz, I can't," and then I steadied myself with my hand on the hood of the car — *still warm, he must have just arrived, when someone . . . when someone . . .* and then my mind blanked again.

A hesitant touch at my elbow jolted me back. "You all right, lady?" the teen with the braids said. The other teen was chattering nervously. "It's the worst thing I ever seen, bruh. For real, that's his *brains* all over the windshield."

I couldn't think, and I had to think. Brad-

287

ley Hartnett had been en route to meet me. Was that a coincidence? Was he killed to stop him from meeting with me? He had spoken of conspiracy.

"What do we do?" the teen with the braids wanted to know.

Just then, the first siren wailed and others joined, growing louder until the first of many emergency vehicles converged at the lot, and then everything seemed to be happening at once. An officer called us witnesses and told us to wait beneath the awning of the grocery store. I didn't like standing under the awning. It felt too exposed. Brad's killer was out there with a gun.

"Sorry, I can't stick around," I said in a voice that was high pitched and panicked, and the officer said, "You'll stay where I tell you until Homicide gets here."

The officer left us to secure the crime scene. The teens were chattering with that wild brew of terror and excitement and disbelief at what they'd just witnessed. I warned them who I was and to be careful what they said, but they kept talking.

One was Darius Brown, twenty, a University of Maryland engineering major and resident of Temple Hills, Maryland. His cousin Harold "Hal" Wylie, eighteen, a senior at Gonzaga High School, lived in the forty-one-hundred block of nearby Fessenden Street, NW.

Darius was scratching the leg of his shiny basketball shorts, up and down, a tic. "We were at the gas station," he said, pointing across the street about twenty yards to a sporty coupe with a gas nozzle still resting in its tank. "Right there, pumping gas, and you know how it takes forever, like how slow it is means somehow you're getting more, because this shit is way too expensive to begin with, and I'm looking around —" He gestured to a stop sign at the end of the block where the businesses ended and the neighborhood houses began. "That's where this skinny white dude was getting off his bike."

I pulled out my notebook. "What kind of bike?"

"I don't know motorcycles. Hal?"

"Not a Harley," Hal said. "All I know."

"Okay." I was scribbling it down, the act of reporting clearing my head and focusing my attention, making me feel like me again. "So this skinny white dude, describe him."

Darius looked at Hal. Hal shrugged. "Maybe my height," he said.

Hal was about five eight or nine, couple of inches taller than me. "What else?"

289

"Stone-cold killer for real," Darius said. "Wearing this trench coat, black leather, like *Shaft*. You see Samuel Jackson in *Shaft*? Badass, like that. He had this black helmet, visor pulled down —"

"Wait. I thought you said he was a white guy. You didn't see his face?"

Darius said, "Nah, but he was carrying out in the open. Brothers can't carry guns in the open."

"Brothers can't even carry a pack of Skittles," Hal said. "The Second Amendment? That shit is for white people."

"Also," Darius said, raising his finger as if to make a point. "Dude's coat was open and you could see his skinny jeans. Now you tell me, what brother you know wears skinny jeans?" He grimaced in distaste. "Makes you look like you got bitch hips."

"Cuz," Hal chastised, tilting his head toward me.

"It's fine," I said. "Tell me whatever you got."

Darius nodded sagely. "Money on it, white dude."

A young lieutenant was walking our way. His jowls fluttered angrily, as he waved toward my notebook. "What are you doing? You can't interview a witness."

"I was told I'm a witness."

"You're a reporter," he accused.

"Look, either I'm the press, which means you let me go so I can work the story, or I'm a witness, kicking it here until Homicide makes its way from downtown. You tell me."

This seemed to confuse him. Eventually, he decided I needed to be separated from the teens at a point several feet away — no, no a few feet farther, he said — which was as silly as admonishing me for talking to a witness. Of course we talked to witnesses. How else did you get the story? What I'd never done was *identify* a witness. I would've explained all this, except that he was too busy making me dance.

"All right here?" I said sweetly.

"I'm calling headquarters to deal with you." He walked off to join the group of officers who had congregated among the cluster of cruisers and emergency equipment shutting down Connecticut Avenue. Yellow crime scene tape crossed the entrance to the parking lot. Behind that tape, the gawkers had arrived en masse. A crime scene tech in her blue MPD windbreaker lifted the tape over her head and ducked under it in a smooth, practiced rhythm.

With the lieutenant gone, I went back to the teens. "Either of you see the gun?"

"Probably a nine," Darius said.

So much for the hope of an exotic weapon. In the District, a nine millimeter was the most commonly carried weapon by criminals and law-enforcement officers alike. "You know guns?" I said.

Darius jerked his chin upward. He knew them. This one he'd seen a little too close and personal. "Dude walked right past us, like we weren't even there, hops the wall beside the Pathfinder, raises the nine, and *bam! bam!*"

I jerked back, more rattled than I'd realized. "What did it seem like? Robbery or attempted carjacking?"

"That piece of shit?" Hal was incredulous. "When the killer has his choice of Benzes all around? Nah, it was like a *hit*."

The blood left my face.

Bradley Hartnett, constitutional law professor at George Washington University, a man I had set up a meeting with, the source in a story of a murdered woman, had been the target of . . . a *hit*? It was unbelievable, and yet the rational part of my brain was already sorting through the idea.

Overhead, a police chopper circled. Its search beam swept across the parking lot to the Pathfinder and slid across the shiny faces of the officers. That first officer even now was watching me out of the corner of his eye, sly, suspicious. One of the crime scene techs, the woman in the windbreaker, was leaning in the open door of the Pathfinder. The dome light was dimmer now, and I wondered sort of vaguely if the battery was failing.

The passenger door, I realized. It had been open the whole time. Why was it open? "Was something taken from the Pathfinder?" I asked them.

"Oh yeah, laptop bag," Darius said. "Remember, Cuz? Like that bag I got for my Mac. Killer grabbed it and ran."

The chopper was directly over us now, the *whamp-whamp-whamp* of its blades making Hal shout: "Dude fired his gun — *bam, bam* — then he opens the door, grabs the bag. Matter of seconds, he was ghost. *Like an assassin.*"

My mouth went dry. If it happened that fast, the killer had to have known to look for a bag. Did he know what was in it — screen shots of Evelyn's phone and documents from her computer? Did he know Brad was coming to meet me?

Was he out there now, watching me?

I forced myself to walk, not run, toward the yellow tape, ignoring the lieutenant shouting and an officer striding toward me, waving his hands. I ran smack into

Michael Ledger.

He was dressed for the cameras, soft black shirt open at the collar and neat gray slacks set off by the gun at his hip. It was such a relief to see a familiar face — until I remembered what the professor had told me.

A conspiracy. Police surveillance. So they could track her. So Ian could kill her.

I took a step back. "I have to get to my live shot."

"In a minute," he said, frowning. "First you'll give me a statement."

So I gave him one that was truthful, if not complete: I'd stopped on Connecticut Avenue for a bite to eat, and had just arrived at the diner when I heard gunshots. I ran out of the diner to find the teens freaking out beside the Pathfinder.

"Lieutenant was supposed to keep you from those witnesses," Michael said. "Witnesses that get named get killed."

"That's why I'm quoting you, not them."

"You're a pain in the ass, you know that?"

"I do," I agreed. "Can I go now?"

"Another minute. So those boys you've been talking to, they saw a motorcycle leave the scene. They get a good look, I suppose?"

"They don't know make or model, but they're good witnesses, very observant. I'd bet they could pick it out of a photo spread.

294

It was gone before I arrived, so unfortunately I can't help."

He slid his hands into his pockets and bounced back on his heels. "You can attribute to me everything those boys told you, except for the motorcycle. We can't have you reporting the motorcycle."

"Come again?"

"Everything else, fine. No vehicle description."

This made no sense. Investigators always wanted the suspect's vehicle look out in the news. That was how they tracked down their suspects.

"Why not?" I said suspiciously.

"We need a couple of days before we're willing to release the description."

"That's an eternity to withhold a critical element of the story." It was also an eternity for a suspect to get away. "What do you need a couple of days for?"

"Play ball on the motorcycle, and I'll reward you with the Carney case. We expect a development soon."

"What kind?"

He gave me a smile I'd seen before. It was meant to make me stop thinking about what might be hidden behind it. Naturally, it only made me more suspicious.

"The kind I'll give only to you," he said.

CHAPTER TWENTY-SIX

The live shot was set up south of the crime scene. Golden girl Heather Buchanan was standing cluelessly in the klieg lights when I arrived. It was bad enough to work a story like this without Ben. Now I had the boss's assistant, a newbie, which meant lots of hand-holding on a skintight deadline, when what I really needed was someone who could pull their own damn weight.

It was a hastily thrown together script, but somehow we got through the live shot. After the control room gave us our good night and the equipment was broken down, I went home and poured a very large drink. Tonight required Jameson, my go-to for the best and worst of nights. It was also Ben's drink of choice, and with that first sip, I wished so suddenly and ardently for him that I imagined his being conjured by the force of my thoughts — or the allure of his favorite whiskey.

If Ben were here, I wouldn't worry about missing some important detail. He had a great eye. So often he caught what I missed. He was also calm when everyone around him was freaking out. I could have used some of that calm tonight.

I wanted Ben. There, I said it. I wanted him and couldn't have him, but maybe I could hear his voice. The clock on my phone showed it was long past midnight, too late to call. If he wasn't asleep, he was probably at some bar with women fawning over him.

That idea didn't make me happy. I dialed his number and left a message about tonight's story: "The victim was a friend of Evelyn's. He was trying to find out who killed her. The shooting, it's not a coincidence, I don't think —" *and I don't know how to say I need you. You make me feel stronger. Not to mention, you're so damned good at your job, you make me better at mine, and I need that, too —*

Instead, I joked: "You would've been all over that story, you big screen hog. So, um, when are you coming back, anyway?"

Early the next morning I called into work and went over Heather's script with the morning show producer. When everything seemed in good shape, I searched the newspapers and websites for reports of Brad's shooting. His name hadn't been released, pending next-of-kin notification, so the articles were thin with detail. If anyone knew about the motorcycle, they weren't reporting it.

When the sun rose a little higher, I called Peter Carney. I asked him about Evelyn's mental state in the weeks leading up to her murder. Had she seemed anxious? Afraid? He hadn't noticed. He'd been distracted by his own difficulties adjusting to civilian life.

"So you don't know if she was being stalked?"

"What?" he said. "Stalked? *No.*"

"Did she mention run-ins with law enforcement or talk about being under surveillance? Any fears that someone might have been monitoring her phone?"

"Is this some kind of joke?" he said, sputtering with disbelief, and then: "Or maybe you're talking about some other Evelyn Carney?"

He had no idea what kind of phone his wife carried, since her employer had provided it, and he'd never heard the name Bradley Hartnett, either. I was starting to wonder what — if anything — he did know about his wife. Was he that clueless? Or was he lying to me now?

"Where were you last night, Peter?"

"I flew in from Syracuse," he said brusquely. "Landed at Reagan National after ten. Took a taxi to my house, got home maybe eleven. It might be on my taxi receipt." After a long pause: "Why? What do you suspect me of now?"

More caution would be needed with Paige Linden. She'd been Brad Hartnett's friend, and since the authorities hadn't yet released his name, she probably didn't know he'd been killed. When she answered the phone, her lovely voice trilled across the line, a joyful sound.

So she didn't know.

This was the terrible part of my job. I asked if we could meet privately. She was headed out for a quick run and had a late-morning appointment, but had a window in about an hour. She suggested we meet at the coffee shop.

I arrived ahead of her, choosing a table in the far corner where I could keep my back to the wall, a good vantage point. A man came in holding a motorcycle helmet in the crook of his arm, and I froze. He paid the cashier and picked up his drink and left without a glance my way. I let out a long, slow breath.

Soon, Paige powered through the door. That's really the only way to describe how she moved through space. She wore running clothes, a bright yellow jersey and sleek black leggings. She was rosy cheeked and vibrant with good health, and everyone in the shop turned to look at her.

From across the room she raised her water bottle in greeting and strode toward me. "So," she said, tapping the bottle against the back of the chair. "What's going on?"

"Would you like to sit down?"

She gave me a shaky smile. "Do I need to?"

I told her there'd been a shooting last night. She merely shrugged. "Saw it on the news," she said. "You'd think that part of town would be safe."

"The victim was Brad Hartnett."

She looked me in the eye steadily. She said nothing.

"I'm so sorry," I said. "Please. Sit."

Her palm moved across her mouth and wandered to the back of her chair, where her long fingers plucked the spokes. "Brad?" she said, shaking her head. "You must be mistaken."

"The authorities will probably release his name later today, after they've made their notifications, but I thought you might want

300

to hear it from a friendly —"

"Excuse me," she said before rushing off to the restroom.

I waited for some time. Paige reemerged with her face scrubbed rosy and glowing again. Whatever storm of emotion she'd suffered was gone.

She dropped into the chair. "I c-can't think," she said. "This must be shock I'm feeling. Why would anyone . . . Brad's just the nicest man . . . I mean, first Evie, now Brad . . ."

"Yes," I said meaningfully. "Evelyn and Brad."

She glanced up at me quickly, her attention now focused. "He asked me to give Evie an interview, so I did . . . for him. Now he's dead, too, and there's a connection?" She lifted the water bottle to her mouth and held its spout between her teeth and gnawed at it anxiously. "Do you think he's in over his head?"

"Who?"

"Michael Ledger," she said. "He was on TV again last night. For him, this is all about getting attention, isn't it?"

"That's not quite fair. Last night he was interviewing people, working the scene."

She went on as if I hadn't spoken. "You ever read that profile *Washingtonian Maga-*

301

zine did of him a few years ago? Total suck-up piece. More about Michael's purported heroics than the poor victims."

I hadn't read it. It'd been published during my Michael blackout period, that time during which I refused to acknowledge all evidence of his existence. In the interest of full disclosure, I explained: "A very long time ago, we . . . dated, I guess he'd say. For me, it was more. He has that Detective Hollywood allure you mentioned, and he really can be brilliant, when he's not a complete jackass."

"Brilliant?" she said with scorn. "These detectives are utterly lost. How many people are going to die before Michael Ledger gets a goddamn clue?"

Before last night, such a statement would have been absurd. This morning, I felt the clock ticking. So I made an instinctive decision. The bartering of information required trust. I'd have to give a little to get what I needed.

"Brad Hartnett was killed en route to a meeting with me," I told her. "He believed Evelyn's phone had been monitored, and thought the likely culprit was law enforcement."

"Why would the police have an interest in Evelyn? She didn't have time to commit crimes. All she did was work and sleep."

I reminded her gently: "She had time for a sexual relationship with an assistant US attorney."

"Not his style."

"What's not?"

"Using the power and reach of his office to stalk a woman. Maybe he's edgy in his intimate relationships, but when it comes to work ethics, Ian Chase is incorruptible."

"Maybe it had something to do with Evie's work, not her personally?" I said. "Brad had documents that belonged to Evie. He was going to show me, but they were stolen from the crime scene."

She paused, gnawing at her lip as she thought about it. "The last time I saw Evie, she was in the coffee room at work," she said slowly, thinking about it. "I asked how she was doing, and she said fine, everything was fine, even though she did seem stressed. But I thought nothing of it. She was working for Bernadette Ryan, after all. Being stressed out is par for the course if you're unlucky enough to be assigned to her team. Bernadette works her people to death, which is ironic, since she doesn't even practice law anymore. She bundles lots of political money for her big-name powerhouse clients who like to push their weight around."

"You really don't like her," I observed.

"You've got it backward," she said. "Bernadette Ryan doesn't like me. After I made partner, I went to make nice with her. I told her I'd been approached to set up an exploratory committee to run for DC delegate and wondered if she'd share her expertise. More than anything, I was trying to connect with her. You know what she said?"

She leaned forward, her shoulders hunched and arms across her chest in an attitude so like mine that I found myself leaning toward her, too.

"She told me I'd lose," she said. "It would be bad for her to support a loser. That's the kind of person Evelyn was working for." She gave me an intense look. "Let me nose around. If Bernadette had anything to do with what happened to Evie, by God, I'll get your proof."

CHAPTER TWENTY-SEVEN

I was late getting back to the station. Our intern was at the reception desk, a phone to one ear, as she held up a finger, making me stop on my way through the newsroom. She hung up and blew out a breath that lifted her bangs.

"Remember how I lost a call for you my first day here?" she said. "When everyone said there was no hope for me, forget about it, you were going to kill me dead?"

"People said I was going to *kill* you?"

"Or get me escorted out of the newsroom forever. Anyhow, part of the problem is sharing this pigsty of a desk. Every day I do a little more cleaning. Like I don't know when somebody spilled soda under the keyboard without wiping it up, totally gross —"

I made an impatient circle with my finger. *Yeah, yeah, get on with it.*

"But that's where I found this." She

handed me a pink sticky note, crumpled and stained but the writing still legible. It noted a caller named Lil' Bit with a District phone number.

"Refresh my memory," I said. "How is this important?"

"She was that drunk girl who saw Evelyn Carney the night she disappeared."

"This person saw Evelyn?" I looked down at the note and back at her and grinned. "Great job. Order yourself lunch on me."

When I turned toward my office, she ran around her desk and stopped me. "I don't know why I was afraid of you," she said. "You're so much nicer than everyone says."

"Well, for God's sake. Don't tell anyone."

Lil' Bit was a street name. Her real name was Sarah Harden, and this Lil' Bit — Sarah — was telling me how she'd changed her mind about talking. She launched into a tirade about the police (the *poh-lice,* she called them), how they refused to give her reward money, and all they ever do is harass, except when they ignore her.

"So tell me," I said. "I'll listen."

"If you pay me."

"That's not how things work. Tell me what you saw, and maybe we'll put you on TV."

She blew out air. "I need money."

"We don't pay for news," I said, and she hung up. I redialed and let it ring until she picked up again, cursing me until I cut in: "Just tell me this. Did you see Evelyn Carney that Sunday night or not?"

"That girl on y'all's news? Yeah, I seen her."

"After she left the restaurant on Prospect Street?"

"Don't know about a restaurant. I was on M Street."

M Street was a handful of blocks south of the restaurant. The hostess told investigators she'd seen Evelyn leave the restaurant and head south on Wisconsin Avenue, the last known sighting by the only reported witness. Now Lil' Bit was saying she'd seen Evelyn *after* the hostess, which made Lil' Bit's account critical. So I threw out what I wasn't even sure I had: "You know Ben Pearce? He wants to meet you. He's very interested in hearing your story."

"Ben *Pearce*?" There was awe in her voice. That's how it always was. The women went for Ben. We set an interview time for two hours hence.

Problem was, I couldn't find Ben. He didn't pick up his cell phone or landline, when he should have picked up. He always picked up. As anchor in charge of bulletins during news emergencies, he was contractually required to.

So Ben was avoiding me.

That left me with no choice except the bait and switch. I asked around the newsroom for Isaiah. One of the writers thought he'd seen Isaiah head up to archives, our seventh-floor warehouse of old tapes and even older film. I took the stairs and went through the door that banged shut and kicked up dust. To my left was a black-draped studio left unused for years, its cameras huddling in the center like penguins against an Antarctic winter. No Isaiah.

I went down the corridor lined with posters of canceled shows and headshots of long-gone correspondents. At the end of the corridor, pillars of boxes were stacked as high as the ceiling, each box marked with a story slug: DC Police Headquarters Shooting, Air Florida Crash, Mount Pleasant Riots, Million Man March, Chandra Levy Missing — on and on the stories went, many stories from before me, barely remembered, all of them considered a big deal at the time.

Around the corner, Isaiah was sitting on a box marked Marion Barry Trial with his feet propped up on Government Shutdown 1995. Across the Persian Gulf War, the first one, his lunch was spread.

The room held the kind of silence you got from places left undisturbed.

"Isaiah?" I whispered.

He turned his head as if it pained him.

"What are you doing here?" I said.

"Thinking."

I moved to sit on a box but noticed it was marked 9/11. So I lifted it to where it would be protected above the others.

"Are you all right?" I said, sitting next to him.

"It's surprising how quickly the end comes." He paused and said, "My job, of course."

"Mellay's not getting rid of you. You're critical to the news operation."

"Nobody's critical to anything." Behind his black horn-rims, his gentle eyes held mine. "I tried to teach you everything I knew. Neither of us had anybody, so I thought we could need each other. But you don't anymore."

"That's not true."

"I had a mentor once," he said, as if to himself. "Quentin worked forty-two years in the biz, first when we were radio and made the switch over to television. He lived and breathed the news and taught me to do the same. The company had to force him to retire. On his last day there was a big cake in the newsroom, lots of toasting and drinking. We all drank in the newsroom back then. We were so happy for Quentin. He was always talking about his boat, this eighteen-footer, and now that he was retired, he was going to spend all day fishing the Potomac. But after the party, he took the stairs to the roof and he jumped."

He was looking into the distance at someplace I couldn't see. I rested my hand on his shoulder, which had carried me so far, this man who'd been everything to me — teacher, ally, friend — and I had no idea how to make this better for him.

"What happens next?" he said, sighing. "People said I was important because of this. Without it, I guess I'm nothing."

"Nobody's making you leave your work. Didn't you hear the big speech Mellay gave in the newsroom yesterday?"

"I heard it all right."

"My star is on the rise again, and you go where I go. That's a promise." I stood, brushing the dust from the back of my skirt. "Now I need you to get Ben on the phone."

He shook his head. "Ben's off today."

"Yeah, well, I hate to cut into his minivacation, but I've got a story with now *two* people killed and an interview with a possible witness in only two hours' time. That person will only talk to Ben."

"He's not on vacation," Isaiah said angrily. "He requested three days to deal with personal business, days that I granted. Today is his third day."

"This interview requires Ben. I need him."

"You should have thought of that before you pulled that stunt with the correspondents dinner."

It felt like a slap. "What does that mean?"

He stood now, too. His head was down and his chin tucked to his chest. He glared at me over the top of his glasses. "It means Ben has a life other than this place, and he's smart enough to know it. It also means that in all his years here, he has never once asked me for a favor. Never once taken a personal day. The guy takes his vacation, that's it, and always it's to go home to work on his family's ranch. Because he's not what you make him out to be. Some pretty-boy slacker —"

"I have never suggested —"

"Oh yes, you most certainly have." His finger pointed at me. "You joke about it often, and it's always funny and not a little unfair. He asked me for time off — asked me, not you — and I granted it. Now you'll just have to figure out how to get by without him."

I leaned back against a column of boxes, reconsidering.

"No, Virginia."

"May I borrow your phone?"

"No means no."

"I just want to run it by him," I said, exasperated. "How can he know he doesn't want to do it if he hasn't even heard what it is?"

He still wouldn't budge, so I told him I'd get someone else's phone. Surely he was only postponing the inevitable and making my deadline tighter. Nelson was my next target. Once I found Nelson, I'd have his phone in five seconds flat.

"This is wrong," he said, but held out his phone.

On the second ring, Ben picked up with: "I know it's you."

"As in . . . me?"

"Yes, you." His voice was surly. "It's the oldest trick in the book. My only surprise is that Isaiah still lets you run roughshod."

"Will you let me apologize?"

"No you may not," he said. "Your apologies wear me out."

I told him about Lil' Bit. He had no interest in interviewing her.

"But she saw Evelyn," I pleaded. "She'll talk to no one except you."

"Why hasn't she gone to the police with her story?"

"Apparently they won't listen. She must not fit their mold of credibility."

"That doesn't sound like the DC Police," he scoffed. "Most of their witnesses have credibility issues. Bet they think she's a lunatic."

But in his voice, there'd been a pause, and in that pause I detected his curiosity.

"What if she was the last person to see Evelyn Carney?" I said, and when he hesitated again, I knew he was close: "If we don't get her now, we may never know."

"It's my day off," he complained.

I gave him Lil' Bit's address.

CHAPTER TWENTY-EIGHT

"I give it a year max before somebody bulldozes it," Nelson was saying.

We were on the curb outside of Lil' Bit's house. This block had once lent its name to an infamous drug crew with members long dead or locked up at Lorton Prison. Now it was an area of dizzying transformation, or revitalization, as some people liked to call it. Homes were being destroyed to build shops and high-rises (as high as the US Congress saw fit to let the District build), resulting in a fretful mix of modernity and fixer-uppers not fixed since the '68 riots. The urban pioneers had begun to eyeball even those, seeing only the promise and none of the troubles that had come before.

Lil' Bit lived at the end of the alley in what she'd called a carriage house. More accurately, it was a converted garage in desperate need of fresh paint. From the eaves of its sagging roof, an acoustic guitar swung from a wire.

A short woman opened the front door. She was in her early twenties, wearing a faded 9:30 Club T-shirt exposing her paunch. She had blond hair and a pale, doughy face I had seen before. "*You're* Lil' Bit?"

Her black-lined eyes darted away. "Yeah. So?"

"You bumped into me at Evelyn Carney's vigil in Georgetown. Nearly knocked me over. And I'm pretty sure you lifted my wallet."

"Don't know what you're talking about."

It was so outrageous I laughed. So she might be a thief. Let's just hope she wasn't a liar.

"That's not the rock star," she said, craning her head to look at Nelson coming up the walkway with his cartful of equipment. He lifted the cart onto the porch and rested his hip against it.

"Cool," he said, tapping the body of the guitar and set it spinning. "We doing this, or what?"

"First I'm gonna need to see the money." She put her thumbnail to her mouth, turning the heel of her hand. The fingernail on her pinky was curled like a scoop.

"No money," I said, and introduced Nelson. "He'll be shooting your interview today." Over her shoulder, I had a view of the interior of the front room. It was small and dark and would be difficult to light. But if anyone could make it work, Nelson could. "Mind if we set up while we wait for Ben Pearce? He'll be here any moment."

Inside smelled of cigarette smoke and Chinese takeout. Nelson began setting up by the only window, which looked onto the brick wall of a neighboring house.

Lil' Bit clacked across the parquet. At the bottom of a set of stairs, she called out: "Maaaa —"

Above, a bed frame creaked, and with it, a faint voice grumbling.

"Maaaa," Lil' Bit called again. "Them TV people are here."

"Quit that hollering." It was a woman's voice from upstairs.

"Don't be all pissed off when you see me on TV," Lil' Bit singsonged. "All you gotta do is get down here, and you be on TV, too."

"I'm trying to get some sleep," the woman yelled.

Lil' Bit stomped up the stairs. I heard their argument through the ceiling. Nelson signaled for help to set up before it all fell apart. In my haste, I knocked into an orange milk crate holding dozens of celebrity magazines, *People* and *InStyle* and *Star,* some dog-eared and others with water glass marks, celebrity shots torn in sheets now fanned across the parquet. I scooped up the magazines and slid them back into the crate.

Nelson was arranging chairs beside the window when someone knocked on the door. It was Ben.

"You came," I said, relieved. "Thank you."

He stepped past me. He smelled freshly showered, and his thick dark hair was still damp and wavy with it. He glanced at the ceiling through which we could hear much yelling. "What have we here?"

"Not sure. She hasn't allowed me to preinterview her."

He regarded me coolly. "So I'm going fishing on my day off, but not on my boat."

Upstairs, there was a shriek followed by a slap. Everything went silent, and then the sounds of footsteps across the floorboards — *boom, boom, boom, boom* — followed by heavier, slower steps and a door slamming. Lil' Bit stomped down the stairs. At the bottom, she grabbed the newel post, staring dumbstruck at Ben. She wore bright pink gloss on lips that quivered.

Ben crossed the room and held out his hand, introducing himself. He took her by the arm as though they were at a cotillion and led her to one of the ratty chairs that Nelson had set by the window. He held it out for her.

My perch was against the far wall, out of the shot, where I could watch Nelson make his last-minute adjustments with the lighting and Ben disarm Lil' Bit with personal questions she hadn't let me pose. She told him her name was Sarah Harden. She was twenty years old and had lived in this house her whole life. No, she wasn't in college. She hated school. Kids had been mean to her, calling her trash, even though her people had been on this block for a hundred years, longer than anybody's. When he asked if she wanted to go to college or if she had work ambitions, she stared at Ben as if no one had ever asked her such a question and he might provide some answer.

"Excuse me," he said, holding his white notepad in front of her shirt, so Nelson could set the white balance. "So tell me about the night you saw Evelyn Carney."

"There were a lot of stars out that night. I was sitting on the steps at M Street. You know, the *Exorcist* steps where they made the movie? Nobody bothers you there." She was warmed by his attention. Her chest rose and fell as she spoke with the excitement of her telling. "The lights on the bridge were

318

starry, too. That's when I saw that Evelyn Carney woman."

Ben squinted past the lights to me, asking: "Do you have a picture?"

I pulled Evelyn's flier from my satchel, unfolding it, and handed it to Ben without a word. "This is the woman you saw?" he asked her.

She smiled up at him, her glossy pink lips over sharp little teeth. "That's her. She was walking through the stars on the bridge. The lights had — whadayacallit?" She made a sweeping gesture, flinging her arm outward.

Nelson came out of his crouch behind the camera. "No kidding? The lights had trails?" He was referring to the photographic effect of capturing the movement of light with a long exposure, like making a moving car's taillight appear like a red trail. But I figured she was describing the effects of being high as a kite, hallucinating. That, along with her curved fingernail scoop and suspected theft of my wallet, was making me increasingly uneasy.

"Yeah, but the woman . . . Evelyn" — Lil' Bit corrected herself — "she stopped when everything else was moving. Her face was all lit up and everything moving around her and she just disappeared. Like the night took her or something."

319

"The night did?" I said, unable to help myself.

Ben cut me a silencing glare.

Her lips curled in disgust. "That's how I seen it."

"Okay, I'm ready to go," Nelson said. "We're at speed."

"Let's start again from the beginning," Ben coaxed. "Tell me everything you remember."

She shook her head. "Not when she's looking at me all funny. Like she don't believe a word I say."

"Don't worry, she looks at me like that, too," he said, leaning forward and smiling, as if they were sharing a secret. "Ignore everyone else. It's just me and you talking."

She told the same story. This time, it was recorded.

"Here's what I don't get," Ben said. "Maybe you can help. How'd you see Evelyn's face? It was dark. You were on the steps. Wasn't the M Street traffic between you?"

"There's no traffic on a Sunday night. How it always is."

"Okay," he said. "But from so far away? How can you be sure it was Evelyn Carney? Not a woman who resembled her?"

She put her head down, saying nothing.

"Is someone tapping a foot?" Nelson said. "I'm picking up tapping."

Lil' Bit stilled her foot.

"Take your time," Ben said.

She winced. "I forgot to say I seen her before the bridge."

"That's all right. I forget things all the time."

"She walked by me on the *Exorcist* steps," she whispered.

We waited for more. Ben reached out and clasped both of her small hands and twisted at the waist to talk to Nelson. "How's Sarah framed? You got her tight from the chest up?"

"You're not in the shot," Nelson said.

Ben turned back to her and said: "You were doing real good there. Now tell me about the steps."

When Lil' Bit started talking again, he pulled her hands toward him, and when she paused, he pushed her gently away. It was this weird rowing motion I'd never seen done before, not in any interview, but it got her talking, the story rushing out in a flow no one could halt. She said Evelyn had been walking fast, as if she were scared or upset about something, it was hard to tell. Lil' Bit followed her across the street and onto the bridge. Just to make sure she was okay. Now

321

maybe she did ask Evelyn for some spare change, but that was nothing more than panhandling. Was she hungry, Evelyn wanted to know, and Lil' Bit agreed she sure could use something. Evelyn reached into her little purse, not bothering to count the bills, and handed the money over to Lil' Bit, everything she had, nice as you please.

Ben was as skeptical as I was, asking the follow-up question three different ways. Lil' Bit answered the same way each time: she had no idea why Evelyn gave her that money. Most people walked past her, cutting their eyes away, but not Evelyn. She just said to get some warm food and God bless and kept going across the bridge. Lil' Bit turned back to the city.

"You believe me, right?" And then she turned her attention to me: "I see you thinking I was gonna rob her. You're just like the police."

"Detectives talked to you?" Ben said.

"Bald white cop got those jelly rolls down the back of his neck," she said, waving at her nape.

"Detective Miller," I told Ben. Miller was the lead detective in the Evelyn Carney case.

"Yeah, him. All I'm trying to do is help myself by helping them and get ahold of that reward they promised, but he says 'stop playing me little girl. You keep up, you find yourself in a heap of trouble. You being the last person to see Evelyn Carney and all.' "

But there was no evidence she was playing them. In fact, everything she told us matched precisely what the police were saying. The only new information was that Evelyn Carney had made it onto Key Bridge, which did nothing to turn the investigative theory on its head.

"What did you say to him that you aren't telling us?" I said.

She pulled her hands from Ben's, folding her arms across her chest. A stubborn look crossed her face. I pushed away from the wall and circled the camera, now close enough to catch the scent of her cherry lip gloss, bringing with it an elbow-sharp childhood memory: the sale aisle at Happy Harry's, a yearning for rollerball lip gloss that cost the dollar I didn't have, the yearning so profound I slid my bitten nail beneath the glued edge of its package and slipped the gloss into my pocket before making my way, terrified, past the security guard. Cherry became the scent of poverty and fear, and it was coming off of Sarah Harden in waves, and no wonder: she was young and alone, a witness in a city that killed its witnesses, and her tough-girl camouflage

323

called Lil' Bit was a flimsy defense.

An intuition brought words that had never before fallen from my lips: "Turn off the camera, Nelson."

"What?" Nelson shot up from behind the camera.

Ben studied me for a moment, and then, to Nelson, "You heard her."

"But, Ben," Nelson pleaded.

"She's the producer. Do it."

When Nelson made a big show of turning the camera off and stepping back from it, Lil' Bit whispered, "I feel bad. She was nice to me, that girl that got killed."

"What are you afraid of?" I said.

She flicked her eyes up at me and quickly looked back down again, picking at her fingernail.

I waited. When she said nothing more, I told her: "I'm not going to lie. We can't protect you, but we'll never give up your name."

She hesitated, and then: "That's what he wanted."

"Detective Miller?" I said, and when she nodded, "What did he want?"

"He was hounding me for a name. Look at some pictures, he says, but like I already told him again and again, I never did see a face. Everything happened too fast. That motorcycle blew right by me."

"On the bridge?" I said, barely able to control my excitement. "A motorcycle?"

"Triumph," she said. "One of them monster bikes, I know some guy had one. So anyhow, this bike came tear ass down M Street and idled at the light, growling like they do. Then it takes off again, on the bridge and stops beside that Evelyn girl. She backed up against the rail, holding her arms out like *Titanic*."

"Were they fighting? This rider and Evelyn?"

"Not that I could tell."

"What were they doing?"

"Couldn't say. I rolled out pretty fast."

"But you described the motorcycle to Detective Miller, right?" I said. "That's what he told you to keep quiet?"

"Yeah."

"Did he say why?"

She shook her head. "Just keep my big yap shut, that's all."

"Okay, so let me make sure I understand you," I said. "You didn't see anything beyond the rider backing Evelyn against the rail? You didn't see Evelyn go over the rail?"

"Nope."

"What about sounds? You hear fighting or Evelyn screaming for help or gunshots —

anything like that?"

"Nope, nothing but wind," she said, and shivered. "Then that bike took off, roaring loud as the devil himself. I looked back, and she was gone. I told you. It was like the night swallowed her up."

CHAPTER TWENTY-NINE

Ben caught up with me on the curb outside the carriage house. "Whoa, slow down, Speedy," he said. "What's our plan?"

His use of *our* was a great kindness, especially given the arm twisting it took to get him here. I told him about the motorcycle seen fleeing the professor's murder, how an official had also asked me not to report it.

"So Ledger knows a motorcycle was at both scenes," Ben said dryly. "He doesn't want to tip the fine folks of Northwest they've got a killer in their midst with a body tally of two."

If we were talking about any official other than Michael, I might buy it, but Michael didn't mind the hot glare of attention. The hotter, the better, and he never worried that he'd close his case, since he usually did.

"Last night, the gunman parked beneath a streetlight just off Connecticut Avenue," I said, working it out aloud. "Bold as you please. Then he strolls past two witnesses, not even trying to hide his gun, like he didn't care if he was seen. Almost as if he wanted a witness to see him."

"Taunting investigators?"

"Maybe." I pulled at my lip and considered it a moment. "It's as if the shooter was confident that he couldn't — or wouldn't — be arrested. Don't you think?"

"You're thinking police corruption?" he said in a low, careful voice. "That's what got you so rattled in the interview?"

I didn't like the way Detective Miller had talked to Sarah Harden. Then again, the Metropolitan Police Department as a whole was not known for its cordiality toward certain groups of people. But threatening the witness if she talked? Or had Lil' Bit misunderstood the detective's intentions? Maybe he'd warned her not to talk because talk was dangerous. Maybe it was for her protection. After all, two people had been killed.

"She has to be protected," I said. "If that means we don't use the information she gave us, so be it."

"More than one way to skin a cat," he said, winking. "I'll find somebody else to go on record, and no one will ever know we talked to her."

"Be careful with your law-enforcement sources."

"Nah, I think I'll hit the street." He wanted to talk to residents along the route on which Lil' Bit had seen Evelyn. See if any shop owners noticed Evelyn or a motorcycle or anything that might corroborate Sarah's story. "Most of the shops were probably closed by that time on a Sunday night," he said. "But what about security video? It's lucky the vehicle we're looking for is a Triumph. They're pretty rare around these parts, and when you see one, you notice it. Maybe someone will remember one prowling the area?"

By now, Nelson had joined us on the street by his Tahoe and was opening the lift gate. He ducked into the back and rifled through a crate until he pulled out a media card he'd been meaning to give me, he said. It stored the unedited video of Evelyn Carney and Ian Chase at the meeting in Rock Creek Park. The editor, Doug, had told Nelson I'd been looking for it.

"This has the footage of Evelyn watching Ian Chase at the podium?"

"From what I remember," Nelson said before sliding it into the camera.

A series of shots flickered across the

camera's LCD screen: neighbors chatting with police officials inside a meeting room, the mayor glad-handing and the police chief working the crowd and finally, everyone taking their places. Then, Ian at the podium, giving his remarks and behind him, a wall of white shirts: the MPD chief and a commander from the Second District, officials from US Park Police, some suits I assumed to be FBI. Ian was still at the podium, when the video turned suddenly, and there was Evelyn Carney —

"Pause it," I said with relief. So Evelyn had been gazing at Ian Chase with a nearly palpable heat. "That's it, good," I said, and noticed again how she pulled attention from those around her, the gray-haired man sweating in his elegant suit, the bored woman in her gold brocade jacket. My eye kept being drawn back to Evelyn.

"Play to the end," I told him. "See if anything else is usable."

From the moment Nelson hit the red button, he would never stop recording, not even when he changed camera positions. This was his method. And so there was video of the meeting as it was breaking up and people were moving about, some making their way to the doors, and the camera swung wildly again, reestablishing for another shot and settling on a corner of the auditorium, where a dark-haired man in a stylish navy jacket leaned back on his heels. His hands were in his pockets, and the butt of a handgun peeked out from his jacket. His face was averted, as he spoke to a companion hidden from the camera's view.

But I knew that profile anywhere, the line of the jaw, the sleek runner's body. It was Michael Ledger. His torso twisted as he reached out, his palm sliding across his companion's waist. In doing so, he created a brief line of sight.

"Back," I said, my voice hoarse. "Go back. There, pause it."

The video froze on Michael's companion. She had Disney princess eyes that tilted upward. Her lips were thinned, tight against teeth, what appeared to be the barest hint of a frown.

It was Evelyn Carney.

Michael Ledger had never met Evelyn Carney. That's what he'd told me, anyway. Of course, Michael Ledger was a liar. Now it was true, he had lied to me more often than I could count, but that was *in a relationship.* Those lies were hurtful but unsurprising. This time he had lied to me *as a source.* That was unforgivable, and he would answer

331

for it sooner rather than later, and in person, not over the phone, where he'd fob me off with some bullshit excuse, if not avoid my call altogether.

Nope, I was going to corner the rat in his nest.

So there I was in the lobby at headquarters, temper roiling, foot tapping impatiently as I waited in line at the magnetometers. There was no real plan. You couldn't just walk up to the commander of CID. Once you got past the magnetometers, there were armed officers at every entrance and locked doors opened only by swiping an identification card. These made CID, especially the Homicide Branch, completely inaccessible to the casual passerby. Probably the most effective security measures were the watchful eyes and suspicious natures of men and women who expected to be attacked in their workplace at any moment, with Michael Ledger the most suspicious of all.

Years ago, before the magnetometers had been installed, a gunman had sauntered through this lobby with a Tec-9 concealed in his coat. He'd taken the elevator to the third floor and strolled into the anteroom that housed an elite team of investigators, including a young Detective Michael Ledger, although Michael had been testifying at court at the time. A handful of Michael's coworkers, federal agents and city detectives, were busy working behind their desks when the gunman came into the office and opened fire. A detective was killed immediately, two federal agents critically wounded. Michael's partner, Abby Sanders, took cover behind Michael's desk and returned fire, disabling the Tec-9 in what must have been a magnificent shot, or a damn lucky one.

Her back was to the wall when the gunman lunged for her. They wrestled for her gun. She was already wounded but had much to live for. She was young and in love and had a dinner date with her husband not three hours away, and so she struggled with the gunman who killed her coworkers to get to the man she loved. But she was alone and losing blood, and the gunman was bigger and stronger and he wrenched her gun away.

In the time I knew Michael, he'd spoken of Abby only once. *Killed with her own gun,* he'd said. *I should've been there. I would've done something.*

It had been a bad idea to let Michael investigate: working that crime scene, attending his partner's autopsy, tracking the illegal gun. During a nighttime raid on the gang that sold the Tec-9, one suspect had reached for something that resembled a weapon but turned out to be a phone, and the most celebrated detective in the city emptied his service weapon, killing two men and wounding the others. Prosecutors said it was self-defense, a justified use of force. I'd asked if he'd been afraid.

"Terrified," he said in a tone that suggested anything but.

"Don't be such a hard-ass. It's okay to admit it was difficult. Killing another human being —"

"Is easy with a Glock 9," he'd said, tapping twice at the spot over my heart. "Two to the chest, love. Always aim for the biggest part of the target, where you know you won't miss."

A couple of detectives were waiting by the elevator. The older had a thin, intelligent face with pursed lips. He bounced rhythmically on his toes. His companion, younger and hairier, appeared more thug than cop. He wore jeans frayed at the hem and his flannel shirttail out. His badge hung from a ball chain around his neck.

The elevator opened, and they got in ahead of me. The younger detective was at the control panel: "What floor, sugar?"

"Three, please," I said, stepping in.

"No kidding?" A grin emerged from his unkempt beard. He was giving me the full body scan. I ignored him.

At the third floor, I got out. It was a long, empty corridor of closed doors. At the end of the hallway, a plaque: Criminal Investigations Division. I pulled the door handle. Of course, it didn't open.

There was a light shuffling behind me. I glanced over my shoulder at the thug detective.

"Need some help there, sugar?"

"I'm supposed to meet Commander Ledger." I showed him my press passes. He leaned forward with his hands behind his back, making a big performance out of reading the passes.

"Well, Virginia Knightly," he said. "Didn't Commander explain the rules? You go up to the fifth floor, look for the Public Information Office. State your purpose, they give you an escort. You know PIO?"

What I knew was that the Public Information Office was a lose-lose proposition. They wouldn't escort me, and they might even leak my visit with Michael to other television stations, if only to sound like they were in the know.

"Commander Ledger said come to him

335

directly."

"Did he now?" He smiled with his eyes stuck someplace south of my neck. "Maybe if you're friendly, I'll walk you back."

"What do you mean?" I said, even though I knew what was coming, what came with such frequency it was really very disturbing. But if he was going to be a dumbass and give me the words, I could surely use them now.

"Meaning you give me your digits," he said, "so we can hang out later."

"Hang out?"

He took a step forward, too close. "Hook up. Whatever you're good for."

I studied the detective badge hanging from his chain. Number 442. "What's your name, Detective?" And when he told me, I tested it out: "Detective Roark, here's an idea. Instead of giving you my phone number, why don't I wait here while you run on back to your commander and tell him I'm staking out his front door?"

He seemed to consider this for a moment, and then: "Why would I do that?"

"Because if Ledger doesn't come out, I'm taking the elevator to the chief's office, not PIO, and I'll pose my questions to her instead. While I'm there, I'll mention your charming offer to sell out headquarters security for a strange woman's phone number and a hookup."

He glared at me.

"Fifteen minutes, Detective." I pulled out my phone and set its stopwatch.

His white teeth flashed in his dark beard. Not a smile, something ugly. "That phone tells you what day it is, too?" When I didn't say anything, he went on: "Meaning if it's Thursday after shift, Commander's at the Dubliner enjoying a Guinness or two with his pals, like every Thursday afternoon. What you might know if you really had an appointment with Commander."

"Thank you, Detective," I said with a genuine smile now. The Dubliner was only a short walk away. "That's very helpful."

When I hurried off, his voice carried across the empty corridor: "Bitch."

Like I'd never been called that before.

CHAPTER THIRTY

The Dubliner was my kind of bar, all dark wood and forest-green walls and subdued lighting, mirrors advertising whiskey and Gaelic blessings etched in stained glass. Today it was crowded and loud with the raucous cheering of folks watching the basketball tournament on the television above the bar. Michael was alone at a four-top, his attention on the basketball game, or so I thought.

"Nice surprise," he said without looking away from the television. "I was going to call you."

Another lie. "Save it, you great braying jackass."

Behind me, a deep guffaw, as a man's voice said, "Truth to power." He was carrying a couple of drafts and handed one to Michael.

Michael introduced his drinking partner as Ray Callum, the mayor's chief of staff.

Ray was a slender man of medium height wearing a bow tie and a generous smile. He looked me in the eye, as if searching for something in particular, and having found it, smiled wider. "Very good to put a face to a name," he said, shaking my hand. "I watch your news exclusively."

This was emphatically untrue. Someone like Ray Callum would be an idiot to watch only one source of news.

Michael's cool gray eyes rested on me, challenging. "Should we share the tidings of great joy?" he said with sarcasm.

"Why not?" Ray set his beer on the table. "The administration has informed the mayor's office that there's a new US attorney for the District of Columbia." He grinned and said, "Derek Mantis."

Of course I knew who Derek was, but listened to the chief of staff's spiel: Derek Mantis was the son of a single mom from a poor neighborhood east of the Anacostia. He'd been brought up in DC, a product of the city's public schools, and was a Harvard Law grad. He'd done a dozen years of exemplary work in the prosecutor's office. All in all, he was a brilliant and capable man who'd do the District proud, and I liked Derek, but the timing made me suspicious.

Michael's gaze wandered before it settled

on a mirror advertising Harp beer. In it, he studied my reflection, as if I were a problem that vexed him greatly.

Ray slapped Michael's shoulder. "We got our guy, Mike." Ray was giddy.

"Mayor got *his* guy," Michael corrected. "The rest remains to be seen."

Ray pulled a vibrating phone from an inside jacket pocket. "I have to take this. Catch you later, Mike. A pleasure, Virginia." The phone was to his ear. On the way to the door, he pulled the phone back suddenly, his palm over the mouthpiece. "A feel-good story, right?" Ray said to me. "Not a neighborhood Mantis doesn't know. One of DC's own, born and bred. Break it tonight, if you want. White House announcement tomorrow at four." He raised his phone in farewell and ducked out of the doorway.

"Nice of you to clear Ian Chase out of the way for Mantis," I said bitterly.

He got up and held out a chair for me. "Sit, please," he said. "I prefer relative comfort when a woman yells at me. If you're very entertaining about it, I'll buy you a drink. You still a Jameson girl?"

I took my time, needing the moment. "For the record," I said evenly, "you're a complete jackass."

"Braying, you said." He settled across from me, easing back into the chair with a careless grace.

"How can you not expect blowback?"

"Afraid I'm not following."

"You know, for how cleverly you dispatched Ian. No evidence for an arrest warrant? No problem. News has neither due process nor burden of proof. Just leak your so-called investigative theory to a producer who trusted you as an investigator if not as a man, and throw in some fancy forensic talk from the medical examiner to corroborate your theory of Ian as this so-called person of interest. Said producer breaks the exclusive, so she's happy, right?" I leaned forward on my elbows, about as angry as I'd ever been, and said: "Too bad the *story's not true.* I wonder if you ever suspected Ian at all."

"You reported he was a person of interest," he said pleasantly. He lifted his glass in toast. "At the time I was interested. So you're good. No worries."

My face grew hot. "I'm . . . good?"

"To use your parlance, you're accurate. Mr. Chase still hasn't been cleared. He has no alibi." He held out his hand and ticked off with each finger: "Two, he has a history of being, shall we say, overly physical with

341

his sexual partners. Violent might be a better word. Three, he has motive, the pregnancy —"

"On further consideration, I find that debatable. Most men are thrilled to have children. Has Ian given you any reason to believe otherwise?"

He ticked off another finger. "Four, he admittedly planned to meet Evelyn that night. We believe she did meet him. That's called opportunity."

"Does Ian Chase own a motorcycle?"

He gave me a look of pure arrogance, and then: "You know, any other reporter would be kissing my ass for information instead of reaming me a new one. I find myself very close to cutting you off."

"Funny how I've arrived at the same conclusion about you. To my way of thinking, a lying source is no source at all."

"I'm . . . *lying*?" He laughed. "Careful now. That's a pretty strong accusation."

"That raw video of Evelyn at the community meeting in Rock Creek?" I said. "The one where she first met Ian? I found it."

"Excellent. Where's my copy you promised?"

"One of the exterior shots shows an unmarked cruiser parked outside the meeting. That cruiser has a dent in the front quarter-panel, exactly like the dent in the car you drive, the one that carried me to the correspondents dinner."

"I'm uncertain if it's the narrow streets or the traffic," he said, scratching the stubble on his jaw thoughtfully. "If I had a dollar for every banged-up cruiser in our fleet, I wouldn't need my pension."

"You're saying you weren't at that meeting with Evelyn?"

"I attend more meetings than I'd ever thought possible as a starry-eyed detective dreaming of the climb up the ladder to officialdom, and no, I do not specifically recall that meeting." With that, he took a long swallow of his Guinness. He smacked his lips with satisfaction.

"Would it help if I showed the video of you in a dark corner with Evelyn Carney?" I said.

He didn't blink. His face remained expressionless. No hint of worry or guilt, no anger that I'd caught him. Not even a concession that he was caught.

"Before the camera panned away," I went on, "you reached over and touched her waist. It was an intimate gesture, Michael."

He pulled out his phone and scrolled through his messages, as if bored. He talked

343

down to his phone, frowning. "Your camera caught me groping a woman. Big deal."

"Were you intimate with Evelyn Carney?" I said. "Did you come clean to the chief? Has anyone asked for *your* alibi?"

"Be serious, would you? Do you have any idea how many people recognize me and start up a conversation, wanting to know about this or that case or whatever. She's just one of those people who used to hang around the Hill —"

"Evelyn?"

"Sure. I'd run into her time to time, once with her colleague Paige. She asked me about jobs at Justice, that kind of work. She thought it was all very glamorous — poor deluded girl — and wondered if I'd introduce her to certain people who might help her."

"She wanted you to get her a job?"

"That was her suggestion."

"And let me guess. You *helped* her?" Help, up in air quotes.

"Of course not. But she was okay to talk to, easier to look at. That's all that happened."

"So why not say so from the beginning?" I said.

He gave me a hard look. "Now that has got to be the stupidest question you've ever

344

asked. You know what people would say. That's why you're not going to pursue it."

"I'm not?"

"No."

"I shouldn't ask what kind of relationship you had with the victim whose murder is being investigated by *your* detectives? Or how that relationship impacts *your* investigation? Did you okay the surveillance of Evelyn Carney?"

"*What?* No. That's nuts."

"Maybe you stalked her. Were you obsessed with her?"

"Get real . . . stalk a woman." He let out a harsh laugh. "That would risk my job. I've never cared that much about anyone."

That at least had the ring of truth.

"Seriously, this is a waste of your time," he said smugly, and then explained: the chief had requested him specifically to oversee the investigation because he was the best she had, simple as that. She was aware the decedent was a person known to him, but that sort of thing happened in a city so small, more often than you'd think. Throughout the investigation, he made certain the chief and the mayor were consulted and that his superiors green-lighted each avenue pursued and all information released.

Besides, he told me, the only reputation injured by a rumor of relationship would be Evelyn's. If people caught wind of a scandal, they'd believe the worst of her, and the worst would be everywhere. After all, dead women sold stories. Add to that the unfounded allegations of a love triangle involving a cop and a prosecutor, and every smarmy television executive and newspaper editor would pump the story onto Web pages and cable stations 24/7, as though it were somehow true or relevant to the investigation. And Evelyn Carney would become the face of gruesome fantasy for predators and perverts to indulge in while passing their twisted judgment: sexy girls and girls who like sex got what they deserved, and sometimes that's death.

"A message that sells a million ads," he said, "but I don't see you unleashing it."

It was a stirring speech from a surprising source, and I really didn't think he believed a word of it. But that was Michael's genius. Everybody else in this city bought or bullied you into thinking their way. Not Michael. He figured out your fear and worked it against you.

I leaned forward on my elbows, staring him down. "You don't get to tell my news division what's worthy of our air. We make our own determinations of importance and relevance and yes, factor in sensitivity to the victim, independent of your preferences and those of other government officials." I paused. "Consider that fair warning, Michael. Don't get complacent."

"Back at you, love," he said with a grim smile. "Try not to forget that old saying about curiosity."

CHAPTER THIRTY-ONE

While I was spinning my wheels with Michael Ledger, Ben was charming the owner of a Georgetown gift shop into handing over her store's surveillance video. The shop was on M Street at the base of the Key Bridge, and its video came from the camera over the front door that recorded movement on the street. The video, date stamped the night Evelyn Carney was killed, showed a woman who appeared to be Evelyn as she walked past the store and waited at a traffic light to cross M Street. Clips from a few minutes later showed an empty sidewalk, but in the background, Ben could make out a motorcycle waiting at the light.

He was telling me this over the phone as I sped across town.

"Detectives wanted the original," Ben said, "but the owner only gave up a copy. She's not into what she calls the police state. Not sure if that's politics or paranoia, but lucky for us, she's a huge fan of the Fourth Estate, and thinks I — Ben Pearce — am her best defense against unlimited state power. So she gave me a copy, too. Cool, huh?"

"I'll start writing soon as I get there," I said into the speakerphone. "The surveillance video should go at the top of the script."

"Yep. Already called for it after the lead-in."

"You wrote the script already?" I said, and then: "Read it to me."

It was terrific, easily the best he'd ever written, and it gave me an uneasy feeling. Basically, Ben was born for television news, with the exception of his writing. That had been his Achilles heel. If that struggle was over, he needed no one. Not even me. Which was good, right?

"Well done, Ben."

He snorted. "Try not to sound as surprised as I was. What's your ETA, anyhow?"

Twenty minutes later I was rolling up on our satellite truck parked the wrong way on a cobblestone street at the corner of M. The truck, which blocked a loading zone, also took up two premier parking spots. The manager of the condominium that owned those spots was screaming and pointing at our truck operator, George. For just such occasions, George wore earbuds. If he listened to people shouting at him, he'd never find a place to put a truck that size.

I climbed out of my car into sheer chaos: Ben pleading with the condo manager screaming at George, who was bobbing his head to whatever music blasted in his earbuds as he worked the controls that lifted the satellite dish. Nelson scampered around them, running cables from the truck to his camera. The truck's motor thundered as the satellite dish went up with its weird pings and metallic groans.

"That woman whose body was found in the Potomac?" Ben was shouting over the sound of the motor. "She was last seen here. We can only be live from here."

"Not using my parking spaces," the manager said.

"There's important new information we have to report. Pictures that could identify the killer of a woman who walked *right past* your condominium."

The manager threated to have us towed.

I popped my trunk where my secret stash was kept and scooped an armful of sweatshirts embossed with our network's logo. What the hell, a stack of baseball caps, too.

I carried it all to Ben and dumped it wordlessly in his arms.

Ben offered the armful to the manager, who soon began nodding about this great misunderstanding. Wasn't it terrible what happened to the young woman? Sure we could stay, as long as we left the minute the show was over. Sending one last poisonous glare at George, the manager took the shirts and hats and stomped off.

Station swag. Worked every time.

"Come see the surveillance," Ben said, waving for me to follow him to the truck.

The video was black and white, and it jumped as Evelyn — or a woman who appeared to be Evelyn — moved quickly through the frames. She was swathed in a dark coat and her face was so pixelated that I couldn't make out her features, let alone her expression. We played with the zoom, but it only got worse.

"Video's terribly degraded," I said.

"Yeah," he sighed. "It's the copy of an original that wasn't great to begin with. But it's her, right? I mean, look at her."

"I can't see how it'd be anyone else. The location and the time stamp matches what Lil' Bit told us. But I think we need the ID to come from authorities."

"All right. Who works them? You or me?"

We batted the question around for a bit. The complication was this: investigators always released this kind of video to the media, and yet they'd been sitting on this for a week. We didn't want to run into an official telling us not to use it.

"Question is, why didn't the police put the video out to the public?" Ben said. "You think they're burying evidence?"

Certainly Michael had chosen not to tell me about the video. It was becoming increasingly clear that Michael had been feeding me just enough information to get what he wanted reported on air, while diverting my attention from Lil' Bit's motorcycle sighting, and now, from his acquaintance with Evelyn — or whatever the relationship was. What else was he hiding?

"It'd be interesting to know if MPD investigators shared this video with the prosecutor's office," I mused aloud. "Show me the other video."

The motorcycle was shot from too great a distance. You could tell it was a motorcycle with a rider, and you could watch the motorcycle move out of the frame, and that was all.

Nelson bounced over to us. "Director wants you in front of the camera," he told Ben. "Live tease at top of the hour."

"Be right there," Ben said, and then to me: "Do we use the motorcycle or not?"

We talked it out. I'd promised not to report the motorcycle *leaving the professor's homicide scene*. Now it was true, Michael Ledger was a lying jackass, but my promise was a promise, and a journalist who couldn't keep her promise was a hack. So we agreed the motorcycle was out of bounds for me and for reporting the professor's crime scene, but the surveillance of M Street that Ben had gotten from the shop owner? As long as he could get a confirmation from the prosecutor's office, it could be used.

I thought of one of Ben's lovelies: "That girl from the US Attorney's still crushing on you?" I teased.

"She's a source," he said, frowning. "Not a girl."

"Oh, right, sorry." It was the kind of dumb joke we used to make before that night in my office. Now it was poor taste. "Ignore me. Not my business anyway."

"It most certainly is."

I waved my hand for silence. "So this video —"

"Virginia, stop."

He was looking at me with warm dark eyes that crinkled in the corners, and his skin was burnished gold in the last of the day's

353

sun. Memories flickered from the night of the correspondents dinner, how I'd kissed him in my office and wrapped myself around his bulk and whispered those wild, needy words.

His smile spread slowly.

Nelson came up behind us. "If you'd stop making eyes at the talent," he complained to me, "maybe I could get him in front of the camera. Earth to Ben."

"Plenty of time," he said, still looking at me, and repeated: "I'm making it your business. You have the right to ask me about any relationship, and after we dig our way out of this story, I'm going to ask for that right in return. We're going to talk this out."

Terrifying thought.

"There's an open mike not five feet away," Nelson hissed.

Ben ignored him. "You owe me a talk, Virginia."

"I know it."

"As in, *the control room can hear you,*" Nelson said. "Now get in front of the damn camera."

Ben made a face. "Let me knock out this tease, then I'll make my strictly professional call."

He sauntered over to the camera and bent down, checking his hair in the lens, before he straightened again, giving his usual greeting, "Ben here, howdy," to the control room, and then he was on air. After the tease, he pulled off his microphone and draped it over the top of the camera and walked back to me, talking animatedly with his cell phone to his ear.

Ben's source at the prosecutor's office confirmed the motorcycle sighting on M Street but was unaware of any surveillance video. She was troubled that her office hadn't been told of what seemed a crucial piece of evidence, and promised to get answers from police officials as soon as she got off the phone. Soon, Ben's cell phone was ringing. One of his best police sources wanted Ben to hold off on reporting the motorcycle. When Ben asked for a valid investigatory or public safety reason, he got threats from someone he'd once considered a drinking buddy. Ben, who was always calm, was red-faced when he hung up the phone.

"Put the motorcycle video on air," he said curtly.

After the live shot in Georgetown was clear, I drove home to find a man camped out on my goddamn porch again. This time it was J. Thomas Winthrop, attorney for Ian Chase, sitting on my Adirondack chair as if it belonged to him. What did dudes not get about how uncool it was to jump out at night at a woman who lived alone?

I grabbed the Maglite under my driver's seat and got out to confront my visitor. "Did I miss your call?" I said. "Seriously, how hard is it to give a girl a head's-up that you're dropping by?"

He rose from the chair with great dignity. "I have information, on background for now. If you can corroborate, this interview could be used as the second source. You interested?"

"Who am I interviewing? You?"

"Do you have your phone on you?"

"Why?"

"Get rid of it or I walk."

I unlocked my front door and made a big show of dropping the phone on the entry table before resetting the alarm system and locking the door. When I turned back, my hands were up. "Afraid I'll record you?"

"Let's go." He escorted me down the walkway to a black Escalade parked at the corner and opened the door to the backseat, telling me to get in. The dome light was turned off, but in the gloom, I picked out blond hair, a proud tilt of a head. Ian Chase waited for me.

"Please," he said. "Can we talk?"

Winthrop slammed my door and rounded the Escalade to the driver's seat. We pulled from the curb in an awkward silence. When the Escalade turned onto Rock Creek Parkway, Ian began talking in a low, formal voice. "I know your source is well placed and you trust him, but please believe me, I've never struck a woman in my life. I'm not into — what your source told you. I never hit Evie. Not even accidentally."

"But you had a sexual relationship with Evelyn Carney?"

"Yes. I was in love with her."

The Escalade was taking the parkway curves at high speeds, and every now and again, we'd round a corner and the headlight from an oncoming car would fill the windshield and illuminate Ian's pallor before we were plunged in darkness again.

"She broke it off with me," he said. "That was nearly two months ago now. She had to stay with her husband, because he needed her. He wasn't well. She thought it better, easier, if we didn't contact each other. It was to be a clean break. Then one morning she called me out of the blue, asking if we could meet."

"That was the Sunday morning before she disappeared?"

He nodded. "I canceled dinner plans with friends from law school, giving excuses that police tell me sound suspicious. But you have to understand the state I was in. I let myself hope she was coming back. All night I waited for her."

It had to be asked. "Did you kill Evelyn?"

"No," he said with a catch in his breath, and then louder: "I didn't kill Evie."

His lawyer was watching me in the rear-view mirror. When our eyes met, he said, "My client has consented to a paternity test requested by the MPD. This is an absurd waste of time. Even if there is a DNA match, what crime does that prove? Certainly not homicide."

"I believe there will be a match," Ian said quietly.

Winthrop glanced in the mirror again. "When the results come back, we can expect another round of leaks from our dear friends in blue. We ask that you consider the results within the context of what Ian has told you, and also that you give our side a chance to respond."

"Yes, of course," I said.

Ian turned in his seat as streetlight flashed across his face, illuminating the high planes of his cheeks and long eyebrows over shadowed eyes. "You believe me, don't you?" he said.

"What you're telling me sounds credible."

That seemed to ease him. He settled back into the leather seat. "I keep thinking this part of it, at least, will go away. The longer they waste time trying to charge me, the more likely the real killer will get away with this. I hope the phone recovery helps them."

"Evelyn's phone?" I said, turning to him. "Investigators found it?"

Ian gazed at me curiously. "No, they have Brad Hartnett's. He didn't tell you?"

I felt completely at sea. "Who?"

"Your . . . *source,*" he said, bitterly, and then to Winthrop: "What goes on in his head? I understand protecting the investigation, but this isn't about her as a member of the press."

"So tell her," Winthrop said.

He said that Hartnett had left his cell phone in his apartment before he drove off to meet me on the night he was killed. During a search of Hartnett's apartment, investigators recovered his cell phone and turned it over to the FBI at Quantico, where it was examined by digital forensics. Agents found a spy app called CovertWizard installed on Hartnett's phone. CovertWizard, already under federal investigation, was known for

359

its ability to turn on phones remotely and record private conversations in violation of federal wiretapping laws.

"Agents traced the spy app on Hartnett's phone to an account on a server in suburban Virginia," Ian went on. "On the account, they found several other phone numbers, also targets. One number was for the phone that Evie carried the night she was killed. It's unclear who installed the app on her and Hartnett's phones, as it was registered to an alias and paid for by an offshore account."

It was complicated, but I thought I understood: "So agents found a spy app on Hartnett's phone. This was the same app monitoring Evelyn Carney's phone. Which is how she was tracked to the bridge, right? Someone followed her phone's movement, the same way Professor Hartnett was tracked to the grocery store parking lot?"

"It's the same suspect, yes. But the professor left his phone at home on the night he was killed. A lucky break for investigators."

I nodded.

"Most likely, the suspect overheard your plans to meet with Hartnett that night," he said, carefully — too carefully. "That's how the suspect knew where to find him."

That didn't make sense. "The suspect

bugged the phone Brad borrowed from his friend?"

"No," he said, gazing at me with a pity that unnerved me.

My mouth went dry. "They found my cell phone number on the account, didn't they?"

"Michael Ledger should have warned you." He paused and gave me a grim smile. "It appears that Evie's killer has been monitoring your phone, too."

CHAPTER THIRTY-TWO

The escalade dropped me off in front of my house. I went inside and locked the door, turning the safety bolt. On the entry table was my cell phone that Ian had told me was bugged.

It was unbelievable. Someone was listening in on my calls — me! I thought about calling the police on a landline, or maybe I could call Michael, and then I stopped myself. Michael already knew and hadn't told me. Why hadn't he told me?

What had Brad Hartnett warned? A conspiracy, he'd said. Justice might be in on it.

Which had sounded crazy, completely paranoid at the time, beyond the realm of possibilities. Then half an hour later, Brad Hartnett was shot to death. And his killer had tracked him by eavesdropping on my phone.

All right, no calls to Michael. Hell, I didn't know who I could trust. All I could think of was — run! But I had no idea who I was running from or where I could go or even if I'd know when I was safe.

So I picked up the cell phone and sat with it on the hard marble floor, willing myself to be calm. I would figure this out. I was always able to figure things out if I kept a clear head.

I approached it as I would a news story about anyone other than me. First, I tried to locate the app on the phone. See what information I could find on the registry. Part of me stayed focused, thumbing through the apps list and settings, much as I knew how, as another part of me listened to every creak and groan of the house and the street noises outside the door. After a long frustrating search, I gave up. I needed an expert's help.

Meantime, I could figure out how this happened. If there was an app on the phone, it had to have been installed, and if it was installed, someone had to have taken possession of my phone. I thought about the day my phone had gone MIA. It was the same day Evelyn's body had been recovered.

I went through the events of that day: calling the station at dawn for a live truck and crew. Seeing Evelyn's mutilated body, and that crippling panic attack I suffered after.

Had I lost the phone then? No, it was in my hip pocket after I'd climbed the ravine to the live truck and called in a script to the station.

So how about when I changed into the evening gown and drank whiskey in the office with Ben? Or after, when I escorted Michael to the correspondents dinner, and we socialized with dozens of colleagues? I couldn't see the phone anymore. Had I put the phone in my evening bag? Had someone stolen it from my bag?

Had Ben taken it? Had Michael?

Not Ben, no. That I couldn't believe.

Michael?

There were problems with suspecting Michael. For one thing, law enforcement had access to devices more sophisticated than a spy app. If Michael wanted to monitor me, he wouldn't risk stealing my phone to put an app on it.

If not Michael, then whom?

I had a terrifying thought. My phone was always within arm's reach, so whoever had taken it was someone who'd gotten close, someone I liked and trusted, a part of my inner circle. I let few people that close.

Who had slipped past my guard?

The next morning, I went into the office

early. I went through my usual routine, checking the newspapers and television news websites. None of my competitors had anything on the spy app. That was good for us professionally — we weren't getting beat — but not so good for me personally. Just this once, I wouldn't mind getting answers from the newspaper.

I was off to a good start researching spyware when Ben burst into my office, looking like he'd slept in his clothes. Beneath the brim of his ball cap, his eyes were wild. "Where's your phone?" he said.

So the news was out. Dammit. I put my finger to my lips to shush him and plucked the phone from my satchel and carried it to the newsroom, where I left it next to some noisy scanners.

When I returned, Ben was sitting on my sofa, scowling at me. "My source at MPD wanted me to warn you about your phone. It appears you already know."

"I found out late last night." I told him everything. How Ian got the information from his friends at the FBI, that the digital forensic guys tracked the app to a server that hid the user's true identity, but that agents were also nearly certain it was the same user who'd tracked Evelyn and Brad

Hartnett. "At first, this seemed . . . worri-some."

"Being stalked *worried* you?" he said dryly.

"Well, okay, it scared me. But now that I've thought about it, the app could be useful. You know, if we can figure out how to track it back to the suspect."

Ben was staring at me, slack-jawed, as if I'd lost my mind.

Not exactly the response I had hoped for.

"Admittedly, it's a little out of the box," I said. "Think about it. The app is a piece of evidence, like a fingerprint. Now we find who it belongs to."

"Are you insane?" he said, springing up from the sofa. He began pacing. "You just said this suspect probably killed two people. What if this guy isn't just curious about what people are telling you? Have you thought of that? You could get hurt . . . or *worse.*"

"Of course I've thought of it." But I'd also thought of Brad Hartnett as he'd been in the front seat of the Pathfinder. He'd been my source, and he'd been killed bringing information to me. It'd been my duty to protect him, and I'd failed.

I had to try to use the app. Shouldn't I at least try? "I'm open to suggestions about how to minimize the risk."

"My suggestion?" he said. "Throw the damn phone into the Potomac."

"No, Ben, think about it. Wouldn't it be satisfying to catch the killer using the phone he bugged? Then we point a TV camera into whatever hellhole he's hiding in and his face would be everywhere. Then he's on the run, not me."

"Worst idea I've ever heard," he said, but I could tell he was thinking about it. I gave him the time he needed. Finally, his shoulder moved in that impatient way of his, and he frowned, saying, "You have to carry a burner phone, in case you need to talk to me or call for help. That's nonnegotiable."

"So you'll help?"

"What a question. You know I will," he said. "First things first, let's have Isaiah take a look at your phone."

I was shaking my head. "The less people who know, the better. Besides, Isaiah is already stressed about Mellay and the layoffs, and he's not particularly supportive of me working this story. The last thing he needs is one more thing to worry about."

His eyes narrowed. "In other words, you know he'll try to talk you out of this harebrained idea?"

"He won't succeed," I said. "So why argue about it?"

Ben reached into his pocket and pulled out the pocketknife that had been a gift from his father and that he carried with him always. He gazed fondly at it, caressing the worn ivory handle, and then held it out to me.

"This is more good luck charm than anything else," he said. "A weapon of last resort."

CHAPTER THIRTY-THREE

It's easy to keep your game face on when you're surrounded by friends and coworkers and a team of security guards. The television station was a safe place, where I felt invulnerable, free. But driving to my empty house was altogether different. My anxiety grew with each block. I turned into my neighborhood and slowed as I went past the cathedral. The red light in its tower was blinking over me like a weary eye.

I circled my block, looking for a parking space. On the second pass, I noticed the car. It was a clunker, boxy-brown 1990s sedan, parked in front of my neighbor's house. My headlights flashed across the rear window, showing someone in the driver's seat. The car had no lights on, no engine running, and it was parked facing my house — the perfect vantage point. Exactly where I'd park for a stakeout.

Was someone staking out my house?

As I drove past, I sank a little in my seat, which was silly. If someone had my address, they probably got the make of my car, too. At the end of the block I swung the car against the curb under the stop sign. It was an illegal spot, too close to the intersection, but made for an easy getaway. I killed the lights and sat with the engine running, my knuckles white against the steering wheel, working up the nerve to walk past the clunker to my house.

There was an old trick I'd learned from bouncing between foster homes: act like you feared nothing, and the fear would ease. I reached under the seat for the heavy Maglite. Its weight and the texture of its barrel felt good in my hand. *Fear nothing,* I told myself again, and climbed out of the car.

Halfway to my front door, headlights came on and flooded the street. I was caught in the light, blinded for an awful moment before I ran. An engine revved and the light slid away as the clunker made a u turn and sped off.

It wasn't until I was behind the locked door in my house that I realized: *the license plate.* Goddamn it all to hell, I ran instead of getting the tag numbers. Isaiah could have used them to get the owner's name. We could have known the identity of the stalker, now, tonight.

How could I be so goddamn stupid?

Maybe it was all too much. The murder of my source. The bugged phone. The stakeout of my house. Maybe I couldn't handle this alone. Maybe I should call Ben. He'd know what to do. Ben would help me. And then I caught my reflection in the mirror beside the door.

My lips were bloodless, and my skin pale as death. It was the scared little woman face that mocked everything I'd worked for. The face of a woman too frightened to break news stories, who let other people take her risks, the real journalists who were no less vulnerable to bullets or blackjacks or stalking but who had somehow found the courage to carry out a simple plan. I had nothing but disdain for this face. I dropped the bugged phone on the table and raced up the stairs two at a time.

In my bedroom, I pulled off my dark suit and tossed it onto the bed before changing into my old American U sweatshirt and a pair of nylon running pants. My tangled hair got swept back in a tight ponytail. I went to the bathroom sink and scrubbed my skin until the blood was back in my face. That was a start. Not such a scared rabbit now.

I thought of Paige Linden, how she'd been

that first night I met her, decisive, indomitable, prepared for whatever the world threw at her. She'd moved like an athlete — if an injured one. Something about her shoulder during a training session. For self-defense, she'd said. My mind seized on the idea. Paige Linden would have known what to do tonight. She would have stood her ground and gotten that goddamn license plate number. She would have kept her wits about her. Why couldn't I be more like Paige Linden?

From downstairs, I retrieved the burner phone that Ben had gotten me and placed a call to Paige to find out where she trained. She didn't pick up.

What had she told me about the gym? Not its name, but that it was across town, somewhere off of Georgia Avenue. There were listings for several gyms fitting that description, and I called them all, dropping Paige's name as a reference. During the last call, a gruff-sounding trainer turned friendly and asked how Paige was. He offered an introductory class.

"Can you teach me to kick ass? That's what I really need."

The guy laughed. "You know it. Kicking ass is what we do."

"Sign me up."

■ ■ ■ ■

The gym was in an old warehouse near the Fourth District police station. It had a reception area that was clean but utilitarian with folding chairs and an old-fashioned water fountain that hummed. Dozens of trophies were lined in a glass case. A young woman behind the counter glanced up from her *Essence* magazine. When I told her I was looking for Leroy, she gave me the once-over. "You the police?"

That made me laugh. "No, a prospective student."

She smiled widely and asked, "Why didn't you say so?" and set her open magazine flat on the counter before she went to the door. She curled her fingers that had long red nails like talons and punched a button with her knuckle. The door clicked open.

This gym was for real. No warmed hand towels or juice bars or fancy cardio machines with LCD monitors. This was for serious athletes — punching bags and pull-up bars and thick mats for throw downs and free weights that ran the length of a wall. A boxing ring was in the middle of it all. Sweat smells competed with lemon cleaner and oiled leather. Not a bad mix, surprisingly. Deep male laughter rose and fell amid the trash talking, and coursing through the laughter, the percussive *bump, bada, bump, bada* of go-go pumping out of speakers.

The receptionist cupped her hands around her mouth and shouted "Leroy" toward a group of men. A clean-shaven, fifty-something man of carved muscle separated from the others and approached us with a grin. A diamond stud winked in his ear.

"You a friend of my girl's?" he said in a thick Gulf accent. He told me any friend of Paige's gets a free session with him. "We're all so proud of Paige, coming up like she did. Her daddy and me, we go way back. Since she was no bigger than a minute."

How this friendly man knew Paige's family, he didn't say, nor could I get a word in edgewise. Leroy was on a roll about his Paige. "I haven't seen her since I don't know when. Got to be months. Guess she's getting ready for her politics. Always said she'd run the world, and you best believe what Paige says, she'll do. How's she been anyway?"

That confused me. "You didn't see her last week? Are we talking about the same Paige *Linden*? Blond hair, athletic, couple of inches taller than I am?"

"That's my girl, yeah."

I glanced around the gym, wondering if I'd come to the wrong place after all. "But she trains here regularly, right? Well, not this week. Not since she was injured — when was it, last Tuesday?"

"Paige *hurt* herself?"

She'd told me about it that first night I'd met her, when she held out my coffee, barely able to lift her arm. Slowly, trying to remember the details, I said: "She'd been sparring at the gym — this one, I thought — and took a hard jab to the shoulder. Said she'd been distracted with worry about a friend."

He held up a huge fist, playfully. "Well, you tell Miss Thing she's in serious trouble with old Leroy. Getting herself beat up in somebody else's gym. Sparring with somebody who don't know what he's doing."

There were lots of gyms in town, I reasoned. She'd spoken of this gym, when she'd meant another. But the mix-up was troubling. Paige Linden was my best source, central to our reporting of Evelyn's story. What else had I misunderstood?

"So how do you know Paige's father?" I said.

I left the gym in a hurry and drove home to

put in another call to Paige. Her voice mail picked up again: *"I'm out of the office until Friday. If you need immediate assistance, call my secretary — "*

Well, I'd have to find her, that's all. She had to explain why she misled me. Of course, everybody misled the press. Many flat-out lied. We called it spin, to be polite about it, because what else could you do? You couldn't go around calling people liars. Nobody would talk to you if you did.

Why mislead me with information as innocuous as how she grew up? She led me to believe she was a social peer of Ian Chase, born into comfortable affluence with a family name that opened doors to the law and politics. I'd asked for none of it.

She told me she'd mentored Evelyn, taught her how to behave in a professional setting, how to dress and wear her hair and tone down her makeup. She'd even nixed Evelyn's shoes. All of which seemed oddly controlling, narcissistic, now that I thought about it. Had she tried to turn Evelyn into a mini-Paige? Or had none of it happened? Had it all been a lie, too?

If Leroy was to be believed, Paige Linden grew up in a much less stable environment than Evelyn. Paige's father had served with Leroy as a mechanic in the Coast Guard, and had been discharged after another "dustup" with the local police. Leroy described Paige's father as a man who liked to drink, and when drunk, liked to fight, sometimes with the police. After his discharge, Paige's family had bounced from place to place, struggling to make ends meet.

Paige had told me Ian Chase struck her during sex. Last night, Ian said he'd never struck any woman, ever, and I found him credible — which was a very serious problem. Much of my reporting had relied on Paige's narrative. If Paige Linden was a liar, then that reporting was in trouble. I was in trouble.

I went to the freezer and pulled out a bottle of Absolut and poured it. I carried the glass to the kitchen table and sat down to rethink what we'd reported. Across the table were the pictures I'd collected. That first missing person poster of Evelyn, her face a dark mask with those creepy eyes. The wedding photograph of Peter dancing with Evelyn. The cutaway shot of Evelyn gazing ardently at Ian Chase.

In an outer ring, the other photographs: Ian at the podium. Paige's law firm portrait. Professor Hartnett from the George Washington University website, which was the picture we'd been using on our air. Surveillance from the gift shop in Georgetown: the frame of Evelyn at the crosswalk to the bridge, another of the motorcycle and rider, its detail lost in the distance.

A photograph of Michael belonged next to Paige's, since the information he gave me echoed hers. No, not an echo. More like a duet of alternating calls, him then her: Michael leaking Ian's alleged violence with his lovers, Paige confirming. Did those allegations come from Paige? Or had he asked Paige to lie for him?

At the Dubliner today, Michael had admitted running into Evelyn on the Hill, once when Paige had been with her. At the time, his reference to Paige slipped by me, but now I wondered, what was Paige to Michael? An acquaintance? A friend? An informant?

I turned on my laptop and ran searches of Michael Ledger and Paige Linden together, looking for intersections or signs of relationship or connections to people they might know, but found no direct links.

There was a wonderful photograph of Michael from a *Washingtonian* feature, several years old now. The article profiled Michael's pursuit of a killer over the Canadian border and into the wilds of the Northwest Territories, where Michael pulled his suspect from a remote shack near the Arctic Circle. Glancing at the article, you'd never know Michael had worked with a task force made up of Canadian authorities and federal agents. No, this feature story read like Jack London fiction: Michael the hero who fought man and nature and won. Its photo gallery seemed more like a promotion for a feature film, with the last picture showing off the rugged good looks of a younger, and airbrushed, Michael Ledger, relaxed in a black leather jacket, his dark hair ruffled against a cantankerous DC sky.

He was astride a motorcycle.

I blinked, unable to believe what I was seeing. The make was written boldly in silver letters across the gas tank, the same make that Lil' Bit had described seeing on the Key Bridge with Evelyn.

One of them monster bikes, Lil' Bit had said. *Loud as the devil himself.*

Michael had a Triumph.

Next to the computer screen, I held up the surveillance photo of the rider turning onto Key Bridge. The photo was shot from too great a distance, but I could make out its basic shape, which appeared similar.

There must be hundreds of motorcycles like it in the District, I reminded myself.

This particular article was nearly four years old. If Michael had once owned this Triumph, he may have sold it by now. There could be any number of explanations.

On the burner phone, I texted Isaiah for a list of all vehicles registered to Michael's name and address and any other residents of that address. Anything owned within the last five years.

Isaiah called back immediately, sputtering: "As in *Commander Ledger*? MPD? What the hell am I looking for?"

"A motorcycle."

CHAPTER THIRTY-FOUR

The eleven o'clock news had gone to commercial break when Paige Linden returned my call. I didn't want to talk on the phone. I wanted to watch Paige's face when she explained why she lied to me. "Can you meet first thing tomorrow?" I said. "Earlier the better."

She put me on hold on while she checked her calendar. It seemed her morning was booked solid. "Why not now?" she said. "I just got back from out of town, and I'm all revved up. Sleep's not happening anytime soon."

I went to the front windows and peeked through the gap in the curtains. The clunker was parked in front of my house again. It was impossible to tell if anyone was in the car. I stepped back, saying, "I need a few minutes to get ready." Not to mention the time needed to ditch the clunker.

"I'll be awake." She gave me her address.

I went through my house and flicked off every light as I would when turning in for the evening. The last room to go dark was my bedroom. I sat on the bed and waited for what felt like forever but was probably only fifteen minutes or so. I shoved the burner phone into my jacket pocket and felt my way through the dark hallway and down the stairs to the back door. The alley was clear. A couple of dogs barked as I sprinted to the car half a block away. If my ride was being watched, there was nothing to do.

But no one followed. Not that I could tell anyway.

Paige Linden answered her door, dressed in all black, a gritty column of boots and jeans and long-sleeved T-shirt. Her ash blond hair was a windblown mess, and she was giving off an odd vibe I couldn't pinpoint. Was this Paige being "revved up?" Nervous? Excited? Whatever it was, she nearly pulsed with it.

We stood in her foyer. I explained that Ian Chase was no longer a person of interest in Evelyn's homicide. The whole theory had fallen apart, and federal investigators were now involved, pursuing another angle entirely. I paused, waiting for her reaction. She merely watched me, silently, without expression.

"The old theory relied on a rumor of Ian's violence with sexual partners," I reminded her. "Allegations that you confirmed."

"No," she said, evenly. "I didn't."

"You didn't what?"

"I confirmed no such thing."

"Yes," I said emphatically. "You did."

"I told you Ian hit me once. I do not allow myself to be hit."

"You said you'd dated Ian Chase long ago but that he was rough in bed, and you broke up with him when he hit you near your eye. That was your exact quote. Where you said he hit you, by the way, is the same area where Evelyn was struck, a detail left out of our reporting. Something only the police and the medical examiner know. Did someone in the police department ask you to tell me that?"

She held my stare. Her pupils were enlarged, giving her eyes a strange, vacant look, and I had no idea what she was thinking.

"Ian denied hitting any woman ever," I said.

"What do you expect him to say? What do men like him say?" She was growing angry and trying hard not to show it. It would be bad to anger her before I got answers. She might kick me out.

I blew out a breath. "Okay, let me start over. Maybe we're getting caught up in the language. When Ian hit you, it was during a sexual encounter, right? So maybe what you called hitting was what he thought of as role play?"

"Look, you asked me a question I didn't want to answer," she said with scorn. "But I trusted you weren't one of those sellouts forever questioning the integrity of a woman but never the man." She came closer, moving like an athlete does, strong and graceful, until she was towering over me. "Even if I prove he hurt me, there's always another hoop, isn't there? If I didn't want it, why didn't I *do something*? As if recourse existed, especially against a law-enforcement official. So instead of giving an answer you won't believe anyway, maybe I should ask — why are you selling me out?"

I felt my face flush but wouldn't let her unsettle me. "I met your friend Leroy at his gym. He said he's known you since you were a child. His depiction of your childhood was very different than what you'd offered up — information I never asked you for."

"You asked Leroy about Dad?" she said almost wistfully.

"So that's another inconsistency. Have

you been lying to me, Paige?"

She inclined her head, staring at me for a long moment.

"Don't you understand?" I said angrily. "I can't use any of your information if you lie to me. I *hate* lies."

"That's not what you hate."

"Oh yes, more than anything, lies are precisely what I hate."

"What you hate," she said, "is that you understand that particular lie too well. Yes, I lied about where I came from, because I'm ashamed of it — in that very same way you're ashamed of your old life."

My jaw clenched shut. I didn't trust myself to speak.

"What you also understand? How that shame pushes us to succeed, to take control over our life, even when it drags at us. Strange gift, isn't it?" Her voice dropped and took on a musical sound that was lulling. "First day I met you, I recognized how alike we are. It was in what you said about the investigators, how you question everything. It's even in the way you move."

"The way . . . I move?" I said, feeling my face go hot again.

"Your watchfulness. The way you look over your shoulder. You expect everyone to deceive you, don't you? Even the people who care." She paused, and nodding, said, "But I was glad to see you felt better after visiting your father."

Through my teeth, I managed: "How the hell . . . do you know . . . about that?"

"I called last weekend about the story," she said. "Your office told me you'd gone out of town for a family emergency. I was concerned. After everything you've done for Evelyn, for the help you gave me at the vigil, the least I could do is ask if you needed anything."

We were caught in a stare down. Her eyes were calm and clear. I was anything but. My temper whipped viciously against a vague awareness that I was probably over-reacting.

You expect everyone to deceive you, even people who care.

About that, at least, she was right.

"Listen, I don't talk about certain things," I said. "It's not because I'm ashamed or have an issue with authority. I don't discuss those things *because they're mine.*"

She took a quick step back. A hurt look crossed her face. "I hadn't meant to upset you. I invited you here to tell you about — well, it really doesn't matter now. You don't trust me, and I get it, believe me." She went to the door. "Maybe you should go."

"Tell me what?"

Her hands went up in a defensive position. "That I saw your news tonight. Whatever. It's not something we should discuss now."

I eyed her suspiciously. "What about my news?"

"There was a motorcycle in the story about Evelyn," she said, sighing. "I wanted to run it past you, before I called the police. I have an idea where it could be."

CHAPTER THIRTY-FIVE

The vodka I'd drunk earlier must've made me slow, almost stupid. My head was damn near spinning. "You recognized the motorcycle in the surveillance photo?" I sputtered. Talk about burying the lead. "Where is it?"

She glanced away with that hurt look again. "You won't believe me."

"Why not?"

"You don't trust me," she said. "Maybe I shouldn't trust you, either."

It was the way she said it — *maybe I shouldn't trust you* — as if she wanted to, or needed to. As if she had no one else, which is why she'd called me.

I apologized for quarreling with her, for thinking the worst, and for making judgments before giving her a chance to explain.

She hesitated. "I don't know."

"Please tell me."

She began with a vague story about the District, how its people were crowded too close together, tangled by the same roots. Take Michael and Ian and Evelyn, she said. Turns out they'd run into each other far more often than Michael had led me to believe. It could be like that in a city so small, especially in that smaller federal center around the courts and the Hill.

During the time Paige had dated Ian, she'd heard tell of his long-standing animosity for Michael Ledger, who Ian called an upstart who never saw a line he wouldn't cross. Paige took Ian's word for it. She'd heard of Michael's exploits and seen him around, but had avoided him until last summer.

After a big win at court, she treated Evelyn to a drink at the Dubliner. Michael approached them at the bar, introducing himself to Paige. Could he buy Paige and her friend a drink? He was more charming than Ian had described. He told funny tales and was particularly attentive to Evelyn. It was an enjoyable evening, but it was also a work night. Paige drank a glass of wine and then left Evelyn with Michael and headed home. After that, she saw Michael from time to time, and always he went out of his way to say hello.

Last Monday, he called her office, asking if Paige knew where Evelyn might be. "He told me someone had reported Evie missing," she said. "He was looking into it personally. I knew she'd missed work without calling in, but nothing more. He asked that if anything came to mind, could I be in touch?"

"And did you reach out?"

"Sure," she said. "He's the head of Criminal Investigations concerned about Evie. And it seemed to me at the time, a nice enough man. I called him with even the silliest rumors, just as he asked. We talked often. I came to like him a lot more than I'd expected. When I started hearing things about my firm, I wanted to tell him, but wasn't quite sure if I trusted him enough."

"What kind of things?"

"The kind you can't report, okay?" she said.

It was funny the way she said it. For a moment, she sounded so like Michael, and then she began telling me about auditors seen upstairs in Bernadette's suite of offices. A well-regarded private eye had been hired. There was talk of misuse of funds, money stolen, but nobody knew for sure. Bernadette Ryan wasn't talking.

"You told Michael the rumors?"

"Well, yes — but not immediately." Her hand sifted through her hair nervously. "It was a difficult decision. What if auditors had nothing to do with Evie's death? Telling a police official about rumor of a financial crime is pretty much the same as making a report. Nobody wants law enforcement nosing around the books. And this is my firm, which I have an ownership stake in, where all my money is tied up. Then again, I also have an obligation to Evie. Should I have waited for the firm to finish its due diligence?"

"You told him?"

"On the drive home from a late night at the office, I thought, the hell with it. I was tired of the indecision and called Michael from the car. His cell phone signal was going in and out, but I understood that he was having car problems, and was stranded near the Chain Bridge, which is literally minutes from here." She gestured to the ground on which we stood. "So I drove out to help him, but he wasn't there."

"Where was he?"

"I drove up and down Chain Bridge Road several times. No Michael. No broken-down car. Finally, I figured I heard him wrong, blamed it on the bad cell phone signal, and headed back to the city. That's when I saw him, stepping out of the woods."

"What was he doing there?"

She lifted her shoulders. "No idea. But he was not happy to see me, I can tell you that. He took the ride, grudgingly, as if he were doing me some favor. He was quiet the whole ride. When I told him about the auditors and private eye, he said, great, we'll look into it. Totally blew me off."

I tried to see it but couldn't. Not any of it. Michael was not a woodsy guy, and why would he hang out there at night? "You said it was late, right? Can you break down the tick-tock for me?"

"Between around nine thirty, maybe close to ten, on Wednesday —"

"Wednesday?"

"Yeah, I get stuck late at work every Wednesday night. That's when we do the conference call with our partners on the West Coast."

Wednesday was the night Brad Hartnett was killed. "You must be mistaken," I said. "Michael was at headquarters that night, not the woods. The lieutenant told me to wait at the scene for Michael. He said Michael was coming from downtown."

She stared at me, dumbstruck. "Your lieutenant was wrong, or he lied for Michael," she said finally. "On the night Brad was killed, Michael Ledger was in my car, getting a ride from the bridge to his house in upper northwest."

With the same sick feeling that came every time I thought of that night, I made myself remember the conversation with Brad, the promise to meet him at the diner, how I'd held open the door by the cashier stand and surveyed the patrons, looking for him. The neon clock above the counter read 9:07 when I heard the shots.

After that, everything was a blur. I'd made it to the satellite truck in time to call in a script and prepare Heather for the live shot at the top of the eleven o'clock show. But I'd only just made it. Michael had been the holdup. He'd made me answer those questions.

Attribute to me what those boys told you, except for the motorcycle, he'd said. *We can't have you reporting the motorcycle.*

I put my hand over my throat. "You recognized the motorcycle on the news?"

"From the night I met Michael at the Dubliner. There was one like it, parked out front, bold as day. You couldn't help but notice it. It was a big, flashy bike."

"A Triumph?"

She nodded. "He mentioned it at the bar. Promised to give Evie a lift home, if she didn't mind riding on the back of a motor-cycle."

I wondered if she understood what she was suggesting about Michael Ledger, legendary detective, police official. One step at a time, I thought. "You drove up and down Chain Bridge Road and there was no car broken down, as he'd told you."

"No car."

"You spotted Michael Ledger coming out of the woods, alone?" I said, and when she nodded, I went on: "How did he behave when he got in your car?"

"You know how he's always flirty and chatty and quick with the crime stories? Not that night. It's like his brain was somewhere else entirely."

Because he was thinking about what he'd just done? Dumped his motorcycle used in a homicide off of Chain Bridge Road? Hiding evidence for the killer?

Was he the killer?

The bridge was four or five miles from the crime scene. Given the lack of traffic in the late evening, it would have been easy to get to the bridge in fifteen minutes, max. The shooting occurred at 9:08. Paige picked Michael up sometime after nine thirty but before ten.

Was I really thinking Michael Ledger was involved in the murder of Brad Hartnett?

"You think he dumped his Triumph?"

Her lip trembled. She bit it. "It sounds crazy, right?"

I dug the burner phone from my satchel and brought up a satellite map of the bridge and held the screen out to her. "Show me where. Since it's so close, I'll swing by. Take a look."

"*Now?* It's late."

I explained that lots of news happened late at night. If there was a piece of evidence dumped in a lonely place in the dark of the night, we had to get video of it. That's what we did. But I also told her not to worry. I'd go alone, quickly, without her. She was a source and should go nowhere near evidence, and I'd protect her identity. What I didn't say: no way would I let what happened to Brad Hartnett happen to her.

"If I find a motorcycle, I'll report it to the authorities as an anonymous tip." Which wasn't a lie. I'd promised Paige Linden anonymity from the beginning.

She studied the map for some time, widening the screen and playing with the zoom, moving the map around in frustration. "I can't say definitively from this view."

"Take your time."

She glanced up from the phone with a frown. "We should let the police handle this."

"Not until morning, please." I begged her. If there was a motorcycle, I had to get a shot of it before the police impounded it inside the garage at Mobile Crime, where I'd never get a picture. Or, if my worst imaginings were even remotely true, that this was the police corruption Brad had hinted at, I had to get to it before they destroyed it as evidence or dumped it where it'd never be found.

I took the burner phone from her and shoved it into my pocket and turned to the door to go.

"You're going out there, aren't you?" she said quietly.

"Yes."

"Maybe if I drove out with you? I might recognize the spot if I see it."

It was a bad idea. I should have argued, but if I were to have a chance in hell of finding this bike? "It would make things easier," I agreed reluctantly. "If you stay in the car. Out of sight." And then I thought about it some more. "There's a reason we protect witness identities, you know? It could be dangerous."

She laughed nervously. "Then we'd better go quickly, before I think better of it."

From the trunk of my car, I pulled out my

video camera. It was the latest model Canon, a nifty little professional grade with a terrific lens. I replaced its batteries and those of my Maglite, too.

We climbed into the car and started up the road under yellow lights that blinked over sleeping neighborhoods. My eyes flickered to the rearview mirror, but no one followed. The streets were empty.

A game plan was playing out in my head: if I found a motorcycle, I'd shoot it before calling a real photographer — Nelson, if I could wake him. When Nelson arrived, he could keep an eye on the scene while I drove Paige home. After Paige was tucked safely away, I'd call the authorities, and Nelson could shoot police activity when they arrived. It was a good, workable plan. Best of all, it would get Paige back home in a hurry.

I glanced over at her. She was staring ahead, her posture rigid and the muscles in her neck protruding. My Maglite was in her lap. She was fiddling with it anxiously, clicking it on and off. The clicks were setting off my nerves.

"You're going to run down my new batteries," I said in a gentle voice.

She flinched, glancing down as if only now noticing the flashlight, and said, "Oh, yeah," with a sigh and turned it off again.

We were on Canal Road now, following the river out of the city. I forgot how dark the night could be. Dark video was bad video. "Wish I had a light kit," I muttered. "Even a floodlight would do."

She lifted the heavy Maglite. "I can help," she said, pointing the flashlight outward like a sword, showing off the lean muscles of her strong arm, and if she could hold the light steady, it might even work.

The car went silent again, except for Paige fidgeting on the leather seat.

"Don't worry." I hoped to sound more convincing than I felt. "It'll be fine."

CHAPTER THIRTY-SIX

The chain bridge was the smallest of the Potomac crossings, connecting upper Northwest DC to the tony Virginia suburbs. The bridge had a remote feeling, surrounded as it was by federal parkland and estates on the cliffs high above. Just beyond the bridge, Paige told me to slow down. "This is it," she said, indicating a gap in the trees. "Where I picked Michael up."

I turned into a small, unpaved pullover lot that was surrounded by trees. There was no light of any kind. It was hard to figure out the lot's purpose. A lover's lane? A pullover for road crews? A surveillance hide-away for police? It was impossible to say. There were no nearby stores or restaurants or neighborhoods, nothing except the woods and the bridge and the river far below.

"He was over there." She was pointing toward the farthest corner of the lot, where the brush and tree limbs had taken over. Its darkness seemed impenetrable. On the opposite side closest to the bridge, a low wall made of stone kept cars from pitching over the cliff. I backed the car against the wall and aimed the headlights where Paige had pointed.

We got out. It was spooky quiet.

"Stay by the car," I told her, taking the Maglite. With the camera slung across my shoulder, I walked through the high beams. There was no sign of any motorcycle, nothing being wheeled or dragged across the lot. Only an old fishing lure and crushed beer can. No sign of any vehicle at all, dammit.

"You sure it was here?" I called back over my shoulder.

From across the lot: "Yes," she shouted.

The trees were tall and thick, and the overgrown brambles formed a barrier in the gap between the trees that was impassable. I swung the flashlight like a searchlight and came across a good-sized break that tunneled deep into the woods. By the looks of the broken edges of the branches, a large animal had passed through — a bear, a buck, a man. No way to know without following the trail.

But I didn't like it. Anything could be back there. Anyone.

"What's wrong?" Paige said. She'd come

up from behind me, startling me.

I put my finger to my lips, listening for movement. There was the sound of the wind high in the trees, and that was all.

She guided my hand holding the flashlight and whispered, "What's that?" A piece of fabric fluttered on a branch. It was a narrow strip, black, maybe two inches long. She plucked it off the branch and handed it to me.

It felt smooth, silky. A delicate texture from an article of expensive clothing, perhaps a scarf or the tail of a shirt, the lining of a coat, something like that.

"What was Michael wearing?" I whispered.

She struggled to remember. "We were in the car such a short time. A dark jacket, I think. Maybe leather. Yes, I think that's right. It had that distinctive smell of leather."

The witness to Brad Hartnett's murder, Darius, had said the shooter wore a trench coat. Black leather. *Badass* —

"Like the one Samuel Jackson wore in *Shaft*?" I murmured.

"Who?"

Deep in the woods there was the shriek of an owl followed by the cry of its prey, disturbingly like the cry of an injured child.

401

I shouldn't be here. But then I chastised myself: that was an owl, not an omen. I was letting my imagination run wild, when I should be doing my job. Sometimes that job meant coming up on crime scenes at night and running through alleys and banging on lonely doors, never knowing who might be on the other side.

But this was different. I was afraid of the dark woods, the way they closed you in, trapped you. The thought of going into those woods made me light-headed, yet I knew I was going to do it.

"Are you scared?"

"Go back to the car," I said in a voice surprisingly steady. "You're my source. I don't know how to protect you here."

"You think I'm afraid of a bunch of trees? A herd of deer?"

"No, Paige, but it's not a good idea. Not for you."

"I'll admit it. I was scared in the car, but not now. Now I want to know if he was hiding something." She put out her hand. "Give me the flashlight."

She slipped her hand through the silk cord at the base of the Mag and slid sideways through the gap in the trees.

"Paige, slow down."

But she was gone. I heard her stumbling

around, and then there was silence. It was as if the woods had swallowed her up.

"Goddamn it, wait!" I went in after her. Thorns and branches scratched me, catching my hair and clothing, and then I was through the brambles and in some kind of clearing. I could feel its openness, but it was too dark to tell its size. The fragrance of pine and moist earth and decayed leaves was strong.

"Over here," Paige said from some distance. A beam slid across the forest floor between us, lighting a path. "Watch your step," she said.

Beneath my foot, a downed branch cracked with what seemed the loudest sound in the world. Only a little farther, I told myself. Just a few more steps. I reached out and put my hand on Paige's shoulder like a swimmer who'd gone too deep reaches for the pool wall.

"What is this place?" I whispered.

"Some kind of camp . . . look." She swung the beam across the ground. There were remnants of an old fire and some crushed beer cans, their labels long worn away. The beam of light moved outward along the perimeter and then to the farthest edge of the clearing where it met the trees — and bounced across a flash of chrome.

"Hold it," I said excitedly.

The light jerked back, and there it was, caught in the beam — a beautiful beast of a motorcycle. Muscular and dangerous looking and as thrillingly sexy as only bad can be. Even at rest it gave the appearance of heart-stopping speed.

From my shoulder I slipped the camera and clicked the record button, and when the red light came on, crept up slowly on the bike, as if it were a mirage that might disappear with one wrong move.

My palm ran along its cover that was as cool and smooth as glass. The windscreen was shaped aggressively. How well this bike suited its rider. I sorted through my memory that captured every piece of video I'd ever seen, even those I'd rather forget, and honed in on Michael's photograph in the *Washingtonian* article.

Under a gray sky. Squat white building in the background — police headquarters. Michael, bigger than life, astride his Triumph, hands resting comfortably — no, that wasn't right — resting *possessively* on the handlebars. Seated so tall, proud —

Something didn't fit this motorcycle. What was it?

I took a step back, setting down the camera. It was something about the handlebars. Something was . . . different.

"What is it?" Paige said in a terrified whisper.

It made no sense. This was the same make and model and color, the same bold *Triumph* written across the gas tank in exactly the same way. In every way, in fact, this bike matched the one in the photograph — every way, that is, except the angle of the handlebars . . .

The answer was a punch to the heart. I spun around, looking for Paige. "We have to get out of here," I said, breathlessly. "Back to the car."

She aimed the beam at my face, blinding me, and then suddenly the light went out. We were plunged into a darkness that felt alive with menace, that seemed to be breathing, and then I realized the sound was my own short, panicked gasps.

I reached out to get my bearings. "Paige?"

"I'm here," she said quietly.

She clicked the Mag on again, holding it to her side, pointing downward and creating a narrow circle of light on the forest floor. My eyes were already adjusting, and I glimpsed the faintest outline of her body.

Tall and strong, narrow, thin-hipped —
Bitch hips.

The witness, Darius. What did he say?

"Makes you look like you got bitch hips."

A woman's hips.

A woman —

The world turned upside down, nightmarish, dazing me. The words tumbled out: "It was *you*?" No more than a whisper. "*You* killed Brad? Evelyn?"

She came toward me slowly, and in the eerie shadows thrown by the bobbing flashlight, it was as if she were hunting . . . me. I told myself to run, but couldn't. My legs had gone rubbery.

"Give me your keys." She spoke in a low monotone, a horror soundtrack of a voice. It had the effect of a siren going off. I scampered back until I bumped into the bike.

"Don't make me ask again," she said.

Suddenly she was in front of me. The Maglite flashed. I got a forearm up before her blow came crashing down on it. I stumbled but stayed on my feet.

"Give me the fucking keys."

I yanked them from my hip pocket and tossed them wide of her. She went over and scooped them up. By then, I'd put the motorcycle between us.

"Now the phone," she said.

I shook my head, near tears. My phone was my call for help. But she lifted the flashlight again, hefting it against her shoulder, threatening to hit me again. In the distance, that damn owl let out another shriek.

"Give me your phone and I'll let you go," she said. "I don't want to hurt you."

"Like you hurt Evelyn?" I was circling the motorcycle, closer to the path out of the woods, closer —

"What a fool, that Evie. She let herself be a pawn. It was a mistake to hurt a pawn. Like it'd be to hurt you." She paused, and then: "What could I do? Bernadette's out to destroy me."

"Bernadette Ryan?" This was about Evelyn — and now me — not her boss. Her fixating even here made her crazy as a shithouse rat. My mind went cold and sharp: she brought me here for one purpose, and that purpose was not to let me go. She was holding that Maglite as if she would beat me the same way she hit Evelyn before shoving her off the bridge.

Fight or flight? She was bigger. That meant flight.

I took another step, inching closer to the path, and reached into my pocket for the phone. There, alongside it, was a smooth handle.

A pocketknife. It was Ben's knife.

My thumbnail slid along its edge, and the blade flicked open. The tip was sharp.

Mother of God, I had a weapon.

With the knife in my fist, I ran like hell, stumbling over downed branches and tree roots, and finally I got to the brambles and barreled through. My shoes hit gravel. But I could hear her gaining.

From behind she tackled me, and I went down hard, slammed onto the ground, the wind knocked out. It was a nasty, graceless tussle, boots clattering, us rolling painfully on the gravel. I swiped at her with the knife. She jerked back with a grunt and swung the Maglite, smashing my forearm again, and I dropped the knife.

And then she was on top of me, pinning me with the Maglite across the base of my throat.

I can't breathe. I'm going to die.

The fury of it blackened my mind. I fought back, pushing up and up and up, all shaking adrenaline. The weight against my throat went away, as the Maglite arched up again, and I grabbed the knife. She swung the flashlight at the same time I lunged up to meet her — this time with the knife. I felt the give of skin beneath the blade and the warm wetness on my hand, just before the pain on the side of my head exploded.

Everything went to black.

When I came to, I found myself sitting on the gravel, blinking at the dots in my vision, trying hard to stay still. Movement made me queasy. I blinked again, and my eyes cleared, and I saw Paige. She lay near me, unconscious.

I struggled to my feet and stumbled to the car before I remembered — no key. I reached into my pocket for my phone, and shards of glass scraped my fingertips. The screen was shattered. No phone service.

No help.

Across the parking lot, Paige remained still, deathly so. I went back and stood over her. "Paige?" I whispered. Her eyelids didn't flicker. And then a little louder, I said, "Paige?"

It was like talking to a dead person. I squatted down and looked closer. In the trickle of light coming off the bridge, her skin had a bluish cast that was as pale as her hair that had fallen across her face. There was a stain on the collar of her jacket. It was blood.

I killed her.

CHAPTER THIRTY-SEVEN

I ran across the bridge. I kept running until the adrenaline seeped away and my lungs were on fire and all I knew was injury. Aching forearm. Tender throat. Head throbbing. The dirt trail along Canal Road, the trees, and the streetlamps were all curiously distant, and the trek back to the city much farther than I remembered.

Yet the night itself was close, intimate, as if it had welcomed me and shown me its secret, and I was a part of it now, and its breath was my own. I never noticed how the night breathed, how patient it was, content now that I joined it. Nor had I noticed the terrible beauty of its variant shades — the midnight-blue sky beaded with stars, the ebony of trees, and the charcoal of space between the trees — and far below, the darkest place of all, the river.

The night had a song that was low and somber, punctuated by the sharp note of the owl as it hunted, its piercing shriek followed by the anguished cry of its prey. Paige had been like the owl, but then she became prey, and that, too, had been revealed by the night.

The blood from the knife had dried on my fist, the knife an extension of my hand, and it was true, I had wanted her to die by it. I could remember the intention distinctly. What did that make me? Was I a killer?

At Arizona Avenue, I went up the hill, feeling weightless, without any size or heft, as if the slightest breeze might carry me away. A Citibank sign told the time and temperature — 3:26, fifty-four degrees. Good to know, I thought vaguely. Better yet if I could find my way home. The maze of city streets disoriented me.

There were brownstones on the corner, one with a porch light on. I should bang on its door and ask to use the phone to call the police and tell them — what? That Paige had tracked and killed Evelyn and Brad and had tried to kill me.

Evie let herself be a pawn.

For whom?

Paige had said, *What else could I do?*

So I killed Paige. What else could I have done?

My thoughts were dark, incoherent, speed-

411

ing without any control. If I told the police, I'd sound crazy, just like Paige Linden was obviously crazy but also smart. Would they believe me? What would they do to me?

I turned from the brownstones and made my way up the hill. At the crest, there was a wide field, and in the field, a children's park. I'd never noticed this park before. An empty swing set was a shadow against the sky, and above that shadow, a full moon hovered.

It was the moon of Diana, lunar virgin, goddess of the hunt, protector of young girls and woodland creatures, a moon so beautiful it hurt. Much like those stories told by my father had hurt, his stories of Mama. How she'd flung herself into motherhood as she had into the marriage and the move north to an industrial world she could scarcely comprehend. How she would never put her child down, though he'd warned her: *you're going to spoil that child, Diana.* But she'd wrap me in blankets and carry me into the night and point to a sky bright with constellations, a sky much like tonight's, and she'd whisper her star stories of heroes challenging their gods.

Before she died, she told me the story of the moon. How a woman was like the moon, always there, watchful over sleeping children, luminous against the darkness. See

412

how the moon appears differently tonight, more shadowed than in nights previous? But her essence never changes. Her eye never wavers. She's only moving through her phases as if changing a beautiful dress, following the rhythms of a life that is good because all of life is good, even when the darkness threatens. So it is with women.

With a deep sigh I tucked the bloody knife into my hip pocket and set my shoulders against the night. Under that moon, I made my way home.

CHAPTER THIRTY-EIGHT

I went inside and called Michael with the idea of turning myself in. He laughed. When I explained, he stopped laughing. Within the half hour he was banging on my front door.

He took Ben's knife and bagged it as evidence. His gaze kept flitting to my neck. "Those bruises look bad," he said. "How about we get you checked out at a hospital? All right, love?"

No way was I going to any hospital, but he was being nice, and it made me feel terrible. "You weren't by Chain Bridge the night Brad Hartnett was killed, were you?"

"Nope, I was at headquarters all night," he said with a sad smile. "When the call came in requesting the homicide unit, I was at my desk. Promise."

I winced. "Sorry I mistook you for a killer."

He picked up his camera and pointed it

playfully at my expression, laughing as he photographed it. *Click.*

"That was my guy at your house," he said. "The one you made."

His guy. The one who scared me witless? "The brown sedan? That was yours?"

He took my hand gingerly, extending my arm, the one that'd been bashed by the Maglite, and took pictures of the bruising. *Click.* "Good. Now hold your hair up and slide your collar down so I can — yes, that's fine." He whistled softly as he took the picture. "So my guy camped out in front of your house? He was looking out for you. Needless to say, he was pretty upset to see you hobbling home at 4 a.m. — three sheets to the wind, he reported — when you were supposed to be tucked in. How is it you never do what's expected?" He was being playful, trying to keep it light, but I just wasn't feeling it.

"I killed someone," I said in a rough voice.

"Stick to the story. You did what you had to do to come home."

Just then, his phone rang. He turned away from me and talked in a low voice to an official from the scene, I presumed.

"Scene secure?" he said. "Uh-huh . . . no . . . well, that's a problem . . . yeah, be there soon as I can." He turned back, saying, "Your car is gone. We've put out an APB."

"My car?"

The lines between his eyebrows deepened. "There was no body, either."

"What?"

He tilted his head and studied me for a moment, and then: "Did you touch her, check her pulse?"

"I — no." I felt my face flush with embarrassment. "It was dark. There was blood on her collar, a lot of it, and my head — it hurt to think." What I couldn't admit: I had panicked and ran. "So what are you saying?"

"Her body was not at the scene."

"No body?" I repeated dumbly.

"It means she got away."

"She's alive." It was unbelievable, and then, hopefully: "I didn't kill her?"

His cool gray eyes narrowed wickedly. "That would've been too lucky."

We crossed the bridge in Michael's cruiser. At the entrance to the pullover lot, a uniformed officer stood guard. Michael flipped his identification, and the officer waved us in and showed Michael where to park. He got out to chat with the supervisor at the scene.

I stayed in the car and waited for my nerves to settle. In the thin light of the early morning, crime scene techs were searching for evidence. A trail of yellow flags marked where I assumed blood had been found, the largest cluster of flags where I'd fought Paige. The trail thinned to the stone barrier where my car had been parked.

Slowly, painfully, I climbed out of the cruiser, my shoulder and arm screaming where it was bruised, and walked away from the techs to the other end of the lot where I found the break in the brambles that led back to the woods. It was wider than it'd seemed last night, but deep. My stomach trembled, and the trembling radiated outward.

Michael came up behind me. "Ready to show me?"

I hesitated, staring into the woods, remembering.

"It's okay," he said. "Take your time."

"She lured me back there to kill me."

"Yes."

"Can you believe I gave her my flashlight?" I laughed without humor, and then: "I handed her a weapon to kill me, like she killed Evelyn with her husband's blackjack." The path back into the woods was shadowy even in the morning light. "What if she'd

417

brought the gun she used to shoot Brad?"

"She probably tossed the gun," he said in a soft voice, surprisingly gentle. "I'd say she prefers to get someone's weapon away from them and use it against them — until you put up a fight. That must have surprised her. Or maybe she enjoyed the fight."

She enjoyed it. Hurting me.

It had been a game to her.

"Paige had been monitoring Evelyn's calls," I said. "She heard Evelyn ask Ian for a meeting. That's how she got the time and place and was able to track Evelyn's route."

He nodded. "Sounds about right."

What to make of the Triumph? She had one like Michael's, which suggested she'd planned to set up Michael for Evelyn's murder, right?

I thought about the spreadsheets Evelyn had given to Brad Hartnett. For safekeeping, Evelyn had told him, and he was going to give them to me, but Paige killed him.

"What did Paige tell you about the audit?" I said.

"What audit?"

"Rumors of money missing from a client account? I guess she lied about that, too."

"Sure you're okay? You look like you're going to be sick."

"Yeah," I said, rubbing my temple. "Let's

418

get this over with."

We followed the path into the clearing. At the far edge was the Triumph, that big, beautiful bike, and near it, the Canon where I'd dropped it. I picked up the camera and swept pine needles off. The batteries were dead, but otherwise, it seemed in working order. No dents or busted switches or buttons.

Michael had gone straight for the bike, circling it as I had last night. He was scratching the stubble along his jaw, perplexed. After a long silence, he muttered, "Same as mine."

I glanced up. "Not exactly. Handlebars are different."

He tilted his head. "You're right. They are." There was curiosity in his voice. He put his hand on his hip and turned to me. "How do you know that?"

He wouldn't believe it, so I shrugged. "It's a gift."

"A . . . gift?"

"It's also my job to observe. I'm very good at my job."

His eyes narrowed. "What's that in your hand?"

"This is called a video camera, as you must know, since every time you see one, you go all Detective Hollywood. But these batteries are in fact dead. There'll be no glamour-boy photo ops today."

"Smart-ass. How'd it get here?"

I explained how I'd brought it to shoot the motorcycle, but dropped it before the fight. "It must have recorded until it ran out of power."

"So you have video of Paige attacking you?"

"Nah, we beat each other up in the parking lot, not here," I said. "Besides, the lens was face down in leaves, so no pictures."

His jaw tightened, giving him a sleek, aggressive look. "Give it to me."

"Why?"

"It could be evidence."

"I'd have to run that past the company lawyers first." As he well knew, the camera was property of the station, not mine to give, and he couldn't make me. Any video was protected under the First Amendment as working notes of the press and protected legally. "If you really want it, I'll take it to the attorneys. Tell them it's a rush job."

Just then, an official came to the edge of the clearing. "We found a flashlight," the captain told Michael, glancing warily at me. "And the second team is ready to get started back here."

Michael nodded once, his jaw stubbornly

set. "We need a few minutes. Keep the others away for now." When the official left, Michael turned back to me. "Give me the camera."

"What? No."

He was struggling with his temper. "After all I've done for you."

"I feel I've done a lot for you, too," I said. "I closed your case for you, and I'm willing to testify, which is better than any dark video of leaves." And then I stopped, realizing what he really wanted — the audio.

He was worried about *what conversations* the camera recorded.

"Go ahead," I said, sighing. "Ask me if we talked about your relationship with Evelyn Carney."

He glanced over, surprised. "Paige say I had sex with Evie?"

"Not on tape."

"I never hooked up with Evie. I was never even alone with her. Paige Linden is a skillful liar."

That was certainly true, but it was also true that Paige's skill came from great confidence. The puzzle that had nagged at me on my walk home: she'd used a motorcycle like Michael's to set him up, but how could she be so confident? It was a great risk going after the head of the investigation, Michael with the privilege all law enforcement enjoyed, that his every word would be accepted as fact, and in a court of law, his godlike testimony held above all others.

In fact, her plan to frame Michael had been so perilous that it was stupid, and Paige Linden was not stupid. The only way it could work?

"You never told me where you were the night Evelyn Carney was killed," I said. "At the Dubliner, I asked several times. Each time you ducked it."

His cheeks bloomed with color. "I wasn't with Evie," he said angrily. "I was never alone with that woman, not once, certainly not that night. But you won't believe me, will you? You never trusted anyone, especially not me. Not in all the time I've known you."

That was just bluster. He was trying to make me mad and throw me off my stride. "Actually, I believe you never had a sexual relationship with Evelyn."

He blew out a breath. "Thank you."

"For days I've had all these scenarios running through my head, making me crazy. I remembered what you admitted about Evelyn, how you ran into her at bars around Capitol Hill, and once Paige had been with her. That's quite a roundabout way of admitting you hung out with Paige, too."

He gave me a level look. "What are you getting at?"

"Just musing aloud about what runs through my head," I said, shrugging. "You know how it is, all these inconsistencies, unanswered questions, how they nag." I set the camera on the ground and straightened again. "The camera's not recording. Why not tell me where you were the night Evelyn disappeared?"

His jaw moved slightly, but that was all.

"Know what I think? You were with Paige Linden that night," I said, and when he remained silent, his face a blank mask, I went on: "That's why Paige was confident pointing her finger at you. She was your alibi." Which left me struggling with the terrible conclusion: "Did you help Paige kill Evelyn?"

His head moved vaguely, a shake no or a nod yes, it was impossible to tell.

"Helped clean up the crime scene? Dispose of the body? You'd know the best way to do that, wouldn't you?" He'd been with Paige, but beyond that, I couldn't see. "You know I won't stop until I know. If need be, I'll go above your head to find out."

"Are you trying to ruin me?" His voice

was hoarse.

"You were with the suspect the night she committed a murder. How many people have you sat across from in an interview room and pressured into a confession with a similar scenario? I haven't ruined you. This is just how the terrible game goes."

He glanced off into the distance, figuring how to play me. I was in no rush. He could take the time he needed because I had him and he knew it, but he also had to come to terms with it. His expression was stoic when he began his tale.

"I was hanging out at the Dubliner with friends; that's what we do Sunday nights. We were drinking half yards of black and tans, watching the hockey game at the bar. The Caps were winning. I was feeling good. Paige strolled in alone, looking for me. That's the kind of relationship we had." He hesitated for a long moment, and then: "Somehow I ended up at her house."

"Somehow?"

"Yeah, I don't know. I was kind of inebriated."

I cut him a look. "If you want to help me figure how to keep you out of the story, you'd better explain how you're not news. Right now, you're looking like a lead — a double murderer's alibi at best, at worst an accomplice."

"Do you have to be so hard?"

"Do you have to insult my intelligence with bullshit?"

He lifted his hands helplessly. "Like I said, she came in. My buddies picked up the sexy vibe she was throwing down, and they left. Paige and I had a couple of shots. After that, I wasn't feeling so good anymore. She helped me out of the bar, gave me a ride. That's about it."

"So drunk you can't remember?" I scoffed.

"From the time I left the bar to the next morning when I woke up on her couch, there's a black hole." He was pacing now. His hands raked through his hair. He was about as worked up as I'd ever seen him.

"You're not a blackout drunk," I said with skepticism.

"No."

"Yet you blacked out on two shots and a beer?"

"It was like coming out of a coma, my arms and legs numb, my brain all fogged up, and not a fucking clue what happened to me. And Paige, boy was she pissed. She complained she'd had to take care of me all night. I'd been sick and made all kinds of mess, which I couldn't remember, either."

He ducked his head, but not before I'd seen his cheeks redden. "She mocked me for not holding my liquor. It wasn't until much later that my head cleared enough to think it through."

"What's that mean?"

He went on, as if to himself. "Hindsight, with those symptoms, I could've gone to Washington Hospital Center for testing. Then again, most of that stuff is undetectable after a handful of hours, so the lab wouldn't have —"

"Wait. What are you saying?" I almost laughed, it seemed so absurd. "Paige Linden slipped you *a date rape drug*?"

"I can't prove it," he said. "Which means no one will believe me. No one."

We stared at each other in silence.

"You must find this ironic," he said bitterly.

It was ironic. It was also cruel.

"You, of all people," he said. "The keeper of my secrets."

"Yeah," I told him gently. "Me."

"Can I give you something for your silence?"

He was a victim now, and victims deserved privacy, if that's what they chose, and I would have given my silence for free. But he wouldn't trust it. Michael Ledger wasn't

426

a man to accept kindness.

I kept it all as normal as I could by listing familiar demands: "Keep me in the loop with the investigation. I want to be first everywhere, all the time, and my photographers get special access —"

"Done."

"If by some stroke of luck you find Paige Linden, I have to be there for the arrest. No matter where or when, I want it exclusively."

"You have my word." His eyes glittered with malice as he stared out into some vision of a future bleak and vindictive. "And Virginia? It's not going to be luck when I find her."

CHAPTER THIRTY-NINE

Later that day, the police found my car in a suburban commuter lot within walking distance to a train station and Baltimore-Washington airport. There were no signs of Paige Linden. My money was on Paige jetting from BWI to some exotic island. I imagined her reclining on a lounge chair beneath the equatorial sun, reading the latest police procedural. Not e-book, though. She'd forgo Wi-Fi and cell towers for some time.

Michael disagreed. There was no way she'd gotten so far so fast and certainly not through airport security or its watch list. But what did Michael really know of Paige's capabilities? He'd been as close to her as a man could be to a woman, and he'd missed it all. Michael Ledger, the great investigator, had seen Paige Linden as nothing more than an object for his pleasure, even as she slipped a drug in his drink and made him her alibi and used his blindness as her shield.

He had no clue why Paige killed Evelyn Carney. Nobody did.

I went over the timeline again: Evelyn had an extramarital affair with Ian Chase, whom she met last August. By Ian's account, the two fell in love, and she promised to leave her husband. When Peter Carney came home from deployment, he was suffering from what appeared to be a form of PTSD or a related anxiety disorder — or perhaps exhaustion that anyone might get from returning again and again to foreign war zones with no end in sight. In any case, Evelyn broke it off with Ian and stayed to help her husband. In the five or six weeks that followed, Ian and Evelyn had no contact with each other.

Until the morning of March 8, when Evelyn called Ian out of the blue, asking to meet with him that evening, no reason given. That night, Paige tracked her to the Key Bridge and hit her with Evelyn's blackjack and threw her over the bridge.

It was the morning call to Ian that started everything in motion. I was nearly certain of it. Which suggested the call posed a threat to Paige — but what kind? Why did Paige have to keep Evelyn from meeting Ian? Evelyn was a first-year associate, a young woman who, after breaking it off with Ian, had no one who might help her, except an ill husband who had too many problems of his own to notice hers.

Or was Ian Chase the threat? In his role as a federal prosecutor, or as someone who'd protect the woman he loved? Why was Paige afraid of Ian and Evelyn together?

I called Isaiah. "Can you run a background check on Paige Linden?"

"Your . . . *source*?"

"Yeah, and a full background on immediate family. Any available financials, property tax and vehicle records, business partnerships outside the firm, employment and education history — the whole shebang. See if you can work your magic with medical and psych records, and yes, I know HIPAA bars it, but give it a shot. Oh, and court records. I'm especially interested in criminal —"

"Slow down," he said. "You want criminal and psych records *for Paige Linden*? What's going on, Virginia?"

"Actually, scratch that. She wouldn't have been admitted to the DC bar with a criminal record, you're right. Listen, I'm working on a script now. Don't tell anyone until I send it to you and Ben to file. Just know it's an exclusive and should lead the show. If Ben has questions, tell him to call me at home. I'm working here today and all weekend."

"Why are you being so secretive?" His voice had gone wary. "And you sound angry."

"Nope, just focused." But along with the wariness, I'd picked up something unexpected. He sounded . . . guilty? "Is there a reason I should be angry?"

He paused. "What's the deadline for the research?"

"Yesterday."

Later, a flurry of calls to anyone I could find from Paige's past, looking for hidden criminality everyone had missed. Childhood schoolmates gave the same description of Paige as a fearless kid who excelled in academics and played sports on the boys' teams and seemed to lead every group she ever joined. People joked about the girls she ran with, what they called the "cult of Paige" and whispered her name with reverence. A few people hated her guts.

One long-ago neighbor, Estelle Becket, described Paige as a bold girl who adapted to the roving lifestyle of her parents, who moved from one cheap apartment to the next, following a trail of lost jobs and failed business ventures, not to mention a few outstanding warrants. She told of one summer morning when a gun went off in Paige's apartment. "Poor child was no more than thirteen, fourteen at the time. Her mama was shouting how she'd heard every stupid thing Paige's daddy was ever going to say and then *bam,* a gunshot. Her mama missed from not even ten feet away. The old man was pouring whiskey into his morning coffee and didn't spill a drop."

Maggie Loftman of Wichita, Kansas, had been touring the District several years ago when her third-grader fell into the Potomac near the Tidal Basin. When everyone else froze, Paige dove in and rescued the kid. Maggie tried to reward her, but Paige wouldn't hear of it. She was a strong swimmer. The river presented a challenge, not a threat.

Which was untrue, and Paige knew it. The brackish Potomac with its wild undercurrents had a hundred ways to pull you under. What had she said? I found the quote: *I didn't want the boy to wash away.*

She knew he'd disappear.

The first hint of possible motive came from the family financials Isaiah emailed me. Paige's father owned an auto repair shop, for which he'd filed bankruptcy six months ago. Soon after the filing, the papers were withdrawn, the business suddenly solvent. During that same time, property records showed a home purchase for Paige's parents. It appeared to have been paid by cash, no mortgage.

Who could write a check for a house? Especially since Paige must have been worrying about funds for that campaign she promised to run. Unless she was using outside funding? Bernadette had refused to back her, Paige had said.

I called Bernadette Ryan's office. While waiting for the callback, I researched the firm. Simmons, McFadden & Ryan was at the forefront of election law. Bernadette provided "top-notch expertise representing corporations in the ever-growing field of political law" and had "an impressive roster of clients including top corporations and nonprofit organizations."

Of Bernadette's life outside the firm, there were a few links, and those showed how quietly she moved through the upper echelon of Washington society, among administration officials and powerful legislators. There was a rumored sighting, but no picture, of Bernadette at the Washington Opera, chatting with a Supreme Court justice at intermission.

A long-form article about campaign financing laws referenced "powerhouse Bernadette Ryan" cozying up to a member of the Senate leadership at the Capitol Grille. This time, there was a picture: a tall, white-haired senator arm in arm with Bernadette Ryan.

My palms went flat on the table as I leaned in. Of course I recognized her. She'd been in the cutaway shot next to Evelyn, an older, elegant woman, perfectly coiffed with chin-length blond hair. She'd worn a gold brocade jacket that shimmered in the light.

And she'd been with Evelyn the night she met Ian Chase.

Bernadette was ducking my calls. I left messages, and over the weekend, staked out her home from outside the gated community she lived in. That was particularly miserable in the cold March rain. My injured shoulder stiffened up, and my arm ached endlessly. I got nothing but wet shoes.

On Monday morning, I called the Federal Election Commission and left a message asking for any filings from Bernadette's firm, especially those that referred to or otherwise named Evelyn Carney. An hour later, there was still no return call. I drove down to E Street and announced myself in the small lobby of FEC headquarters and waited. And waited. I called back to the press office, and again no one picked up, so I settled in.

Around noon, a woman darted past me, as if she wore blinders. She had bright red hair and wore a plum-colored pantsuit and sneakers, a combination that struck me as quirky, maybe eccentric. She stopped at the door and turned back suddenly, looking me full in the face, and gave a quick wave she hid from the security officer, before she rushed into the hallway.

I followed her, calling out a hello as she passed the elevator and went into the stairwell. It was a long way down, nine floors, and since she was wearing Converse and I was wearing heels, she made better time than I did. The stairwell door slammed at the lobby level, and I still had another flight to go.

At the corner of E Street, I caught her flash of red hair as she entered the Hard Rock Café. The restaurant was packed with tourists, but the bar was empty, except for the redhead now sitting at the end farthest from the door. I left an empty seat between us, and said hello again and waited. She didn't acknowledge me.

"I'd like a hurricane, please," she said to

the bartender.

My eyebrows lifted, but I said nothing.

She turned her head slightly my way and talked out of the corner of her mouth, saying, "That's so I can tell my boss I was too drunk to remember how you cornered me against my will."

"I did . . . what?"

"This is so not nice of you. There was a much better way to do this. That's the first thing I'd like to make very clear."

"You're from the press office, right?" I said, confused. "I'm the press. What's all the drama about?"

"If I didn't call you back, it was because I couldn't talk. Obviously." She huffed with indignation. "And then you just show up at my office. For everyone to see! So now, when you get something to report — *and you people always get something to report* — it's going to look like I did it. And yes, it's true, I hate my job, but I have these normal human needs, like a roof over my head, food on my table, that kind of thing, and even though it's not a great salary, it's my salary, and I need it. That is, until I find another job." She turned and looked me full in the face and gave me a wary smile. "You wouldn't know of anybody hiring on your side of the fence, would you?"

I was struggling to keep up with her. "Why would you get in trouble? I'm asking for public information, any documents that are part of the public record."

Her drink arrived. It was a red monstrosity with skewered fruit clipped to the edge of the curved glass. She pulled the cherry off the skewer and chewed it.

"Seriously, aren't we both doing our jobs, here?" I said.

"You can't go dropping names like Bernadette Ryan on a phone line that everyone has access to. You're asking about Bernadette Ryan, queen of political fund-raising, who, by the way, is very friendly with half our members. The other half, of course, thinks she's evil incarnate, but that's the split personality we've got going. Half the office wears a red cap, the other wears blue, and nothing gets done. That's the mandate to the press officers, too. Dodge and dissemble, if we have to. Do anything to hold off questions from people like you."

Her shoulders slumped, as her frantic mood seemed to crash. "It was so sad, though. Poor Evelyn Carney." She sighed and put her hand over her heart, whispering: "Did you know we went to the same school? Although she was quite a bit younger. But really, to think one of our alums could be . . . *murdered.* And she also worked in political fund-raising? Same school, same business, and I can't help but think: wow, if that could happen to her, it could happen to me."

That was my opening. "You could help."

"Why else am I here?" She took a long sip from her straw, surveying the restaurant with the straw between her teeth. She picked up a drink menu that was long and built like a book and set it on her lap. "What I have here is a public document that you could get from anyone," she said as she reached into her handbag and pulled out a thick envelope and slipped the envelope between the pages of the drink menu. She slid the menu across the bar. "So pick any name, except mine."

I let it sit there for a moment. "This is what I need?"

She laughed suddenly. "You don't even know what you need, do you? I figured you were clueless to call me like that. This is the copy of a 990, an IRS form filed by a political nonprofit called the Order First Fund. You'll find all the basic information: fund officers, purpose of the fund, its revenues and costs. An attached schedule lists donors, but I had to redact the names. It's illegal to release the names of donors for these funds,

438

and I *am* sorry for Evelyn Carney, but not enough to get hauled in front of some congressional hearing, or good heavens, go to prison. Take a look on page six. That's where the keeper of the books is named — Evelyn Carney."

"Evelyn was in charge of the fund?"

"Yes."

I slipped the envelope into my satchel. "When I have questions, can I call you?"

"Oh gads, no." She scribbled a name and number on a cocktail napkin and slid it across the bar. "This is my friend, a counterpart over at the IRS who works in the section that handles these nonprofits. He's been crazy busy, though. Justice came through and had the whole office working through the weekend. He had tickets to the tournament, too. Boy was he pissed."

That set my news ping off. "Justice?"

"Department of," she said, looking at me quizzically. "How do you think I got your doc so fast? He'd already pulled it for the prosecutors." She leaned forward to take a sip of her drink and stopped suddenly, snapping her a finger. "Ohhhh darn it, I almost forgot to flag you to the important thing. The diversion of assets."

"The what?"

"Money missing from the fund," she said.

"Looks like Evelyn Carney embezzled a whole lot of money. If the poor thing hadn't been killed, surely she'd have gone to jail."

I got out of the Hard Rock in a hurry. No way in hell was anybody blaming Evelyn Carney. The feds could make a fall guy out of every lawyer on K Street and half of Capitol Hill for all I cared, but Evelyn?

Hell, no. Not if I could help it.

As I ran, my thumb skipped across my phone, through its contact list until I got to Ian Chase. When he picked up, I started talking, "Evelyn's being set up. You have to help me. Give me a name, whoever is investigating —"

"Miss Knightly?" he said soothingly. "Slow down, it's okay."

"No, it's not." Christ, I sounded rattled. Emotional. When I sounded emotional, people disregarded what I said even though it was real, so I could not be emotional. I stopped and leaned against the wall of an office building and forced myself to start again, from the beginning. "There's money missing from the fund Evelyn oversaw, but she didn't do it. Paige got into the fund, I'm nearly certain of it, and she set up Evelyn. That's why Paige killed Evelyn and tossed her over the side of the bridge into the river. She said Evelyn had been a pawn, that it'd been a mistake to kill someone so lowly as a pawn."

He didn't say anything for a long moment, and then: "Have you recovered from your injuries, Miss Knightly?"

So he knew about the fight; good. I had no time to talk about it.

"This isn't about me getting hit in the head," I said. "It's about people getting washed away in the river. When Paige saved that boy all those years ago, she said the Potomac is so wild, brackish, bodies get washed away forever. Don't you see? She planned for Evelyn to wash away — disappear — and everyone would think Evelyn took the money and ran. She was laying the groundwork for that story the first day I met her. *She was using me.*"

"She used a lot of people," he said gently, in that soft southern lilt.

"But the police started looking into you, and CID got involved. And then Evelyn's body washed up in the cove with that head trauma. Paige had a backup plan for that, too," I said, talking over him, when he tried to interrupt. I was panting now. "If the ME ruled it a homicide, she could always pin it on Michael Ledger. She actually thought ahead like that. *Who the hell thinks like that?*"

"Someone who enjoys it," he said calmly.

Christ, my head was throbbing.

"You have to help me," I said. "Evelyn was coming to you that night about Paige — well, I don't think she knew it was Paige, but she knew there was money missing and she was in trouble, and you — that was your expertise, right? You prosecuted the mayor's cronies over improper use of campaign funds, right?"

"It was embezzlement, and yes, I'd know how to spot it. I could have helped her."

"So you knew?"

"Not that day. She never told me why. But now that I'm vindicated — if that's what you call this — I've been able to think more clearly and piece things together with the help of my friends." There was bitterness in his drawl. "You know how tribal the city is. My tribe never stopped believing in me, they swear it. Of course, they weren't going out on any limb for me, either. But they're making it up to me. They've let me back in the loop again."

"My source says Justice has the IRS filings for the fund Evelyn worked on, and yes, there's money missing and she was in charge of the bookkeeping, but she didn't do it."

"Nobody's going to blame Evie, not on

my watch." And then, after a long pause, he said, "Know what? Everyone let Evie down, except for you. You kept searching, and I owe you for that. But you have to understand, I no longer work at Justice, and this isn't my investigation."

I slid down to my haunches with my back to the building. My head fell forward and my hair fell over my face, so no one could see my frustration.

Ian Chase had been my best hope.

"So you didn't hear it from me, okay?" he said, and then: "You ever hear of dark money, Miss Knightly?"

CHAPTER FORTY

Ian was talking about political fund-raising in which anonymous donors could give unlimited amounts of so-called dark money to non-profit groups, sometimes called PACs. These political nonprofits acted like middlemen between donors and candidates who fit the groups' ideology. People called their donations dark not because they were necessarily bad, but because they were made in secret.

When investigators searched Brad Hartnett's apartment, they found in his computer a USB memory card that belonged to Evelyn Carney. Saved on the card were documents for the Order First Fund. Some of the documents recorded communications. Others were spreadsheets coded by a series of numbers and letters. Agents cracked the fund's code and linked dark-money donors to judicial candidates in dozens of states around the country.

"The fund itself is legal," Ian said. "Or at least gives the appearance of being legal. The big problem is the type of donor who gives to this fund."

One donor was a for-profit prison corporation that paid for the campaign of a senior judge, Lawrence Euclid. For-profit prisons were a growing industry worth billions of dollars with an increasingly aggressive lobby, Ian said. "They make money by filling beds and keeping as many incarcerated for as long as possible. That's why donations from these types of corporations should be allowed nowhere near a judicial campaign."

"But if the law says the Order First Fund can accept donations from any corporation, it's doing what the fund was legally set up to do, right?" I said. "Whether you approve of that industry or not."

"Except with this fund, some of the donations were specifically designated for certain judges," Ian argued. "In the case of one Judge Euclid, for example, you have to ask if these donations are kickbacks for maximum sentencing. You know, locking up kids for campaign cash. Because, boy, does Euclid like a long sentence."

I drew a sharp breath. "The documents show evidence of this?"

"The docs are a starting point. Whether there's enough hard evidence to prosecute, it's impossible to say at this point." He paused thoughtfully, and then in a low, passionate voice, said, "But if voters knew what kind of prison Euclid appears to have sold these kids into, the neglect and assault and sex abuse, his reelection prospects would be toast."

He was pitching the story. Usually my mind romped giddily at a new lead, but the prospect of this story was dismaying. I'd have to look into children trapped, cast away, and sold out, forgotten by the state.

"There are other problems," Ian said. "Some of the donors have business before the court. You know, if the donor corporations think they can't win their case, they'll attempt to sway the election to a judge more favorable to them — or their money. Other evidence shows the fund skirting rules against direct communication with campaigns — that's called coordination, and it's illegal. But frankly, nearly everyone does that. Thankfully, coordination won't be too much of a problem for Bernadette."

His tone surprised me. "You sound like you're letting Bernadette off the hook."

"Well, she's likely ruined," he said. "Once her clients hear about a federal investigation, they'll desert her. No campaign can afford to be associated with someone under investigation, even if those same campaigns took advantage of her fund." He let out a deep sigh. "Maybe my fondness for Bernadette blinds me. It's hard to believe she had knowledge about some of the goings-on in the fund."

"I hadn't realized you were friends with her."

"If it hadn't been for Bernadette, I'd never have met Evie. She introduced us."

"*Bernadette* did?"

He laughed caustically. "The grande dame of the political scene, playing cupid. She told Evie, *'Let's go meet the next US Attorney for the District.'* If Evie was going to work for her, she had to have strong connections. It was a prerequisite."

"She nudged you together?" I said. "That didn't strike you as manipulative?"

"It's what people do. What do I care, if it brings me Evie?"

I thought of the cutaway shot of Bernadette Ryan in her gold brocade jacket, seated next to a vibrant Evelyn Carney. Bernadette had taken her to meet Ian, and Evelyn was enamored.

"You said there were two prongs to the investigation," I said. "The other is the missing money?"

"The embezzlement," he corrected. "Small amounts began disappearing as early as a year ago. They were assumed to be accounting errors. Recently, the amounts grew larger as the suspect appeared to grow more confident."

"How much did Paige Linden skim?"

He hesitated.

"Ballpark?"

"There was a wire transfer in the early evening prior to your attack," he said. "The Order First Fund was cleaned out. I'm told the figure is in the millions."

It was staggering. "Of dollars?"

"The low estimate is ten," he said. "But again, the audits have just begun."

"Ten . . . *million*?" I stammered, slumping back in my chair, completely in awe. She had done it. Paige Linden had committed the perfect crime. She'd stolen from a fund that could not bear the scrutiny of law enforcement. If the embezzlement were investigated, unlawful activity in the fund would be discovered, donors would become public record, and everything would be out in the open.

None of which Bernadette Ryan could risk.

For Paige, the revenge must have been

thrilling. The money was the fund's illusory power, and by stealing the money, she'd stolen Bernadette's power over her. She had millions of Bernadette's dark-money dollars. With that kind of cash, you could disappear forever.

The low estimate was *ten million,* which came from only *one* fund. "How do we keep faith in a judiciary that's awash in secret money?"

He didn't say anything for a long moment, and then: "You know that inscription on the pretty white building on First Street?" He was talking about the United States Supreme Court. On its facade it was written: Equal Justice Under Law.

"I've read it."

"A beautiful dream, isn't it?" he said mournfully. "But nowhere close to reality. Know what's worse? Nobody cares."

CHAPTER FORTY-ONE

The next morning I sent a package with written questions to Bernadette Ryan at her law office. In the cover letter, I explained that I was working on a story of alleged embezzlement of her Order First Fund, and that investigators believed the crime was linked to two murders. Subsequently, the Department of Justice opened an investigation into whether donors used the Order First Fund to influence judicial outcomes. I offered an opportunity to comment. If she chose not to respond, I'd report that, too.

Fifteen minutes after the courier confirmed my package had been signed for at the firm, I got a call from Bernadette Ryan's secretary. Ms. Ryan would see me at noon.

The firm was housed in a Federal-period mansion obscured by an enormous magnolia tree. Beside the front door, a small brass plaque read Simmons, McFadden & Ryan. Inside, it was all lemon-polished wood and wide-planked flooring that creaked as I crossed and heavy doors that kept secrets. Even the phones rang quietly. A thin man escorted me up narrow stairs to a suite of offices.

Bernadette Ryan was seated behind her desk. She wore an expensive suit that must've been a size two, and her infinity scarf was meticulously folded. Her lips moved in what might've been a smile. "I cannot imagine why this meeting is necessary," she said. "My lawyers are composing answers to your questions as we speak."

And yet you invited me here.

"As you know, I'm working on a story about the Order First Fund," I said. "I've been told a considerable amount of money was stolen from it. Can you comment?"

On her desk, there was an old-fashioned apothecary jar filled with gold-wrapped candies. She lifted the lid and chose one, studying its wrapper with great attention.

"You were aware money was missing?" I said.

She unwrapped the chocolate and popped it into her mouth. She chewed the candy thoughtfully. After a long moment, she said, "It was brought to my attention. At what point, I cannot recall. But you must know, I don't involve myself with minutiae. My role is to lend my name to bring in donors."

"You'd define millions of dollars missing as minutiae?"

She lifted an elegant shoulder. "The fund is one of the smaller and less consequential funds, yes. As such, it was off my radar, unfortunately."

"Whose radar was it on?"

She tossed her blond bangs from her eyes assertively, but did not ask me to leave. I think she wanted me to feel her power, to intimidate me, and I was intimidated. But that should never stop a person from doing her job.

"Evelyn Carney was assigned to the fund, yes?" I said.

She complained about my asking questions I knew the answer to. She said it was a waste of her time. "Do you have any idea what rate I bill out at?"

"So to avoid cutting into those billable hours, I'll be blunt, shall I?" I glanced down at my notepad. "The thrust of the story, based on evidence gathered by law enforcement, goes like this: on Sunday, March 8, an employee under your direct supervision, Evelyn Carney, went missing while en route to an evening meeting with Assistant US Attorney Ian Chase. She was going to ask Ian for help."

452

"Is there a question here?" she said.

"For months your auditors and private investigators failed to find money that went missing from the Order First Fund. All internal efforts were also a bust. You knew Ian Chase had vast experience with white-collar crime, particularly embezzlement. You also knew he was romantically involved with Evelyn Carney and would help her as he would no one else. So you sent Evelyn to ask Ian if he could take a peek at your so-called 'diversion of assets' problem."

This last had been supposition. She took a moment to adjust. "You still haven't asked a question."

"Problem is, there's no way that fund can withstand an official federal inquiry, right?" I said, and when she didn't answer, I went on: "From what I understand, illegal co-ordination with campaigns is the least of your worries. Which makes Evelyn's assignment tricky, doesn't it? She has to make sure an upstanding federal prosecutor turns a blind eye to the pesky illegal fund activity that could tie you up in a lengthy federal investigation. So you assign Evelyn as keeper of the books. Now it's Evelyn's fund, not yours, and she's in trouble, not you. That's how you get Ian Chase's help on the sly. You figured he'd do whatever it took to

453

save the woman he loves."

"You may report it was Evelyn's fund, because it was Evelyn's fund," she said in a low, hoarse voice. "There's documented evidence to prove it."

"I'll take that as a comment, yes?" I wrote it down. "Here's what I can't figure out. How did you get Evelyn to agree to go to Ian's that night?" For a long moment, I stared down at my pen, considering the possibilities, and then I tapped my notepad with it. This is the part I'd have to riff.

"Why go to Ian's?" I tapped out each word. "Evelyn was pregnant and alone and feared she was being followed. How does she overcome that fear? Why doesn't she say, screw Bernadette Ryan and her corrupt fund-raising activities, and *let you hang*?" Tap-tap-tap. "Why put herself at risk? Unless it was you she feared." I thought about that for a moment. "She knew you'd hired investigators. She thought they had intercepted her phone. Maybe it wasn't only Paige Linden tracking Evelyn the night she was killed. Did you have someone following her, too?"

"You have a rich imagination."

"Is that a yes or a no?"

She said nothing, merely lifted the lid of the apothecary jar with hands that were no longer steady. As she'd grown more nervous, I'd become less so. The lid clattered back on, and she folded her hands in her lap.

"Feel free to jump in anytime you want to comment on what I plan to report," I said. "It begins with the Order First Fund getting skimmed around a year ago. In the beginning, it's not much money, barely noticeable. When did you realize it wasn't an accounting error?"

"I couldn't say."

"August of last year, at the latest, right?" When she said nothing, I went on: "I have video of an August community meeting where you'd taken Evelyn Carney to meet AUSA Ian Chase. That's how you got your inside line with a powerful federal prosecutor. Soon thereafter, you put her to work on the embezzled fund."

I paused, waiting for her denial, but she remained still, silent. Her face was sickly white, and I knew: "You set up Evelyn to discover the fund shortage. Then you blamed her, since as you say, she's in charge of the fund. Is that accurate?"

She stood up. "That's enough. This meeting is over."

"That's not a denial," I said, remaining in my seat. "Is that a confirmation?"

"I'd like you to leave."

"I'll take that as a no comment, fair?" I said, and without waiting for her response: "Now Evelyn's in deep shit. If she doesn't find your money, she could be disbarred, maybe even prosecuted. At the very least, her career in this town is over. After all, you are Bernadette Ryan, doyenne of the Washington political scene. You attend opera with Supreme Court justices and private luncheons with US senators. But you're not all threats. You dangle the carrot, don't you? If Evelyn figures out where the money went, you'll reward her. Ian seemed to think Evelyn had been promised a promotion working directly for you."

She interrupted: "I never told Evelyn Carney where to go on the night of Sunday, March 8."

"Fine, thank you." I wrote that down, too, quoting her.

"What's more, I believe you're losing sight of the villain here," she said angrily. "Paige Linden stole vast sums of money and killed two people to cover it up. All because she didn't get what she wanted, campaign money for a rumor of a candidacy. Paige Linden may have talked herself up all she liked, but I had already warned donors about her. What does she do? *She took the money anyway.*"

Paige had said Bernadette tried to destroy her. That night in the woods she'd told me. I'd thought she was batshit crazy.

A chill went down my neck. "You started a whisper campaign against Paige?"

"They're my colleagues, allies. It was my duty," she said. "From the first day she walked into this firm, I *saw* her. I knew exactly what she was. Not my idiot partners. Against my instruction, they recruited a person who, as I warned them, was sneeringly ambitious, grandiose, and narcissistic with no respect for tradition or authority. Yet they voted her in. They gave her partnership in my firm."

I thought of the spy app Paige had used. She'd monitored Evelyn and Brad and me. Ian Chase thought there were others.

"When you plotted against her, it was over the phone?" I said.

Where she was eavesdropping on you.

"My partners laughed off my warnings, said I felt threatened by her. Me, Bernadette Ryan, threatened." She was flushed with anger. "So I built a case and argued it to each partner, one by one, until I could get rid of her. Was I wrong? *Look at what she's done to my firm.*"

Quietly, I said, "I haven't forgotten that Paige Linden killed two people. But I also

457

can't forget that when Evelyn Carney went missing, you told investigators you regretted you could not help. That can't be right, can it? You knew where Evelyn had gone, that she must be in danger, and *you did nothing?*"

She picked up the phone on her desk and called security. I heard the ring and a gruff response on the other side of the door, and then the door was opening.

I rose from my chair. "To you, Evelyn Carney was expendable. Her life wasn't worth your firm or your power or whatever ideology you're peddling."

The security guard grabbed my arm. I pulled away. "Don't touch me. I'm going."

"Ms. Knightly?" she called out.

I stopped at the door and turned back.

"When I look at you, I see a woman wasting her talents," she said. "You could be anything. You could work for the Senate or House leadership. Maybe the White House is more your style. There are lobbying firms all over town that'd pay enormous amounts to a woman with your savvy. Instead, you chase perilous stories. Why put yourself at such risk when I can get you more prestige and power than you ever dared dream?"

Give up my story for an embarrassment of riches. Through the years, Bernadette had probably delivered on many such promises. She'd been the magician who turned fools into kings, and those kings owed her big. But Paige had stolen the money that was Bernadette's magic. Soon her kings would know the magic was gone, and they'd abandon her. They always did.

"Save your deal making for Justice," I said. "Those prosecutors are appointed, not paid for, but maybe you'll find one to let you plea out."

CHAPTER FORTY-TWO

A few days later, I got a tip from Ian Chase. Paige Linden had been taken into custody at a beach in Santa Marta by Colombian officials, and was now being flown into Reagan National on a Gulfstream owned by the US Marshals. The plane was expected to land in little over three hours.

Her capture had come shockingly fast. It seemed Paige Linden had accounted for everything except social media. American tourists on spring break had recognized Paige's face from her picture in my story trending on Twitter.

"I need to know which terminal," I told Ian. "A tail number for the plane would be good, too."

"If you're going to the airport, you'll need an escort. Let me get someone out there to meet you."

The money shot was the perp walk, that

video of Paige Linden being led away in handcuffs. If we got it — and we had to get it — it would lead the show and keep us out in front of the story. It was the shot we'd use again and again.

There was other video needed, too. I assigned Isaiah to monitor what we called the Citycam, our robotic camera mounted on a high-rise used to shoot the river and the bridges and the traffic along the bridges. In a pinch, that camera could pan to shoot video of an aircraft on its flight path into National. Isaiah was in charge of getting the Gulfstream's descent.

Ground shots were more complex. For those, we broke into two teams: Ben and his photographer would cover the runway from their stakeout on a grassy area beyond airport property. Nelson and I would go to the tarmac where the government jets deplaned — or as close as my escort would take me.

"Let's swap," Ben said. "I get the suspect. You get the runway."

"Nope. If my escort is a no-show, you're more likely to be recognized and therefore hassled by security and you can't be detained. I need you live at the top of the six. Besides," I said, showing my teeth, "Paige Linden is mine."

He nodded slowly. "Makes sense, except for your thinking nobody's going to notice you."

"I'm smaller. I blend in. I get the perp walk."

"You look in the mirror lately?" His eyebrow shot up. "You don't blend. You turn heads."

"Try not to be ridiculous," I said, ignoring the quick jolt to my insides. It must have been my adrenaline, which was spiking. There was no room for error on this shoot. "How much longer do we wait?"

"If she's not here in another minute, I'll get her," Nelson said. We were idling in his Tahoe, waiting for Kendal, Ben's photographer. Just then Kendal loped out, weighed down by her camera and tripod. She went to the back of the truck. There was some thumping as she stored her gear, and then the lift gate slammed shut. We were off.

I checked my phone again. Ian Chase hadn't called with the name of my escort. That worried me. I put in another call to him, but he didn't pick up.

"Airports Authority cleared us for the live shot on airport grounds at six," I said, going over the plan again to make sure everyone was clear. "For the eleven o'clock show, we'll go back to the studio. So Kendal, after you get the runway shot, I need you to hustle back to set up the live shot — unless Nelson calls for help with the walk. First priority is Paige Linden's walk. A suit from the FBI is supposed to help. My source was working on it, anyway," I muttered, checking my phone again. "He never called back. Maybe I should've taken care of that myself."

Ben reached around the headrest and caressed my shoulder. "You got it all covered. No worries."

I could feel Kendal staring a hole in the back of my head. Nelson was grinning at her through the rearview mirror. "You ever been in the field with these two?" he asked.

"You talk too much," Ben said, and surprisingly, that shut Nelson up. A tense silence came over the Tahoe as we sped along the parkway. When we were past the airport beyond Four Mile Run, we pulled over. Nelson got out to help Kendal unload her gear. Ben stayed in the Tahoe with me.

I twisted around the seat, saying, "Once Kendal gets the landing, hurry to the live shot location to feed that video. I'll radio as soon as I'm clear at the terminal."

He was staring at me, a warm, soft look.

"What?"

"You're going to get her," he said quietly.

"Oh yeah. Consider it done."

He leaned forward and kissed me quick and got out of the car.

Nelson and I doubled back to the airport. I told him to slow down by the long-term parking lot. "I'll hoof it from there."

"Without me?"

I reached into my satchel and pulled out my video camera. "Find a safe distance where you can shoot the perp walk," I said, checking through the camera settings. "Somewhere you won't get hassled by security. No matter what happens, I need to know you're on that perp walk. I'll go to the terminal alone and find my escort."

"We're supposed to stay together. That was the plan."

"This is the new one."

"Ben told me to watch your back. He made me promise."

"Look at me," I said, and when he did: "I'm your boss, not Ben. If you don't do what I tell you, I will put you on the National Zoo beat. You'll be shooting baby pandas and tourists until your retirement. You want that?"

He slammed the brakes. "Hell no."

"Good man." I climbed out and stood in the doorway, clipping the two-way radio to my belt. I shoved the phone into the pocket

464

of my jacket and the camera back into the satchel, which I slung over my shoulder. "You're the best we have, so you get the money shot. That perp walk will open the show tonight and many nights to come. It's the most important piece of video there is. No matter what happens —"

"I'll be on it," he said.

"Good." I slammed the door and cut through the parking lot for Air Cargo and walked along the access road that went far south of the passenger terminals, where I got my first view of the tarmac. Twin blue Suburbans with tinted windows were parked next to the southernmost terminal, which was owned by the feds.

My camera zoomed in on the license plates. Both had US government tags. Bingo, the transport vehicles. So the Gulfstream would deplane and the Marshals would walk Paige Linden to one of these Suburbans. I looked around for Michael and wondered why he wasn't here.

A brawny guy with a flattop and wearing a suit that screamed fed got out of the Suburban and leaned against the hood. He was fiddling with his phone, and glancing up, turned his sunglasses my way and stayed on me for a long moment. I waited for his acknowledgment, but he put his head back down to his phone.

Not my escort, then. Someone had given him a heads-up about me, but he'd neither help nor hinder. That was fine. I walked across the parking lot toward the Suburban.

From a distance behind, someone shouted, "stop." I kept walking, hoping the command was for someone else, anyone other than me. I didn't dare look back. The fed with the flattop gazed my way idly, and then got up and went inside the terminal.

The voice behind me was louder, angrier. "Ma'am. You're in a restricted area."

Damn.

I turned to face a uniformed airport police officer. He was short and slightly plump and panting from exertion. "I'm sorry, Officer. You're talking to me?"

"Show some ID."

"Certainly." I reached behind my neck and lifted the lanyard that held my press passes. It dangled between us. He glanced at it in distaste.

"An official ID," he said. "A driver's license."

"I didn't drive, but these are official. There's a Hill pass, one for the White House, and here's DOD."

He flipped through the tags. "I don't see an Airports Authority pass."

466

"Not a hard pass, but Airport Ops cleared me for today. My escort from Justice will be here momentarily."

"We haven't been notified. You don't have proper ID. You have to leave."

"My escort will be here." I glanced around wildly. Where the hell was my escort?

"I'm not going to tell you again."

"But Airport Ops cleared me," I said, trying to buy time. "Can't you call them to confirm it? Or ask my escort when he gets here?"

"Are you disobeying a lawful order?"

Before I could answer, he called on his radio, asking for backup. I couldn't believe it. "Are you calling for backup — for me? This is ridiculous."

His face turned red. "I'm ridiculous?"

"What? No. Let me call my contact to clear this up." I reached for my phone in my pocket and he stepped back, yelling, "Keep your hands where I can see them."

His hand was on his holster. He pulled *his gun* out of the holster.

There was nothing else in the world except that gun. It was big and black and pointed to the ground with both his hands on its grip.

"Don't," I said, or thought I said. It was what I kept hearing in my head.

"You have a weapon in your coat?"

"No." And then, louder: "No weapon."

"What's in your coat then?"

"Phone. Radio. Camera in bag."

"Drop your bag to the ground slowly," he said, and then, "Take your coat off. Hands visible at all times."

Everything happened slowly. My hands moved to the lapels, and the coat slipped from my shoulders and onto the blacktop — and all that time my eyes were on the gun. I stood in the puddle of my coat and held my hands out like starfish, shaking.

Coming out of the government terminal was the brawny man with the flattop. He was joined by what had to be the most beautiful person I'd ever seen, no less because I was praying she was my escort, or my guardian angel. She was running across the tarmac, holding up an identification folder, heading straight for me.

"Special Agent Roubillard, Washington Field Office." She addressed the officer in a voice as calm and as warm as her brown skin. "This is my guest. Is she being detained?"

"I caught her trespassing without proper ID."

"She was confused about where to meet," she said, and turning to me, "Forgive me. I waited for you at the *front entrance* of the terminal. You were walking toward the rear entrance. It is an understandable mistake."

"She refused an order."

"Not her first order, which was to meet me at the terminal," she said. "Now that we've cleared up the confusion, I'll take it from here."

His face turned red again. "This is an unauthorized area."

"This tarmac is federal, not airport property. You are a few dozen steps beyond the access road, which is where your jurisdiction ends." She gave him a blinding smile beneath her mirrored shades. "Thank you, Officer."

We stood side by side, watching the officer return to his cruiser at the edge of the tarmac. Finally, I picked up my satchel and coat from the ground.

"I owe you," I said. "I don't even know you."

Without looking at me, she murmured, "Michael Ledger keeps his promises."

"Michael? I thought —"

"He's a political animal," she went on, "and I believe, also quite paranoid. He feels he needs plausible deniability. It was no great favor to do this for him, because I never confirm or deny anything. I don't

469

have to. I'm FBI."

She was talking to me, but looking outward toward the police cruiser, or beyond that to the runways. It was impossible to tell with her glasses. "You're going to report that officer to his supervisors?" she murmured.

Ah, the blue line. "I'm here for video, not trouble."

She tipped her glasses down. Her eyes were a radiant hazel against her brown skin. She pinned me with her stare. "He escalated, hoping you'd give him a reason to arrest you, then pulled his service weapon on *you* — a fancy white chick in a designer suit. Now imagine if you'd been a Latina or a sister." She slid her glasses up her nose and turned her attention back to the runway. "File the complaint," she said.

My two-way crackled to life: "Got a Gulfstream on Citycam one. Recording its descent." Isaiah read out the tail number to confirm. I glanced over at Special Agent Roubillard, and she nodded.

I eased the radio from my belt. "Roger that," I said.

"I'm in position." That was Nelson.

There was the double clicking sound of Kendal's affirmation.

"Over the Jefferson now," Isaiah said.

"About a minute to National." The radio went silent. I turned the volume down and shoved it back onto my belt and grabbed my camera from the satchel. It checked out. I began recording.

In the distance, the Gulfstream touched down. It slowed and made its turn before it taxied toward us. The jet came to a stop and steps lowered. Michael climbed out first. He was wearing his blue MPD windbreaker, the kind he never wore except when cameras were around. Special Agent Roubillard met him at the bottom of the steps.

"Commander Ledger, welcome back stateside," she said, holding out her hand. They shook. "My SAC sends his regards. Congratulations on yet another successful apprehension by the joint task force."

"Always a pleasure to work with the Washington field office," he said in a voice meant to carry. He never once glanced at my camera.

The two Suburbans pulled up. In the door of the jet, a Marshal appeared and led a figure in a black hoodie down the steps. Her head was down, hands behind her back. Michael met her at the bottom.

The hood obscured her face. I couldn't get a shot. I called out her name.

She lifted her head. In a sharp, vicious

471

movement, Michael tore off her hood. Paige's appearance was shocking. Her hair was dyed black and cut short around her face, and she had an angular, hungry look. A square bandage marred her long white neck where I'd cut her.

"Why'd you kill Evelyn Carney?" I said.

Her mouth curled up in a smile. It was worth more than any denial she might have made, and she was looking right into the camera.

I got her.

CHAPTER FORTY-THREE

There's a high that comes with breaking that kind of exclusive. You feel at the top of your game, that your powers are limitless, and you never want to let the feeling go. Of course, the flipside is knowing this is temporary, as all feelings are, and that the work will be forgotten, as all work is forgotten, and sooner rather than later all anybody will ask is: What have you got for us today?

But for now, the moment was perfect. I would allow nothing to intrude on it, not Isaiah talking about how to expand the story for tomorrow's news, or Nelson badgering me to celebrate at Chads, where Mellay was buying everyone drinks, or the network requesting my interview on their morning show, and if not that, what could I do? How soon?

I ignored it all, locking myself away in my office. From behind the bookshelf I pulled the bottle of whiskey and poured a shot and carried it to the television, where I stood like a symphony conductor and waited for my story to air. The show opened with the video of Paige smiling, and then the anchors tossed to Ben on the set. He read as he always did, as if his viewers were friends with whom he was sharing an amazing story, a telling that was as smooth and satisfying as the whiskey in my hand.

After the show was over and everyone left the station to celebrate, I drifted around the empty newsroom, enjoying the quiet, stacking newspapers and press releases, turning off the lights. When I got to the conference room, Ben was coming out of his office at the end of the hallway, locking his door. I went still, startled out of my private moment.

His back was to me. I thought about calling out. Maybe he wanted company, as suddenly I wanted his company, and we could celebrate or talk or whatever he wanted — and then I thought of that quick kiss in the Tahoe, and the words stuck in my throat.

So I left it to chance. If he turns my way, fine. If not, I'd head home.

He rattled the doorknob to check the lock, and shoving the keys into his pocket, turned away from me toward the stairs. I stayed silent in the dark corridor, watching him go.

■ ■ ■

The next morning, my cell phone went off at an ungodly hour. The caller left a message that beeped and then the damn phone started ringing again.

It was Mellay's secretary talking about some big postmortem at noon in Mellay's office. The head of the News Division and the vice president of legal affairs were coming down from New York on the Acela and wanted to meet. No, she had no idea what it was about. No, there were no concerns about the story or trouble with the staff, not that she had heard anyway — unless I was refusing to come in? Should she tell Mellay I was refusing?

"No, but I'm tired," I said, exasperated. "I worked a sixteen-hour day yesterday. I'll come in for this meeting at noon, but no earlier. If Mellay has a problem with that, he can call me himself."

The chairs in Mellay's office were arranged like an inquest. He pointed to a chair that faced three others, and my anxiety jumped. "Sit, sit," he said, and introduced me to the bigwigs. The lawyer — Henry was his name — was a good-looking older man, very stiff in the torso. He also had a funny way of talking, keeping his face expressionless with only his mouth moving. He talked a lot.

Javier was the head of the News Division, the big boss in charge of us all. He was a tougher read. He had a lean, intelligent face and he listened attentively, letting others speak, which was a rarity in television news. I liked the way he'd stood when I had come in and remained standing until I took my chair, and especially the way he looked me in the eye when he shook my hand and congratulated me for yesterday's story.

This was obviously Mellay's meeting, though. He and Henry took their seats across from me and grilled me about the fight with Paige by the Chain Bridge. I kept it brief and emotionless, as if I were reporting what had happened to someone else, a news summary. Yes, the suspect had been my source, although much of what she'd told me checked out by other sources and therefore raised no red flags. She'd shown no hints of violence, let alone any indication of her role in two murders. The police investigators, some with over twenty years of experience investigating homicides and who'd interviewed Paige Linden themselves, hadn't suspected her, either.

"She fooled everyone she came in contact

with," I told Mellay. "She'd have fooled you, too. Frankly, I don't know how much more careful I could've been."

Henry's mouth thinned peevishly, as he stared pointedly at my neck. "Surely you could've been more careful, or you wouldn't have those bruises."

"Those are her war wounds," Javier said, wandering from the window with his hands clasped behind his back. He stopped in front of me. "They came during the performance of her duty to the News Division, for which she should be commended, not interrogated."

"Of course, Javier," Henry agreed. "This is no criticism of the story itself."

"It sounded critical to me."

"The concern back at corporate is for a larger pattern of risky behavior that could jeopardize the company, and her personal safety as well. That is our duty to the News Division."

"With every great story comes risk," Javier said flatly. "She has dealt with that risk admirably and answered your questions to my satisfaction. Move on."

There was a knock at the door. Mellay's secretary carried a tray with bowls of fruit and cookies and sandwiches cut in quarters. She set the tray on a low table between the row of chairs and left. No one touched the food.

"Well, then." Mellay tugged at the knot in his tie and shifted toward Javier. When Javier nodded, Mellay told me: "We brought you in today to thank you for a job well done. As a reward, we'd like to give you your old title back."

I blinked, struggling with the abrupt change in direction. "My . . . show?"

Mellay swept his hand across the air as if unfurling an imaginary banner. "Executive producer of the *Morning Show.*"

It was stunning. "The *Morning Show*? That's not my show. Mine is the *Evening News.* That's what was taken from me."

"There's currently no opening on the *Evening News,*" Mellay said.

"The *Evening News* is my show," I repeated. "It was for that show I brought in a story that shot our ratings through the roof. It also increased our Web traffic a hundredfold. I walked through fire for that story — Ben Pearce and I both did — and he's the *Evening News* anchor. That's the kind of story we're capable of. That's why we belong on the highest-rated and most-watched show."

Henry's mouth thinned again. "Unfortunately, Pearce is gone."

"*Gone?*" I said, sputtering. "*Pearce* . . . as in Ben?" I glanced from each man to the next. "Ben's gone where?"

"I'm here to negotiate his buyout," he told me.

My mind jumped through the possibilities. First, Henry had to be lying. Ben would never take a buyout. Not without telling me, anyway. He certainly would have told me he was leaving. And then Henry started talking about how Ben will take *this* buyout — future tense — and I understood. "Ben doesn't know yet, does he?"

Mellay didn't say anything. He didn't have to. Mellay had never liked Ben. From day one, Mellay had fussed over costs, and Ben's was the highest dollar contract and therefore a target.

"We toss Ben, we lose female viewers," I said.

He drew the key demographic advertisers most coveted: eighteen- to thirty-four-year-old women held a powerful economic sway, and they didn't even know it. But Mellay knew. He was fiddling with the knot on his tie again.

"Women love Ben," I said. "If he goes, that audience is irrecoverable. Do you really want to lose the gains from these past weeks?"

"This is about the money we save on an outrageous contract. It's not about holding on to a shrinking demographic," Mellay said, and then to Javier: "As I told you, I have a fresh young anchor named Heather Buchanan —"

"Who has talent but no experience," I argued. "One day she may be as good as Ben Pearce, she really might, but that day is far in the future."

The lawyer chimed in: "We've drawn up a package for Ben that's extremely generous."

"Ben's got a ranch back home that needs a constant influx of cash," Mellay said, and jerked his chin toward me. "There's no noncompete clause in the package. If we let him stay in town, she'll talk him into signing."

What an outrageous assumption. "I'm not talking Ben into anything," I said.

"Why should she have to?" Javier asked Mellay. "I was told you have a high-dollar employee who'd expressed interest in a buyout. If that's not the case, why am I here?"

I caught Mellay's brief glance at Henry. So they were in this together. Javier was the odd man out.

"Ben and I have an inside line on follow-up stories to yesterday's exclusive," I said, directing my comments to Javier. "There are also a number of investigative stories that have emerged during the course of the Evelyn Carney investigation, stories of government corruption and illegal campaign money. These stories are available only to me." And then, because there was no other possibility I could feel good about, I said: "If Ben goes, I go, and I take my stories with me."

"You can't use stories as a bargaining chip," Henry said furiously. "They belong to the company, not you."

It was such a silly lawyer thing to say, I just laughed.

"You've received an offer from a competitor?" Javier said.

This strained the meaning of Leila Gupta's *let's have lunch* offer at the correspondents dinner, but I didn't correct him. Let him think what he would. Besides, if I had to jump with nowhere to land, I'd do it. No way would I let them hurt Ben.

"State the terms of the offer," Javier said. "Whatever it is, I'll match it."

"Ben Pearce remains anchor of the *Evening News.*"

"Done."

Mellay jumped up from his chair. Henry cut him a look of caution.

In a formal voice, Javier asked if he might use Mellay's office to speak with me privately. Mellay looked as if he'd been slapped. "Gentlemen?" Javier said, dismissing them.

After they left, Javier took a seat across from me. "I want your stories on my station," he said. "Let's get down to the specifics. What will it take?"

CHAPTER FORTY-FOUR

The screen door creaked when I opened it and pounded on the front door. Ben answered with a huge grin that faded quickly. "What's wrong?" he said.

"I had a meeting with Mellay. Some corporate bigwigs came down from New York. Can we talk?"

"Let me guess. Mellay was an ass."

"Does the sun rise in the east?"

He stepped back to let me in, and the screen door thwacked behind me. "I'm glad you came by," he was saying. "I've got some things to tell you about, too. Give me a minute, though. I'll be right back," he said, and was gone.

He left me in the front room, which was meant to be a formal receiving room. Despite its elegant bones, it was crowded with a huge television and old leather couches and heavy wood tables piled with sports magazines and paperback novels, a handful of remotes.

On the bay window were photographs of Ben's family — lots of big, dark-haired men — and there were pictures, too, of his farm with mountains in the distance. I picked up one of Ben and me at an awards ceremony a couple of years ago. He was in a tux, and I was in a black gown, and we held the statue of a winged woman between us. We wore the same smile, a grin from ear to ear.

"That was a good night for us," he said from the doorway. He'd spruced himself up, changed out of sweats and an old T-shirt into a button-down and khakis, and his hair was wet with comb lines. "I didn't care about that Emmy," he went on. "But I went to see you get what you worked so hard for. That's when I realized what you meant to me."

A warm feeling flooded my chest.

"My official statement on the record," he said, his mouth twisting wryly. "For when you get mad at me."

"At you? You must be joking." I put the photograph back in its place, impatient to get back to the news. "You won't believe what Mellay tried to pull this time."

I told him how Mellay had tried to use me to break Ben's contract. I was talking fast, excited now that it was all over, feeling that same breaking-news euphoria — except that this time it came from outsmarting Mellay and saving Ben.

Ben didn't seem surprised. I said, "You knew Mellay was after you?"

"Honey, I didn't just fall off the apple-cart," he drawled softly. "Course I knew. He's been trying to get rid of me from day one. It only pissed me off when he went after you to get to me."

I held up my hand, needing a minute. "Mellay took away my show," I said, finally, *"to piss you off?"*

"That time, I nearly bit. If I hadn't gotten out of the building to work on Evelyn's story with you, I might have done something stupid. I really might have."

It was astonishing. All the time I'd thought Mellay was coming after me, when in truth, I'd been nothing more than a tool to get to Ben. A demotion should at least be about the person demoted, for Christ's sake. It should've been about me.

But it was also a relief. Mellay was a bad boss and needed to be pushed out the door, which meant I had no regrets.

"You deserve so much better than this dump," Ben was saying. "You should be where your strengths are rewarded. That's what I've been working on." He was prat-

485

tling on nervously. "Will you give me a minute to show you?"

"But you're missing the good part. The deal with Javier."

He held up a finger. "Just one minute. All I'm asking."

"No, listen." I went to him in the doorway. "Javier asked what else I wanted, other than you, so I did it. I told him what I really wanted, secretly, all this time."

"You got your show back."

"No," I said, feeling the wild rush again, all the excitement. "I'm the news director."

His mouth opened. There were no words. I waited for him to say something, but he kept gaping at me.

"You think it was heavy-handed?" I said. "Not so nice of me to take Mellay's job?"

"Mellay," he said, as if the name was a curse. "He was never good enough to answer your phones. You've been carrying this dump for years, which is obvious to anybody with half a brain. Javier is that rarity in upper management, a dude with a working brain."

"Then why are you so angry?"

"Not at you." He moved his shoulder in frustration, as if fighting against a terrible constraint. "I should have seen this coming. We're so alike, the way we charge ahead

486

without looking."

Little pinpricks of anxiety tickled my spine. "I don't understand what's happening here." He guided me to the sofa, handling me as if he were afraid I'd get away, and I complained: "You're treating me like that girl we interviewed, Lil' Bit."

"No, not like a reluctant interview," he said gently. "Like my best friend, the person I'd rather be with than any other. My statement on the record, remember?"

He was handling me, all right, and I didn't like it.

"Whatever this is, just say it."

So he did. Since Mellay had come to town, Ben had been testing the waters for other jobs. The network expressed a serious interest. There was an immediate opening for a national correspondent position, very prestigious, great salary and bennies, and best of all, it was closer to his home. He would be based out of the Chicago bureau.

Chicago was all I heard. There was a punch of heat to my chest, unbelievably painful. He was leaving, and it was an entire world away. *Chicago.*

"But I hesitated," he said. "I couldn't leave you. My agent negotiated into the contract my choice of producers, so you could come. It's a good offer. I knew you'd be tempted. Then Evelyn Carney disappeared. The network took notice of our reporting. Well, that's an understatement. Now they're frothing at the mouth. I told them you broke it, not me, that the brilliance was all you." He gave me a nervous, boyish smile. "They want you, badly. I bet we could negotiate for you a higher salary."

"But, Ben . . . Chicago?" I said, trying to slow it all down.

He clasped my hands and pulled them close to his chest.

"Come with me," he said. "It's the network. Deep pockets for the kind of investigations you like. More resources. Better work environment." He was gripping my hands so tightly they hurt. "Take a chance. I promise you'll never regret it. You know my word is good."

I looked down at our hands together, his, which were big and rough with those little half-moon scars over the knuckles, and I believed him. His word *was* good.

But I pulled away and got up and wandered the room, my thoughts jumping. He was talking about working for the network in Chicago, a steppingstone to New York and even bigger opportunities. He might someday have his own network show. There really was no limit for Ben. This was a serious offer. He'd be a fool not to take it.

"Whatever Javier offered you, we could get the network to match," he said.

I needed a good excuse but couldn't think of one. I was trying too hard to keep my thoughts from my face. But he had already seen, and he knew. "For you, it's not about the money, is it?" he said. "This, here, running the station, you said this is what you've dreamed of?"

"It is, yes."

He was waiting for me to say more, and I had no idea what. I made my way to the window and ran my fingertip across the picture of us holding the Emmy, and talking down to it, I said, "This is the beginning of great things for you."

He hesitated. "For me, the network move makes sense."

"Of course it does," I said quickly, still looking down at the picture. "I understand."

"Chicago is closer to where I feel more at home."

"You need a bigger skyline, fewer people."

He got up and came to me and turned my shoulders until I faced him. He lifted his hand to my cheek. "I like the women here, one in particular, very much." His voice had gone thick.

My smile wobbled. "And those women

will all wear black when you leave." This was the old joke that never truly fit, but I was trying to keep it light, failing miserably. It was settling in now, and with it, the panic. What would I do without him?

One thing I learned, you can't make a person stay. Begging was out. Trapping him with pity was beyond contempt. When you lost a person, you had to let him go. But the words rushed out: "What if I wanted you to stay?"

He said nothing. I couldn't read him, dammit.

"What I mean is, is there anything that might keep you here?" I went on. "More money? Longer contract? More annual leave to spend time at home?"

After a moment, he said carefully, "As the anchor, you're saying? You want to know how to keep me on the set of the *Evening News*?"

It was terrible and selfish, and I was ashamed.

"That's what I'm asking," I said.

He took a step closer. "Do you need me, Virginia?" His voice was deep and husky, and oh, how I'd miss that voice.

But did I need him?

"To stick around until you can get your news director feet wet?" he went on. "You know I'll do what you need, but it's not a great idea. Working for you with the way I feel about you."

I paused before nodding and saying, "You might be right," and then he nodded with me, and we were in this together, talking quietly with polite words, afraid to say the wrong thing. "You were always more at ease with yourself than I am," I murmured. "You're a bit of a romantic. That's the big difference between us. I would like to be. I might have been, but could never afford it."

He was studying me. "Why is that, do you think?"

"For me, it feels dangerous."

"Because you can be hurt."

"I don't know how to explain." I was frustrated, struggling with this part of me I'd never understood, and not understanding it, had pushed it aside for too long. "It's a feeling I get," I said haltingly. "I know it's not real, it's just — well, it feels like I'm lost in the dark and someone is with me but hidden. I keep waiting for him to show himself for who he is or what he wants."

"To hurt you?"

"Not you," I said quickly. "You're the finest person I know and I trust you. But that's what comes over me, and the feeling's not rational, but I've never figured out how to make it go away."

He got a distant, thoughtful look. I'd been afraid he'd mock or disregard my feelings out of hand, but he didn't. He was actually trying to see something quite alien to him, and this seemed a generosity so rare and precious, so Ben-like, that it hurt.

"I understand," he said.

I blinked up at him. "You do?"

"You think I don't worry? Or have my own fears? Because I'm a man or because I'm a pretty big guy, I can't be hurt?" Emotions flickered across his face, tenderness and something else too complex to comprehend, and I knew I'd be wondering about that look for a long time.

Then he said gently, "If I let myself, I could easily fall in love with you. Which is why I can't work for you. Every day I'd look at you and want to touch you. It'd be bad for me, but worse for you. There'd be gossip. It'd undercut your authority, everything you're going to accomplish."

He touched my cheek again briefly and said, "I won't hurt you like that," and then he walked away.

I dropped to the sofa with my head in my hands, stunned, like when you cut yourself accidentally and wonder at the depth of the slice and why you don't feel pain in that brief, dazed moment before the blood rushes out.

Soon there were heavy footsteps in the hallway. I lifted my head from my hands. Ben was holding an envelope.

"What's that?"

He dropped it onto the table in front of me. My name was written across it in his big, bold scrawl. "You know what it is," he said.

Chapter Forty-Five

The next morning it rained. My car was still impounded in the Mobile Crime lot, and I needed a cab. You can never find a cab in bad weather, so I walked to work in the nasty sideways downpour that flipped up my umbrella and soaked my pants legs and ruined my shoes, the *squish-squish-squish* matching my mood admirably.

Tucked deep in my satchel was the sealed letter Ben had given me. I didn't have to read it. I knew what it said. But as long as it remained sealed, it was not yet real to me, so I didn't have to act on it. Besides, there was always the chance Ben might change his mind. If he changed his mind, it'd be easier if I hadn't accepted his resignation. He could slide onto the anchor desk as if nothing more than his leave of absence had happened.

So began my first day as news director.

■ ■ ■ ■

I slipped in through the rear door by the loading dock and came up the back stairs rather than the elevator, hoping to avoid my staff, at least until I'd dried out and put myself together for questions I didn't feel like answering yet. That was my hope, anyway. But I came around the corner to find Heather Buchanan, Mellay's young protégée, waiting outside my office. She was slouching on the floor with her back to the wall, as if she'd been there for some time.

She wore a buttoned cardigan, no makeup, and her glorious blond hair was pulled back tight. The black frames of her glasses were thick. I was impressed. She looked less the beauty queen and more the nerdy kid, and it was a smart way to approach me.

She asked for a letter of recommendation. "Nick Mellay said you might give me one if I promised to leave without a fuss."

"You're leaving?"

"Now that Nick is gone," she said, showing nerves now. "I know you don't like me."

"Let's be honest. I disliked your method of using Mellay. It's harmful to you and totally unnecessary, although it does suggest you have no idea how naturally talented you are."

Her jaw dropped.

"What I also don't like?" I went on. "Riding the coattail of some lame news director who wants to turn you into eye candy with a short shelf life. It's a terrible future for anyone, and ridiculous for someone with your talent. What you need is a mentor, someone who will teach you to gather news, build sources, and learn how to balance stories fairly and think objectively. You have to learn to report before you can become a good anchor, but those are all things Isaiah or I could teach you."

"*Y-you'd* teach me?" she stammered.

"Honestly, Isaiah's more patient and easygoing. With me, there are no shortcuts, and I don't give a damn how pretty you are. All I care about is competence, and frankly, that's all you should care about, too. If you're good at what you do, no one can steal it from you, and you'll carry your skill wherever you go. Being good at what you do is the closest thing to freedom a woman can find."

I put the key into the lock and opened the door. "Let me know what you decide," I said, dismissing her.

It was that time of transition, when one

story file closes and another begins. I paused over Evelyn's file, not yet ready to let her go. Instead, I eased back in my chair and closed my eyes and let myself see her as I had in the beginning — Evelyn walking on that same dark street I frequented, her coat swirling about her, her hair as wild and tangled as her feelings, searching for the help she'd never find . . .

She'd been so close. If only she could have made it across the bridge.

Why had that mattered so much to me? I still couldn't say.

Or maybe I was asking the wrong question again. Maybe it wasn't who she was or what she meant. Maybe it was what I'd wished to be for her and for all the lost women who are flung into a world vaguely hostile to them, women harassed and assaulted and sometimes killed for their female bodies, a violence that never ended. I'd protect them all, if I could, even though I hadn't been able to save Evelyn. She was dead before I knew her name.

Evelyn Carney made me remember. Not just the work I wanted to do, but also how good the work could be when it was a power that helped, not hurt. Maybe she even reminded me how good I could be.

That was what I never dared say: I wanted

to do good work in the world. That sounds pretty naïve, I guess, but I couldn't help it. I wanted it so badly.

My office door creaked open, and Isaiah peeked in. He gave me a soft smile, gazing over the top of his glasses. "Hey, boss," he said. "You're late for your own meeting. Not an auspicious start."

I shot up from the desk, shrugged on my jacket, and stepped into my wet shoes. We cut through the newsroom to the conference room with its glass walls through which we could see the full staff assembled. Every seat was taken except ours. The rest were standing. There was a palpable energy.

When Isaiah reached for the door, I stopped him. What the hell, I thought. I couldn't keep pretending it didn't happen.

"Why did you give my phone to Paige Linden?" I said quietly. "Please don't deny it. She knew about my father, which she could have only gotten from you, since I only entrusted you. Also, you returned my phone to me."

He put his head down. He didn't say anything.

I felt my face getting hot. "You gave her my phone, and she put a spy app on it."

He went around the corner, away from the glass walls and prying eyes of the staff. I dogged his heels across the newsroom and into the stairwell, where he paced on the landing.

"I didn't realize how dangerous she was," he said. "My first hint of any problems was your request for Paige's background check. This, by the way, was after you dashed out to meet her, which I only learned when I saw your attack reported *on our news*. I found out about the bugged phone *in the same report.*"

I narrowed my eyes. "So this is my fault?"

"You stopped talking to me." His outrage was striking, bouncing off the hard surfaces of the stairwell, the concrete landing and metal steps, the cinder blocks painted an underwater green. "While you were visiting your father, she called the station looking for you. Like any other call, I asked if I should track you down, if she needed you urgently. She said not to bother you during a family emergency. She also told me you had the story wrong. That Ledger was using you and our shows to destroy an innocent person with whom he had a political vendetta, and that our show's reputation would surely suffer. She said Ledger tricked you, which wasn't surprising. You'd fallen for his tricks in the past."

"She lied to you," I said. "That's what she does."

"So I watched you when you came back. I gave you the benefit of the doubt, and you know what? You were acting just as she described, running yourself crazy, obsessing over this woman, and Ledger was using you. All of this was observably true. What's more? You were hiding things. There was a time we used to talk about everything, and during the Evelyn Carney story, you just stopped. You cut me out of the loop."

His words were hurtful — and true — but his mouth trembled. That worried me. His mouth showed weakness, not anger at all, and he still hadn't given me a straight answer about the phone.

"How could you give Paige Linden my phone?"

"The night you took Ledger to the correspondents dinner, you left your phone in your office, so I took it. I did that. You wouldn't come clean about Ledger, so I looked through your history. It was over drinks at Chads."

"Paige Linden was with you?"

"I was so angry with you," he said. "Remember that day up in archives? I told you how bad things were. You knew Mellay was making cuts, but did you even ask what kind? He told me there was room for only one of us — you or me."

"Let me guess. Paige helped you look for something incriminating on my phone, so Mellay could pick you?"

"So I could confront you," he said. "So I could make you stop putting the show in jeopardy — or else."

"That Evelyn Carney story saved us."

"How could I have known it would turn out that way? I trusted Paige because you'd trusted her. You'd done the credibility checks. She was your source. She knew Ledger's private numbers and helped me go through the phone."

He put his head down again and ran his palm across his scalp, his problem-solving gesture, although what there was to solve, I had no idea. It was a fait accompli.

"When I got our drinks at the bar, I left the phone on the table," he said. "It was out of sight only a couple of minutes. I had no idea what she'd done. I'm so sorry."

His words echoed in the stairwell. *I'm sorry. So sorry.*

I rubbed that spot over my heart where my press passes hung. "I didn't keep my promise to you. You're right. Mellay was coming after you, and I didn't protect you."

When he looked up at me, his face was

full of suffering. "I'm sixty years old," he said. "I have no family. I have nothing except this one employer I've worked for my entire career. Who will hire me after this? Where do I go? Do you know what I have to look forward to? Do you?"

Suddenly I hated the business within the business, the climbing and deals and scheming for basic survival. Someone like Isaiah should've been beyond all this. In a world that made sense, he'd be coasting until he chose to let go. For his years of dedication to the news, he deserved at least that.

And you had to look at the totality of a person's life, didn't you? Through the years, he'd done so much for me. He'd protected and mentored me. He taught me everything I knew about the news. He treated me as his own, as a father might.

We had to forgive our fathers, didn't we? Because they were taught to appear strong even when they weren't and fearless when riddled with our same fears, and sometimes that fear made them do terrible things. Sometimes our fathers betrayed us.

"Stealing my phone is a fireable offense," I told him.

He lifted his chin for the punch. "So it is."

"Don't do it again."

When I turned to leave, he grabbed my arm and held me firmly. "You're not firing me?"

"Ah, no. You're not getting off that easy," I said, and left him standing there, slack-jawed, alone in the stairwell. I crossed the newsroom and went into the conference room, and everyone stopped talking. So they'd already known what I was about to say. Of course, they did. They were news-people, the best in the city.

I took my seat at the head of the table. "First, I'd like to confirm the rumor." I paused to take them all in, my gaze moving from each face, one to the next, my staff. They were all so dear to me. When I got to the chair left vacant for Ben, I glanced away.

"The good news is that you know who I am, and that I don't change, and everything will be as it always was for the most part . . ."

My voice drifted off. The announcement about Ben would have to wait. Besides, any minute now he might come sauntering in, his Grizzlies cap flipped backward, grinning his good morning. He'd slouch in his chair and consider the stories being pitched before sharing his opinion about what to pursue. I had always relied on his judgment and his calm, his sense that this was a great game that we would surely win, or at least pull off by show time. He'd made it all so fun.

I put my head down and pretended to flip through the newspapers on the table in front of me. Ben wasn't running late. He was gone. I'd sent him away. Somehow, very stupidly, I had broken my own heart.

"Virginia?" Nelson prodded.

They were all staring at me, waiting for their marching orders. The door opened, and Isaiah came in. He took his seat to the right of me.

"You're here, good," I said. "Tell us, Isaiah, what's the news today?"

ACKNOWLEDGEMENTS

With profound gratitude to my extraordinary agent and friend, Dan Conaway. Thank you for finding me. This would not be this without you.

Deepest thanks to my editor, the brilliant Dawn Davis, publisher of 37 INK, for her clarity of vision, steady hand, and terrific taste in shoes.

Thanks also: to Judith Curr and the wonderful team at Atria Books: Lisa Keim, David Brown, Hillary Tisman, Albert Tang, and Woodrow Dismukes. And the folks at Writer's House, especially Taylor Templeton for her fine reads.

To my circle of talented writer friends for sharing their insights: particularly James Mathews, who was with me from the beginning of this journey and got me to Hildie Block, who helped me through that first really rough draft; and Jim Beane, Catherine Bell, Carmelinda Blagg, Dana Cann, and

Kathleen Wheaton. Thank you all.

Most of all, to my family, for their unflagging love and patience, especially Sharon Taylor, who gave me my first words; Kimberly Sneed, who never questioned my sanity; and Lauren Loebach and Jaclyn Loebach, both of whom inspire and give me hope for a better future.

And of course, always and above all, to Joe Loebach.

ABOUT THE AUTHOR

Christina Kovac worked for seventeen years managing Washington, DC, newsrooms and producing crime and political stories in the District. Her career as a television journalist began with Fox 5's *Ten O'Clock News,* and after that, the ABC affiliate in Washington. For the last nine years, she worked at NBC News, where she worked for Tim Russert and provided news coverage for *Meet the Press,* the *Today* show, *Nightly News,* and others.

Christina Kovac lives with her family outside of Washington, DC.

The Cutaway is her first novel.